NONE WITHOUT SIN

A FIRST STATE MYSTERY

NONE WITHOUT SIN

A FIRST STATE MYSTERY

MICHAEL BRADLEY

CamCat
Books

CamCat Publishing, LLC
Brentwood, Tennessee 37027
camcatpublishing.com

Hardcover ISBN 9780744305951
Paperback ISBN 9780744305814
Large-Print Paperback ISBN 9780744305623
eBook ISBN 9780744305517
Audiobook ISBN 9780744305982

Library of Congress Control Number: 2021952249

Cover and book design by Maryann Appel

5   3   1   2   4

For Dennis "Elwood" Gallo and Michael "Jake" Canonica,
both of whom taught me the allure of creativity,
the value of having fun,
and the importance of being my authentic self.

"Some rise by sin, and some by virtue fall."

—William Shakespeare

WEEK
1

CHAPTER ONE

Saturday

The loaf of brown bread looked distinctly out of place resting on the dead man's chest, leaving Candice Miller to wonder if all crime scenes contained such incongruities. She expected blood. Yellow police tape? Definitely. But baked goods? This seemed outrageous even for the most imaginative of minds. Yet, there it was, reminding her of the artisan bread she would get at the steakhouse near the mall. *Never going to eat there again*, she thought.

The scene was not gory, at least not to the degree she had expected. What blood there was had pooled around the man's sternum and left a crimson stain on the front of his white Oxford shirt. The round loaf of bread was split down the middle, and the bottom of each half soaked up enough plasma to darken the crust to almost pitch-black. The corpse of Robbie Reynolds was stretched out on a black leather sofa along the far wall. His face—which was turned toward the door—was pale and lifeless. His vacant eyes stared at her from across the room. A sensation like a cold finger touched the back of her neck for one brief second.

Everything else looked normal. The pool table in the center of the room showed signs of a game in progress, with balls scattered across the green felt. A cue lay nearby on the plush beige carpet, as if it had been dropped on the floor by the dead man. Otherwise, there was no sign of violence. If not for the blood, Candice might have thought Robbie was just napping.

Chief Lyle Jenkins nudged her away from the doorway. "Down here, Reverend." The police chief moved between her and the door—presumably to block her view—and then gestured toward an archway a few steps down the hall.

Candice took one last glance at the dead man. She should have felt a sense of revulsion or been horrified by her first murder scene. But there was only a sense of curiosity, of wonder. *Who killed him? Why leave behind a loaf of bread?*

She stepped from the door and moved along the hall in the direction the police chief had indicated. "Such a shame."

"That's life," Lyle said, his voice deep and brusque.

Her jaw tightened with his words. His callousness angered her, but she knew Lyle Jenkins had a reputation of being an unfeeling hard-ass. She refused to be goaded by his insensitivity and tried to ignore his remark.

She passed through the archway across the hall into the sprawling living room. The early afternoon sun blazed through high windows, bathing everything in a warm light. Detective Mick Flanagan stood beside a stone fireplace opposite the archway. His ginger hair was tussled, his clothing wrinkled, as if he had dressed haphazardly before rushing to the crime scene. A silver badge dangled on a thin chain from his neck. He smiled momentarily, then his lips sank into a grave frown. He crossed the room to greet Candice.

"How is Andrea?" she asked.

"Not good." Mick ran his hand through his hair. "Thanks for coming."

Chief Jenkins leaned in and asked, "Did she say anything yet?"

"Nothing new," Mick said. "Just what she told you earlier."

Candice touched Mick's shoulder. "Let me talk to her. She needs comfort, not questions."

The police chief grunted. "That's all fine and dandy, but we've got a crime scene to process. The sooner we can get the family out of here the better." He turned abruptly and walked from the room.

Mick rubbed the back of his neck. "Sorry about that."

Candice rolled her eyes and shook her head. "What happened?"

He shrugged. "Your guess is as good as mine. She found the body when she came home an hour ago. That's all she told us."

"I can't understand why anyone would want to kill him." This seemed like the right thing to say about a murder victim, but Candice knew Robbie Reynolds well enough to know he wasn't without his secrets. In a small city like Newark, rumors were always easy to find.

"He helped my wife and I buy our first home," Mick said.

"Give me a few minutes with her."

Candice moved to the long Chesterfield sofa facing the fireplace. Its tan leather was cracked and worn. Andrea Reynolds sat with her head bowed, her shoulders quaking with each sob. Long ash brown hair fell forward and obscured her face from view.

Andrea clutched a balled-up tissue in her hand. She didn't seem to notice Candice's arrival.

Seated at the opposite end of the sofa was Marissa, the Reynolds's pre-teen daughter. Her hands were folded in her lap, and her eyes held a blank stare. The girl's blonde hair looked shorter than it had on Sunday. *Must have got a haircut this week.* The Reynolds family always sat in the front row during Sunday service, and it was hard to miss the beaming smile on Marissa's face. The ten-year-old girl had pushed herself as far into the corner of the sofa as possible, as if trying to escape the horror around her. Marissa glanced up at Candice, then dropped her eyes to the floor.

Candice approached the sofa and took a seat next to Andrea. She wrapped her arm around the shoulders of the grieving woman, who glanced up to give Candice a feeble smile. Bloodshot eyes bore witness to her anguish.

"Oh, Candice." Andrea sniffed, then wiped her nose with the tissue. "Who would do this?" Her voice was broken and soft.

Candice stared at her for a long moment, searching for the right words. Despite her time at seminary and her short experience as an Episcopalian priest, she'd always struggled with providing comfort to grieving families in the wake of a loss. Her words seemed inadequate, even trite. There was nothing she could say that wouldn't sound like a cliché, like some canned response to grief. "Time heals all wounds." "He's in a better place." "God will get you through this." That last one, in particular, had been a source of contention for her lately.

"Andrea, I know it may not seem like it right now, but this pain will pass," Candice said, cringing within as she spoke.

Andrea broke into an uncontrolled sob and buried her face in Candice's shoulder. As the woman cried, Candice glanced at Mick.

He rolled his eyes and folded his arms as a faint sigh slipped from his lips. She suppressed a semi-panicked urge to giggle. *Five years on the force, and he gets more like Chief Jenkins every day.* Then, after a further moment's thought, she caught the irony and chastised herself for her own callousness.

The seemingly endless stream of Andrea's tears dampened the collar of Candice's blouse. When she lifted her head, the woman blotted at her swollen eyes with a tissue. Her face was red and blotchy, with a network of little purple veins on her nose.

"Mick needs to ask you some questions," Candice said. "Do you feel up to talking?"

Andrea blew her nose on the tissue. "I think so."

Candice took hold of Andrea's hand and squeezed it. "I'll be right here beside you."

Mick mouthed a silent "thank you" to Candice, and then said, "Andrea, I know this is a difficult time for you, but the sooner you can tell me what happened—"

Andrea cut him off. "We'd gone up to New York City yesterday." She gestured to her daughter at the other end of the sofa. "A girls' night out."

Andrea dabbed once again at her eyes with a tissue to wipe away fresh tears. "Marissa and I took the train up to see a Broadway show. We had dinner before the show and stayed the night at a hotel on Times Square."

"When did you return home?" Mick asked.

"About an hour ago," Andrea replied. "We'd planned to be home earlier, but the train was running late."

Candice toyed with a hangnail on her right ring finger.

She felt a flutter of guilt for not saying or doing more. But, how to behave at a crime scene had not been part of the curriculum at seminary. *First murder scene and I didn't even pray with the widow. Way to go.*

She looked toward Marissa. The young girl—wearing pale blue jeans with sequins in the shape of a flower on the right pant leg—hadn't moved. She looked distant and afraid. Very different from the affable, high-spirited preteen Candice was used to seeing on Sundays. It seemed as if everyone had forgotten Marissa was even in the room. This was not the type of conversation the girl should hear.

"Sorry to interrupt," Candice said. "What about Marissa? Does she need to be here?"

At the mention of her name, Marissa looked up at them. Her eyes were wide.

"Until we've cleared the crime scene, you won't be able to stay in the house," Mick said to Andrea. "Do you have someplace the two of you can go?"

Andrea toyed with the tissue in her hand. The flimsy material was creased and shredded. "We can stay at my mother's house." She gestured toward Candice. "I called her right after I called you. She can take care of Marissa while I . . ." Her words drifted off.

Candice rose from the sofa. "Why don't I take Marissa upstairs and help her get a bag packed? You can stay here. Talk to Mick. Do what you need to do."

Andrea stared at her for a moment. Her eyes welled with tears, and she reached out her hand. "Thank you."

Candice smiled, took the woman's hand, and gave it a reassuring squeeze. "Will you be okay?"

"Yeah." There was some hesitation in Andrea's voice.

Candice walked to the other side of the sofa and knelt before the young girl. "Marissa, how about you come with me? We'll go up to your room and pack your suitcase. You're going to spend a few days at Grandma's house."

Marissa didn't move at first.

"Sweetie, go with Pastor Miller," Andrea said.

After a brief glance at her mother, the young girl slipped from the sofa. Candice took the girl's hand and led her from the room. As they moved down the hall toward the stairs, Candice glanced back at the doorway of the room where Robbie Reynolds lay dead. The blood-soaked loaf of bread resurfaced in her memory. That was downright odd. Why would someone leave a loaf of bread on a dead man's chest? Yet, the concept seemed eerily familiar some-how. A distant memory she couldn't quite reach.

The girl's bedroom looked as if every Disney princess movie had detonated within it. Movie posters from *Moana*, *Frozen*, and *Tangled* hung on the walls. Images from *Beauty and the Beast* covered the comforter on the twin bed. Small statuettes of the seven dwarfs lined the top of the nearby bookshelf. Candice hadn't been to Disney World, but she imagined this was what almost every gift shop in the park might look like.

Marissa crossed the room and sat on the bed; her head bowed, staring at her feet. She bit her bottom lip and said nothing. Candice reached over and put her arm around Marissa's shoulders.

The young girl looked up at Candice. Her blue eyes were puffy and bloodshot. "Is Daddy okay?"

The question shocked Candice and left her reeling for an answer. How could Marissa not know her father was dead? Wasn't she in the house when Andrea discovered the body? Candice struggled to find the right words. Talking with children had never been her strength. As an only child, she had never had a younger sibling to bond with. Never learned the art of relating to adolescents. Her jaw tightened at the idea of being the harbinger of tragic news. "Let's not worry about that. Let's pack a few things and get you outside. Your grandma will be here soon."

Marissa didn't move, just turned her gaze to the floor and stared. "I saw the blood. Mommy doesn't think I saw it, but I did."

"You saw it?" Candice bit her bottom lip. *She's going to need years of therapy.*

The girl nodded. "She told me not to look, but I did." There was a pause. "Is Daddy dead?"

Candice pulled the girl closer, giving her a comforting squeeze. Marissa stared up at her. A young life untouched by tragedy . . . until now. As much as she wanted to, Candice knew she couldn't shirk this responsibility. "Yes. Your father's dead."

She waited for the girl to break down. To burst into tears. To kick and scream. To run from the room. But nothing happened. Marissa was silent. Her big eyes filled with sadness; her mouth curled down in a frown. But her grief seemed subdued, almost controlled, as if the girl had already come to terms with her father's death. Candice touched the girl's arm. "Let's pack up a few things. Do you have a bag?"

Marissa nodded, then climbed from the bed and drew a small Cinderella suitcase from beneath it. She set it on the bed and flipped open the top.

"Pick out some clothes for an overnight stay," Candice said. "Make that a few days' stay."

Marissa wandered over to the nearby dresser and pulled open the top drawer. The young girl picked through her clothes as if having trouble deciding what to take. Candice allowed her gaze to drift to the end table. A paperback rested face down next to the Little Mermaid bedside lamp. She turned it over and read the title. It was a Nancy Drew mystery. She smiled. *The Mystery at Lilac Inn. I remember that one*, she thought. *Ghostly apparitions. A stolen inheritance. No murder. Just one in a series of stories that always come with a happy ending. No one gets hurt and the world is perfect on the last page.* When she set the book back down on the bedside table, a glint from the nearby bookshelf caught her eye. She spied a small crystal statuette of an angel sitting on the second shelf. Her pulse quickened for an instant.

With the suitcase packed, Candice led the girl from the bedroom and down the stairs. A uniformed police officer waited at the bottom. Two overlapping sheets of plastic had been hung over the doorway leading into the "death" room. The sheets were attached along the edges of the doorframe with yellow tape. Blurred shapes and figures were all that could be seen through the semi-transparent plastic. Candice was grateful Marissa would be spared any further horror. She nodded at the officer, then led Marissa out of the house and into the afternoon sun.

CHAPTER TWO

B rian Wilder downshifted and halted for the traffic light at the bottom of the off-ramp. His two-hour drive along Delaware's beach expressway from Rehoboth Beach had been a blur. The Friday night birthday party had gone into the early hours of the morning, forcing him to crash on the couch of Chris Carson, the birthday boy himself.

Amber Fox, morning host at WREB-FM, had thrown a surprise birthday party for her co-host, Chris. Brian had the dubious responsibility of getting him to the Mexican restaurant for the party. He never realized how difficult it would be to keep a surprise from a blind man. They'd only just stepped across the restaurant's threshold when Chris leaned toward Brian to ask how many people were waiting in the back room for them. It wasn't until later in the evening that Chris explained how he knew.

"Did someone let slip about the party?" Brian had asked.

Chris shook his head. "Not at all. It was a perfectly planned surprise party."

"But, how—"

"How did I know?" Chris said. "Do you remember the loud music playing when we entered the restaurant?"

"Yeah, but what's—"

"What about the soccer game on the bar TV?"

"No . . ."

Chris smiled. "And the woman at the bar nagging her husband about his drinking?"

Brian shook his head. "Nope."

"Then, you probably didn't hear Amber in the back room trying to shush everyone when we arrived."

"No." Brian sighed. "Can't say I did."

He had known Chris Carson for years before the accident that robbed the radio DJ of his sight. Chris was just as much a smart-ass now as he had been then. Perhaps more so.

When the light changed, Brian turned left, heading toward downtown Newark. The fifty-plus-year-old car roared up the street and brought a smile to his face. The candy apple-red Mustang was one of the few luxuries he allowed himself. Brian was meticulous in his care and maintenance of the Mustang. If only he'd put that level of care into his relationship with Allison, his daughter. A sense of guilt washed over him.

He glanced at his mobile phone on the passenger seat. He toyed with the idea of calling her, but their last call had ended in a fierce argument, just like so many others. *No point in upsetting her weekend,* he thought.

The car raced across an overpass. Northbound traffic on the interstate below was backed up, creeping along. Early beachgoers on their way to the Jersey shore. Although the morning was windy, the weekend was shaping up to be the first nice one of the month. Rain, cold temperatures, and the occasional snow flurry had made the first two weeks of March less than pleasant. This third week—with temps in the mid-sixties—seemed to be the trigger for everyone to emerge from a self-induced winter hibernation.

As he glided past a slow-moving U-Haul, his mobile phone rang. He slipped the hands-free earpiece into his ear and pressed the button to answer.

"Yo Brian, where are you?" Jessica O'Rourke asked. The part-time newspaper photographer spoke quickly, her young throaty voice full of excitement.

"Just got off the highway," he said. "Maybe ten minutes out. Why?"

"The police scanner's blowing up. Something's rotten in Newark. Cops and paramedics have converged on Annabelle Street. Sounds serious," she said, her words coming out in rapid fire.

Brian narrowed his eyes. Annabelle Street was in a select neighborhood on the north side of Newark. Half-million-dollar houses. Land Rovers and Mercedes in driveways. The mayor had a house in the neighborhood. So did the dean of Northern Delaware University. "Thanks for the tip."

"Look," Jessica said, a hint of hesitation in her voice. "I've got a wedding to shoot in three hours. I can't meet you there."

Brian smiled. "No worries. I've got my camera in the trunk." His years as a journalist had taught him to be flexible, often taking photos for his own articles. A photographer by his side was a luxury he'd learned to do without. His pictures would never be as good as Jessica's, but they'd be just fine for the newspaper. "You can criticize my picture-taking skills later."

"How was the party?" she asked.

Heavy traffic slowed Brian's approach into the city of Newark. He braked as the line of cars ahead came to a crawl. "You missed a good time." He thought again about the previous night. "Chris was disappointed you weren't there."

She sighed. Chris Carson's "crush" on Jessica was public knowledge—as was her unwillingness to be tied down in any relationship. "He'll get over it," she said.

Brian laughed. "Go to the wedding. Enjoy yourself."

Three police cars were parked in front of a house on Annabelle Street, and an ambulance was backed into the driveway. Brian parked the Mustang along the curb a few houses up the block. Before climbing from the car, he reached into the glovebox and dug out a spiral notebook and a pen. From the trunk, he grabbed a black camera bag and slung it over his shoulder.

As he walked along the sidewalk, he noticed a small crowd of onlookers across the street. The house at the center of everyone's attention was a modern take on a classic Victorian. A police officer leaned on the white railing of the wraparound porch. A two-story turret rose high above the house, black shingles covering its peak. The white siding was bright in the afternoon sun. Brian recognized the house.

It belonged to Robbie Reynolds.

He sifted through a mental dossier of the man. Robbie Reynolds. Mid-forties. Married with one child. Wife's name is Andrea. Born and raised in Delaware. Attended and dropped out of Northern Delaware University. Local real estate agent. No, local real estate mogul. Self-proclaimed "king of Newark real estate."

The facts came readily to mind, as did the rumors. Egotist. Gambler. Womanizer.

As Brian approached a nearby police car, he was surprised to find Father Andrew Blake in conversation with Sergeant Stacy Devonport. The priest's black hair was peppered with specks of gray; a few strands above his forehead waved with the afternoon breeze. He wore his customary black tab collar shirt and slacks. A black jacket hung awkwardly from Andrew's gaunt frame, looking like it was a size too big. The priest's presence was puzzling. As far as Brian knew, the Reynolds family wasn't Catholic.

Stacy shook Brian's hand and smiled. "I bet I can guess what brings you here."

"Same reason that brought you." He turned to Andrew. "I'm surprised. I don't recall ever seeing the Reynolds at St. Matthew's."

"How would you know, Brian?" Andrew folded his arms and tilted his head to the side. "You're not exactly a regular attendee at Sunday Mass."

Stacy laughed at the priest's rebuke. "He's got you there."

Brian shrugged off their remarks. "I've been busy." It was easier to lie than try to explain why he'd not been to church in a while. He gestured toward the house. "What's going on, Stacy? Why the heavy police presence?"

"I can't tell you much." She rested the roll of crime scene tape on the trunk of the police car. "I've been relegated to crowd control. Haven't been inside."

Brian glanced at the crowd across the street. Ten, maybe eleven people. "Yeah. I see you've got your work cut out for you."

Stacy folded her arms. "Hey, if that throng gets out of hand—"

"That's a throng?" Brian raised an eyebrow. He let the moment linger before straightening up and narrowing his eyes. "Seriously, what's going on?"

"Suspicious death." Stacy turned her gaze toward the house, then back at Brian. "Robbie."

A slight heaviness pressed down on his shoulders. Brian's dealings with the real estate agent were infrequent and always all business. Robbie ran a weekly half-page ad in the Monday edition of the newspaper, but often sent it, along with a check, in the mail. Brian's only other dealings with the man had been when he first arrived in Newark.

Robbie was the real estate agent who helped Brian find the building that now served as the office of the *Newark Observer*. Since then, Brian rarely had to see the man face-to-face. But that only meant the pang of grief was momentary. A death was still a death after all. "How?"

"All I know is it's suspicious." She shrugged. "Nothing else."

Brian gestured toward a black Dodge Charger parked up the street. "I see he's here already."

"The chief? Yeah, he's in there now. Want me to tell him you're here?"

Brian gave a nod, and Stacy spoke into the radio mic attached to her shoulder. He flipped open the notebook, made a couple notations, and closed it again.

"He'll be right out," she said. "Word of warning. He's not in the best of moods. He's missing his grandson's Little League game for this."

"Thanks for the heads-up. Where's Flanagan? Couldn't he handle this?"

Stacy gestured toward the house. "He's here, too, but you know how the chief is. He's got to stick his nose into every investigation." She looked over at the crowd, which had now grown to twelve people. "If you'll excuse me . . ."

As Stacy strode off, Brian turned back to Andrew. The priest stared across the lawn at the Reynolds's family home, arms hanging limp at his sides, his eyes wet and dull.

Brian touched the priest's shoulder. "Andrew?"

"Man's propensity to commit violence against another never ceases to amaze me." Andrew slipped his hands into his trouser pockets and sighed. "You've probably seen that more than most people. How do you get used to it?"

Brian mulled over the remark.

A twenty-two-year journalism career had certainly shown him the darkest sides of human brutality. He'd covered two wars in the Middle East. Been at ground zero on 9/11. Reported on the violence between the drug cartels in South America. Then there were more natural disasters than he could remember. All for *Time, Newsweek*, and a dozen other magazines and newspapers. He'd seen more death than one man probably should. "You don't," he finally said.

Brian watched the black van from the county medical examiner's office drive past and pull into the driveway. "Why are you here?"

Andrew rocked on the balls of his feet. "I'm just a chauffeur. Do you know Candice Miller, pastor at Trinity Episcopal Church? No?" He paused for a second; his lips thinned to a downward arch. "Remind me to introduce you. Anyway, we were meeting at the rectory for our weekly chess game."

Brian knew of the church on the corner of Haines Street and Delaware Avenue, but he couldn't recall ever meeting the pastor. He made a mental note to take Andrew up on his offer of an introduction. "You found a sucker who doesn't mind losing all the time?"

Andrew snorted with amusement. "We're pretty evenly matched, thank you very much. We were just settling down to play when Candice got the call about Robbie. His wife called. They go to Candice's church. I offered to drive her."

"So, driving Ms. Miller?"

Andrew turned to look at the house. "You could say that."

A flurry of activity outside the house caught Brian's eye. Police chief Lyle Jenkins stepped from the house, paused at the base of the porch steps, then moved across the lawn toward Brian and Andrew with purposeful strides. A moment later, two additional people emerged from the house. Brian recognized Marissa Reynolds, but the woman with her was a stranger. She was petite with dark hair and wore a lavender windbreaker. The woman carried a small, bright-colored suitcase. She guided Marissa to a porch swing, and they sat together.

Brian was still studying the pair when Lyle Jenkins approached. The stout police chief—dressed in faded blue jeans and a gray polo—wore his holster and gun belt low on his waist. A gold badge hung from his neck on a silver chain and bounced off his chest. The touch of gray in his black hair was highlighted by his dark complexion. "Wilder, how did I know you'd show up here?" He held out his hand.

Brian returned the hardy handshake. "You going to give me a scoop? Or do I have to wait for the press conference?"

Lyle cocked his head. "How exclusive can you really be with that rag of yours?"

Brian snorted, knowing the chief had a point. The *Newark Observer* was a twice-weekly newspaper. Even if he was the first to a story, the larger news outlets would have covered it ad nauseam before the next issue of the *Observer* hit the streets.

"I hear its murder," Brian said.

Andrew shook his head and made a *tsk-tsk* sound. "I believe the words used were 'suspicious death.'"

"That's all you're getting at the moment," Lyle said. He then leaned toward Brian, conspiratorially. "Off the record, Flanagan's got his hands full with this one." He glanced around, then hitched his thumb into his belt. "Where's your sidekick?"

"Shooting a wedding." Brian tapped the camera slung over his shoulder. "I'm on my own."

A gray Chevy Malibu slowly pulled up to the entrance of the driveway. The driver seemed confused as to where to park, first attempting to pull into the driveway behind the medical examiner's van. Then, thinking better of it, the driver backed up and drove past the house to park along the curb. An elderly woman climbed from the car and headed for the house. She was stopped at the end of the driveway by two police officers. Their conversation started cordially enough. But when it was clear the officers weren't going to let her pass, she became more animated. Her arms flew in wild gestures, pointing at the house. From where he stood, Brian heard the woman's voice grow louder as she became more frustrated.

". . . daughter needs me! Don't you have any sympathy for what's happened here?" The woman placed her hands on her hips, almost as if she were daring the officer to stand in her way. Obviously, she was a force to be reckoned with. Brian took pity on the officer. It was probably not going to be a battle he would win.

"Grandma!"

The cry came from the front porch. Marissa leapt from the porch swing and ran down the steps. The grandmother pushed past the police officers and met her granddaughter halfway. They embraced, and Marissa appeared to break down into tears.

Lyle let out a gruff sigh and shook his head. "I need to take care of this."

"Chief, I'd like to check on Candice, if you don't mind," Andrew said.

Lyle's eyes tightened and his lips curled down. He pointed at the house. "That is a crime scene, not a social club."

Andrew folded his arms. "Even the comforter needs to be comforted sometimes."

Lyle allowed a loud sigh to slip from his lips—a clear sign of reluctant capitulation. "Fine. Come with me," Lyle finally said. "You can go as far as the porch. But, stay out of the house, understand?"

The police chief turned and started toward the house, Andrew just steps behind. Brian shrugged his shoulders and took a step forward to follow.

"Not you, Wilder," Lyle said, without looking back.

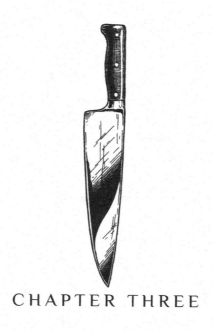

CHAPTER THREE

C andice carried Marissa's suitcase down the driveway to where the girl and her grandmother were standing. The young girl was enveloped in the elderly woman's embrace, sobbing. Candice had only met Andrea's mother once before.

She tried to remember her name. Audrey? Susan? *I'm sure it started with an S.* A flash of recognition appeared in the other woman's eyes.

"Pastor Miller, thank you," the elderly woman said. The skin on her hand was pale and translucent, with blue veins bulging in streaks across the back. "Not sure if you remember . . . we've met before. I'm Andrea's mother, Nancy Barrett."

Candice shook Nancy's hand, feeling the knuckles ravaged by years of arthritis beneath her fingers. "Yes, I remember." *Not with an S.*

"Thank you for bringing Marissa out to me," Nancy said. "Have you seen my daughter? How's she doing?"

Candice felt a sudden chill. She wasn't sure if it was from the faint breeze that blew across the yard, or the horror of the crime scene within the house. "The police are talking to Andrea now. She's holding it together, but only just."

"Please tell Andrea to call me when the police are done with her. I'll come back and pick her up." Nancy patted Marissa gently on the shoulder and gazed down at the young girl. "Let's get you home with Grandpa."

After Marissa left with her grandmother, Candice walked back toward the house. She was surprised to find Andrew waiting for her near the porch steps. His hands were deep in his trouser pockets, arms pressed close to his body, and his shoulders were hunched forward, as if he were cold, too.

He smiled as she approached. "Just wanted to check on you."

"I'm sorry," Candice said. With all that was happening, she'd forgotten Andrew had driven her to the crime scene. A twinge of guilt surfaced in her mind. "I've ruined your afternoon. Go ahead and leave. I'm sure I can get a lift back from the police."

"No, no." Andrew waved his hand. "I'm happy to wait. I wanted to see how you were holding up."

Before she could respond, movement in the nearby doorway caught Candice's attention. Two officers were carrying a stretcher out of the house; a black body bag was strapped on top. Candice touched Andrew's arm and guided him out of the way.

"I'm fine," she lied. She was supposed to be a well-trained, devout minister, able to cope with the death of her parishioners. But, at that moment, she felt more like a snake oil salesman. She knew all the words and all the actions, but did she believe them herself? She gestured toward the door. "I should go back in and see how Andrea's getting along."

"You want me to go with you?"

She waved him away. "I think Lyle would have an aneurysm if he caught you in there with me."

Andrew gave her an encouraging smile. "Do what you have to. I'll be waiting out here, whenever you're ready to leave."

Queasiness surged in her stomach at the thought of re-entering the house. It wasn't so much about the corpse, which wasn't even in there anymore. Robbie Reynolds was dead, and nothing she could do would change that. It was the living she didn't want to face. She didn't want to see Andrea or Mick again. Didn't want to return to a state of fruitless inaction. Donning the mask of faithful comforter was an unwelcome duty she could've done without. Candice drew in a deep breath like one she might take before diving into deep water, then climbed the porch steps toward the door.

Inside, she found that the plastic sheeting that had earlier covered the door of the "death" room was pushed aside. Although the body had been removed, the signs of what had happened remained. Candice could see a pool of congealed blood on the leather sofa where Robbie had lain. A police officer snapped photos of every item in the room from multiple angles. The repeated flashes of bright light from the camera left gray orbs in her vision. The bread sat on the pool table, sealed in an evidence bag. Something kept nudging at the dark recesses of her mind. A sense of familiarity, but she couldn't figure out why.

Candice returned to the living room, and instead of sitting on the sofa, stood near the fireplace behind Mick. Andrea was—for the second or perhaps third time—repeating the details of the discovery of her husband's body.

"Robbie doesn't . . . didn't care much for the theater. That's why he didn't go with us," Andrea said.

Candice studied her face from across the room. The cracks of frustration and exhaustion showed in Andrea's expression; the deep furrow of her brow, heavy eye lids, downward slope of her lips showed the toll this had taken. Andrea seemed to have aged a couple years just in the minutes Candice had been out of the room.

Mick continued his questioning. "How have things been with your husband's business? Any issues lately?"

"None that I know of. I'm involved with the business in name only. He listed me as a majority owner to take advantage of incentives offered to women-owned businesses." Andrea thought for a moment, then added, "He's been anxious about something over the past few weeks."

Mick's eyes brightened. "Do you know what?"

"No. He wouldn't tell me."

"Did your husband have any enemies?" Mick said.

Candice snorted aloud. It was such a clichéd question that she thought they only asked it in television cop shows. Mick glanced at her with a puzzled look, then continued with his questioning.

———

The sun had sunk beneath the horizon by the time she emerged again from the house. The small crowd across the street was gone; the spectacle having grown boring to watch now that the ambulance and much of the police presence was gone. Candice found Andrew sitting on the porch swing, rocking slowly back and forth.

His head was low, and he picked at the cuticles of his fingers. The porch light bathed his face in shadow, making his sunken cheeks appear as great chasms in his face. As she approached, he rose to his feet and smiled.

"Ready?" he asked.

Candice nodded, feeling too exhausted to speak. She followed him off the porch and along the sidewalk toward his car. As she walked, Candice fought the urge to look back at the house. Like Lot's wife, she knew casting a backward glance would bring un-welcome consequences, but the urge was too strong. She turned to look at the Reynolds house. Her mind flooded with all-too-fresh memories of Robbie's vacant expression; his cold empty stare was unlike anything she'd seen before. In her experience, the dead didn't stare back. Their eyes were always closed when she saw them at the funeral. She didn't have to stare deep into the dark void of their empty soul.

On their ride back to the rectory at St. Matthew's Catholic Church, neither of them seemed interested in talking. Candice caught glimpses of Andrew's face beneath the passing streetlights. His eyes were fixed on the road ahead; his gaze seemed distant. Candice slouched in the passenger seat and fingered the small ob-ject in her jacket pocket. She glanced at one of the houses they passed along N. Chapel Street, noting the obvious evidence of a party in its infancy. College students lounged on the front porch, plastic Solo cups in every visible hand. Muffled music drifted from the open front door. The early evening revelry seemed to be in op-position to the anguish still being felt only a few blocks away.

Once in the driveway of the rectory, Andrew turned off the car, and the two of them sat in silence beneath the gleam cast from the dim light above the garage door. Neither moved to exit the vehicle.

Candice stared out the window at the silhouette of the church at the end of the block. St. Matthew's towered over the other buildings, and the centuries-old church looked ominous beneath the moonlight.

Candice turned toward Andrew. "Have you ever dealt with a murder before?" she asked.

At first, it seemed like Andrew hadn't heard her. He kept his gaze straight ahead, as if he were refusing to look at her. When he did speak, his voice was almost a whisper. "Murders are rare in Newark."

She turned her gaze away from him and stared out the windshield at the darkened windows of the garage door. The blackness beyond the glass seemed to swallow all light. "Probably won't sleep well for a few days," she said.

"Violence can leave an indelible mark on even the casual observer."

Candice checked her watch and sighed. It was 8:35 already and she still had to put the finishing touches on her sermon for the next morning's service. "I'd better go. Thanks for being there today. It meant a lot."

Her Subaru was parked along the street just up from the rectory. Once in her car, Candice reached into the pocket of her windbreaker and her fingers wrapped around the small, cold object. She held it up to the windshield so the light from a nearby streetlamp reflected off the crystal angel. The light twinkled off the ridges of the tiny wings when she turned it around in her fingers.

She sighed. Another shiny object she hadn't been able to resist. *Stealing from the daughter of a murder victim.* Candice slipped it back into her pocket, started her car, and drove off.

CHAPTER FOUR

Sunday

S weat beaded on Candice's forehead as she jogged up her driveway and stopped by the front door of her cottage. She bent
forward—hands on her knees—and gasped for air for several moments. Her early morning three-mile run usually served to energize
her for the busy day ahead. It was particularly important for her
on Sundays to be alert and clear-minded to lead her congregation
through the morning service.

But this morning, Candice was so exhausted that she barely
made it a mile before turning back. Although she'd arrived at home
before nine o'clock the night before, she found herself pacing her
small house, still tossing the events of the day around in her head.

When she eventually did make it to bed, sleep eluded her. Candice tossed and turned and thought about Robbie Reynolds, his wife and daughter, and the murder scene. But what really had kept her from sleeping was the loaf of bread.

Once her breathing had slowed, Candice unlocked the door and stepped into her house. She went straight to the kitchen, made herself a fruit smoothie, and carried the cold drink upstairs to her small bedroom. At the desk in the corner, she lifted the lid of her laptop. The blue light from the screen radiated through the darkened bedroom. Candice yawned as she studied the text displayed on the screen for that morning's sermon. *Riveting stuff. I'm putting myself to sleep.*

After showering and dressing, she returned to the computer and pulled up a local television station website. At the top of the screen, she found an article covering yesterday's murder. There were not a lot of details. Just a general summarization of the few facts that police made available: approximate time the body was discovered, the victim's name, a brief bio about Robbie Reynolds, and the usual "police are still investigating" statements. To her surprise, there was no mention of the bread she saw at the crime scene.

Candice leaned back. A loaf of bread resting on a corpse at a murder scene couldn't possibly be normal. It was the kind of thing that would cause a sensation and be listed as an unusual side note in any true crime book or television show. But, besides watching old reruns of *Unsolved Mysteries* when she was a kid, Candice wasn't much into that kind of entertainment. So why did it seem familiar?

She checked the alarm clock on the bedside table. She had twenty minutes to kill before it was time to head over to the church for the morning service. On the laptop, she started a series of Internet searches, changing up her key search words each time. The first search resulted in several so-called "killer" bread recipes, links to various bakeries, and a news article about a mother who had murdered her two-year-old child by stuffing his mouth with bread. She cringed at that last one, wondering what would drive a parent to commit such a heinous act. Additional searches brought more recipes, and several more news articles where bread played a part in a crime. But nothing seemed to match what she had seen the day before.

The loaf of bread on Robbie Reynolds's chest had been cleanly split down the middle. Its positioning almost made it look like some kind of ritual or sacrifice. She expanded her Internet search and found several biblical references to the Last Supper, but nothing else that seemed relevant. She pushed back from the desk, interlocked her fingers, and stretched.

Candice arrived at church fifteen minutes late. Sylvia Bavistock was already waiting on the front steps. The elderly church organist squinted through tortoiseshell glasses with pursed lips that conveyed her irritation at Candice's tardiness. There were still forty-five minutes before the service started, but Sylvia was almost zealot-like in her preparatory timetable, which included a full hour of warm-up before the service began.

While Sylvia scurried off to the organ, Candice lit the candles around the sanctuary and went through her usual Sunday morning routine. It was a mindless tedium that she followed like an automaton. As she prepared for the service, Candice wondered how she should address Robbie's death with the congregation. Or, if she even should? Most of the congregation would've heard the news by now. There was little that Candice could add to what had already been reported.

As her congregants began to filter into the church, Candice noted several people clustering together in fervent conversation. The topic of discussion, she assumed, had to be Robbie Reynolds. On any normal Sunday morning, Candice would wait until it was time to start the service to emerge from the vestry, the back room that served as a dressing room of sorts. But today, she decided to emerge early and mingle. She felt an overwhelming desire to hear what her flock was saying, thinking, and feeling about Robbie's death.

Her cassock danced effortlessly across the sanctuary floor as Candice moved slowly from one small group to another, greeting individuals and eavesdropping on conversations. Much of what she heard were words of shock and grief. A few had words of praise for Robbie's generosity with local charities. Some spoke of their concern for Robbie's grieving wife and child. But one or two had darker words.

"Wonder if Andrea finally got sick of his antics," someone said.

"He wasn't the most faithful of husbands," another remarked.

A moment of annoyance gripped Candice. She gritted her teeth and moved off to a silent corner of the sanctuary. The man was dead, and yet some people still resorted to gossip. She clenched her fists as the temptation to substitute her sermon with a lecture on respecting the dead rose from within, but it faded moments later as the hypocrisy dawned on her. No point in lambasting her whole congregation for the words of a few inconsiderate . . . assholes. She snorted at the thought. That wasn't a word she readily used, and for it to surface now made her wonder if she was far more exhausted than she realized.

"Pastor Miller," a frail voice said.

Candice hadn't seen Agatha Bowman approach, and was startled at the elderly lady's voice. She studied the lines of Agatha's face and marveled at the eighty-three-year-old history engraved there. Folds of pale, translucent skin hung from her chin. Her gray hair was thinning in front and looked dry and brittle. Agatha held a cane in one hand and a plate covered with aluminum foil in the other.

"I heard about Robbie," Agatha said. "So sad."

"Yes. It's a real tragedy."

"I heard about it on the news late last night. You were probably up late providing comfort to Andrea."

"It was a bit late," Candice admitted.

"I figured you'd need a pick-me-up today." Agatha peeled back the aluminum foil and held the plate out to Candice. "I baked you a batch of chocolate chip cookies."

"Thank you," Candice said, smiling. She reached for a cookie and took a bite. Her annoyance melted away as the sweetness of the chocolate filled her mouth.

Agatha pressed the plate into Candice's hand. "They're all for you."

Candice carried the plate into the vestry and left it on the table in the corner. Before stepping back into the sanctuary, she paused and reached for another cookie.

The organ summoned the congregation to their seats. Candice climbed the three steps to the carved wooden pulpit and watched as people filed into the pews and picked up their hymnals.

She raised her outstretched arms. "Welcome everyone. It's a beautiful day to be in the Lord's house. Before we begin, I'm sure that you've all heard the tragic news about Robbie Reynolds. I'm not going to dwell on his death during today's service. But, if any-one needs to talk, please feel free to reach out to me. My door is always open."

Even as her words hung in the air of the silent sanctuary, Candice knew no one would take her up on the invitation. They never did. In her two years at the church, only one person had sought her guidance. That was Robbie Reynolds, and all he'd wanted was the name of a good therapist.

The organ came to life again, filling the sanctuary with a low rumble. As Candice prepared to lead the congregation in the first hymn, she gazed down at the empty first row. A row that she never remembered being empty before. The row where Robbie Reynolds and his family sat every Sunday.

CHAPTER FIVE

B rian slipped quietly into St. Matthew's Catholic Church and
took a seat in the last pew at the back. Sunday mass had already begun. Andrew's white and green robes were embroidered in
gold thread, creating an intricate vertical design of what looked like
intertwined vines down the front. He stood before the altar with
his hands clasped in front of him.

"The Lord be with you," the priest said.

In unison, the congregation responded, "And with your spirit."

Brian muttered the responses along with everyone else. As
a child, Brian had been indoctrinated into the rituals and tradi-
tions of the Catholic Church. His parents had been devout in their

beliefs and had ensured he received his education at the best Catholic School in the Asheville area, Paul VI High School. Although they never said it aloud, Brian thought his parents had a secret hope he'd become a priest. He'd seen the faint look of disappointment in his mother's eyes when he announced his intention of becoming a journalist. The search for tangible truths outweighed that of the intangible. Faith in the unseen was far more difficult to encapsulate into two thousand words.

Brian now considered himself a lapsed Catholic, showing up for mass on the odd Sunday. It was usually Sarah's prompting that would get him out of his apartment and into the church.

"Go talk to Father Blake," she'd say.

Out of guilt, Brian would give in and make an appearance at St. Matthew's. He'd sit in the back, recite the litany of responses with the rest of the congregation, and at the end of mass, talk to Andrew. The conversation would be friendly and mundane. Afterward, he'd feel guilty for not mentioning the real reason he was there. Or the real reason he needed to talk. He simply couldn't bring himself to admit that he needed help.

Andrew led the congregation through Sunday mass while Brian observed quietly from the back row. Something was off about the priest's delivery. He stumbled over his words through the Gospel reading, as well as the Homily. Brian even noticed a tremble in Andrew's hands when he lifted the chalice of wine into the air during the blessing. At one point during the prayer after Communion, Andrew paused awkwardly, seeming to lose his train of thought. Unable to resume the prayer, the priest quickly ended it with an abrupt "Amen," leaving the congregation confused.

After the mass ended, people dispersed and began to file out of the church. A few congregants stood in the center aisle and chatted while inattentive, bored children distracted themselves by crawling along the pews. Brian made his way up the side aisle of the church, passing a young mother in a pale blue dress. She was deep in conversation with two other women while her young son tugged again and again at her arm. A futile attempt to persuade her that it was time to leave. She seemed quite adept at ignoring her child's pestering.

A few pews ahead, Andrew was speaking with a man whom Brian vaguely recognized. A few moments of rummaging through his memories returned the recollection of a banquet at the university. The man with the thinning hairline was a lecturer, but Brian still struggled to put a name to the face. When he approached the two men, Andrew lifted his eyebrows in mock surprise.

"The prodigal son returns." He extended his hand, which Brian shook heartily.

"Mr. Wilder. It's good to see you again," the other man said.

Andrew looked between them. "Alex, you've met Brian?"

It was Brian who answered. "Yes. At a university function."

"The honor society banquet," Alex added.

Alex Brennen. The name emerged from Brian's memory. He smiled as he recalled a pretentious evening of speeches, students in ill-fitting suits, and stuffy academics who babbled incessantly about their chosen topic. Not the most exciting story he'd covered. Alex Brennen's own level of pomposity that evening, as Brian remembered, had been the lowest among those in attendance.

Andrew placed his hand on Brian's shoulder and smiled. "What brings you back to the church, my son? Have you turned over a new leaf?" Andrew's touch was gentle but firm.

Brian laughed. "You make it sound like I haven't been here for years. It's been a month, two at tops."

"At least you're here. That's what matters."

Before any of them could say another word, a woman—dressed plainly in a navy dress and gray cardigan—appeared beside Alex. Her salt-and-pepper hair was drawn back away from her round face. The pudgy cheeks were red, and her eyes were cast down toward the floor. She clutched a battered hymnal against her chest. Alex gave her a passing glance, then frowned, as if her presence came as an unwelcome intrusion.

"Brian," he said, "you may remember my wife, Antonia?"

Brian didn't remember seeing her at the banquet but nodded politely anyway. Her only response was a momentary glance in his direction, then her eyes returned to stare at the floor.

Turning to the priest, Brian said, "You got a second to talk about yesterday?"

Andrew's shoulders shuddered and the color seemed to fade from his face. It took a moment for him to recover some composure. "Horrible business. Absolutely horrible."

"The Reynolds murder?" Alex asked.

Brian nodded but said nothing. He preferred to speak with Andrew alone and now regretted bringing up the topic in front of Alex.

"Such a shame," Alex said. "I heard it was a brutal scene."

Brian wondered where Alex got his information. He'd had little luck yesterday getting even the most basic details out of Chief Jenkins. He was hoping Mick Flanagan would be more forthcoming tomorrow. He glanced at Alex. "Did you know Robbie?"

Alex shrugged. "Everyone in Newark knew Robbie Reynolds, but I was never personally acquainted with the man."

Andrew clasped his hands together. "He was quite a stalwart in the business community. His death will certainly be felt for a long time."

A slight movement caught Brian's eye. Alex's wife was fidgeting quietly behind her husband. She'd remained so quiet Brian had almost forgotten she was there. When he glanced in her direction, she shifted further behind Alex, pressing herself into his back. Alex, for his part, whipped around, glaring down at his spouse.

His voice was low and gruff. "What? Can't you see I'm talking?"

She whispered something Brian didn't quite hear. Alex turned briefly to excuse himself, then gripped her arm and led her a few feet away. Brian watched while the couple spoke in hushed tones. He couldn't help but notice the white-knuckle grip Alex had on his wife's arm. Although she looked uncomfortable, Antonia made no attempt to break free. She remained silent, giving almost imperceptible nods as her husband spoke at length. Brian glanced at Andrew, who looked uncomfortable and had diverted his attention away from the couple.

After a few moments, Alex released his wife's arm with a slight push. She shrank away and moved along the aisle toward the church doors. Alex stepped back toward Brian and Andrew. The smile on his face looked forced. "My apologies. Toni's not feeling well. She's a bit distressed over the news about Robbie Reynolds." He shrugged his shoulders. "Actually, she's quite stupid about things like this. Very stupid indeed."

Brian exchanged a glance with Andrew. They seemed to share the same distaste for Alex's choice of words.

"I should be on my way," continued Alex. "Need to get her home and set her straight, if you know what I mean."

As Alex walked off, Andrew shook his head, and spoke softly so only Brian could hear. "That poor woman. I've never seen any signs of actual physical abuse, but she's certainly been beaten into submission."

They let their conversation fall into a silence as the remaining congregants worked their way out of the church. A few were still clustered in the corners, talking, and laughing amongst themselves. Brian recalled similar moments from his childhood. His parents had been active in their Asheville church, and he could always count on the hour-long Mass being followed by an hour of socializing. He remembered patiently waiting every Sunday for his parents to finish talking with their friends. Then it was off to the local diner for lunch. He had the same sense of isolation in church now as he did when he was a child. It was a world of beliefs and rituals with which he'd never quite become comfortable.

He glanced at Andrew. "You got a few minutes?"

Andrew didn't answer immediately. He, instead, stared blankly toward the back of the church. His lips formed a frown and his eyelid twitched. Then he said, "Sorry, Brian. I forgot I've got to be somewhere." Andrew made a point of glancing at his watch. "Actually, I'm late. We'll talk later."

With that, Andrew turned and walked swiftly toward a door off the right side of the altar. The priest's flowing robes skirted along the floor with each rapid footstep. Brian watched his departure with curiosity. He'd never known the priest to run from a discussion, at least not without a solid explanation.

CHAPTER SIX

Monday

Brian rose early Monday morning. He'd struggled to sleep the night before, tossing and turning most of the night. He crossed to the windows at the front of his apartment and opened the blinds to gaze down on Main Street. With the sunrise still an hour away, the thoroughfare was shrouded in darkness. The second-floor apartment—above the office of the *Newark Observer*—was small, with two back bedrooms and an eat-in kitchen off the living room. It wasn't much, but it was home.

Outside, a faint mist was coating the street and sidewalks with a glistening sheen of moisture. It would only worsen into rain as the day went on, if the weather forecast held up to its prediction.

The Dunkin' Donuts across the street and the Starbucks a block down were the only stores showing any activity at five in the morning. Brian watched a young couple exit the coffee shop—large cups in hand—and walk along Main Street toward the university. He noted the man held an umbrella but had neglected to put it up.

Brian moved into the kitchen and rummaged through the refrigerator. He found the ingredients for an omelet and set them out on the counter. As he sliced the onion, he heard a noise behind him and glanced over his shoulder. Sarah sat at the table watching him with her ice-blue eyes. She wore a red silk dragon kimono. Brian had brought it home from his last trip to Japan, nine or maybe ten years ago.

"How'd you sleep?" she said.

"As good as can be expected." He felt a tear form in his eye. Was it the onion? Or something else? He drove the knife down into the cutting board just a fraction harder than before.

"You went to church yesterday. Did you talk to Father Blake?"

He shook his head. "Didn't seem like it was a good time."

"You really should talk to him. He might be able to help you let go."

Brian glanced at her, admiring the almost flawless skin on her heart-shaped face. He'd always loved the faint dusting of freckles around her nose. Her cheeks, so soft. He wiped his eye on his shirt sleeve, then piled the chopped onion to the corner of the cutting board.

He grabbed a green pepper and started to chop again.

"He seemed shaken up during mass. Whatever happened at the Reynolds's house affected him badly. He barely got through the homily."

"You're skirting around the issue."

Brian grabbed two eggs and cracked each into a glass bowl. With a fork, he stirred the eggs vigorously. "I'm not. Just telling you what happened yesterday. Don't you want to know about my day?"

"I want you to move on."

Brian turned up the heat on the stove. "I need to see Lyle and Mick today. See if I can get more details about Saturday. They were tight-lipped when they left the Reynolds's place. Mick even looked a bit shaken up."

"Brian . . ."

He dumped the chopped peppers and onions into the skillet and caught their aroma as they began to sizzle. "The *Post-Gazette* stuck a story about it on page three. Just a couple paragraphs. Looks like they know about as much as I do." With a spatula, he shuffled the vegetables around the pan. "I wish you could've been at Chris's party Friday night. What a great time. He's a riot. You'd like him."

Brian pulled a pitcher of orange juice from the refrigerator and filled a small glass. Leaning against the counter, he sipped from the glass and studied her, taking in every detail. Even without makeup, she was as gorgeous as ever. He recalled with vividness their first meeting. He'd been passing through Atlanta's Hartford-Jackson International Airport, on his way to cover an important meeting of the United Nations Security Council. She was headed home to a family reunion in Louisiana. Their flights were both delayed, turning a chance conversation into dinner at the airport's TGI Fridays. Through fourteen years of marriage, she had seemed to defy the passing of time, remaining just as lovely as when they'd first met. A few strands of her tawny hair fell across her right eye. She didn't move to correct it.

"You're staring at me," she said.

"Have I told you lately that I love you?"

She smiled at him, nodding her head. "Yes."

"Sometimes I think I don't say it enough."

She frowned and closed her eyes. "You say it too much. Far too much these days."

"I can't help it."

Sarah leaned forward. "When was the last time you told Allison you loved her?"

Brian chewed on his bottom lip. It was a low blow, but not one that he didn't expect. His daughter was coming up far more frequently of late as a topic of conversation between them. Sarah usually used it as a rebuke of sorts. He refused to get angry at the subtle reprimand. After all, Sarah was right. It had been far too long since he last spoke to Allison.

"Your veggies are burning," Sarah said, calmly.

The acrid odor behind him was strong. He spun around and was greeted by whiffs of smoke rising from the skillet. The green peppers and onions were blackened. He lifted the pan from the stove, and, with a spatula, toyed with the scorched vegetables before letting the charred remains of his breakfast slide from the skillet into the nearby trash can. Brian sighed, set the pan in the sink, and turned back toward the table. The room was empty.

Brian strode into the Newark Municipal Building, waved at Erica Taylor—the young police officer seated behind the reception desk—and made a beeline across the marble-floored foyer toward the two elevators on the far wall. One floor down, he was greeted by another police officer seated behind a half-wall topped with a thick, glass partition.

A voice crackled through a small speaker embedded in the glass. "Hey Brian. Come on through."

The door to the right of the counter buzzed, then clicked. Brian pulled on the handle and stepped through the open doorway. A thickset officer rose from his chair and reached over the counter to shake Brian's hand. "What brings you here?"

"I'm looking for decorating tips, Frank." Brian smiled. "Is Lyle around?"

The police officer snorted, then leaned on the counter, his elbows propping up his broad chest and shoulders. "Nope. He's up with the mayor." He paused, as if checking to see if anyone was within earshot. "The chief is on a rampage this morning. Stewie is looking for ways to . . ." He raised his hands and made air quotes with his fingers. ". . . reallocate the budget again."

Brian smirked at the irreverent nickname for Jacob Stuart, the city's mayor. The animosity between the police force and the mayor's office had become a bit of a legend around the city. "I'll try to steer clear. Is Mick here?"

Frank thumbed over his shoulder toward the hall behind him. "In his office."

"Thanks."

Brian made his way along the hallway, passing the squad room on the left. Four rows of empty chairs faced a solitary podium at the front of the room. Further down, Brian stopped at a partially open door. The silver nameplate beside it read, "Michael Flanagan, Detective." Brian knocked on the door frame.

"Yeah?"

Mick glanced up from behind his desk when Brian pushed open the door and stepped into the office. A blue-striped tie hung loose from the collar of Mick's white Oxford shirt. Brushed back and neat, his ginger hair was the opposite of the tousled mess it had been on Saturday. A day or two of stubble was around his mouth and chin.

"Trying for a goatee again?"

"Did you come here to mock the facial hair-challenged?" The detective closed the manila folder he'd been reading, left it in the middle of the desk, and waved toward a nearby chair. "Come in. Sit down."

Once seated, Brian said, "You going to fill me in on Saturday?"

"What? No 'hello?' No 'good to see you?' No 'how's the family?'"

A laugh escaped from Brian's lips. "Hello. Good to see you, Mick. How's the family?"

"Fine. Thanks for asking. Did you know that Cheryl's pregnant?"

"No! Congratulations, Mick! Your first, right?" Brian said, recalling the excitement he'd felt years ago when Sarah had told him she was pregnant. It seemed like only yesterday that he had held his own daughter—Allison—in his arms. He feigned a smile to hide a sudden pang of heartbreak and guilt.

Mick nodded, his face beaming with pride. "Yep."

Brian gestured to the black-and-white photo framed on the wall behind the detective. A young man in a dark suit, posing beside a 1940s police car. "Your great-grandfather would be proud."

Mick spun his chair around and looked up at the photo. His smile was broad when he turned back. They'd spoken many times before of the great esteem that Mick had for his ancestor, the first detective on the Newark police force.

"Yeah, he would be, wouldn't he?"

Brian gave him a nod, pulled a notepad and pen from his coat pocket, then said, "Now, tell me about Saturday's murder."

Mick tapped his fingers on the desk, then leaned back in his chair. "Robert Reynolds. Stabbed once in the heart. His wife and daughter found him sprawled out on the sofa. They'd gone to NYC the evening before to catch a Broadway show. Found him when they returned on Saturday."

Brian clicked his tongue and shook his head. "Hell of a thing to find. Any suspects?"

The detective's mouth turned down. "You know I can't tell you that."

"Robbie Reynolds was a big name in this area. One might say he was Newark's self-proclaimed real estate king."

"Self-proclaimed is right," the detective said. "Ever been to his office? Not overly impressive for someone who's supposed to be a hotshot real estate agent."

"Maybe he doesn't like to appear too flashy."

"Have you heard his radio ads?" There was a sarcastic edge in his voice.

Brian snickered, recalling the over-the-top commercials on the local Delaware radio station that had made Robert Reynolds a minor celebrity around Newark. "Anything else you can tell me?"

Mick's hands rested on the folder. "Not at the moment."

Brian eyed the folder. From his angle, he couldn't read the words on the label, but could imagine what they said.

A loud voice bellowed into the office from down the hall. "Flanagan!"

"The chief's back." Mick rose from his chair. "I'd better go see what he wants. If I'm not back in five minutes . . ."

Brian smiled and waved at him. "I know. I'll let myself out."

Once alone, Brian checked the door. Mick had left it half open, blocking most of the view into the office for any passerby in the hall. Brian reached over the desk and picked up the manila folder. Mick's crime scene notes were on top. He skimmed through the details about the placement of the body, witness statements, and evidence gathered by the county's forensics team. He reread one paragraph twice. *A loaf of bread?*

Further in the folder, he found the crime scene photos. Brian glanced over his shoulder at the door and listened for approaching footsteps. Nothing, so he stole a glance at the first photo, then flipped through the rest in the pile. One photo showed Robbie's body stretched out on a leather sofa. The spotlessness of the room surrounding the corpse stood in stark contrast to the crimson stain of blood on Robbie's white shirt. Brian's eyes were drawn to the loaf of bread amid the blood. He jotted down a few notes in his notebook.

The next photo was a close-up of the loaf of bread. It had been split in two, with each piece soaking up blood like a sponge. Between the two pieces, a stubby handle protruded from the dead man's chest. The diminutive knife handle was wood clad, a rich golden-honey color. The wood looked unused, as if the knife was brand new.

The sound of footsteps from the hall reached Brian's ear. He hurriedly closed the folder and placed it back on Mick's desk. He had just enough time to settle back into his chair when the detective came through the door.

"Sorry about that," Mick said. "The chief wanted to rant about Stewie again."

"No worries," Brian said. "I should probably go anyway."

He rose from his chair as Mick patted the folder with his hand.

"Did you see everything you needed to?" Mick asked.

Brian chuckled. "Yeah, I think so."

"Did you see the message?"

Brian lowered himself back into the chair. "What message?"

"The one on Robbie's forearm." Mick opened the folder and sorted through the photos. He pulled one from the back of the stack, a photo Brian hadn't had enough time to see. "This is off the record."

Brian took the photo from Mick and studied it. The close-up of the dead man's forearm showed a jagged line of letters scrawled in crimson. The handwriting was clumsy and irregular. The dried blood still held a faint congealed sheen in the light of the camera flash. The seven capital letters spelled a single word. CHEATER.

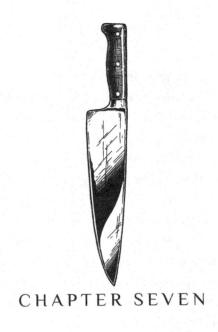

CHAPTER SEVEN

C andice pushed open the large arched door of St. Matthew's Catholic Church and stepped into the dim sanctuary. Her gaze drifted along the center aisle and then up toward the ceiling. The woodwork of the vast cathedral was ornate and picturesque, far more than her own church. The gray morning light filtered in through eight stained glass windows that ran the length of the church, four on either side. The reds, greens, blues, and yellows were muted by the overcast weather outside, the sun hidden behind clouds. Shadows draped across the rows of wooden pews like a painter's drop cloth. She allowed the thick wooden door to swing closed behind her with a deep thud. The sound reverberated through the vaulted ceiling. The Monday morning gloom matched her mood. She'd not slept well Saturday or Sunday night. She'd tossed and turned, haunted by Robbie's blank eyes in her dreams. After Sunday's church service, Candice had tried to call Andrea at her parents' house to find out how she was doing. But there had been no answer. Perhaps the grieving widow preferred to be left alone right now.

Candice moved down the aisle toward the church's single occupant. Andrew was seated in the first row facing the altar and didn't seem to notice her approach. He stared at the immense golden crucifix hanging from the wall behind the marble altar. The face of the crucified Christ was bowed and seemed to peer into the sanctuary with half-closed eyes and a deep, painful frown. It was a striking contrast to the simple wooden cross that hung in her own church.

"Hey, Andrew," she said.

He didn't acknowledge her greeting.

"I wasn't sure if you'd be in here," she continued. "But when you didn't answer the door at the rectory . . ."

He remained still and silent. Candice peered down at him. Andrew's hands were clasped on his lap. They were trembling.

She placed her hand on his shoulder. "Andrew?"

He jumped at her touch, turned, and glared up at her. For a moment, there was fear in his eyes. A soul-wrenching fear from the darkest depths of the heart. Then a sense of recognition filled his face, and he tried to smile. It looked forced.

"Sorry," he said. "I didn't know you were here."

"I didn't mean to startle you." Candice studied him for a moment. There were shadows beneath his eyes, and his salt-and-pepper hair was disheveled. He turned his gaze back to the giant crucifix on the wall. He wrung his hands together.

She took a seat next to him. "Are you okay? You look as if you haven't slept."

He waved away her concern. "Yeah, just had too much coffee yesterday." He averted his eyes. "What brings you here? I hope it isn't to play chess. Not really in the mood this morning."

Chess was the furthest thing from her mind. She shook her head. "No chess. Just needed to talk."

Andrew straightened up and turned her way. His eyes lit up, and the fatigue she'd seen in his face a moment ago seemed to wash away. That was something she'd always admired about him. His ability to instantly transform into a caring man of God no matter his own current plight.

She wished she had that superpower.

"How can I help?" he said.

Candice took a moment to wrangle her muddled thoughts into something marginally coherent. "I can't stop thinking about Robbie Reynolds," she finally said. "I had nightmares about him."

Andrew nodded as if he understood. "Violent crime can come as a real shock to someone who isn't used to it." He looked through her with a gaze that was a million miles away. "You think you can handle it. Control the emotional rupture it creates. You put on a brave face and hope no one notices." He breathed deeply. "But it burrows into your soul. The violence replays itself again and again. Reminding you of your own impotence against it." He stopped speaking, his eyes still locked on something unseen behind her.

"Andrew?"

Her words broke the spell. He looked at her and smiled. "Sorry. Was thinking of something else."

Candice turned to stare at the altar. "This is something way outside of anything I've experienced before." She clasped her hands and rested them in her lap. "I grew up in a small Kansas town where we left our doors unlocked at night. Crime was a nonentity in Bridgewater Falls." She glanced at him. He nodded as if to direct her to continue. "In seminary, they taught me how to provide spiritual comfort to those who were suffering. Taught me how to pray. How to say all the right words. Helping people cope with death was something I expected with this vocation. But . . ." She closed her eyes, recalling the ghostly pale complexion of Robbie's face. "They never told me how to cope with murder."

Andrew reached over, took her hand, and gave it a gentle squeeze. "It's the same thing. Death is death, violent or not. The family needs comfort either way."

Candice rose from the pew, turned, and looked down the aisle toward the back of the church. The vast empty sanctuary suddenly felt oppressive. The dark shadows seemed to be closing in on her. "But where do ministers go for comfort? Who relieves our burdens and our grief?"

"Isn't that what God's for?"

Candice grunted. "I was hoping for something a little more tangible."

Andrew frowned. "You've got me." There was disappointment in his voice.

She gazed at him and smiled. "Sorry. I didn't mean—"

"I know what you meant." He grinned at her. "Just remember that I'm here for you."

She returned to her seat and leaned forward, allowing her hands to dangle between her knees. "It's just . . . I'm not used to staring death in the face." Candice leaned back and felt the hard wood of the pew press against her spine. "Did you ever meet Robbie?"

"No. Can't say I have."

Candice looked down at her shoes. Her blue canvas Vans were faded, the once-white rubber soles were more of a faint gray from years of use. They were the perfect analogy for her waning faith. "A great guy," she said. *If you don't believe the many rumors,* she added in her head. "Always there with a smile for anyone who needed it." *Then again, smiles are cheap.*

"Quite the marketer. I doubt there's anyone in Delaware who didn't know who he was," Andrew said.

She opened her mouth to speak but was interrupted by creaking hinges on the door at the back of the church. Candice turned and caught sight of a figure silhouetted against the gloomy light from outside. The man stepped into the church and pushed the door closed behind him. His footsteps echoed through the sanctuary as he walked along the center aisle toward them.

"Andrew," he said. He halted when he saw Candice. "Sorry, didn't realize you had company."

Andrew rose from the pew and smiled. "No worries. We were just chatting."

Candice felt the warmth on her cheeks, a mix of annoyance and embarrassment. She didn't have a monopoly on Andrew's time, but the interruption seemed ill-timed. She had a momentary urge to shout, "I was here first." But she balked at the thought. How would that sound? A thirty-three-year-old minister whining like a child over a popular playground ride. But she wanted—no, needed—Andrew's help and advice.

As the newcomer approached, she assessed him with an eye that was a tad more judgmental than she knew it should be. The man wore a brown tweed sports coat and faded jeans. The coat hung open and looked as if it would be impossible to button because of the rotund stomach that protruded from beneath its folds.

Beads of sweat formed along his high forehead and his breathing was slightly labored.

Andrew shook hands with the man, then gestured to her. "Have you met Candice Miller?"

"No, I don't believe I've had the pleasure." The man extended his hand toward her. His grip was firm, and his palm sweaty. She tried not to flinch at his touch.

"Alex, Candice serves at Trinity Episcopal Church over on the corner of Haines Street and Delaware Avenue. She's an exceptional chess player. Sometimes she even puts me to shame." He turned to Candice. "Meet Alex Brennen, a professor of religious history at the university. He's written a couple books, been to the Holy Land, and has guest lectured at half the seminaries in the country at one time or another."

The man blushed at the priest's embellished introduction. He turned his eyes downward for a moment, and then smiled. "That intro gets more grandiose every time you tell it. Next, you'll have me finding the tomb of Christ."

Andrew chuckled, but Candice sensed a tired edge to his laugh.

"Religious history was always my Achilles' heel in seminary," she said. "Except for Martin Luther. I did my thesis on him. Fascinating man."

"Really." His eyes narrowed as he studied her. "That's interesting. Very interesting."

His eyes locked on hers and lingered.

She suddenly felt vulnerable, almost stripped naked before the intensity of Alex's stare. The back of her neck prickled, and Candice found it hard to pull away from such a domineering gaze. She finally stepped back and turned away from Alex. "Andrew, I better go."

Andrew frowned. "So soon?"

"Don't leave on my account," Alex said.

"I've got a few errands to run," Candice lied. She looked at Andrew. "I'll call you later."

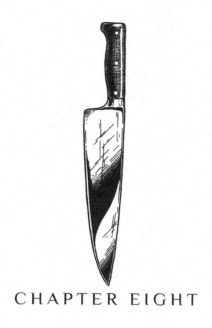

CHAPTER EIGHT

Sitting at his desk, Brian reread the first line of the article on the front page of that morning's *Newark Observer*. He didn't like it any more now than when he wrote it Saturday evening. It had been a rush to get the edition sent off to the printer before Sunday. He'd worked feverishly through the night changing the front page to accommodate the breaking news about Robbie Reynolds's death. On Saturday night, there had been little to report other than the death itself and that it was under investigation. But Brian made sure to deliver all the facts he knew to his dwindling readership.

He set the newspaper down on his desk. *How much longer can I keep this going?* The newspaper was barely limping along. In the five years that he had owned it, the *Newark Observer* had only made money in one year. Every other year, it barely broke even, and the past year it had lost money. He figured he had another two—possibly three years—left before it threatened to eat through what was left of the settlement money. When it was all over, what would he have? One building with an empty office on Newark's Main Street, and an apartment on the second floor.

Over the past couple years, he'd had offers to buy the *Observer*. A regional conglomerate that ran over twenty small town newspapers had expressed interest in purchasing the newspaper from him. These days it was all about consolidation of resources. Cover the broadest of territories with the fewest number of journalists. Despite his previous global journalistic status, Brian believed that the best journalism came from locally based reporters with solid relationships rooted in the community, like those he'd established with Newark's police department, the mayor's office, the university's administration, and many others.

A car honk from outside drew his eyes to the large picture window of the *Observer* office. The early afternoon traffic on Main appeared unusually heavy. He was half-tempted to step out to see if there was an accident further up the one-way thoroughfare that might account for the increased bottleneck. But he resisted the urge.

Brian looked over at the three nearby empty desks. The newspaper kept a small staff: himself, two part-time reporters, and Jessica, his photographer. Liam Poole—the youngest of the two reporters—had gone up to the university to cover a press conference, while the other, Chloe Williams, was away on vacation. He smiled when his eyes fell on the third desk. Jessica would wander in when she wandered in. Getting her to keep regular office hours wasn't worth the aggravation.

Across the office, a ceaseless clicking drew his attention to the front desk. The needles in Mildred Smith's hands flashed like lightning. The sixty-seven-year-old receptionist was absorbed in her knitting, drawing lavender-colored yarn from a bag that sat on the floor beneath her desk. He tried to recall what she was making without success. A scarf? A sweater? Or even for whom she was making it. His hope was that it wasn't for him. He smiled as her head bobbed in time with each click of her needles. Her dark wavy hair was only speckled with gray, making her appear younger than she was.

Mildred had joined the small newspaper two years ago after finding her retirement from the post office to be far less exciting than she'd anticipated. Her willingness to answer phones and manage the newspaper's correspondence had been a godsend for Brian. As the newspaper's owner, editor, and only full-time reporter, he'd been struggling to keep the day-to-day operations running smoothly while also pursuing stories for the next edition. There was one other thing that Mildred brought to the newspaper that had become invaluable to him. Information. Mildred was an interminable gossip.

He leaned back in his chair. "What do you know about the Reynolds family?"

"I'm not one to talk ill of the dead, but they're the biggest bunch of liars and cheats in Newark." She stopped knitting and set her needles on the desk. She glanced in his direction. "Well, excluding our illustrious mayor."

"I'm not sure I'd say Jacob Stuart is—"

"Word on the street is that Robbie was having an affair."

Brian laughed, knowing that her "word on the street" was a group of elderly women who met every Saturday at the Main Street

Diner for lunch and an afternoon of gossip. "An affair? I thought he was—"

"You know I'd never say a bad word about anyone, but odds favor that bimbo who answers the phones at his office. Big boobs and a personality as light as a helium-filled balloon. At least that's what I hear. Real airhead, if you know what I mean. What would you expect from someone who calls herself Cupcake?"

"So, he wasn't a shining example to husbands everywhere?"

"Nope. And that wife of his? She isn't much better. A drunken little shrew. That's what Andrea Reynolds is. Just about every Saturday night you can find her at Gaelic Arms with her snoot full." Mildred shook her head as if in disgust. "Usually needs to get an Uber home because she can barely find her car, let alone drive it. Sylvia Bavistock sees her at church every Sunday. Dark glasses, and a puss that looks like she's been sucking lemons."

Brian knew about the Irish pub on South College Avenue. He'd been there more than once himself. "Isn't Saturday karaoke night?"

"Yes, and the drunker she gets, the worse she sings. Not that she could sing to start with. Sounds like someone's dragging a porcupine across violin strings. So I've been told."

"What about their daughter?"

She frowned at him. "Brian, you know I don't like to gossip, especially about children."

"Sorry, I didn't—"

"There was a bit of bother back when she was born. A story was floating around that she wasn't Robert's child. Andrea was seen quite a bit with some student from the university. He left town shortly after she got pregnant. Someone told me there might have been a payoff involved."

Brian picked up a pencil from his desk and twirled it between his fingers. "Raises some interesting questions." *Maybe the real father came back to stake a claim.*

The office door swung open, and the sounds of the busy street filtered in along with Jessica, dressed in gray cargo pants and a blue T-shirt.

"Hi guys, how's it?"

Brian waved at her. "Hi, Jess."

Jessica crossed to a desk in the far corner, tossed her black canvas messenger bag onto the chair, and hiked herself up on the desktop. Her black combat boots thudded against the desk as she folded her legs beneath her.

"How was the wedding?" said Mildred.

Jessica pulled the hairband from her ponytail and ran her fingers through her strawberry blonde hair. "Totally betchin'." Gathering a handful of her shoulder-length hair behind her head, she slipped the hairband back into place and then fanned the newly made ponytail out with her fingers. "Got some unreal shots that completely rock. They're gonna love the proofs."

Brian smiled at the spunky twenty-three-year-old. Her sharp pale green eyes were masterful behind a camera viewfinder, taking photos that a veteran photojournalist would envy. He had no doubt she had the raw talent to be highly sought after by all the top magazines. In many ways, she reminded Brian of himself when he was her age. Hardworking. Enthusiastic. Unaware of the true potential behind her talent. The difference between them was that Brian had ventured forth, making a name for himself within the industry. Jessica was satisfied with remaining in Newark, building a reputation as a top-rated wedding photographer as well as the *Newark Observer*'s photojournalist. She was still young.

Give it another few years and things might change.

Jessica said, "So Chris's shindig rocked?"

"Yeah. It's a shame you couldn't make it," said Brian.

"He's a little creepy," Jessica said. "You don't just ask to feel someone's face."

"He's blind, Jess. How else is he supposed to know what you look like?"

"It's just . . . weird." Jessica slid out her legs and let them hang over the edge of the desk. "Heard Robbie Reynolds got whacked over the weekend."

"We were just talking about it when you came in," Mildred said.

"Don't let me stop you. Let's hear all the juicy details."

"I was up to see Mick this morning. There isn't much to tell yet." Brian rose from his chair and crossed to the coffee machine along the far wall. "Stabbed with one upward thrust to the heart. He was laid out on the sofa."

"Perhaps Andrea had had enough of his little games," Mildred said.

He poured himself a cup of coffee, then shook his head. "Seems she has an alibi for Friday night." Brian took a sip from his mug. "Mildred, do you know anything about Candice Miller? The priest at the Episcopal church on Haines Street?"

"Not much, why? Do you think she had something to do with the murder?"

Brian snickered. "No. Just wondering. She was at the Reynolds house after the murder. Father Andrew drove her over."

"Does Flanagan have any suspects?" Jessica asked.

Brian returned to his seat. "None that he'd tell me about." He set his coffee mug onto the desk. "It's all a bit out of the ordinary, Jess."

"In what way?"

Brian proceeded to detail the crime scene photo that Mick Flanagan had shown him. Jessica sat attentive as he detailed the torn loaf of bread and the bloody word written on the dead man's arm. Mildred seemed to take the second point as vindication of her earlier analysis of Robbie Reynolds's character. She wore an "I told you so" smugness in her half-smile and mumbled inarticulate words of affirmation. When he concluded his narrative, Brian fell silent, and waited for his companions to comment. Jessica was the first to speak up.

"Wicked."

Brian leaned forward and rested his elbows on the desk. "I'm glad you're so enthusiastic."

Jessica's shoulders dropped and she let out an exasperated exhale. "Damn. You want me to do something, don't you?"

"With all the wedding work you do, I figure you've got an inside contact over at Barley's Bakery."

"I guess," Jessica said. All her enthusiasm was suddenly gone.

"See if they make a dark, artisan bread like the one found at the murder scene. If they don't, ask if they know any area bakeries that do."

As it closed in on five, Mildred began to pack up her knitting and slipped the work-in-progress into her bag along with her needles. Jessica had left the office half an hour earlier.

"Don't stay too late," Mildred said.

Brian looked up from his computer, nodding. "I'll try not to."

She frowned. "Brian Wilder, don't patronize me. It's not good for you to work all the time."

He couldn't help but chuckle. Mildred's admonishment was a regular occurrence, and rightly so. He spent far too many nights working late in the office. But it beat the alternative of returning to his apartment and wallowing in his own grief.

Mildred's rebuke continued. "You need to get out. Find yourself a nice girl."

Brian forced a grin. He had a nice girl. One he loved deeply. But he didn't dare tell Mildred that. "Perhaps you're right."

"Stella Fairchild's daughter is single. You and she would make a lovely couple." Mildred slung her knitting bag over her shoulder. "I could speak to her . . ."

Brian shook his head, rose from behind the desk, and crossed the office. *Better to leave now, before she starts taking her matchmaking too seriously.* He placed a gentle hand on Mildred's shoulder. "Come on, let's close up shop for the night. I'll walk you out."

The evening's chilly air sent a shiver down his back as they stepped out of the office. Brian pulled the door closed and turned the key in the lock. The block letters on the plate glass picture window beside the door read *Newark Observer*. No glitz or glamour. Just matter of fact. He'd often thought, over the past five years, about updating the lettering to something a bit flashier, more modern. But after spending a week mulling over the idea, Brian would always decide to leave the window the way it was. No point in messing with a classic.

He glanced up and down the street and noted the college crowds that were already filtering out of their dorms for an evening's revelry. Brian turned to Mildred, who'd pulled a shawl over her shoulders to stave off the brisk March air.

She gestured to the second-floor windows of the *Newark Observer* building. "Don't you go up there and work."

His eyes followed hers up the tan brickwork to the darkened double windows of his apartment's living room. They looked empty and lifeless. "I won't. See you in the morning."

Mildred shook her head, as if to tell him she knew he was lying. "Good night, Brian."

He watched her walk almost a block down Main Street before moving the short distance to a solitary white door situated on the opposite side of the office window. The brass knocker on the door was tarnished with age. The narrow black mailbox that hung beside the door contained three pieces of correspondence: one bill, one solicitation from a charity, and a sales flyer from a local grocery store. Brian unlocked the door and climbed the stairs to his apartment above.

He paused at the top of the stairs. His gaze fell upon an 8 x 10" photograph, framed in black, hanging on the wall. It greeted him every night. As much as it hurt for him to see it, he never moved the photo from its place at the top of the stairs.

Brian peered at the woman and young girl centered in the picture. The woman's ash brown hair was brushed over the right side of her face. Her blue eyes stared forward as if looking straight at him. Her white sleeveless blouse was appropriate for the beach, which acted as the photograph's background. He remembered the beach well, on a small Caribbean Island called Saint Marie. The young girl was resting her head on the woman's arm, eyes closed as if asleep. The girl's hair—the same color as the woman's—was pulled back into a ponytail.

He touched the lower corner of the frame. "I miss you, Sarah."

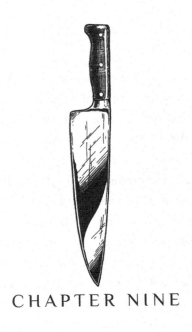

CHAPTER NINE

Candice leaned out of the elevator and glanced around. Seeing no one, she stepped out and moved down the hall. The thud of her footsteps on the tile floor echoed off the whitewashed walls. As she passed, Candice glanced at the door for the office of Newark Dentistry and completely ignored the next one, which was for Dr. Biddick, an ear, nose, and throat specialist. She strode to the end of the hall and paused outside the last door. The small black plaque beside it was simple and unadorned. It read Blackwell Counseling Services. She checked her watch before going in. 6:40 p.m. The last client would be long gone, as well as two of the therapists. She slipped through the door into a silent and empty waiting room.

Another door was across the room, and she wasted no time passing through that into the suite of offices beyond. Candice stepped past the empty reception area with a sliding window that looked back into the waiting room where she'd just been. A nearby door stood open, and the sound of someone typing on a keyboard drifted into the hall. She peeked around the doorframe and glanced into the office beyond. It was scarcely furnished. A paisley sofa sat along the wall near the door. The sunken cushions bore witness to years of use. The evening sunset shone through the floor-to-ceiling window along the opposite wall. The long curtains that draped down either side framed the window in pale blue. A meager wooden desk sat before the window. The room's only occupant was behind the desk, leaning over a laptop and typing feverishly.

Candice rapped on the door frame with her knuckles. Samantha Blackwell glanced up with a smile, which quickly changed to a momentary look of surprise. "Oh, Candice. I . . . um . . . wasn't expecting you."

Candice moved into the office and took a seat on the sofa. "I figured you'd still be here."

Samantha gestured to the laptop. "Just catching up on my notes from today's sessions. What brings you over here?"

Candice studied Samantha for a second before responding. Something seemed off. The top two buttons on her beige silk blouse were undone, revealing quite a bit of flesh. She'd never known Samantha to be so careless about her appearance, particularly when facing clients. "Uh, do you usually . . ." Candice felt a rush of heat on her face.

"What?" Samantha asked.

"You're showing quite a bit of . . ." Candice gestured toward Samantha's neckline.

Samantha glanced down, then laughed. "Sorry, didn't realize that button had popped." She quickly fumbled with the button. "Damn, I hope it wasn't like that all day." The comment and the laugh that followed seemed forced.

Candice sank back into the sofa and folded her arms. "I assume you heard about Robbie."

"Yeah. What a tragedy." Samantha's eyes darted toward the door, then back at Candice. "Have you spoken to his wife?"

"I was there on Saturday . . . after his body was discovered." Candice closed her eyes and shook her head. "It wasn't pleasant."

"Death never is." Samantha checked her watch. "How are you holding up?"

Candice rubbed the back of her neck and grunted. "I've been better."

"You don't look like you've slept much."

Candice didn't respond at first. The fatigue from the last few restless nights weighed heavily on her. "That's the understatement of the decade."

"Have you pilfered anything lately?"

"What?" The sudden change in subject unsettled Candice. A hot tingle rushed up her cheeks as she stumbled over her response. "No . . . well . . . I . . . it was . . . maybe . . ."

Samantha held her hand up as she laughed. "Say no more." Then she leaned forward, elbows on the desk. "You do realize, I can help you with this."

Candice shifted in her seat and averted her eyes. "I still think I can beat this on my own." Samantha was her solitary confidante regarding her kleptomania, but she was not ready for therapy.

Samantha shrugged. "Okay. I'm here when you change your mind."

The room fell silent, and a sudden awkwardness hung in the air. Candice recalled the glass angel she'd stolen from Marissa Reynolds's room. It had been so easy to pocket the tiny figurine. She'd become a resourceful thief over the years. A master at the sleight-of-hand needed to abscond with her prize even in a crowded room. She never stole anything of great worth, mostly just shiny trinkets that caught her eye. But the shame and regret that loomed over her always seemed disproportionate to her crime, like she'd stolen a dollar bill but was being punished for robbing a bank.

Candice decided it was time to change the subject. "Was Robbie still coming to see you?"

"Yes, he was still a client."

"He's been seeing you for a while. It's been—what, a year—since I referred him to you?" Candice said.

"You know I'm not supposed to talk about this with you."

Candice held out her open palm. "Why was he seeing you? When he asked me if I knew any good therapists, he never told me why he needed one." She furrowed her brow and added, "What if he was killed because of something he was discussing with you?"

Samantha said, "All my sessions are confidential, but if the—" Her words ended abruptly.

Candice heard movement by the door. She followed Samantha's gaze and found Alex Brennen standing in the doorway. He looked at Candice, and for a moment, she thought his eyes darkened with a mix of surprise and anger. Then he smiled, and his eyes were suddenly bright and welcoming once again.

He glanced at Samantha. "I'm sorry. I didn't realize that you had company."

"Not to worry." A sudden change washed over Samantha. Her words became breathy, her eyes brightened. She reached for the top button on her blouse—the one that had been undone earlier—and began to finger the round piece of plastic. "We were just chatting." She gestured toward Candice. "Do you know . . ."

Alex interrupted. "We've met."

Candice added, "Just this morning."

Without taking her eyes off Alex, Samantha rose from her seat and rounded the desk. "Candice, I've got some business to attend to with Alex. Can we continue this discussion later?"

Candice eyed the therapist for a moment, then stood. "Sure. I'll give you a call."

Samantha was quick to usher Candice through the waiting room and open the outer office door. Before exiting the waiting room, Candice glanced back at the door that led to the inner parts of the office. She wondered how long the affair had been going on, because she was sure that was what was going on between them. Although Samantha wasn't married, she was certain that Alex Brennen was. She'd noticed a gold wedding band on his finger that morning when they'd met at St. Matthew's. He wasn't wearing it a few minutes ago, but there was a distinct indentation around his finger to indicate that he usually wore the ring. Probably took it off before coming into the office. Did Samantha know that he was married?

Candice had known her for two years, and in that time, they'd become close. There wasn't a lot that she didn't know about Samantha. But discussions about the therapist's love life were often met with resistance. Now, Candice understood why. "Didn't know you had office hours this late," she said.

Samantha stammered for a moment. "I . . . um . . . no, I usually don't see clients this late."

"He's a client?"

Samantha's jaw tightened. "No . . . I mean, I can't talk about why people come here to see me." She inched the door closed, forcing Candice to step out into the hallway. "I'll talk to you later. Not tonight. Let's talk tomorrow." The sentence was punctuated with a click as the door closed, and another click as the door lock was engaged.

CHAPTER TEN

Tuesday

B rian waited by the second-floor elevator in Northern Delaware University's Hennessy Hall. His morning meeting with Roger Halderman, dean of the University's journalism department, had ended earlier than he'd anticipated, which freed up the rest of his morning. The meeting—a discussion about the continuation of the journalism internships at the *Newark Observer*—consisted primarily of Roger inquiring if Brian wanted to continue with the internships for the fall semester and Brian saying yes. The remainder of the twenty-minute meeting was idle chit-chat between the two men, swapping stories from their years in journalism. Roger, fifteen years Brian's senior, had his own long illustrious career at a Chicago newspaper before coming to the university. Brian enjoyed hearing tales of the day-to-day insanity of a busy Windy City newsroom. At the pinnacle of his own career, he'd rarely stepped into a newsroom, instead filing his stories remotely while en route to cover the next.

The elevator doors opened, and Brian was surprised when Alex Brennen stepped out. The man was carrying an overstuffed leather briefcase. The zipper was wide open, and Brian doubted it would close even if someone had tried. A bundle of papers and a thick textbook peeked out of the opening. The shoulder strap strained beneath the weight. With Alex was a young student—tall and gaunt, with wavy dark hair. The student was chattering away and gesticulating wildly. From Alex's creased brow and the tightness in his jaw, it was obvious that it was a conversation that he wanted no part of.

"—and if there is unity between the three persons—" the student said.

When Alex caught sight of Brian, his face lit up with a mix of excitement and relief. He thrust his hand forward. "Brian, sorry I'm late. My last class ran over."

Brian was momentarily startled by the greeting, but quickly picked up on his cue. "No problem. I was a little late myself."

The student, unaware that he had lost his audience, continued to prattle on. "—said that the Trinity was more about the relationship—"

Alex turned to the student. "Phillip, I've a meeting with Mr. Wilder. We need to continue this conversation later."

The student shook his head in protest. "But professor—"

Alex glared back at him with a reddening face and nostrils flaring. His words came out slow, deliberate, and hard. "I said later."

As Phillip walked away—shoulders hunched and head down like a puppy that had just been scolded—Alex returned his gaze to Brian and smiled. "Thanks for playing along. I would've been stuck listening to his inane commentary on my lecture for an hour. Some students don't know when to quit."

Alex began to move down the hallway, and Brian decided to walk with him. He gestured over his shoulder. "Is he a bad student?"

"Phillip Baxter?" Alex shrugged. "He's actually a brilliant student. But he thinks that every fact and philosophy should be questioned ad nauseam. And I usually take the brunt of the questioning. It gets old after a while."

"Refresh my memory: You teach religious studies?"

Alex shifted the heavy bag from one shoulder to the other. "Among other things. The administration likes to get every drop of blood it can out of us."

Brian noted the sarcasm in Alex's words. It was a similar story in journalism as well. Many of his friends in the industry often complained it was becoming increasingly difficult to focus on one particular area of news when budget and headcount were constantly being slashed. "Welcome to the modern workforce. Do more with less," he said.

Alex halted by a door; the brass plate emblazoned with his name. He unlocked the door, and they entered a small, cluttered office. The most prominent piece of furniture was the oak desk at the opposite side of the room. The intricate carving around the desktop's edge and the tongue-and-groove construction revealed that this was not typical university-issued furniture. There was only a small surface area visible among the papers stacked in uneven piles. Two side-by-side bookshelves along the wall overflowed with volumes, both modern textbooks and antique editions. A single leather club chair—chocolate-brown in color and cracked with wear—was positioned before the desk.

"Have a seat," Alex said, gesturing to the chair. He rounded the desk and rested the briefcase in between two heaps of paper. "You're a bit of an enigma to me. Of course, I'm familiar with your ‑background. An award-winning journalist of the highest caliber. Father Blake has nothing but good things to say about you. Yet, here you sit, running a small newspaper in a small town. I can't figure it out." Alex pulled some papers from his bag and placed them on the desk.

Brian's mouth formed a lazy grin, but inside his stomach tightened into a knot. This was a conversation topic that surfaced more often than he'd like. It was difficult to separate himself from his past. He realized it was only logical that people would find his presence in Newark to be a curiosity. How long must he live here before people stopped being curious?

"I was looking for a change," Brian said.

Alex lifted the thick textbook out of the briefcase, briefly searched the desk for a spot to set it, then placed the book on the front edge of the desk. As Alex withdrew his hand, his elbow pushed into one of the heaps of paper, sending the top twenty or so sheets fluttering to the floor. He tried to make a quick grab for the first few sheets and in doing so, inadvertently pushed the briefcase forward on the desk. The case hit the textbook and sent it tumbling onto the floor at Brian's feet.

Brian watched the comedy of errors unfold, trying to stifle a laugh. As Alex scrambled to gather up the spilt paperwork, Brian leaned forward to pick up the fallen textbook. As he lifted it from the floor, a slip of folded notepaper fell from between the pages.

Brian snatched it up and got a glimpse of the six words printed on the note.

He set the book back on the desk. "This fell out of your textbook." Brian held the note out to Alex. "Do your students usually send threatening letters?"

Alex took the note from Brian and read it aloud. "You won't get away with this."

"Any idea what it means?" Brian asked.

A smile broke on Alex's lips. "It's probably just some . . ." Then the color suddenly rushed from his face. The smile faded. "I just remembered. I've got an important meeting to get to." Alex rounded the desk and moved quickly to the door. He pulled it open and stood to the side. "Sorry to rush you out. Thanks for stopping by."

Brian took the hint. He rose from the chair and moved through the door. In the hallway, Brian turned to speak to Alex once more, but found the door was already closing behind him.

———— · ————

Brian stepped back into the outer office of Roger Halderman's suite. The dean's receptionist, Rachel Wallin, looked up from her computer and greeted him with a broad smile. She brushed her black hair away from her face. "Back so soon? Roger's not here. He had another meeting across campus."

Brian placed his hands on the desk and leaned forward. "I'm actually here to see you."

Rachel let out a soft moan. "Really? Intriguing." She tilted her head and toyed with a few strands of her hair. Her voice was warm and inviting, almost sultry. "And what does Brian Wilder want with me?"

"Information."

Rachel's sigh was loud like a pressure release on a newly opened bottle of soda. "Is that all I am to you? An information source?" She leaned forward, looked up, and locked eyes with him. "When are you going to take me out for dinner?"

Brian felt his face flush. "Rachel—"

She looked at him with pouty lips and doe-like eyes. "We should go out," she said. "We would be awesome together."

Now it was Brian's turn to sigh. "I'm not interested in seeing anyone right now, but when I am—"

Rachel waved to dismiss his words. "Yeah, yeah. Whatever. What do you need this time?"

"Anything you can get me on Alex Brennen."

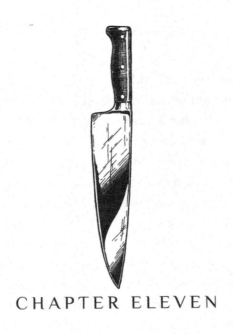

CHAPTER ELEVEN

An afternoon mist coated the windshield of the Mustang as Brian pulled into the parking lot of Reynolds Real Estate. The lot was empty except for a yellow late model Volkswagen Beetle. The license plate caught his eye. CUPK8KE. He smiled.

As he stepped through the front door, the young woman behind the front desk looked up from her computer screen. Her long, ash-colored hair had a streak of purple on the left side. A victim of too much mousse, it fell in brittle strands over her shoulders. He figured she was twenty-three, possibly twenty-four at the most. A sweet perfume that he couldn't identify hung thick in the air and caught in his throat as he breathed.

"Can I help you?" she said.

He caught sight of the name plate on the desk. Mandy Pullman. Brian handed her a business card. "I'm Brian Wilder from the *Newark Observer*." He glanced at the office space behind her. There'd been an attempt to tidy up, but he could still tell the police had been through the files and drawers.

"If you're looking to sell us something, it's not a good time."

Brian smiled, then shook his head. "Not selling anything. I'm a former client of Robbie's." He'd learned long ago to read the situation and go with what garnered the most access to information. "Just wanted to stop in and pay my respects. It's such a tragic thing to have happened." He didn't feel even a moment's guilt in deceiving her.

She didn't reply, instead looked briefly down at her desk. When Mandy looked up at him again, her eyes were moist beneath the heavy layer of mascara and eyeshadow. "We shouldn't be open today, you know." She clutched a balled-up tissue and dabbed at her eyes. "But two of the other realtors have deals in flight . . ." She gestured behind her. "But, like, they're not even here. Probably at home, enjoying a day off."

He studied her face. She seemed to teeter between sorrow and indignation. But it lacked the distress of a lover in mourning. This was going to take tact. A wrong word in either direction, and she might clam up instantly. Brian gestured behind her. "I see the police have been here."

She nodded. "Yeah. Came in yesterday. Tore through everything and left a big mess." She thumbed over her shoulder at the file cabinets behind her desk, then added, "Guess who had to clean it up." She rolled her eyes to signify her displeasure.

He nodded his understanding. "The police aren't known for being compassionate during their searches." *Except perhaps Mick*

Flanagan. The most compassionate cop he'd ever met. "Did they seize much of Robbie's stuff?"

"They, like, emptied his desk." Mandy leaned an elbow on her desk and rested her chin in her palm. "Took his laptop, too. Kept asking me if Robbie . . . Mr. Reynolds had an appointment book. I told 'em, everything's on the computer."

He made a quick mental note of her slip of the tongue. He wondered if there might be some truth to Mildred's rumor about Robbie's alleged affair with his receptionist. "I'm sure Robbie had everything password protected. Probably even encrypted," he said.

"Encrypted? Don't know nothing about that. But damn straight about passwords." She glanced around as if checking the empty office for eavesdroppers. There were none. "Didn't tell 'em I had access."

Brian lifted his eyebrows in faux surprise. "You have access?"

She raised her head, looking proud of herself. "Yep. Had to. I kept track of his appointments. Got access to everybody's calendars."

Brian folded his arms and frowned. "Robbie always struck me as someone who didn't like to give up control of anything. I doubt he'd give anyone access to his calendar, even you."

Mandy's lips tightened and she pressed a few keys on her computer keyboard. Then she spun the screen around toward him. "See."

Brian leaned over the desk and scanned down the list of entries. Two weeks of appointments were visible: last week and this week. His eyes stopped on the entries for the previous Friday. There were several appointments throughout the business day. They looked innocuous enough. There was one, however, that held his gaze.

10:00 p.m.—AB

"I stand corrected," he said. "My apologies for doubting you."

She returned the computer monitor to its original position. Her smile held a faint smug satisfaction. "That's okay. I'm smarter than people think, ya know." She brushed a few strands of hair back from her face. "They think I'm dumb because I don't have some fancy college degree. But I listen. I know more than everybody thinks."

Time to tread carefully. Brian had been able to get her talking, but she was opening up more than he expected. He mimicked her earlier search for eavesdroppers, and then sat on the edge of the desk, folding his arms across his chest. "Probably a lot of secrets in a place like this."

Mandy grinned and leaned back in her chair. "You got no idea. I won't name names, but one of the realtors . . ." She glanced over her shoulder to one of the desks behind her. ". . . gives more than just tours in the houses up for sale. If you know what I mean."

"I guess you knew about Robbie, too?"

She straightened her back, turned her eyes away from him, and made a poor job of feigning ignorance. "What about Robbie?"

"You know. There were rumors all over town about it. People talk."

Mandy looked away, seeming to ponder his words for a moment. Then she sighed, shaking her head. "I told him." She lifted the crumpled tissue to her eyes, dabbing lightly at the outer edge of each. "Told him people would find out."

"It's not the sort of thing you can keep secret for too long."

She looked up at Brian, eyes like a sad puppy dog. "Do the police know?"

Brian shook his head. "Not yet. But it's only a matter of time."

Mandy leaned back in her chair again, folding her arms. "He was so stupid. I'm always up for a trip to the casinos in Philly, but Robbie . . . He went all the time. Loved to play cards, he did."

"Gambling?"

Mandy gave him a quick nod. "Yeah, what'd ya think?"

Brian was forced to suppress a snicker. He'd been prepared for the tear-filled admission of an affair from the dead man's mistress. Not a hidden gambling addiction. "Did he lose much money?"

"Shitloads. That wife of his wasn't too happy 'bout it either."

Brian opened his mouth to ask her a further question but withheld it when the front door swung open. A slim man strode in, exuding the confident air of someone who held himself in high esteem. His gray trousers and silken shirt looked starched and precisely pressed. A blue and black striped tie hung loosely from his collar. Brian knew Jamie Wilkerson by reputation only. It wasn't the most flattering of reputations. Womanizer, and arrogant son of a bitch, as Mildred had put it. It was no wonder that Jamie worked for Robbie.

The two probably got along like a house on fire.

Jamie stopped at the front desk—barely noticing Brian's presence—and leered down at the receptionist, his eyes focused on her low neckline. "Hey Mands, any messages for me?"

Mandy gave the realtor an abrupt shake of her head and disdainful frown. Jamie turned to Brian, as if he'd just become aware of the journalist. He thrust his hand forward. "Jamie Wilkerson. Are you buying or selling?"

"Brian Wilder. Neither."

Jamie's handshake faltered quickly with Brian's response, as if the energy required to be cordial couldn't be spared for anyone not in need of a realtor.

"Just here to pay my respects," Brian explained.

The realtor's disinterest was evident when his gaze drifted toward a desk in the far corner. "Yeah, well . . . Thanks for coming in." He moved away from the reception desk and headed toward the coffee machine along the back wall.

Brian leaned forward, lowering his voice. "Doesn't seem too upset to have just lost his boss."

Mandy frowned. "He figures he's next in line to run this place." She paused to glance over her shoulder. "He's gonna be in for a surprise."

Brian looked back toward the coffee machine to find Jamie scooping sugar into a black coffee mug. "You know something he doesn't?"

Her frown turned to a sneer. "Robbie told me all kinds of stuff."

"Really, you two must have been close."

She held up her hand and crossed her fingers. "Like that . . . sometimes." She flashed a smile that oozed with double entendre.

Jamie crossed to the far corner desk. The realtor didn't seem to be paying them any attention. Brian leaned a little closer to Mandy. "Were you and Robbie having an affair?"

She let out a gasp and huffed in disgust. "What kind of girl do you think I am? I'd never have an affair with a married man."

Brian smiled, as he looked forward to telling Mildred that her precious gossip mill was wrong.

And then Mandy said, "All we ever did was have sex."

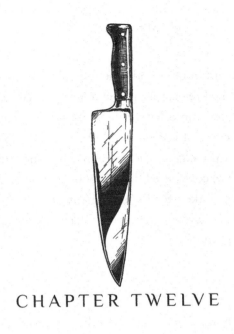

CHAPTER TWELVE

Candice stared at the screen of her laptop and reread the opening line of the sermon she was writing for Sunday's service. She'd spent most of the afternoon writing the first draft, but now as she reread it, she was as disappointed by the effort as she figured her congregation would be on Sunday. This was going to need a lot of revision. She pushed back from the desk and rolled her shoulders to relieve some of the tension. Her mind was cloudy, probably from staring at the computer screen for too long. There was a mild ache behind her eyes. She squeezed the bridge of her nose and groaned.

She stepped out of her small church office and wandered out to the sanctuary and took a seat in the front row. Candice revisited the crime scene again in her mind. The mental image was as clear as a photograph. The bread still intrigued her. Her continued Internet searches had come up empty. But it still seemed familiar. Broken bread on the chest of a dead man. Or perhaps a dying man. The answer was on the edge of her memory, but she still struggled to reach it. Candice considered the symbolism of bread in the church, and how it was linked to the atonement of sins. Then it hit her. Religious history class in seminary. That was where she'd heard about them: sin eaters.

———————

Later that evening, Candice climbed the steps to the front porch of a Victorian-style house on W. Main Street. She was five minutes early for her arranged 6:30 appointment. Light blazed from the broad windows on the first floor, casting a golden aura over the front yard. Once on the porch, she glanced behind her at the street, and then across the street at the Newark Country Club. The parking lot was teeming with cars. Tuesday was Surf and Turf night. She smiled, then pushed the doorbell.

The woman who greeted her had stringy, graying hair that flopped on her shoulder without form or body. She wasn't what Candice would call obese, but the woman wasn't thin either. Her hands—pudgy and small—clutched a dish towel.

"Yes?" The woman's voice was soft and reticent.

"I'm Reverend Candice Miller. Your husband told me to stop by." She paused, then added, "He was going to call to let you know."

The woman's pale lips turned up at the edge to form the slightest of smiles. She wiped her hands on the dish towel, then extended her hand. "Toni Brennan, Alex's wife. Please come in."

As Candice crossed the threshold, she was arrested by a tantalizing aroma that filled the foyer. She stopped for a moment to inhale deeply and allowed her pleasure to escape as a moan. "Smells good."

Toni's face flushed. "Thanks, I had some baking to do for this weekend's bake sale at St. Matthew's." She led the way toward the living room. "My husband isn't here yet. Said he'd be right home, so I don't know what's keeping him." She gestured to a dark mauve Chesterfield.

Lowering herself onto the sofa, Candice brushed her hand along the lush fabric. Was it velvet? She couldn't remember the last time she'd seen a sofa covered in velvet. Toni took a seat in a leather club chair, crossed her legs, and then adjusted the hem of the pale blue skirt to cover her knees.

"You have a nice house." Candice gestured toward the roll-top desk across the room. "Some beautiful antiques."

Toni nodded, then mumbled, "Thank you."

A long silence fell over the room. Toni remained still with her hands folded in her lap, her gaze directed down toward the floor in front of her.

"Have you and Alex lived in Newark long?" Candice asked, mainly to break the awkward silence.

"Over twenty years."

The room fell silent again. Candice tapped the sofa arm gently with her fingers. Her gaze wandered around the room and fell on the sizable portrait which hung over the fireplace at the far end. It was an oil replica of the Michelangelo fresco *The Creation of Adam*.

The silence in the room shattered as the front door opened and Alex Brennan hurried in. Sweat dripped from his ruddy face as he kicked the door closed behind him and swiftly moved toward the living room.

Michael Bradley

"I'm so sorry. I got waylaid by John DeNicola on my way out. Sociology professor and royal pain in the ass." He glanced at Candice with wide eyes. "Sorry. Pardon my language."

She grinned. "No worries. I hear far worse at the annual inter-parish softball game. We Episcopal ministers can curse up a storm when we want to."

He laughed, then turned his gaze to Toni, who still sat silently in the chair. The jocularity behind his voice turned stern. "I'll need my gray trousers, and a white shirt for tomorrow. Please make sure they are pressed and ready."

Toni nodded, then rose from the chair and left the room.

"Nice meeting you," Candice said as Toni disappeared.

Alex gave a wave of dismissal. "Don't mind her. She's just shy. Come to my study." He turned and walked from the living room. "I was surprised to hear from you. It's not often these days that I get a call from a woman I just met."

His remark made her think of the previous evening. She wondered how Samantha and Alex had ended up together. Who made the first move in the affair? She hoped it was Alex. She wanted to think of Samantha as the seduced and not the seducer.

Candice followed him across the hall and through a dark-stained oak door. The room beyond wasn't so much a study as it was a small library. Every inch of wall space—from floor to ceiling—consisted of bookshelves. Books filled every available spot on the shelves with volumes stacked side-by-side, and even on top of each other. Leatherbound, hardback, paperback, and textbook—all manner of books were represented throughout the room.

Alex crossed to an antique oak desk, which was centered in the library. A double globe antique brass lamp stood on the corner of the desk. Several leatherbound volumes were stacked nearby.

A black digital voice recorder sat on the desk beside a decorative oak stand. The light gleamed off the silver buttons of the recorder, catching Candice's eye. Cradled in the oak stand was an empty letter opener sheath.

Alex sat down in the chair behind the desk. "So, how can I help you? Something about religious history?"

"Yes," Candice said. "What can you tell me about sin eaters?"

He became animated upon hearing her question. He rubbed his hands together and smiled broadly. "It's funny you should ask. Sin eaters are a hobby horse of mine. Perhaps obsession would be a better word." He crossed to a nearby bookshelf and scanned the book spines. "I gave a lecture on them just last month."

Candice said, "I remember a few details from seminary, but it—"

"Wasn't something your lecturers spent much time on?" He laughed. "Not surprising. It's a bit of a taboo, really. An obscure part of the church's history." He slipped a book from the shelf and crossed to the desk. "It's in here, *Brand's Popular Antiquities of Great Britain*."

He rested the book on the desk and flipped through the pages. Candice circled around until she stood beside him. The leatherbound book looked old, perhaps a century and a half or more. As he turned the pages, a musty smell rose from the book. Her eyes were only able to catch the occasional word and the faintest of glimpses at the intricate artwork. She feared that his rapid thumbing of the pages would tear the yellowed paper.

"Here," he said, finally finding what he was searching for. He pointed to the page.

Candice leaned forward and gazed at the elaborate engraving. Despite the book's age, the coloring of the image was vibrant. It depicted an eighteenth-century parlor, a small gathering of people dressed in, what Candice assumed, was the finest of mourning fashion of the time. They stood at a distance from a coffin centered in the illustration. Standing beside the coffin was a solitary man; his tattered apparel was in distinct contrast to that of the other mourners. His arms were outstretched over the coffin, holding a round loaf of bread.

"The sin eater. One of the worst career choices in history," Alex said. "It was the wealthy's way of trying to skirt the consequences of their sin."

"It was mainly practiced in Europe, wasn't it?"

"England, Scotland, and Wales mostly. When a wealthy family member was dying, the grieving family would seek out a sin eater. A loaf of bread would be placed on the chest of the dying. The bread absorbed all of the departing soul's sins, or so the belief went."

Candice filled in the details as memories from seminary returned, "And the sin eater would eat the bread, hence taking on the sins of the dying."

Alex turned and smiled at her. "See, you remember more than you think. Usually, the sin eater would come from the poorest of the poor. They get the bread, a little ale, and a small payment for their service. But you had to be extremely desperate to pawn your eternal soul."

She folded her arms and reflected on the concept. "It holds certain parallels with the sacrifice of Christ. But, even in that day and age, they must have understood enough scripture to know that a common man can't wipe away someone's sin."

"Can't they? Isn't that what Father Blake does every Saturday during confession?"

"That's part of a never-ending theological debate." She paused for a moment. Was that a note of doubt she heard in his question? "I thought you were Catholic. Don't you go to St. Matthew's?"

Before he could answer, there was a knock on the study door. Alex crossed the room with a rapid step and yanked the door open. His voice was hushed, but not enough that Candice didn't hear his harsh words.

"I thought I told you not to bother me."

She saw Toni Brennan's face through the crack between the door and the frame. Her eyes were hung low, and half closed in what looked like fear. She couldn't hear what Toni said, only Alex's response.

"No, she doesn't want any." He paused. "No, get back to the kitchen, and don't interrupt again."

CHAPTER THIRTEEN

C andice pushed the front door to her cottage closed and dropped her keys and mobile phone on the small table by the door. She slipped off her jacket as she moved to the kitchen. After draping the windbreaker over a chair, she poured a glass of iced tea and leaned back against the kitchen counter. Her conversation with Alex Brennen had been enlightening. His interpretation of the practice of sin eating had aligned with what she remembered from seminary. The concept behind the archaic ritual seemed outlandish, especially when compared with theological doctrines of the modern church. Candice felt certain that she'd be hard-pressed to find any minister these days who would find the practice to be legitimately supported by biblical principles. However, as Candice considered the crime scene, she struggled to see how the ritual of the sin eater might fit into the murder.

Was the killer trying to absolve Robbie of some sin before he died? If the killer had been trying to emulate a sin eater, they'd made a serious error by leaving the bread behind.

Candice finished her iced tea and placed the glass in the kitchen sink. Maybe she was overthinking this whole thing. Probably making connections that weren't there. Suddenly, she felt silly for considering the possibility that Robbie's murder was related to the sin eaters. At least no one knew the absurdity she'd been toying with in her mind. Alex was the only person who knew of her sudden interest in sin eaters, and Candice had evaded his repeated questions about her curiosity. No harm done.

She grabbed the windbreaker from the chair, moved from the kitchen, and climbed the stairs to her bedroom. After hanging the jacket on a hook behind the door, she undressed and slipped into a lavender sleeveless T-shirt and matching sleep shorts.

Candice hopped onto the bed, and with her legs folded beneath her, turned on the television and flipped aimlessly through the channels. When she didn't find anything of interest to watch, she turned to CNN and muted the television. She reached for the cordless phone on the bedside table.

Andrew answered her call on the third ring. "Twice in one day. This is a surprise," he said.

She fluffed one of the pillows on the bed, then placed it on top of the other. "Just wanted to thank you for giving me Alex's number this afternoon."

"Glad to help." His tremulous voice sounded distant and distracted. "Did he have what you were looking for?"

"Yeah." She laid her head on the pile of pillows. Sometimes her late-night calls with Andrew reminded her of those midnight gossip sessions she used to have in high school with her best friend. "He was very helpful."

"Good."

She stared up, watching the shadows from the spinning blades of the ceiling fan dance across the popcorn texture of the ceiling. How long had she known Andrew? Two years? "I met his wife."

"Toni? She's a lovely woman. So kind, and always willing to help. She's taught Sunday school for more years than I can remember. Likes to teach the older kids. She probably knows every child in my congregation."

"I think every church has someone like that." The name that immediately popped into Candice's mind was Agatha Bowman. The elderly woman probably held the church record for having the most lifetime volunteer hours, not that anyone was counting. But Agatha, even at her advanced age, still volunteered to help at almost every church and community event. "Mine is named Agatha."

"Oh, Agatha Bowman is a real blessing."

Candice widened her eyes in surprise. "You know Agatha?"

"Anyone who has been to Newark Day knows Agatha," Andrew said.

Candice chuckled, remembering how Agatha singlehandedly manned the information tent every year at the annual spring event. The eighty-three-year-old woman was incredibly adept at pointing people in the right direction.

Although Candice had only been in town for two Newark Days, she'd heard all about how—when Agatha had turned eighty—the mayor presented her with a proclamation honoring her years of service.

"Toni and Alex seem like an odd couple," Candice said, abruptly changing the subject.

Alex seemed to hesitate before responding. "I'm not sure I know what you mean."

"He's so outgoing and forthright." *And possibly an adulterer.* She bit her tongue on the last thought. It would be inappropriate to voice her suspicions without proof. Particularly to Andrew. "And she seems so . . ." She struggled for the right word.

Andrew tried to help with his own suggestion. "Dutiful?"

"What do you know about them?"

There was another hesitation on the phone. She wondered if she was crossing a line.

Her curiosity bordered on the edge of gossip. Their close friendship sometimes made her forget that he was bound—like herself—with certain doctrinal bonds related to confidentiality; his a bit more stringent than hers. "Sorry, I probably shouldn't have asked that," she said.

"No, that's fine," Andrew said. "I don't know too many details. They met at Princeton University. She was a student, and he was a lecturer. From what I hear, her father was quite wealthy and left her with a nice little trust fund. That's a touchy subject with Alex. Apparently, the stipulations of the fund are very strict. They don't have kids. They've lived here in Newark for almost twenty years."

"Does Toni have a job?" Candice asked.

"No. She's a stay-at-home housewife." Andrew yawned. "Alex seems to prefer that."

She thought again about Alex's visit to Samantha's office the night before. It was possible that she'd misinterpreted the incident, but it was hard to shake Samantha's obvious excitement when Alex arrived. "Do you think their marriage is happy?"

"Who's to say? Happiness comes in many forms. They could very well be blissfully in love."

Candice glanced at the clock on the bedside table. 9:45. Andrew sounded as tired as she felt. "I don't want to keep you. Thanks again for giving me Alex's phone number."

"Any time I can be of service," he said.

After the call ended, Candice stretched out on the bed and closed her eyes. She didn't feel like getting out of bed to turn off the light. Maybe she could sleep with it on. Her head sank into the pillows as she tried to clear her mind. She tried a meditation exercise she'd learned in seminary. Breathe in, breathe out. Breathe in, breathe out. Breathe in. It didn't help. Her mind still raced. She turned her head and glanced at the bedroom door.

Out of bed, she moved to the door and dug through the pockets of her jacket, which still hung on the hook. When her hand emerged, it was holding a small digital voice recorder. Candice studied it as she turned it over and over in her hands. The recorder itself was black, but the buttons, speaker, and microphone were all a glossy silver. Lustrous enough to catch her eye. When she'd passed around the desk to get a better view of the book Alex had pulled from the bookshelf, her hand had run along the desktop casually, cupping the small recorder and slipping it in her pocket. It'd been almost instinctual, to the point that she barely remembered the theft herself.

She dropped to her knees before the bed and shifted the mattress to reveal a cavity in the box spring below. She reached in, lifted out a plastic box, and set it on the floor before her. With the lid off, she stared at the assortment of small objects within. It was an odd collection of trinkets, some appearing to be more valuable than others. There'd never been much rhyme or reason to what she stole, the only constant being that it had to be small enough for her to slip into her pocket. Among the hodgepodge, there was the gold pocket watch she'd taken from a senior lecturer at seminary, the silver charm bracelet from a choir member at her first church, and a circular white opal brooch she'd taken from an elderly member of her Newark congregation. She dipped her hand into the box and lifted out a string of black rosary beads. A tinge of guilt filled Candice as she let the beads dangle between her fingers. She'd stolen them from Andrew's house almost a year ago.

Candice replaced the rosary in the box, then placed the digital voice recorder in as well. As she closed the lid of the box, she said a quick prayer for forgiveness.

CHAPTER FOURTEEN

Wednesday

When Brian arrived at the *Newark Observer* office on Wednesday morning, he knew it would be a long day. On Wednesdays, he submitted the next edition of the newspaper to the printer. As he walked through the front door, he ran through a mental checklist of what he still needed to do before the day was over. In the morning, he needed to proofread all the stories, including those submitted by three journalism interns from the university.

Brian would be lashed to his desk in the afternoon working through the formatting and layout for the Thursday edition. Despite having become adept at the placement of stories, photographs, and advertisements over the years, the layout process still took

Brian hours, often keeping him in the office well into the evening. It would be an exhausting day, but the work was always worth it when the next edition hit the streets the following morning.

To add to his already busy Wednesday schedule, he had a lunch appointment with Mick Flanagan at noon. Brian had heard through the grapevine that the autopsy report for Robbie Reynolds had been completed by the county coroner and handed off to the Newark Police. He was hoping Mick would be forthcoming with the details over lunch. The reception desk was empty. Wednesday was Mildred's day off. Until Jessica arrived, Brian would have the office to himself. He settled himself at his desk and started working his way through his proofreading.

Brian was forty-five minutes into his efforts when the phone on his desk rang. He was tempted to let the call go to voicemail, preferring to not be interrupted. But on the fourth ring, he reached for the phone and was greeted by Rachel Wallin's singsong voice.

"You asked for info on Alex Brennen," she said. "I couldn't find much of interest, but I got a few tidbits for you."

"Great. Tell me all you know."

"He taught two years in Princeton before coming here. He was the youngest professor to ever get hired here at the university. I guess teaching at an Ivy League school breaks all the barriers. He's got a clean record here as well. No official complaints from students or faculty. But there were some rumors that he tended to get overly friendly with some of his female students."

"Sexual harassment?" Brian asked.

"Not harassment. Consensual. At least that's what I hear. Apparently, he was quite the charmer in his younger days. Impressionable young students would fawn all over him." Rachel laughed. "I don't think that happens much anymore."

Brian scribbled a few notes on a nearby notepad. "The university had no issue with his behavior?"

"Nothing was ever officially reported. If there isn't a complaint, the administration doesn't care." The cynicism in her voice was evident.

"Thanks for digging this up," Brian said.

"There's one other thing. Again, this is just hearsay, but many of his colleagues think he lives way beyond his means. Working here pays well, but one of the professors told me Alex has a Patek Philippe watch for each day of the week."

"Maybe he got them on sale," Brian said. Rachel didn't laugh at his little joke. He added, "That gives me a lot to think about."

"While you're thinking about that, think about when you're going to take me out to dinner. You owe me that at least," Rachel said.

Brian stammered through his response. "I . . . um . . . I'll give it some thought."

"Come on, Brian. It'd be a hoot. You can't tell me you're not at least curious about how a date with me would go."

Brian wasn't sure how to reply. He did find Rachel attractive and found the idea of a possible relationship with her to be enticing. He looked forward to seeing her whenever he came on campus to meet with her boss. But the thought of going on a date with another woman still felt like a betrayal, as if he were cheating on Sarah.

"I'll give it some thought, but I'm not making any promises," he said reluctantly. "Thanks for the info."

Shortly before noon, Brian walked up Main Street to Tipsy McStaggers Irish Pub. The lunchtime crowd was already filtering in, creating a twenty-minute wait for a table. Luckily, he caught sight of Mick already seated in the back corner.

"How's Cheryl?" Brian asked as he dropped into the seat across from Mick. The acoustics in the corner kept the din of the lunchtime crowd to a dull roar.

Mick nodded and smiled. "Good." Then he frowned and shook his head. "Pretty horrible, actually. Nauseous all the time. She can't even sit at the dinner table without wanting to throw up."

Brian snickered. "Is she getting any strange cravings yet?"

"Radishes and Jell-O. Lime Jell-O."

Brian turned his head and cringed. "Sarah craved fish sticks dipped in chocolate sauce." He glanced over the menu and set it down on the table. The red laminate tabletop was sticky to the touch.

Mick frowned and shook his head. "Not sure which is worse. But I might have just lost my appetite."

The waitress arrived at the table with two glasses of water, and they placed their orders: a chicken Caesar salad for Mick, and for Brian, shepherd's pie. When she walked away, Brian took a long sip from his water glass and studied the thirty-something-year-old detective's face over the rim. His youthful looks were eclipsed by the dark shadows beneath his eyes.

"Cheryl must be keeping you up all hours," Brian said. "You look bushed."

Mick nodded. "Yeah. And having an ongoing murder investigation doesn't help."

The waitress returned with their drinks, setting them on the table, then walked away. Brian stirred his Coke with a straw and watched the ice cubes swirl around the glass.

Brian said, "Speaking of murder cases . . ."

A broad smile crossed Mick's lips. "I knew there was a reason you wanted to have lunch. There's always an ulterior motive with you."

"You should know me by now. I always have at least five ulterior motives at any given time." Brian laughed. "What can you tell me?"

"The autopsy confirmed the cause of death. Stabbed. Single upward thrust to the heart."

"What about the knife?"

Mick smiled. "From this point on, everything is off the record until otherwise announced, okay?"

Brian nodded his acquiescence.

"Not a knife," Mick said. "A brass letter opener."

Brian remained silent, hoping Mick would elaborate. He wasn't disappointed.

"Very ornamental. And—you won't believe this—the blade was engraved."

"Engraved?"

"Yeah. Mainly a bunch of initials and a date. *To AB with love, AC 1995.* Before you ask, no concrete leads on *AB* or *AC* yet. Do you have any idea how many people in Newark have those initials?"

"I can name at least half a dozen. Father Andrew Blake. Amber Butler from the mayor's office. The pharmacist at the downtown CVS." Brian snapped his fingers as he tried to recall the name. "Alonzo Benton."

Mick gestured for Brian to stop. "I don't need you to give me a complete census on everyone in Newark with the initials *AB*."

"Anything interesting come from your search at Robbie's office?"

Mick raised an eyebrow. "You been following me?"

"No, but I stopped by his office yesterday. It was obvious you'd already been through everything."

The conversation paused as the waitress returned. She placed the salad in front of Brian and the shepherd's pie in front of Mick, then walked away. Once she was gone, they both laughed and swapped plates.

"There was nothing remarkable in the office," Mick said. "Forensics is still going through Robbie's laptop. I should know more in a few days. One thing forensics did find was some funny accounting going on with Robbie's business. He might have been skimming off the top."

"Robbie was embezzling money?"

Mick jabbed at his salad. "Yeah. Small amounts almost weekly. When you add them all up, we're talking six figures."

Brian whistled and took a long sip from his iced tea. "Anything else?"

A huge grin crossed Mick's face. "Yeah. You're never going to believe what else the autopsy found."

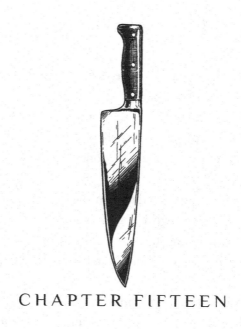

CHAPTER FIFTEEN

The heavy wooden door closed with a thud that echoed through the empty sanctuary of St. Matthew's Catholic Church. Brian stood near the doors and listened to the silence that seemed to float down from the high cathedral ceiling. The intricate carved woodwork on the columns and along the walls and around the windows always filled him with awe. The craftsmanship, the dedication to detail, and the beauty of the ornate patterns in the 150-year-old church took Brian's breath away every time he entered. He wondered if perhaps he should come to mass more often.

As he walked along the left aisle, Brian chastised himself for coming. He still had an enormous amount of work to do on the next edition of the newspaper. On his walk back from the restaurant, he'd passed St. Matthew's and decided to stop in to see if Andrew was in a more talkative mood than he'd been on Sunday.

He walked slowly toward the front of the church out of reverence for the age-old building. His footsteps on the marble floor sounded like a drumbeat. They echoed despite his efforts to step softly. When he reached the front of the sanctuary, he crossed to a door to left of the altar.

He knocked and a faint voice from the other side invited him to enter.

When Brian stepped into the small vestry, he found Andrew standing by an open closet door. Several robes were laid out on a nearby table. Andrew held one of the vestments from a hanger and ran a lint brush over the green cloth. He looked up with a puzzled look as Brian entered.

"Twice in one week," Andrew said. "Has the prodigal turned over a new leaf?"

"Not quite."

Andrew hung the vestment in the closet and set the lint brush on the table. "I guess it's too much to ask for a miracle where you're concerned."

Brian laughed. "Face it. I'm a hopeless cause."

Andrew pulled an empty hanger from the closet and hung a white robe with gold trim over it. "No one is hopeless, but some are harder to reach than others." He made a quick inspection of the robe, then placed it in the closet with the other.

Brian gestured to the remaining robe on the table. "What's all this?"

"Just got them back from the dry cleaner." Andrew gestured to a nearby chair. "Have a seat. I'll be done in a moment."

Brian pulled the wooden chair away from the wall, noting that the tan curved back and matching tan seat with black legs made it look more like something he'd expect to find in a bistro rather than in the back room of a church. He sat down and watched Andrew inspect the remaining red robe before adding it to the others in the closet. Making a study of Andrew, Brian noticed the hunched shoulders and disheveled hair. There were shadows beneath Andrew's eyes that spoke of sleep deprivation. As the priest pushed the closet door closed, his hands seemed to quake. Andrew usually had rock solid hands almost like a surgeon's, leading Brian to wonder if he was ill.

Andrew sat in a chair across the table from Brian. The priest leaned back and folded his arms. "I expect this isn't a social call."

"I was wondering . . ." Brian gazed across the table and hesitated. Sarah stood behind Andrew, her arms folded much like the priest's.

"Talk to him," she said. "He can help you."

Brian averted his eyes for a moment to regain his composure. When he looked back, Sarah was gone. Andrew stared at him across the table as if waiting for Brian's next words.

"Alex and Toni. On Sunday, I couldn't help but notice that she seems quite . . ."

Andrew finished the sentence. "—submissive."

"Frightened of him, was what I was thinking."

Andrew knit his brow and fell silent as if he were pondering his next words carefully. When he finally spoke, he kept his voice low and soft. "I've noticed that behavior many times over the years. It places me in a difficult position." Andrew clasped his hands and rested them on the table. "I've had parishioners in the past who believed in the strict adage that the wife submits to her husband in all things. That kind of submissiveness doesn't necessarily mean there's abuse."

Brian recalled his Sunday morning encounter with the couple. Alex's grip on his wife's arm seemed substantial. Where does one draw the line between intentional obedience and forced submissiveness? "Have you ever seen any definite signs of abuse?"

Andrew shook his head. "You mean physical signs? Bruising and such? No. And I've given her plenty of opportunities to confide in me, but Toni has never said a word. I've done everything short of asking her outright."

"What's their story?" Brian asked.

"I don't know much about their history. They've lived in Newark for a good number of years. Toni teaches the older children in Sunday school. Very good with children. There was a spot of bother a few years ago with one of the girls. I can't remember all the details. She made some wild accusations about Toni. It turned out the girl was lying the whole time. Like I said, Toni is great with kids. But when she gets around Alex . . ."

"Do they have kids of their own?" Brian asked.

"No."

"Any idea why?"

"That's no secret," Andrew said. "They had some infertility issues. I'm not betraying a confidence by telling you. Alex is pretty vocal about it."

Brian nodded to indicate that he understood. The conversation dropped off into silence. Finally, Brian didn't want to hold off any longer.

"Can we talk about Saturday?"

Andrew's eyes widened, and his gaze became distant. "Saturday?"

"Yeah, Robbie's murder."

"Oh, that," Andrew said. His body suddenly crumpled under an unseen burden. He averted his eyes, refusing to meet Brian's gaze. "I . . . don't really know anything about what happened Saturday."

"You got a lot closer to the house than—"

Andrew glanced at his watch and suddenly stood, pushing the chair back roughly. He spoke with a tremulous voice. "I'm late for an appointment." He turned his back on Brian and began to walk away. "Thank you for coming."

Brian rose to his feet. This was the second time that Andrew tried to evade a conversation about Robbie's death. "Are you okay?"

The priest halted but refused to turn and look at Brian. He stammered, "I'm . . . it's . . . I don't know."

"How can I help?"

Andrew ran his hand through his hair; his shoulders slouched forward. "It's nothing. I'll deal with this on my own."

In the six years that they'd been friends, there had only been one thing that disturbed the priest like this. Brian was one of the few people in Newark who knew about Andrew's past. About his previous parish. He feared asking but knew that he would be remiss as a friend if he didn't at least try to help. "Is this about Pittsburgh?" he asked.

Andrew didn't respond. He remained still for a minute; his head down and his hands clenched. Brian hoped he hadn't said the wrong thing. Maybe he should have just left it well enough alone. Then, Andrew began to walk away.

"Thanks for coming, Brian."

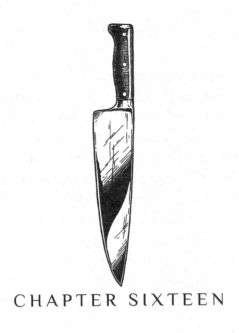

CHAPTER SIXTEEN

C andice stepped out of the Black Stallion Brewery and into the midday sun. Her lunch had been particularly satisfying, with the restaurant's Black and Blue Burger being a nice change from the packed lunch she usually brought from home. She'd had every intention of getting a salad when she arrived at the restaurant, until she had seen the burger on the menu. Yes, she was trying to maintain her figure, but after the stressful few days she'd had, she needed a little comfort food.

The walk back to her church was a short one; only a few blocks at most. Not in a hurry to return to the sermon she was working on, she took leisurely steps along Main Street. Newark's usual lunch crowd brushed past her as if they were in a race against the clock to get back to their offices or classrooms. A student lugging a backpack overflowing with books stormed by her; the bag over his shoulder smacked into her arm. The student didn't seem to notice the collision and kept walking. As Candice passed the pharmacy, the automatic doors slid open and out stepped a woman who was struggling to carry several plastic shopping bags. Her familiar salt-and-pepper hair was pulled back, but loose strands floated out in every direction from the woman's head. It reminded Candice of the experiments she did in elementary school science class with a balloon and static electricity. The woman's face was sullen and her eyes downcast.

"Toni Brennen?" Candice said as she approached.

"Yes?" Toni peered at Candice through wire-rimmed glasses. There was a sense of recognition in her eyes. "Ms. Miller?"

"Please, call me Candice." She gestured to the shopping bags that Toni was wrestling with. "Can I help you with those?"

Toni tried to shift the bags around to get a better grip, perhaps to appear in better control of her parcels than she was. "Oh no. I'll be fine. I don't want to inconvenience you." One of the bags slipped from her grasp and fell to the sidewalk. A plastic bottle of aspirin rolled out of the bag and onto the sidewalk.

"Let me get that," Candice said, lifting the bottle and the bag off the ground. "I can take a few others as well."

After Toni reluctantly handed a couple additional bags to her, Candice said, "Where did you park?"

"Just around the block." Toni's voice was just as soft and reticent as it had been the night before.

As Toni led the way to her parked car, Candice tried to strike up a conversation. "Thanks for your hospitality last night. I know it can be difficult when you get an unexpected guest."

"It was no problem," Toni said. Her response was dry and un-emotional. She didn't look at Candice. Her eyes focused straight ahead, never wavering. She walked with timid footsteps.

"I hear you attended Princeton."

"Yes," Toni said, again with a lack of emotion.

The conversation fell into silence as they turned onto Center Street. The two women walked side-by-side down the side street. Candice found herself becoming more curious with every step. She wanted to know more about this woman. "What was your major?"

Toni didn't answer immediately. It was like she had to think before responding. "Mathematics. I wanted to be a mathematician."

"Really? I'm terrible at math myself," Candice said.

"I thought math was the most beautiful and most powerful creation of the human spirit." Toni became animated for a moment as she spoke. Her face seemed to light up with a spark of excitement. "It is the most precise and concise way of expressing an idea. It's not about numbers, equations, computations, or algorithms: it's about understanding. Understanding the world around me in its purest form." She paused to draw in a breath, then continued with an excited stammer. "I . . . I was fascinated by the Bombieri–Lang conjecture. Have you heard of it?" Toni glanced at Candice, then frowned. "No. No. Of course not. Silly of me. I was . . . was certain I could solve it. But . . ." Then, just as suddenly, Toni's face became downcast again. That momentary passion was gone.

"When did you graduate?" Candice asked.

There was another pause before Toni's reply came. Her jaw tightened as she spoke. "I didn't."

"Oh, was that by choice?" Candice grimaced as soon as she asked the question. It was one of those inquiries where she spoke before thinking. "Sorry, it's none of my business."

"That's fine. I left school after Alex and I got married. With his career taking off, he . . . we felt that it would be best if I stayed at home to take care of the housework, laundry, cooking, and so forth."

They turned into a small parking lot. An elderly man sat in the attendant's booth, his face buried in a book. He glanced up as they passed, gave a thin-lipped grin, and returned his gaze to the page. Candice remained in step with Toni as they crossed the parking lot. Not far from the entrance, Toni halted beside her car. She lifted the trunk of the Honda and placed the first of her bags inside.

"Keeping up that house of yours must be a full-time job," Candice said. "I struggle just to keep my little cottage clean."

Toni placed the rest of her bags into the trunk of the car. "It's my responsibility to keep the house neat and orderly." Again, her voice was flat, without the slightest sense of emotion. "I have my duties, and I fulfill them."

Her archaic choice of words felt like something out of the last century. Candice visualized Toni as being the perfect Stepford wife. Submissive and fawning at her husband's feet. The woman had become so impassioned a few minutes ago when talking about math. What could've driven her to give up on her aspirations so easily? Candice knew there were some fundamental churches with strong teachings about the role of a woman in the household. But Alex and Toni were Catholic. She wasn't aware of that level of submissiveness being part of the Catholic doctrine.

"From what I saw last night, you do an extraordinary job." Candice hadn't seen much of the house, but what she had seen was spotless of clutter and dust. Besides, the compliment couldn't hurt to keep the conversation going. "Alex's study alone must be a day's worth of work. When you add in the living room, kitchen, bedrooms, and even the basement—"

Toni's head suddenly jerked up. Her words came in rapid fire. "Basement? What about the basement?"

Candice tried to explain. "It's just when you add all the other rooms, it must take—"

"Why did you say basement?" Her words sounded like a frantic plea. Toni's eyes became unfocused.

Candice placed a reassuring hand on Toni's shoulder. "Are you okay?"

Toni closed the trunk lid and fumbled with the car keys. "I'm fine. I . . . I . . . have to go."

Candice stood in shock, at a loss for words. Toni opened the driver's door, slipped inside, and drove away, all while muttering, "The basement. Go to the basement. Now."

CHAPTER SEVENTEEN

B rian stared at the empty Chinese takeout container in the center of the kitchen table. He absently twirled a fork around his plate, pushing the remaining grains of white rice in small figure eights. The day had been a long one. He'd finished the work on the *Observer*'s next edition shortly after 7:00 p.m. With the final pages uploaded to the printer, he had walked down Main Street to pick up his dinner and returned to his apartment.

Now, sitting in his dimly lit kitchen, Brian flipped open his notebook to review his latest discoveries about Robbie Reynolds's murder. He scanned the notes he'd jotted down immediately after his lunch with Mick. Most of what he'd learned had been off-the-record, so he couldn't publish it until it had been made public. He glanced further down the page to some scribbled notations that reminded him of his conversation with Jessica that afternoon. He had been focused on laying out the front page for the next edition when Jessica entered the office. She dropped into her office chair. Her combat boots thudded loudly when she lifted her feet up on the desk.

"I've scoured five bakeries for that damn bread," Jessica said. "No one in the area bakes it. Giorgio at Barley's Bakery thinks it might be something he called a Honey Wheat Bushman Bread. I got the recipe if you want it."

Brian dismissed the offer with a wave of his hand.

Jessica continued, "Giorgio told me the only place that would have that bread is the steakhouse at the mall. But they don't bake it in that round shape. Just in those short narrow loaves."

"Why didn't you get the recipe?" Sarah's voice jolted Brian back to the present and to the dim light of his kitchen.

He took his eyes off his notebook and gazed across the table at her, his eyes fixed on her deep blues. Her elbow rested on the table with her chin propped on the palm of her hand.

"You know I can't bake," he said.

"So, no leads on the bread."

Brian shook his head. "Could be an out-of-town bakery. You can order anything online these days. Or maybe homemade."

"Did you tell Mick about the appointment you found?"

"No. They have Robbie's computer," Brian said. "Mick will have found it himself by now."

"Do you think Robbie was embezzling money to pay his gambling debts?"

He slid his chair back and stretched his legs out beneath the table. "It makes sense. Rumor has it that Robbie was a big gambler.

He might've gotten into some hot water with some loan sharks. Could be someone who got tired of waiting for repayment."

"There's always the blackmail angle," she said.

He raised his eyebrows as he considered the possibility. "I hadn't thought of that. A series of payments to a blackmailer certainly would fit the pattern."

"That raises two new questions. If it was blackmail, what was he being blackmailed for? And who was blackmailing him?"

Brian leaned back and stretched his arms above his head. "Cheater."

"What?"

He rested his elbows on the table and clasped his fingers together. "That was the word written on his arm. He was having an affair with his receptionist. Perhaps someone found out and was threatening to expose him if he didn't pay up. What about his wife?"

Sarah gave him an incredulous look. "Why would Andrea blackmail her own husband?"

"Not blackmail. What if she found out about the affair?"

Sarah leaned back and folded her arms. "Why is the wife always the prime suspect?"

"I'm just speculating—"

Sarah shook her head and interrupted. "No, you were casting her as the murderer. You were already writing the headline. I could see it in your eyes."

Brian laughed. "Just a minute . . . I was not writing the headline . . . well, maybe just a little . . ."

"I was married to you long enough to know what goes on behind those eyes." The sound of Sarah's laugh sent a pang through his heart.

"There's something else," he said.

"What?"

His face flushed with a sudden wave of heat. "Well . . ."

"You're embarrassed? Just tell me."

Brian averted his eyes. "The coroner found semen in his urethra. He'd ejaculated shortly before death."

Sarah looked at him, puzzled.

"Interesting fact," Brian said. "Men urinate after ejaculation to clear the urethra of leftover semen."

"So, since there was semen in his . . ." Sarah started to say.

"He died immediately, or shortly after." Brian leaned back in his chair. "There were traces of dried saliva found on his—"

Sarah cut him off with a childlike giggle. "A blow job?"

"Possibly. Whatever it was, he was zipped up and presentable when his body was discovered."

Silence fell between them. Sarah's face was a mask of concentration as if she were tumbling the idea through her mind. She cocked her head to one side and opened her mouth to speak, but then sighed and kept silent. Brian studied her face, tracing the soft lines of her jaw. She was just as beautiful as when he'd last seen her. The week before . . . He stifled the memory. No tears.

"Any DNA?" Sarah asked.

He stared at her.

Sarah added some context. "From the blow job."

"Don't know."

Brian leaned forward, resting both arms on the table. "That Friday night appointment bothers me. Did he know his killer was coming? Mick said the time of death was somewhere between nine and eleven."

"What were the initials? AB?"

Brian frowned. "Could be anyone. There are probably hundreds of people in the area with those initials. I can name half a dozen alone." He held up his fingers and started counting them off. "Anna Bannister from the laundromat, Albert Bond, Father Blake from the church . . ."

Before he could add another name to his list, the phone rang. He moved into the living room and checked the caller ID before answering. With a smile, he put the phone to his ear. "Hey Mick. What's up?"

Mick's words were rushed, and his tone urgent. Brian listened carefully for a few moments, making mental notes. Then he said, "Thanks for the tip. I'll head over in a few minutes."

He set the phone down and stood a moment to replay the brief conversation in his mind. Then he said, "That was Mick. There's been another murder."

He turned back toward the kitchen and stared at the empty chair.

CHAPTER EIGHTEEN

H er mobile phone started to ring as soon as Candice walked in the door of her cottage. She dropped her keys on the table and her bag on the floor. She kicked the front door closed with her foot while digging in her pocket for the phone.

It was Andrew.

"I'm . . . I'm sorry to bother you," he said. His voice fluttered with distress, and his words seemed to stumble over his tongue.

"No problem. What's up?"

There was a pause in the conversation, and all she heard on the phone was raspy breathing. "Andrew?"

"Yes, I'm here. Just . . . Deena Cavendish is dead."

The name meant nothing to Candice, but she'd become accustomed to Andrew's habit of mentioning parishioners' names as if everyone knew who he was talking about. "I don't know her."

"Oh . . . she is . . . *was* . . . a lovely child."

Candice frowned. Death was tragic enough, but the death of a child seemed even more so. The innocence lost so young. A life cut short before it barely had time to begin.

Andrew cleared his throat. "I'm a bit shaken up over this news. Would you mind going with me?"

———

As Candice parked her Subaru along the curb, she glanced over at Andrew, who was seated in the passenger seat. His hands clung to a string of rosary beads. He wrapped his fist around them, grinding the beads into his palm. The beads were small, carved from dark-stained wood, and a matching wooden cross hung from the end of the string.

Andrew had once told her he'd been given the rosary years ago while on a missionary trip to South Africa, and that it was one of his few treasured possessions.

Andrew seemed to struggle as he climbed from the car. The small ranch house on Caldwell Place was lit up by the flashing red and blue lights of emergency vehicles. Mick Flanagan met them at the curb. He was quick to insist that they make their visit as brief as possible. He needed to get the crime scene processed, but Audrey Cavendish was being uncooperative.

"Try to convince her to let us do our job," he said, frustration evident in his voice. "I get she's a grieving mother, but she's hysterical and refuses to leave the house. See what you can do."

Mick escorted Candice and Andrew onto the porch and into the house. He led them into the small but comfortably furnished living room just beyond the door. A woman dressed in faded blue jeans and an oversized T-shirt paced the room. She gripped a wad of tissues in her hand. When Andrew entered, she turned and rushed toward him. He held out his arms to embrace her.

Candice hovered near the door. Mick passed her and walked along the hall to the back of the house. She had a peculiar sense of familiarity when she looked at Audrey Cavendish. It took a moment for her to realize that she'd seen Audrey a few weeks ago at St. Matthew's Catholic Church. Candice had been waiting for Andrew to finish Saturday morning confession when Audrey came into the church with two teenage girls. Candice distinctly recalled the older of the two girls being less than enthused by the concept of "confessing her sins," even loudly cracking her gum over and over. The girl's behavior invoked the ire of her mother throughout their brief time in the sanctuary.

"Audrey, I'm so sorry," Andrew said, as the woman cried on his shoulder. He led her toward the sofa and persuaded her to sit. The priest dropped down next to her and gripped the rosary beads, twisting the round orbs between his fingertips. Audrey sobbed softly beside him.

"I don't understand. Why would someone do this to my little girl?" Audrey said.

Andrew grasped her hand, giving it a comforting rub. "Just relax and tell me what happened."

Audrey took a few deep breaths and wiped a tear away from her eye. Black mascara trailed down her cheeks. Candice stood at the far side of the room, observing and not speaking. She felt like an interloper, intruding on the family at this distressful moment.

She'd have stepped out to wait in the car, but something about the way Andrew was fidgeting with the rosary beads had concerned her.

"I took Maggie for her piano lesson this evening. Deena didn't come with us. Just stayed home. We were only gone two hours . . ." The woman started to sob again. "Who could've done this?" Her head fell onto Andrew's shoulder. He gently patted her back and muttered words of comfort. Andrew glanced at Candice. His look aligned with her thoughts. *What happened?*

Voices echoed from down the hall, and Candice couldn't stop herself from eavesdropping. Only one she recognized. Mick's voice.

"No sign of forced entry. She must've known the killer," the detective said.

"Boyfriend, maybe?" the unfamiliar voice said.

"Possibly."

With no one in the living room paying her much heed, Candice inched closer to the doorway in hopes of hearing the hushed words better. Maybe she could find out what happened. Or pick up some hint as to how the girl died.

The unknown voice echoed down the hall. "Is that written in lipstick?"

"Probably. This might be it on the table," Mick said

"Fiery passion? Why would a sixteen-year-old girl wear something like that?"

Curiosity became an overpowering force that Candice couldn't overcome. She wanted to hear more. Candice glanced back at Andrew and the mother. Neither seemed to have noticed her movement. She stepped soundlessly out of the room.

A doorway at the end of the hall opened into a functional eat-in kitchen. The appliances were white and looked as dated as the dark kitchen cabinets. A stack of dishes was piled in the stainless-steel sink, and a greasy frying pan rested on the stove. A round dinette was to the right of the doorway. There was a faint odor in the room that she thought might be urine. Mick and a uniformed officer had their backs to her and didn't appear to have heard Candice approach. Their attention was focused on something else in the room.

At first, Candice could see nothing but a pair of smooth, bare legs on the floor, one twisted back on itself. They were the legs of the young. No blemishes, varicose veins, or signs that age had begun to creep in. The forest green skirt of a school uniform was hiked about midway up the thighs. *My God, she looks so young. Too young to die.*

Then Mick shifted. Candice got her first look at the teenage girl sprawled on the linoleum floor. One arm was outstretched while the other lay across her chest. Her white blouse was rumpled but intact. Her face was blotchy, and the whites of her eyes had turned red, as if every blood vessel had burst, staining her sclera. There was a faint shadow on her neck. The discolored skin looked like a line of small circles rounding her neck from one ear to the other. Like a necklace of round beads, or perhaps pearls. Candice averted her eyes for a moment and said a prayer beneath her breath.

When she looked back, her eyes caught sight of ruby markings scrawled across the girl's forehead. Four rough block letters: LIAR.

CHAPTER NINETEEN

C andice drew in a quick breath. She stepped backward; her shoulder hit the doorframe. A faint yelp escaped from her lips. She cupped her hand to her mouth to stifle the sound, but it was too late.

Mick spun around in surprise and glared at her. "What are you doing?"

Her mouth opened and closed a few times, with half-words sputtering out before she replied. "I . . . I was just praying . . . praying for the poor girl's soul."

The detective folded his arms and advanced toward her. "You shouldn't be here. It's a crime scene." His voice was firm, filled with irritation. "You and that priest shouldn't even be in the house. I was doing both of you a favor." He turned his gaze back to the girl's body. "And this is what you do."

"Sorry . . . sorry." She paused, then asked, "She wasn't . . . violated, was she?"

Mick turned back to Candice. "We won't know until the autopsy is complete." He pointed back up the hall. "Now, please return to the front of the house before the Chief gets here and has my badge."

Candice gave one final glance at the young girl's body, her eyes focusing on the loaf of brown bread that rested on the girl's bosom. The loaf was torn down the middle, crumbs had scattered over her blouse and onto the floor. Candice turned away and moved back up the hall.

She stopped at the doorway leading to the living room, glanced in to see Andrew clasping his rosary beads in one hand and Audrey's hand in the other. His head was bowed, and his lips moved as he prayed softly. The house became stifling. Candice's chest tightened and she found it hard to breathe. Death hung heavy over the home, and her heart seemed on the verge of breaking. Two bodies in less than a week, both murdered. She wasn't prepared for this sort of thing. There hadn't been a "Coping with Murder 101" class in seminary. Other than her own petty thefts, there'd been little crime in the small Kansas town where she'd grown up. Her exposure to violent crime had been nil minus one. This was becoming too much to imagine, almost too much to endure. Her head spun, and Candice felt as if she would pass out. She had to get out, to get fresh air. She darted out the door onto the front porch.

The swirling lights from the police cars broke through the darkness of the night and cast the neighboring houses in red and blue hues. A black van pulled up to the curb. The white letters on the side read "New Castle County Medical Examiner." Candice moved away from the door and further along the porch as another police officer passed into the house. She drew in a deep breath. The cool air filled her lungs and calmed her nerves.

As the medical examiner climbed the porch steps, he nodded at Candice and proceeded into the house. She moved to the far end of the porch and took a seat on the wooden porch swing hanging by chains from the ceiling. The Sin Eater had struck again. She wasn't sure why the thought popped into her head, or why she suddenly felt the need to give the murderer a name. It wasn't the most accurate of names, especially when she considered the historical context of the ritual.

Again, she wondered if she was overthinking the sin eater concept. There could be a reasonable explanation for the presence of the bread at both crime scenes. But she was damned if she could see it.

She scanned the houses in the darkened neighborhood. A perfect picture of small-town USA. Homes of similar size and shape. Middle-income families living their version of the American dream. She wondered how many secrets lived and breathed on this street alone. How many sins were being committed at this very moment? A small crowd had formed on the opposite side of the street. The rumor mill would be in full swing amidst the hushed conversations circulating through the horde. How many of them would slink away into the dark to bury their own misdeeds where none could see?

"Reverend Miller?"

She turned to look over the porch railing. A tall, lean man rested his arms on the white top rail. His face tapered to a chiseled square chin. Even in the dimness of the porch light, his eyes seemed alive with energy. His dark hair shifted with the breeze. He looked familiar, but his name escaped her.

"Brian Wilder. Andrew introduced us the other day at Robbie Reynolds's . . ." His words trailed off as if he didn't want to speak the word *murder*.

Her recall of the introduction was hazy. It had been in passing, shortly before she and Andrew left after a long afternoon spent comforting Andrea Reynolds. Brian's had been one of a dozen faces that she'd seen that day, and Candice hadn't been in the right frame of mind to make new acquaintances. "Mr. Wilder. Sorry, I didn't see you approach."

"Not surprised. Please, call me Brian." His voice was pleasant to her ears, almost soothing.

She forced a smile. "You can call me Candice. I'm surprised to see you this close to the house. Doesn't Chief Jenkins get upset if you wander onto his crime scene?"

"Lyle likes to bluster, but he's just a pussy cat at heart." Brian laughed. "Don't ever tell him I said that." He gave her a conspiratorial smile. "Besides, I happen to know he's up in Philly tonight."

"While the cat's away . . ."

Brian, with a mile-wide smirk on his face, said, "Exactly. I thought I saw Andrew around here somewhere. Are you two tag-teaming again?"

His remark left her feeling a bit perturbed. On one hand, Candice appreciated his subtle humor and found it to be a nice distraction from the dark thoughts spiraling around in her head. But she wondered how someone could be so light-hearted at such a tragic moment as this. A young girl was dead, murdered. Was he just indifferent, or was it his way of coping with the horror?

"I drove Andrew over," she said. "He asked me to accompany him."

Brian gestured toward the front door. "Have you been inside?"

She nodded, knowing full well what his next question would be. He'd want to know details about what had happened, what she'd seen and heard. One question would lead to another, and she would be forced to relive every tragic detail in her mind.

Before Candice could speak, a sudden flurry of activity drew her attention to the front door. The medical examiner and his assistant were carrying the body from the house. They took care going down the steps, then rolled the stretcher along the sidewalk. As they moved toward the black van, Mick Flanagan stepped from the house and began to follow.

Brian glanced at her. "If you'll excuse me . . ."

He left Candice alone on the porch swing and moved off to catch up with the detective. Moments later, Andrew rushed from the house, gave her a passing glance, and chased after Mick and Brian. A brief discussion followed in hushed tones between Andrew and the detective. She couldn't hear anything that was said, but Andrew's words appeared to irritate Mick. There were vehement head shakes and wild hand gestures on the part of both men. In the end, Mick and Andrew moved down the driveway without Brian. They reached the van just as the medical examiner was preparing to load the stretcher. After another brief exchange, the medical examiner unzipped the body bag. Ah, praying for the dead.

She watched as Andrew prayed over the corpse; she whispered her own quick prayer for the girl's soul. When Andrew was done, the medical examiner tried to pull the zipper on the body bag closed. He seemed to struggle, as if the zipper was stuck on something. The stretcher rocked when he tugged and jerked, and, after a few moments' difficulty, the medical examiner was successful in getting the body bag zipped closed again. The stretcher was loaded into the black van, the doors shut, and the medical examiner and his assistant drove away. Mick walked back to talk to Brian while Andrew returned to the house. He gave Candice a brief wave and a half-smile as he passed her on the porch.

But Candice barely noticed it. Her eyes were locked on a patch of grass along the edge of the driveway . . . where a small metallic object had landed when it fell from the body bag.

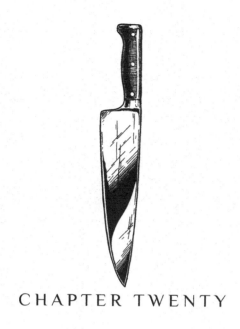

CHAPTER TWENTY

Lucy Hillman placed two glasses of ice water onto the table and waited to take their order.

The waitress smiled warmly at Brian, leaving him to wonder how she stayed so chipper on the overnight shift at the 24-hour diner. He ordered an apple pie with a scoop of vanilla ice cream on the side, then gazed across the table at Jessica, whose face was still buried in the menu.

After a moment, Brian said, "Thought you knew what you wanted."

Jessica waved a dismissive hand in his direction. "Yeah, yeah. A woman can change her mind, can't she?"

Lucy continued to hover, her warm smile quickly fading as Jessica's indecision lingered.

Brian glanced out the window of the diner and watched as a late-night crowd of university students drifted along Main Street. He caught sight of Brenda Robinson, one of the journalism students interning at the *Newark Observer*. She bobbed along the sidewalk among her friends seemingly without a care in the world. He wondered how bad her hangover would be in the morning.

Jessica closed the menu and handed it to the waitress. "Gimme an order of bacon cheese fries and a Diet Coke."

As Lucy walked away, Jessica slouched back in the booth and sighed. Brian took a sip from his ice water. "Thanks for coming out so late. Did you have any luck getting good pictures?"

He knew he didn't need to ask. He'd yet to see a bad photograph come from Jessica's camera. Her skill behind the lens always impressed him.

"Oh yeah! Got plenty. Nothing grisly, mind you. But I think you'll find some good stuff for the front page."

Brian smiled. "Great."

"Got a real good one of your priest doin' his prayer thing with the mother. What's his name, Adam?"

Brian corrected her. "Andrew. Father Andrew."

"Yeah, him." Jessica thought for a moment. "Who was the other dog collar? Didn't recognize her."

"She's from the Episcopal church on Delaware Avenue. Candice Miller's her name."

Lucy returned and set a Diet Coke on the table. Jessica took a sip from the glass, then leaned forward, placed her elbows on the table, and rested her chin in her cupped hands. "Two stiffs in less than a week. Sounds like a serial killer."

"I'm not sure that's how the math works for serial killers." Brian frowned, then shook his head. "There's nothing to tie the deaths together yet."

"Bet there is. Gotta be. People don't get murdered in Newark. At least not in quick succession like this."

Brian took another sip from his glass of water. She had a good point. In the six years that he'd lived in Newark, he could recall two murders, maybe three if he counted that suspicious drowning at White Clay Creek State Park two years ago. It wasn't that Newark was crime-free. If anything, it had its share of violent crimes, but most didn't end in death.

Born and raised in Newark, Jessica had a perspective that Brian didn't. He trusted her instincts, particularly when it came to long-term trends in the small Delaware city. "I'll take that bet. What do we know?" He leaned forward and clasped his hands together in front of him. "First, Robbie Reynolds."

"Stabbed."

Brian rolled his eyes at her brevity. "Yeah, what else?"

"Stabbed with a letter opener."

Brian stared across the table at her. That information hadn't been released to the public by the police. "How did you know that?"

"Mildred told me," Jessica said.

He opened his mouth to comment, then closed it again. The amount of information to which his receptionist had access amazed him. Mick Flanagan had only just told him about the brass letter opener in the strictest of confidence. Mildred seemed to have better sources than he ever had. "Okay, do we know anything else?"

"He was dipping his pen in the company inkwell."

It was one of those cringeworthy comments that he'd come to expect from Jessica. Her salty turns of phrase had taken some getting used to, but now they barely fazed him. He ignored the comment and said, "Mick said there might be something fishy with Robbie's finances. He had a gambling problem. Maybe he was covering his bets with company funds."

"That's what I said." Jessica sighed. "Dipping his pen into the company inkwell."

Brian gave her a puzzled look. "I thought you meant—"

"What?"

"Well . . ." His cheeks grew warm. "He was having an affair with his secretary."

"Was he? That settles it. The wife did it."

The waitress returned to the table and set their orders down. The aroma of his warm apple pie mingled with that of Jessica's bacon cheese fries to create an unnatural yet somehow tantalizing smell. Brian plunged a fork into the flaky crust.

"Doesn't that blow away your theory that the two deaths are linked?"

She slid a cheese-coated French fry in her mouth, then gave a nonchalant shrug. "Yeah, probably."

"How about Deena Cavendish? What do we know?"

"Someone wrung her neck."

Brian nodded. "Strangled. Mick couldn't tell me much else tonight."

He recalled the brief conversation he'd had with the detective outside the bungalow on Caldwell Place. Mick had acknowledged Brian's approach with a nod of his head and frown.

"This is a crime scene, you know. Who let you in?"

"You're starting to sound like your chief." Brian smiled. "I stayed on the sidewalk."

"That's not reassuring."

"What've you got? Can you tell me anything? Is this connected to Robbie Reynolds murder?"

Mick had been brief with his response. All he would say was that it was murder.

A possible strangulation.

"I don't know enough yet," Mick had said.

"Damn it." Jessica's exclamation yanked Brian's thoughts back to the diner. A drop of melted golden cheese had fallen from a forkful of fries, landing on her gray t-shirt. She grabbed a napkin and wiped the messy glob from her shirt.

Brian laughed. "Slob."

Jessica sneered at him. "Not funny. Never gonna get this out." She tossed the crumpled napkin on the table. "What's the deal with that bread at the Reynolds murder?"

Brian shrugged, then swirled a forkful of pie around in his bowl of melting ice cream. "Don't know. Neither does Mick."

"So, Mama Cavendish takes one daughter out for the evening, and the other ends up dead," Jessica said. "Maybe she lets a boy in. She won't put out for him, so he snuffs her."

Brian shook his head. "Still doesn't sound connected to the Reynolds death."

Jessica jabbed at her fries with a fork. "I'm workin' on it." She shoved a forkful into her mouth and continued as she chewed. "Maybe the Cavendish kid was his underage sex slave and Robbie Reynolds's old lady wasn't too happy about it."

Brian leaned back in the booth. He rested his hands on the table before him. "Now you're just being silly."

Jessica gave him a broad smile. "I'll tell you what connects the two."

"What?"

"That priest of yours. He was at both crime scenes. Bet both victims went to his church, didn't they?"

Brian frowned as he thought about her observation. It was brilliant. Why hadn't he noticed that before? He wasn't a regular attendee at St. Matthew's Catholic Church, certainly not enough to know everyone who attended services there. He'd never seen Robbie Reynolds or his wife there. Did the Cavendish family go to St. Matthew's? "I don't know, but it is worth checking out."

As he scooped another forkful of pie off his plate, he turned Jessica's observation around in his head. Andrew Blake wasn't the only common thread between the two murders. Someone else had also been at both crime scenes. Candice Miller.

CHAPTER TWENTY-ONE

B rian switched on the light at the top of the stairs and crossed the living room. He slipped out of his jacket and tossed it over the back of the sofa as he passed.

"You want something to drink?" he asked.

Jessica dropped onto the sofa and placed her feet on the mahogany coffee table. "Nah, I'm good."

Brian grabbed some ice cubes, dropped them in a glass, and filled it with water from the kitchen faucet. As he moved back into the living room, he realized how strange it was to have Jessica seated in his apartment. Brian was protective of his privacy ever since moving to Newark. He'd avoided inviting people into his home.

He preferred instead to keep his friends and colleagues at somewhat of a distance. Too much of his past was in this apartment. Too much access to his personal life would lead to questions he wasn't ready to answer. Jessica was one of the privileged few who'd been granted entry into his inner sanctum.

"Let's have the memory card," he said, holding out his hand to Jessica.

He took the card she gave him and slipped it into a slot in the side of the fifty-inch television that hung on the wall. With the remote, Brian navigated through the photographs from the evening's crime scene. Jessica had taken almost a hundred pictures, and they scrolled through each, giving some a more thorough review than others. Blocked from entering the house by the police, she'd captured shots of all the activity outside. As always, Brian was amazed at how well-framed and in-focus every photograph was.

He reached for the glass of water he'd left on the coffee table and glanced back toward the kitchen. He drew in a quick breath when he glimpsed Sarah in the doorway. She leaned against the door frame with her arms crossed and smiled warmly when their eyes met.

He glanced at Jessica, wondering if she'd noticed his sudden distraction. No. She was studying the photo on the screen. He heard her mumble something about the lighting not being right. He returned his gaze to the kitchen door. Sarah was gone.

Brian and Jessica reviewed images for over a half hour before he paused. The picture on the screen showed the medical examiner standing in the driveway; the occupied stretcher was beside him with the zipper of the black body bag drawn down to reveal the gray pallor of a teenage girl's profile.

"Wait, what's that?" he said.

"I don't see anything."

He glanced at her. Jessica was picking at her teeth with her pinky, not even looking at the big screen. Brian stepped to the television to get a better look. In the photograph, Andrew and Mick stood over the body, and the priest's head was bowed in prayer.

Jessica rose from the sofa and stood beside him. "Took that from the sidewalk. The pigs wouldn't let me get any closer." She crossed her arms and gave him a smug smile. "Best telephoto lens on the market."

Brian gritted his teeth as a momentary wave of irritation rushed over him. "Don't use that term again."

Jessica glared at him. "What, pigs? That's what they are."

"I know you've got some issue with the police. I'm not asking you to tell me what it is. But I am asking for you to show a little respect."

Jessica turned away from him and huffed. "Whatever."

Brian rubbed his eyes and returned his gaze to the photo on the television screen. He zoomed in on the girl's lifeless expression. Her icy complexion was haunting, and her one visible eye was open. Its stare was blank and spiritless. He pointed at the screen. "What's that on her forehead?"

Jessica moved forward to give the image on the screen a more intense study. "Dunno. The letter L?"

"Someone wrote on her forehead?" Brian folded his arms and rocked back and forth on his heels. "With what? A marker?"

Jessica leaned closer to the screen until her face was inches from it. She tilted her head, then said, "Dunno. Could be a Sharpie, paint, or even lipstick."

"Did you get any other shots of her forehead? It looks like there's more than just an L."

Brian scrolled rapidly through the remaining photographs but was disappointed when he reached the last one. There were no other photos with a good angle of the dead girl's forehead. Jessica shrugged her shoulders, moved away from the screen, and ambled around the living room. Brian returned to the photo they'd been looking at earlier and rubbed his chin as he studied the image. He wondered if the mark was even actually a letter. It could just as easily be a smudge. Was he looking for something that wasn't there? Was he trying too hard to make a connection with the Reynolds murder?

He glanced toward Jessica, who stood across the room. Her gaze was locked on his framed Pulitzer Prize. She always seemed to gravitate to it whenever she was in his apartment. But she never asked questions. Never inquired why an award-winning journalist was running a small newspaper in Newark. Never seemed interested in knowing what had driven him out of the limelight into near obscurity. It was better that she didn't ask. Only two people in Newark knew about it. One was a close friend and the other a faithful confidant. And he'd prefer it to stay that way.

He advanced the photos forward again, slower this time. More pictures of Andrew praying over the dead girl. Then some of the medical examiner as he zipped the body bag closed. He stopped on another photo and studied it. Something in the far corner caught his eye. He scrutinized the image, then the next, and then the one after that. *What is she doing?*

Jessica drifted back to his side, folded her arms, and yawned. "I'm outta here. Whatcha gonna do now?"

Brian shrugged. "Talk to Mick again. I'll touch base with him tomorrow."

"Night then." Jessica turned and headed for the stairs that led down to the door.

"Hey Jess," Brian called over his shoulder. She stopped and turned. "Nice work," he added, giving her a smile.

She didn't respond right away, just stood at the top of the stairs. When she did speak, her voice was soft and conciliatory. "Sorry about the pig thing. I'll try to watch my mouth around you."

Once Jessica was gone, Brian moved down the hall. He peeked into the empty bedroom and scanned the shadows. "Sarah?"

Nothing. She was nowhere to be found. He moved back into the living room, turned off the lights, and sat down on the sofa. A faint light from the lampposts on Main Street filtered into the room from around the edges of the curtains. Brian watched the light dance across the ceiling as cars passed on the street below his apartment. With his legs stretched out before him, Brian yawned and closed his eyes, hoping against all odds for a restful night.

CHAPTER TWENTY-TWO

Thursday

It was after midnight when Candice returned to her bungalow on Bassett Place. The small home was secluded within a cluster of old oak trees which cast the house in dark shadows. Even the bright light of the waning gibbous moon couldn't penetrate through the ancient branches of the behemoth topiary. As she approached the front steps, the light beside the door didn't click on as she expected. Was the bulb burned out? She hoped the motion sensor hadn't gone bad already. She'd only had it installed a year ago.

Candice had remained at the Cavendish home with Andrew for almost three hours. The priest offered comfort to Audrey Cavendish while the police asked questions about her daughter's death.

Candice rarely got to watch Andrew at work, but it was always a treat for her to observe when she did. They might not see eye-to-eye on doctrine, but she still could admire his technique. He had fourteen years on her, and those additional years of experience showed when he was interacting with others. His deeply compassionate soul broke through his usual self-conscious shell when it was needed.

She noticed the color rush from his face when the police described the marks around Deena's neck. Andrew's grip tightened on his rosary beads. His voice faltered, cracking every so often as he stumbled over his own words. His eyes continually drifted in the direction of the kitchen, even though the body had already been removed. She'd seen the marks for herself. A line of round bruising that circled her neck, like marbles attached to a long string. Or . . . a string of rosary beads. For the briefest of moments, she felt a cold hand wrap around her heart.

Once in the house, Candice dropped her keys and her mobile phone onto a small table by the door, pushed the front door closed, and reached for the light switch. When she flicked it, the lights failed to come on. She cursed under her breath. The power had to be out. That would explain why the outside light didn't come on as she approached. But then she thought about the rest of the neighborhood. Candice was certain that her neighbor's lights had been on when she pulled into her driveway.

She reopened the front door and glanced up and down the street. Indeed, her neighbor's lights were on as well as most of the nearby houses. Her home seemed to be the only one without electricity. She pushed her door closed and turned to face the darkness of her house. There was a flashlight in her kitchen "junk" drawer. Candice started toward the back of the house but paused by the opening leading into the living room. The heavy odor of potpourri caught her attention. The smell was only ever that strong when she refilled the glass bowl, or if it had been disturbed.

Candice moved into the living room and immediately stumbled over something on the floor. She peered around the darkened room, lit only by the moonlight filtering in through the half-drawn curtains. The dim lighting made it difficult to make out details, but it looked like all that had been in the room was strewn across the floor. Her knees went weak, and she placed a hand on the nearby wall to steady herself. Each breath burst from her mouth in a rapid frenzy.

She backed out into the hall and moved quickly to the kitchen in search of the flashlight. A crunch under her feet as she entered the kitchen told her that the room had suffered a similar fate. The moonlight through the kitchen windows revealed the chaos scattered across the floor. She scrambled over cans, bottles, food containers, and broken dishes to reach the drawer that contained the flashlight.

Candice swept the kitchen with her light. Cabinets and drawers hung open, ransacked. Kitchen utensils were strewn like pickup sticks. A box of Cheerios was torn opened and dumped onto the counter, along with every box of pasta in the cabinets. Her head spun as she surveyed the havoc. Candice breathed deeply, trying to calm her racing pulse. Her chest tightened. An acidic taste rose in her throat.

Candice rushed back to the living room to assess the situation there. The books from her bookshelf were strewn across the tan Berber carpet. The contents from the end table drawer near the sofa lay scattered on the floor. Sofa cushions were tossed in a pile in the center of the room. The glass bowl on the ledge of the bay window lay overturned with the potpourri disbursed carelessly along the windowsill and on the carpet.

With her back pressed against the wall, Candice felt a faint chill run through her body. Who had done this? How had they gotten in? What were they looking for? Money? Valuables? She was an Episcopalian priest, with little of worth in her home. She still had a flip phone, for crying out loud.

She took a moment to slow her breathing, to calm her frazzled nerves. What now? Lights, that's what she needed. Get the lights back on. The neighborhood lights were on, so the issue had to be in her house. Maybe the main circuit breaker was off. She moved back toward the kitchen, using the flashlight to guide herself through the scattered mess on the floor. When Candice swung open the door to the utility room, she felt a cool breeze brush past her face. She swept the small room with the flashlight. A utility sink was to her right just inside the door. Next to the sink was a washer and dryer. A window above the appliances had been forced open. A basket of folded laundry that she'd left on the dryer had been knocked onto the floor.

She moved across the room to the circuit breaker box. The box's metal door was open, and the main breaker was off. She reached up to flip the breaker back on but stopped short when she heard a noise from the second floor of her cottage. It was a thump, like something had fallen in her bedroom. Suddenly, she realized her blunder. She'd assumed that whoever had broken into her home was gone. Now it dawned on her that the burglar may still be in the house. The flashlight beam shook as her hands began to tremble. Her pulse beat like a ticking clock on meth. Had the Sin Eater come to point an accusatory finger at her? Which of her sins would be declared in blood? Perhaps *thief* for her kleptomania?

Or *hypocrite* for her lack of faith?

There was another noise from above. This time it sounded like a footstep. *The police*, she thought. *Got to call the police.* Her hand went to her pocket for her mobile phone but came up empty. She cursed under her breath when she remembered leaving it by the front door. The landline in the house was in her bedroom. She pressed her back against the wall, searching for a rational thought amidst the chaotic panic in her mind. *Got to get out of here.* If she ran for the front door, she could grab her phone and car keys on the way. Then, call for help once she was outside. She was certain the plan had a flaw somewhere, but her only desire now was to get away.

Candice moved back into the kitchen and was about to run toward the front door when more footsteps from upstairs froze her in her tracks. What if the intruder was waiting for her at the door? She swung the flashlight around the kitchen and caught sight of a steak knife in the kitchen sink. Candice grabbed the handle in her quivering hand. The serrated stainless-steel blade glinted in the moonlight from the window above the sink.

Another soft thud came from upstairs. She drew in a quick gasp, and her grip on the knife handle tightened. Candice crept toward the front of the house. When she reached the stairs, she peeked up at the darkened second floor. The house had gone silent again. *Either the intruder knows I'm down here or . . .*

From the darkness, footsteps roared down at her. Before she could move, a dark figure rushed from the top of the stairs. From out of the shadows, she saw only angry eyes and a fierce scowl. The rest of the face was obscured behind a ski mask. She stumbled backward into the front door; her back pressed against the hard wood. The intruder plunged toward her. Her fingers clawed at the wooden door in a frantic search for the doorknob.

The dark figure reached the bottom of the stairs. Candice dropped the flashlight and lashed out haphazardly with the knife. There was a loud cry. Then something struck her in the face. The knife slipped from her grasp. As she spun around, her hand found the doorknob. She yanked at the door, but it didn't open. The deadbolt. She'd forgotten the deadbolt. Someone grabbed her from behind and wrestled her away from the door. She struggled against the powerful grasp, kicking her legs, and flailing her arms. Her assailant's labored breathing was loud in her ear.

"Where is it?" a raspy voice said.

She was jerked violently from right to left. Candice jabbed an elbow back into her assailant. There was a grunt in her ear. Then, in one fierce movement, she was thrown back toward the stairs. As she fell to the floor, her head hit the baseboard. A wave of nausea swept over her. She heard the click of the deadbolt, and the front door opened as she lost consciousness.

CHAPTER TWENTY-THREE

The cold night air brushed Candice's face, sending a chill along her spine, and jolting her awake. The pain along the back of her head pulsed, and the room swam around her as she tried to sit up. Her vision—blurry at first—cleared, and she gazed around her. She felt cold and lightheaded. The front door stood open, allowing the night chill to infiltrate her home. She probed the back of her head and grimaced. A welt had already risen. She checked her fingers. At least there was no blood.

Carefully, she rose to her feet, gripping the wall to steady her legs. Candice stood still for a few moments to allow the room to stop spinning before making another move. She found the flashlight near her foot and used it to search the foyer. The steak knife lay on the floor near the base of the stairs. The edge of the serrated blade had a streak of crimson. Near the door, the beige carpet was speckled with dark red spots.

She gave herself a quick onceover to make sure the blood wasn't hers. Relieved to find no sign of injury apart from her throbbing head, Candice crossed to the door, pushed it closed, then leaned back against it. The jumble of memories in her head were slow to form a coherent narrative. She vaguely recalled lashing out with the knife. Had she managed to strike her assailant and not know it? She remembered hearing what sounded like a shout of pain. How badly had she wounded him? Judging by the small amount of blood, it couldn't have been too bad.

She sidestepped around the bloody knife, grabbed her mobile phone from the table by the door, and moved toward the kitchen. Once she was seated at the dinette table, Candice punched in 9-1-1 on her phone.

"Hello. I need the police," she said. "Someone's broken into my home."

While she waited for the police to arrive, Candice went back to the laundry room to reset the breaker box. The police had said not to touch anything, but she couldn't stand to remain in a darkened house any longer. She wanted—no, needed the light. The whole house seemed to come alive; lights flickered on, and appliances began to hum. The familiar background noises that she barely noticed on a day-to-day basis were suddenly resounding and comforting. She leaned back against the washer and stared down at the laundry that had once been folded but now was a jumbled pile on the floor. A cool breeze tickled the back of her neck. Her eyes widened as Candice realized that she had her back to the open window. The same window that was probably used by the intruder to enter her house.

She turned slowly and backed out of the room.

A sudden loud pounding on the front door startled her. When Candice peered up the hall toward the door, she saw a flash of red and blue light reflected on the wall. She moved quickly to the front of the house and yanked the door open. Two police cars were parked in front of her home. One officer—young and thin with short blonde hair—stood on her front step; his hand rested casually on his hip. Another officer—older than the first, with a bald head and thick around the waist—was standing in the yard, sweeping her house with a bright flashlight.

"Ms. Miller?"

Candice let out a sigh of relief. "Thank God you're here."

"You reported a burglary?"

Candice stood aside and gestured for the police officer to enter. "I did."

While the older officer surveyed the damage in the house, Candice sat at the dinette and recounted her experience to the younger officer. He stopped her narrative on occasion to ask a question or seek clarification on a point. The throbbing in Candice's head subsided to a dull ache as the night went on.

"Any idea why someone would want to break into your house?" the younger officer asked.

Yeah, I'm a kleptomaniac, and a crazed psycho is out to kill me because of my sin, was what she thought.

"No. No idea," was what she said.

Candice rose from bed later than usual. It had been a long night, first with the Cavendish killing, then the break-in, and finally ending with a visit from the police. She sat up in bed, rubbed her eyes, and probed the back of her head with two fingers. The bump had gone down a bit, but it was still tender to the touch.

In the bathroom, she splashed water on her face and considered taking the day off. No one could blame her. Between a burglar ransacking the house and the police searching for evidence, she'd been left with a home in shambles. It would take days to get it back in order.

But she hadn't finished her Sunday sermon yet. And she didn't think she could stand to spend the entire day in the house. Even just the thought gave her a chill.

Back in the bedroom, she moved to the foot of the bed. Her clothes from the previous night were on the floor in a jumbled pile. She picked up her pants and felt around in the pocket, finding a gold ring. The intricate design resembled a tiny rope that circled the ring. She held it to the light. The precious metal must have been beautiful once, but it had lost some of its shine from years of daily "wear and tear." Why would a sixteen-year-old girl have a wedding band?

Candice knew she shouldn't have picked it up. It might be evidence in a murder investigation. But she hadn't been able to resist the urge to steal. She cursed under her breath, then offered up a prayer for forgiveness. With the ring held between her thumb and forefinger, she studied it closer. There were markings visible inside the band. The lettering had faded, but Candice could make out a few of the small letters. There was a *T*, and possibly an *A*. There was *LOV* and another *T.* Followed by some numbers. Perhaps a wedding date. Maybe 1998?

She let the ring drop into the palm of her hand and her fingers tightened around it. The inscription could be a message from one spouse to another. It made sense that a wedding band would be inscribed to commemorate the event. But she returned to her earlier question. Why would a sixteen-year-old have a wedding ring from over twenty years ago? Or, she wondered, had the killer dropped the ring?

Candice could hand the ring over to the police, but how would she explain her actions? There would be awkward questions. Why had she even picked it up? Why hadn't she told the police? Why was she even inside the Cavendish home? She'd seen the dead girl, seen the crime scene, seen more than she should have. To hand the ring over to the police would mean embarrassment, scandal, and possibly the loss of her job and livelihood. No, going to the police was out of the question, at least for now. Candice crossed the room and placed the ring on the dresser. She'd give it some thought and decide what to do later.

After showering and dressing, Candice went down to the kitchen to fix breakfast. She frowned as Cheerios crunched under her feet. Some of the cabinet doors still hung open, the contents spewed across the floor. She stepped gingerly over broken jars, spilt sauces, and flour. *Need to replace all this food,* she thought. She stood in the middle of the kitchen and sighed. It was all too much to tackle before she'd even had breakfast. There was only one thing for her to do. Go out.

CHAPTER TWENTY-FOUR

Although crisp, the morning air was rapidly warming as the sun crept its way up into the sky. Candice zipped up her windbreaker and kept her hands buried in its pockets. The ten-minute walk to the Main Street Diner was a familiar one. She twirled the previous evening's events around in her head. Why would anyone want to break into her house? Anything that did have value had been left untouched.

What was the thief looking for?

Candice was deep in thought as she drew up to the doors of the diner. She barely noticed a man approach from the opposite direction. He reached out and pulled the door open for her.

"Morning. Out for breakfast?" he said.

His voice startled her, and she looked up at his warm smile. "Oh, sorry. I was miles away." She paused, moved into the diner, then said, "Brian, right?"

Brian Wilder was wearing jeans and a pale blue polo. Under his arm was a folded newspaper. He nodded. "You here by yourself?"

"Yes."

He stepped inside behind her. "Mind if I join you?"

Candice wasn't necessarily in the mood for company. She'd hoped for a quiet meal on her own to collect her thoughts. Her mind was like a map with a whirlwind of unconnected dots. She needed time to sort through the dozens of details that alone made no sense, but together might become cohesive. But Brian's smile was inviting. Although she'd only met him recently, Candice knew him by reputation. Was it possible that his appearance was less fortuitous and more about information gathering? He might have questions. Questions Candice might not want to answer. She hesitated before answering. "Uh, sure."

After seating them in a window booth with a view of Main Street, the waitress pulled a notepad from her apron pocket. "You having the usual?" she said, looking at Brian.

"That'd be great, Ellen."

"One short stack. Sausage and bacon on the side, and a medium OJ." She scribbled on her notepad, then turned to Candice, "And what can I get for you?"

Candice glanced from Brian to the waitress and back again. *Does he know everyone in town?* Her eyes fell back to the menu again. She suddenly realized that she didn't have much of an appetite. But she was here now. She couldn't just sit and watch him eat. She ordered an omelet.

Candice slouched in the booth and glanced out the window at the busy thoroughfare. A dozen university students—bunched in small clusters—worked their way along the sidewalk toward campus. She was reminded of a line of worker ants marching toward their nest. Although only thirty-three, she was feeling far older this morning. Maybe it was seeing the young faces as they passed by. Perhaps it was the bruise on her head. Or just the all-over body ache she had from her fight with her assailant.

"I heard someone broke into your house last night. Are you okay?" Brian said.

She was amazed that he already knew about the break-in. She turned toward him, the stiffness in her neck reminding her that it'd been a rough night. "Yeah. I'm okay. The house is a complete mess, but nothing was taken. I consider myself lucky, especially after what else happened last night."

"Terrible business. The poor kid had her whole life ahead of her."

Candice pulled herself up straight when she realized how she must look. Slouching seemed to come far too easily this morning. She tilted her head from right to left to stretch her neck. It didn't help. "Any word yet on what happened?"

Brian ran his hand through his hair. "I was hoping you could tell me. You were in the house, not me."

The waitress returned with their orders, setting the plates on the table without a word. Then she rushed off back toward the kitchen. Candice stared at her plate. The omelet looked delicious, but her stomach churned.

"There's little I can tell you." She thought about the young girl's body, the marks on her neck, the gray pale face . . . the bread. "I wasn't in the house all that long."

Brian shrugged and poured syrup onto a stack of hotcakes that Ellen had brought. "You and Andrew known each other long?"

"A couple years. We met at an exhibition opening at the Delaware Museum of Art. Religious sculptures and such." She picked at her omelet, sliding a piece of tomato off to the side of her plate. Why hadn't she ordered it without tomatoes? She hated tomatoes. "We have a shared love of chess."

Brian nodded. "Hmmm . . ."

Candice shifted another bit of tomato away from her omelet. "Andrew and I play every Saturday over lunch."

"You must be good. I tried to play with him a couple times in the past. Lost every time."

Candice smiled. "I can hold my own." She slid a forkful of egg into her mouth. "How do you know him?"

"I'm a bit of a lapsed Catholic. Met Father Andrew when I first moved to Newark. I consult him occasionally on stories with a religious angle."

She stared across the table at Brian and studied him with a critical eye. Candice didn't know quite what to make of the journalist. Almost anyone who lived in Newark had heard of Brian Wilder. He was the face that you saw at almost every event, celebration, or accident in the city. But it was his career before Newark that she was more familiar with. Candice remembered reading some of his work when she was in seminary. There was an exposé in *Time* magazine on doomsday religious cults that she'd found particularly interesting. And then there was his series of reports from Afghanistan during the war in *USA Today*. When she first moved to Newark, Candice had been surprised to hear that Brian ran the local newspaper. A journalist of his caliber? Hadn't he won the Pulitzer Prize years ago? What would drive someone with his talent to run a small-town newspaper? She'd always intended to ask someone, but her curiosity was short-lived and got lost in the busyness of relocating to a new parish.

He looked up, caught her gaze, and smiled. "Is something wrong? You looked perplexed."

She felt her cheeks heat up and averted her eyes downward. "Sorry. You know, I loved that piece you wrote on cults."

"Thanks."

"As a seminary student, it was eye-opening. Made me realize how lost people are." She toyed with a piece of sausage on her plate. Why not tell him what she knew? It couldn't hurt, could it? "There was something unusual," Candice said suddenly.

"Where?"

"In the house where that girl died."

Candice detailed all that she'd seen the previous night. She spoke briefly of the bruising on the girl's neck, of the unusual round markings. Brian leaned forward with interest when she mentioned the loaf of bread. She went on to tell him about the word written in lipstick on the girl's forehead.

He snapped his fingers and grabbed the folded newspaper off the seat next to him. "That explains this." He laid out the newspaper on the table—front page facing up—and pointed to the article in the sidebar.

The newspaper was the *Delaware Post-Gazette*, a regional daily newspaper that covered the entire state, as well as national and world news. The article in question was about Deena Cavendish's murder and contained only the most basic details about the crime. There weren't any facts in it that she didn't already know. Candice skimmed the article until she got to the paragraph that he indicated.

Sources close to the investigation say that police are linking this murder with the recent killing of local real estate mogul, Robbie Reynolds. A source reported that law enforcement is working under the assumption that both murders were committed by the same suspect, based on handwritten accusations of wrongdoing left at both crime scenes, presumably by the murderer.

"Mick Flanagan is going to flip his lid when he sees this," Brian said. "You said there was a loaf of bread at last night's crime scene?"

Candice glanced up from the newspaper and nodded.

"That's the second one," he said. "Curious."

"You think that's curious," Candice said. "Let me tell you about sin eaters."

CHAPTER TWENTY-FIVE

A few hours later, Candice had just finished lunch and was washing her dish in the church's small kitchenette when she heard the knock on the door at the end of the hall. Odd. She didn't usually get visitors on Thursdays. After her breakfast with Brian, she'd felt a little antsy and staying at home in her cottage was something she couldn't stand at the moment. Yet spending the morning in the church office hadn't exactly eased her anxiety either.

She dried her hands on the dish towel and peeked down the hall toward the plain white door at the rear of the church. A silhouette was framed in the frosted glass of the window. Another knock came on the door, this time a bit louder. Candice moved along the hall, at first with an easy relaxed pace. But as she drew closer to the door, her mind filled with images of Robbie Reynolds and Deena Cavendish. Her shoulders tensed and she froze in the middle of the hall.

The silhouette in the window shifted and then disappeared. Candice stared at the door. The frosted window was now pure white and reminded her of a pristine snow drift. She breathed a sigh of relief, then wondered why she'd been so uptight, so anxious.

Candice drew in a deep breath and moved to the door. She pulled it open and stared out at the church's small parking lot. Hers was the only car present, looking as lost and alone in the empty parking lot as she felt in the empty church. She stepped outside and looked up and down the street. There was the nearby clop of un-even footsteps. Each sounded slow and unsteady. Candice walked to the sidewalk and peered down the street. Half a block away, a short elderly woman walked with unsure footing and a cane. Her shoulders were hunched forward. The head of curly white hair waved in the breeze.

"Agatha," Candice called.

The woman kept walking.

Candice rushed after her and called out again. "Agatha!"

This time, the old woman stopped, then turned as Candice ap-proached. "Ah, Pastor Miller. I thought . . . well, I didn't think you were in."

"Sorry, I was a little slow getting to the door. What can I do for you?"

Agatha looked down as her hand absently squeezed the handle of her cane. "I don't want to interrupt if—"

Candice shook her head and placed a hand on the woman's shoulder. "No, I just finished lunch." The idea of returning to her office alone invoked a sense of dread. "Why don't you come back to the church? I'll fix you a cup of tea."

Agatha's lip quivered. She seemed to vacillate on the cusp between two equally uncomfortable options. The elderly woman looked frailer than she had on Sunday. Her face was pallid; beads of sweat clung to her forehead.

"I don't want to be any trouble. Saw the article in the *Post-Gazette* this morning and needed to talk to someone." Agatha stared past Candice with eyes that were cloudy and distant. "Perhaps I should just go."

Candice touched the woman's elbow, a gentle attempt to steer her toward the church. "You came all this way." She knew Agatha lived across town and would've taken the bus to get there. "Why not come in and tell me what brought you here?"

Candice set the teacup on the table in front of Agatha. The elderly woman had remained silent since they returned to the church, except to provide the answer to questions about how she'd like her tea. Candice sat down at the table, her own warm mug clasped in both hands. There was a chip on the lip of the mug where she had dropped it in the sink a few months ago. She didn't have the heart to throw it away. It had been a birthday gift from her congregation the year before. It was personalized with her name, and said, "World's Best Pastor."

"How are you?" Candice said.

Agatha stared down at her mug, looking as if she hadn't heard the question. She was slouched forward over the table's edge. Her hands rested lazily on the table before her.

Candice leaned forward and tilted her head to look into the woman's eyes. "Agatha?"

"I shouldn't have come," Agatha said, without meeting Candice's gaze. "Should've just left it alone."

Candice reached across the table and placed her hand on top of Agatha's hand. She felt the quaking of delicate fingers beneath her own. "What's wrong? Are you okay?"

"It . . . I saw . . ." Agatha stumbled on her words, as if she couldn't remember what she'd planned to say. "I don't want to be next."

"Next?" Candice titled her head. "I don't follow."

Agatha reached into her sleeve, and pulled out a crumpled tissue, then dabbed at her eyes. A moment later, she returned the tissue to the sleeve. The elderly woman looked up. Her eyes stared past Candice. "I need to talk to someone."

"I'm a good listener," Candice said, but she thought the woman hadn't heard her.

"It's been so long now. I thought I could carry this secret to my grave." Her voice trailed off.

"Agatha, I don't—"

"I have to tell someone . . . I'll be next." There was a long pause before Agatha spoke again. When she did, her words were almost a whisper. "Thought about the police. Maybe they would understand."

Candice narrowed her eyes. She'd known Agatha for only a few years, but in that time the woman appeared to have it all together. But this was a different Agatha. One that seemed confused and uncertain. Almost haunted. Candice withdrew her hand from across the table.

With a sudden motion, Agatha reached over and clamped down on Candice's retreating wrist with an iron grip. "The blood. It was everywhere."

Candice couldn't turn away from the woman's stare. The hazy eyes from earlier seemed to turn dark and frightful, almost like she was possessed.

Agatha looked through her as if Candice wasn't in the room. The elderly woman's neck pulsed, and her hand held firm to Candice's wrist.

"I never meant to hurt anyone." Her jaw tightened as if she was in pain. "It just . . . happened."

Candice pried the woman's fingers from her arm. She sat back and looked at the red marks on her wrist, then back up at Agatha.

Tears were streaming down the elderly woman's face; her shoulders convulsing with each sob. "Oh God, what've I done?"

Afraid of where this conversation was leading, Candice pushed back from the table and bowed her head. She had to get her mind around what she was hearing. The only possibility that came to mind was too outrageous to believe. *It can't be. There's no way.* She scooted her chair around the table and placed her arm around Agatha's shoulders. "I'm not sure I understand. What are you talking about, Agatha?"

The elderly woman continued to sob. Her words and breath came in short gasps. "He was . . . so young. He wasn't doing anything wrong. And now I'll be next."

"Take a deep breath." Candice placed her hand on Agatha's and gave it a reassuring squeeze. "Just relax. Then tell me what this is all about."

Agatha pulled the balled-up tissue from her sleeve again and dabbed at her eyes. Then she slouched forward, her fingers picking the tissue apart, and then abruptly tried to stand.

"No, please stay. You're obviously burdened with something." Candice tried to sound confident but felt far from adequate. She suggested the only thing that came to mind. "Do you want me to call your daughter?"

"No. No." Agatha's shoulders tightened, and her eyes filled with fear. "She can't know. She mustn't . . ."

"What's going on?"

The woman went silent and stared down at her mug of tea.

Candice thought for a moment that Agatha had decided against sharing whatever was troubling her. Although she wanted to be seen as an empathetic resource in times of trouble, Candice couldn't help but feel relieved that the elderly woman had decided to remain silent.

Then, without warning, Agatha muttered, "I've killed someone."

CHAPTER TWENTY-SIX

B rian and Jessica crossed the parking lot of the Marriott, walking toward the lobby doors. The hotel, located near the northwest limits of the city, had recently undergone a year-long renovation, giving it a touch of modern elegance.

The facade of stone, glass, and steel was an eight-story pattern of right angles and straight lines. The landscaping provided a gauge with which to measure just how recent the hotel's facelift has been, with young shrubbery just taking root and grass seedlings barely beginning to sprout.

". . . and the groom went headlong down the church stairs," Jessica said, finishing a story she'd started on the ride over. "The couple spent the whole of their reception at the hospital. Their family still held the party. Can't waste all that food and a DJ."

Brian gave her a smile. "Tragic."

"Tragic? It was wicked! I got every second on video. Even the fight between the groomsmen. Never been to a wedding that was so much fun."

Brian laughed. "You're such a sadist."

When they entered the lobby, the young woman behind the nearby counter glanced up from her computer, smiled, and greeted them pleasantly. After a brief conversation and a quick phone call, the young woman pointed down a nearby passageway. "She's in room 615. Elevators are down there to the right. She's expecting you."

As they waited by the elevators, Brian made a mental review of what he'd learned from Candice over breakfast. He had to admit the concept of a sin eater was new to him. He'd never had much interest in religious history. Even if he did, Brian was certain that sin eaters would probably still have fallen through the cracks. The idea had just enough obscurity to make it one of those high-valued answers no one gets on Jeopardy.

All was silent during their brief elevator ride to the sixth floor. He gave Jessica an appraising look. Brian was impressed by her choice in attire. It was unusual to see her dressed in anything other than dark cargo pants, a t-shirt, and combat boots. The deep green chiffon blouse and black slacks brought out an air of professionalism in her that he'd been trying to instill for as long as she worked for him. On top of that, he couldn't remember ever seeing her in heels before. A brief smile crossed his lips.

"What's so funny?"

He skirted the subject with a lighthearted, "Nothing."

Brian was glad to have her along for this visit. Despite his many years of experience speaking to victims of tragedies, he still felt uncomfortable when he had to speak to a mother about the murder of her child. He'd used the pretense of needing information for the young girl's obituary as an opening to come see the grieving woman. He was hoping it would open opportunities to ask other questions. He didn't know Audrey Cavendish all that well. He'd run into her briefly once or twice at St. Matthew's. He seemed to recall a remark Andrew had made once about Audrey's husband walking out on the family shortly after the younger daughter was born. He wondered if the girl's father had been told about her death, and how he'd taken the news.

Audrey Cavendish answered the hotel room door almost immediately, and quietly gestured for them both to enter. Although newly renovated, the hotel suite had a cookie cutter feel to it. The furniture, wallpaper, even the artwork was generic and seemed as if it had been chosen specifically for its neutrality. The room lacked personality, comfort, and warmth. Everything Brian figured the grieving mother needed right now.

The dark bags beneath Audrey's eyes were a testament to the toll the past thirty-six hours had taken. He wondered if she'd slept at all since her daughter's murder. Thoughts of his own loss surfaced, and he fought momentarily to silence the raw emotions that came with them. He'd learned over the years to control them, compartmentalize them, and hide them away.

Audrey took a seat on a mauve chair and pointed for them to sit on the sofa. Brian glanced through the open double doors that led into the bedroom. The television was on, and Audrey's younger daughter sat—legs folded—in the middle of the king-sized bed. She didn't seem to notice their arrival.

"Can I just say how sorry I am?" Brian said. "Such a tragedy."

Audrey withdrew a balled-up tissue from her clenched hand and dabbed at her eyes. "Thanks. I . . ." She stopped speaking, at a momentary loss for words. ". . . haven't quite processed it all."

"Have you spoken to her father yet? How did he take the news?" Jessica asked.

Audrey dipped her eyes for a moment. "Her father's dead. After he left me, he returned to Florida." Her gaze drifted toward the window, expression vacant, lost somewhere in the past. "We met there while I was on spring break. Oh God, seems like a lifetime ago. Both young and foolish. I got pregnant on our honeymoon." She fell silent, then turned her gaze back to them. "He died a few years ago from a drug overdose."

"Sorry." Brian gave her a sympathetic nod. It seemed as if life was being particularly brutal to Audrey Cavendish. First, the loss of her husband and now her daughter. He'd be apt to say that fate was being a cruel mistress . . . if he believed in fate. He opened his mouth to ask her another question, but a soft voice from the bedroom interrupted.

"Mom? Can I have a soda?"

The young girl had climbed from the bed and stood in the doorway. She was thin, with shoulder-length dark hair and olive skin. The girl avoided eye contact with Brian, her head dipped with shyness.

"Sweetie. You'll have to wait. I'll walk you down to the soda machine when I'm done talking, okay?"

The girl gave a disappointed nod and turned back toward the bedroom.

"Why don't I walk you down?" Jessica rose to her feet. "Is that okay?"

Audrey nodded. "Thanks."

After Jessica and the young girl left, Audrey fell back into her chair. She looked exhausted. "Maggie's dealing with this better than I am."

Brian leaned forward and looked at her with pity. "If I may ask . . . why come to a hotel? Don't you have family nearby?"

Audrey shook her head. "No. My mother lives in California. We haven't spoken in years." She tilted her head over the back of the chair and stared at the ceiling. "Father Blake arranged for us to stay here. He's so kind. I don't know what I'd have done . . ."

Brian felt an uncomfortable lump form in his throat. Before him was a mother who had no one to turn to for support during this traumatic time. It had been very different for him years ago. He'd had plenty of family and friends to lean on, but he chose not to. Instead, he sank into his own deep pit of despair. One that he wasn't sure he'd completely emerged from yet.

"Do you mind talking about what happened?" Brian asked.

She lifted her head off the back of the chair. The motion had a loose, floppiness to it, and her head seemed to rock back and forth. It reminded Brian of a bobblehead doll.

"Must I?" she said after a silent moment.

"No. I'm just here to give my condolences and help with the obit. If you don't want to talk—"

"I've been over it all again and again with the police," she said, her gaze looking beyond Brian to a point unseen. "I was only gone for two hours . . . two hours. What kind of sick person . . . Deena was so innocent. Such a good girl . . . Why?"

Tears fell from her eyes, followed by a soft sob. Brian remained silent and allowed Audrey to grieve. Her anguish was evident with each cry. The magnitude of her loss hung in each wail. He recognized the sound of absolute sorrow. He'd heard it from people in war torn countries, and those in the wake of natural disasters. And he himself had once uttered that cry. There was nothing to be done but wait until the moment of grief passed. He leaned back and let her cry.

———

A half hour later, Brian and Jessica walked toward his Ford Mustang. The humidity of a pending storm hung heavy in the air. They'd not spoken since leaving the hotel room. Brian—lost in thought—barely noticed the silence. Audrey had calmed enough to assist him with writing her daughter's obituary. She seemed to struggle with finding enough to say about Deena's short life. He tossed the events of the past few days around in his mind. So many facts, but none made sense. Two deaths. No apparent connection between the two . . . except for a loaf of bread.

Jessica folded her arms and hugged herself tightly. She shivered against the dropping temperatures. "Worst outfit ever," she said. "Dress professional, you said."

Her remarks made Brian laugh. "I appreciate you coming along."

"No prob. Did ya get any dirt?"

"No," Brian said, shaking his head. "Didn't seem like a good time to ask too many questions."

Jessica's smile broadened into a smug grin. "At least one of us didn't strike out."

Brian opened the driver's side door on the Mustang. He looked across the roof of the car at her. "What's that mean?"

Jessica pulled open the other car door. "Let's just say, me and Maggie. We're tight." She held up her hand and crossed two fingers.

Once inside the Mustang, Jessica explained how forthcoming Maggie Cavendish had been during their walk to the hotel's soda machine.

"Seems Deena had a bit of a dishonest streak in her. She'd lie about anything. Her grades. Sometimes she'd say she was meeting some girlfriends at the diner but end up with a boy for a quick romp in his backseat." Jessica gestured back toward the hotel. "According to Maggie, Mama back there never knew."

"Not as innocent as Mom makes out."

"Hell no," Jessica said. "Sounds like Deena got more in just the past year than I've gotten my whole life."

Brian started the car, then laughed. "TMI, Jess. TMI."

"Deena even tried to get one of her Sunday school teachers in trouble a few years back," Jessica said. "Claimed she saw the woman with a lesbian lover. Luckily, that priest of yours saw through the whole scam, and Deena admitted to the lie."

A revenge killing? Brian wondered. But why wait a few years to exact retribution? He made a mental note to ask Andrew about the incident.

"Explains one thing though," Jessica said.

Brian nodded as he backed the car out of the parking spot. "Yeah. We know why someone wrote 'LIAR' on her forehead."

CHAPTER TWENTY-SEVEN

Candice sat at the small, square table near the back of the Roasted Bean, the coffeeshop on Main Street near the university campus. She sipped tentatively on her double latte and grimaced at the taste. Coffee was never her first drink of choice, but today she felt like she needed the extra dose of caffeine, or she'd never get through the rest of the day. There were only a few customers in the small café, mostly university students who were heads-down working on their laptops at a front table.

She checked her watch and leaned back in the chair. Her mind was still reeling from Agatha Bowman's confession. From what Candice knew, the elderly woman had been a stalwart of good deeds for decades. Volunteering at homeless shelters, the local library, the church, and just about any local charity event for the past sixty years. To think of her as a cold-blooded killer was laughable.

The door to the coffeeshop opened and Samantha Blackwell entered. She glanced around the cafe, caught sight of Candice, and moved toward the back table. The crisp crease in Samantha's navy slacks shifted effortlessly was she approached. Always immaculately dressed. Candice's own gray pants had a sudden inadequacy. They were only a year old, but they seemed so abruptly out of style.

Samantha dropped her leather handbag on the table. "Hiya. How've you been?"

"So-so. Thanks for coming out."

Samantha waved away the comment, "Of course, anytime. But I can only stay for a few minutes. Got a last-minute client appointment at four." She gestured toward the coffeeshop's front counter. "Give me a sec."

While Samantha moved away to order a coffee, Candice lifted her double latte to her lips, caught the aroma and frowned. *Why did I ever order this?* She placed the cup back onto the table and pushed it away. She would just press on through the rest of the day sans stimulant.

Samantha returned to the table moments later. She sat down across from Candice, gestured to the rejected cup, and smiled. "Did you buy a latte again?"

"A double."

Samantha laughed. "What were you thinking?"

"Not sure." Candice shrugged. "Thought the need for caffeine was greater than my revulsion of coffee."

"You sounded troubled on the phone," Samantha said. She tasted her coffee. "What's going on? Does this have to do with Robbie?"

Candice leaned forward; her shoulders hunched over the table. "Sort of. There's more to it than that. I . . . need a little advice."

Samantha checked her watch. "You've got my attention for five minutes. Ten if you'll walk back to the office with me."

"Let's walk." Candice rose from her seat.

Samantha stood and grabbed her bag and coffee cup. "We'll walk slow."

———————————

The door of the Roasted Bean swung closed behind them. The sky was still overcast, the sidewalk still wet from a brief afternoon shower. Although the storm left moderate temperatures, Candice felt a deep chill beneath her skin. It was an icy sensation that had been lingering since the weekend. Nothing she did could make it go away.

She struggled to find the right words to describe this perception of—she laughed to even think about it—evil. Candice wasn't a believer in the concept of evil, but she could not find any other way to comprehend the sensation. Something evil was happening in Newark.

"The past few days have been—"

Samantha interrupted. "Not sleeping?"

"Yeah." Candice nodded. "Do I look that bad?"

"Not too bad, but . . ." Samantha made an idle gesture at Candice. "I can see it in your face."

Samantha and Candice walked along the sidewalk in silence. Traffic moved past on the downtown one-way street at a slow, steady pace. A group of university students brushed past them on their way toward campus.

"What's keeping you up at night?" Samantha asked.

Candice hesitated before answering.

How much should she tell? "I assume you know about the girl who died last night?"

Samantha's smile vanished. "No. What happened?"

"A young girl—Deena Cavendish—was found murdered in her house last evening. Possibly strangled."

Samantha suddenly halted; her jaw dropped opened. "Deena?"

"You know her?" Candice asked.

"She's one of my . . ." Her words stumbled from her mouth. "Yes, I know her."

Candice knew better than to probe further, but Samantha's unfinished sentence suggested Deena had been a client.

"I was there last night, at the house." Candice slipped her hands into her coat pockets.

They started walking again, their pace slower than before. Samantha sipped from her coffee. "Why were you there?"

A young teenager—dressed in black baggy clothes—raced toward them on a skateboard. Candice sidestepped to avoid getting hit. "Andrew Blake asked me to go with him. Deena's family went to his church."

Samantha remained silent until they'd passed the next crosswalk. "It's no wonder you're not sleeping. First, Robbie Reynolds, now Deena. If you're not careful, you'll end up with PTSD."

Candice paused and turned to Samantha. "There's something else." She wavered, unsure of what she could say without betraying Agatha's confidence. "I've been told something. Something that— if true—could mean a lot of trouble for someone who might not deserve it."

Samantha narrowed her eyes. "If true?"

"I have some doubts . . ." Her words trailed off for a moment. "An elderly member of my congregation has confessed to murder. But—"

Samantha interrupted. "You're questioning the state of this person's mind?"

Candice nodded. "It's impossible to picture this person doing anything worse than jaywalking. Even that would probably be a stretch."

They stopped at a street corner and waited for the light to change. As they stood there, Samantha sipped her coffee. "When you say elderly—" she started to say.

"Mid-eighties."

Samantha tilted her head. "Hmm . . . you think she's suffering from dementia?"

The traffic lights changed, and they stepped into the crosswalk. A bustle of footsteps approached from behind. Two young students rushed past them; one jarred Candice's shoulder and muttered a terse apology as he continued on his way. Candice raised her hand to acknowledge the brief words, but the student was already across the street and on down the sidewalk.

"You're the expert," she said. "What do you think?"

Samantha stepped onto the sidewalk, halted, and turned toward Candice. "I can't possibly make a diagnosis without doing an evaluation. Can you talk your . . . murderer into coming to see me?" Samantha made air quotes around the word *murderer*.

Candice reflected on how her conversation with Agatha had ended. At first, she'd waited desperately for the punchline, hoping that it was all just a joke.

"Agatha, tell me what happened Friday night?" Candice had asked.

There was confusion in Agatha's bleary, unfocused eyes. She stared, perplexed, as if the question had been asked in an unintelligible language. "Friday night?"

"Yes," Candice said. "The night you killed Robbie Reynolds."

Agatha's eyes opened wide, and her mouth gapped. "Robbie Reynolds? No, not Robbie. I killed Sam Pyeong."

The name meant nothing to Candice. She'd tried to push for more details, but Agatha had risen abruptly from her chair.

"I'm sorry. I shouldn't have come," Agatha had said. "Please . . . forget what I said. It's all just . . . the ramblings of an old woman."

The memory faded and Candice returned her gaze to Samantha. She shook her head. "I doubt it."

Samantha started moving down the sidewalk again. "Not sure what I can do then."

Candice followed a step behind. "But what should I do? Call the police?"

"You could." Samantha glanced at her watch and quickened her pace. "But I don't know what you'd tell them."

They walked in silence along the next block until they arrived at a crosswalk that stretched across Main Street. Samantha paused for a moment on the curb. "I know you don't want to hear this, but there's nothing you can do. Not until you have more information." Samantha glanced up and down Main Street. "It's probably nothing. Just a mixed-up memory. I got to go."

"Quick question. You've lived here all your life, right?" Candice asked.

Samantha nodded.

"Do you know someone named Sam Pyeong?"

Samantha thought for a moment before shaking her head. "Don't think so. Is that your—"

Candice finished the sentence. "Victim. Yes, at least that's what I was told."

"The name doesn't ring a bell. Sorry." She leaned forward and gave Candice a brief hug. "Call me if you find out more." Then, she stepped into the crosswalk.

Time suddenly seemed to crawl as Candice watched Samantha walk over the white painted stripes in the street. Candice caught a glimpse of a gray Honda as it ran the red light a short block away and accelerated down Main Street. The back of her neck prickled. The car increased speed and swerved over the yellow line. Samantha—head down—scrolled through something on her iPhone and seemed oblivious to the sudden threat bearing down on her.

Candice shouted a warning but didn't seem to hear her own voice. White noise filled her ears. Everything in her periphery blurred. Samantha was all that she could see. Candice shouted again, but Samantha didn't respond. Candice's chest tightened and she fought to catch a breath. Her eyes darted from the fast-approaching Honda to Samantha and back to the car. Before she could think through her actions, Candice lunged into the street. Her shoes felt like they were stuck to the asphalt. The high-pitched rev of the car engine sounded closer than ever. She didn't dare look at it again, for fear it would slow her down. Arms outstretched. Eyes laser focused.

Candice crashed into Samantha's back with her shoulder. The two slammed to the pavement and rolled over the white stripes of the crosswalk. A horn honked. Someone screamed. Tires screeched. A car engine raced.

When Candice opened her eyes, the world was out of focus. Blurred images moved within her field of vision. Something touched her shoulder. Her body raged in pain as she tried to sit up.

The haze in her mind began to fade. Figures came back into focus, and she found a crowd of people huddled over her. Memories of the past few seconds flooded back. She jerked up and searched the crowd.

"Samantha?" she shouted.

"I'm here." The voice was familiar, but weak and trembling.

Candice ignored the searing aches in her body and scrambled to her feet. Samantha was a few feet away; another crowd clustered around her. Candice pushed her way through the mass of people and knelt beside Samantha.

"You okay?"

Samantha nodded. "Bruised and battered but otherwise . . ."

"Where's the car?" Candice said as she rose to her feet. She glanced up and down Main Street. There was no Honda in sight. She turned to one of the bystanders. "Did you see where that car went?"

The young man shrugged and gestured down the street. "It raced off. Didn't even stop."

CHAPTER TWENTY-EIGHT

The front door at the rectory for St. Matthew's had been left a few inches ajar when Candice mounted the three steps to the small concrete porch. She hesitated. Andrew was always conscientious about ensuring that doors were closed and windows latched. He'd never leave a door partially open. Her mind plunged back to the burglary at her own house the night before, mere hours ago. The infusion of fear-driven adrenaline. Her desperation to escape the house. Her struggle with the perpetrator. Her stomach was queasy, and she felt a chill on the back of her neck. What if Andrew was in danger? What if a thief was in the house right now? What if the criminal was waiting for her just inside the door? *What if . . .*

What if... ? The string of *what ifs* vomited from her subconscious to the forefront of her mind.

She fought her desire to flee and stepped forward to listen near the crack at the door's frame. She stood there for only a few seconds, but to Candice, it felt like minutes . . . hours. There was no sound from within the house. She couldn't decide if this was good news or bad. Her heart pounded in her chest. *What if... what if I am blowing this all out of proportion?* The moment of clarity caught her by surprise. She stepped back from the door. Maybe Andrew simply forgot to latch it. What were the odds that a thief would strike in her own home and Andrew's in less than twenty-four hours? It seemed a bit far-fetched to think that she, or Andrew, had anything truly valuable in their homes. Both of their houses were small and modest, and there was nothing remarkable in either of their lifestyles to lead anyone to believe they'd find anything worth stealing in their humble abodes.

Her hand hovered over the doorknob. What if the Sin Eater was waiting inside? Her breath caught in her throat as she withdrew her hand. Why would a religious psychopath target Andrew? She could understand why she might be a target, but Andrew? Surely, he was without sin. But what if it wasn't about sin? What if it was something else? Perhaps the fact that they'd been to both crime scenes? But that made no sense. There was nothing important about their presence in the home of each murder victim . . . except that she'd taken something from both. Her blood ran cold. Was that why someone had been in her house? She shuddered thinking that someone might know about her horrible secret. *No.*

She shook her head, trying to rid herself of the growing paranoia. She looked back at the partially open door. *It's probably nothing . . . just a simple mistake.* Candice wasn't wholly certain that she believed it. She reached for the doorknob and couldn't help but notice her hand was quaking. Candice pushed open the door and crossed the threshold into the living room with a cautious step. She was immediately overwhelmed by a pungent sour odor that reminded her of fermented spaghetti sauce. She turned her face away and wrinkled her nose; her own stomach turning at the stench.

"Andrew?" she said, her voice a restrained shout.

Nothing but silence answered her call. She glanced around the small living room. It contained a smattering of mismatched furniture. A worn green and brown plaid sofa sat near the far wall. A faded pale blue microfiber armchair with a sunken cushion sat in the corner beside a tall brass floor lamp.

Her gaze fell upon the mission-style coffee table in front of the sofa. On the scratched tabletop, a single glass tumbler was on its side next to three empty Jim Beam bottles. A small puddle of liquid crept out from the tumbler and across the table. She'd never known Andrew to be a drinker.

Candice called out again. "Andrew?"

Again, nothing.

She skirted past the coffee table and made her way into the kitchen. A takeout container half-filled with fried rice sat on the dinette table as well as a plate of shrimp and broccoli. The meal looked as if it had barely been touched. A couple of flies were buzzing around the cold plate, scavenging. Candice found several more plates—dirty and covered with half-eaten food—stacked haphazardly in the kitchen sink. The trashcan was overflowing with takeout boxes and bags from several nearby restaurants. Candice was surprised by the mess. Andrew was always conscientious about cleaning up after meals. Would he leave the dishes stack up like this in the sink?

She left the kitchen and made her way along the hall that led to the back of the small house. She glanced into the bathroom. She switched on the light and was shocked to find a beige hand towel balled up in the sink. It was stained and fraying along the edges. She touched it. The towel was dry.

The sour odor that repulsed her when she entered the house was stronger. Her stomach turned and she swallowed hard. Candice moved out of the bathroom and toward the bedroom. The door was open. As she approached, she heard slow rhythmic breathing. When she peeked around the door frame, her nose was assaulted by the forceful smell of vomit. Andrew was sprawled face down on a twin bed. He was wearing a white t-shirt and his usual black trousers. A congealing pool of vomit had spread down the side of the bed and onto the floor.

Candice drew in a breath of surprise, then almost choked on the foul odor that pervaded the air. She stepped into the room and slowly moved to the bed. Andrew appeared to be deep asleep; his steady breathing sometimes tainted with a faint snore. She'd never seen him before out of the long sleeves of his clerical clothing.

The idea that Andrew would drink himself into oblivion was preposterous to Candice. He was mild-mannered. Always in control. He was a spiritual mentor to her. How long had she known him? Two, maybe three years. There was nothing—that she could remember—that would hint at him being an alcoholic . . . or even a drinker at all. Andrew was always a strong, faithful man who seemed infallible. His commanding grasp of doctrine and the scriptures astounded her.

But then she thought about the past week.

She'd seen a different side of Andrew. He'd seemed out of sorts and distracted ever since visiting the crime scene at the Reynolds's home. Deena Cavendish's murder had shaken him as well. She recalled his trembling hands, his vacant eyes. The murders had impacted her as well, of course, but what was so bad that would make Andrew drink himself into unconsciousness?

She moved closer to the bed and reached out to nudge Andrew awake. Her hand hovered over his shoulder. He would be mortified to know she'd seen him like this. She knew Andrew well enough to know he'd distance himself from her, probably end their weekly chess games. At first he'd make excuses for missing the occasional match. Then, as the number of missed afternoons increased, he'd excuse himself from the games altogether. Andrew was the sort who would bear his shame on his shoulders, but never face it head on.

Despite the possibility of losing Andrew, she couldn't leave him to sleep in his own vomit. Candice touched his shoulder and gave it a gentle nudge. He grunted and stirred, then fell back into a rhythmic snoring.

"Andrew," she said softly while nudging him again.

This time, he didn't even stir, and just continued to snore. Waking Andrew was beginning to look like an impossible task. At least until he slept off his drunkenness. She touched his shoulder one more time and nudged harder while calling his name.

He suddenly rolled onto his back. His eyes popped open and stared up at the ceiling. Startled by his sudden movement, Candice jumped back. Andrew flailed back and forth on the bed. His hands clutched the bed covering. He was muttering to himself. The words, at first, were quiet and meaningless. But his voice rose in volume as his thrashing got worse.

"Not dead. Not dead. He's not dead," Andrew said. He repeated the words over again in a voice that quivered with anguish.

"Don't die. Don't die." His last three words came in a scream. "You can't die." His body convulsed, his back arched off the bed. Candice backed to the opposite side of the room in terror. She wrung her hands together as she watched, feeling helpless. Suddenly, Andrew flopped back on the bed, eyes closed and silent.

It was a few moments before Candice realized that Andrew had fallen back asleep. With apprehensive steps, she approached the bed and studied his pale face. Dried vomit still clung to his lower lip and chin. His hair was tousled in every direction. Andrew looked thinner, almost emaciated.

What happened to you, Andrew?

The atmosphere in the room had become stifling, and Candice's own stomach threatened to add to the already formidable smell. Fresh air was what she needed. She had little confidence that Andrew was stable, but it'd become imperative for her to get out of that room, even if just for a few minutes. She touched Andrew's hand. "I'll be in the other room."

Candice moved into the living room and sat on the sofa. What had she just witnessed? A seizure? Had Andrew simply experienced a terrible nightmare? Or was it something worse? She was reminded of the movie *Omen*. Demonic possession? She rolled her eyes and laughed. She'd never subscribe to an idea like that. But another chill raced down her spine. It was the second time in two days that the concept of evil entered her mind. She shook it off. No, nothing otherworldly was at work here. She should call for an ambulance. Get him to a hospital. She glanced back toward the bedroom. The faint sound of snoring drifted down the hall. No ambulance.

"I'm not doing this alone," she said to no one.

Candice grabbed her mobile phone from her pocket and scrolled through her address list. She needed someone who knew

Andrew well, someone who'd be willing to help her handle this discreetly and still get him whatever help he needed. There was only one person who'd fit that bill.

"Hello?" George Hardy answered on the third ring. He had served as deacon at St. Matthew's for years even before Andrew arrived to take over the church. He helped with Sunday services, coordinating the church's Sunday school program, and other outreach efforts. Candice didn't know him all that well, and only had his number because Andrew had given it to her for emergencies.

"It's Candice Miller. Can you come over to the rectory?"

CHAPTER TWENTY-NINE

Friday

B rian looked up from his computer when the postal worker
entered the *Newark Observer* office. The noise of the midday
Main Street traffic followed her in, then ceased as soon as the door
closed behind her. She greeted Mildred and placed a small stack of
envelopes on the front desk. She waved toward Brian.

"Hey Mr. Wilder," she said.

He cringed at the greeting. She looked to be twenty-two, maybe twenty-three at most. Calling him Mr. Wilder just made him
feel old. "Hello, Janice."

"Is it true what they're saying about those two murders? Were
they killed because of some nasty secrets in their past?"

This was the fourth time in twenty-four hours that someone was concerned about being the next victim because of their less-than innocent lifestyle. The *Delaware Post-Gazette* had a lot to answer for. "I'm not sure that's quite what was reported."

"I've got too many skeletons in my closet," Janice said. "Don't want to be the next to end up dead."

Brian tried to reassure her. "I don't think you've got anything to worry about."

Janice smiled, slung her letter bag over her shoulder, and then pushed through the door and out onto Main Street.

After the Janice was gone, Mildred looked up from the mail she'd been sorting. "That girl better be doubly careful. I've heard about the shenanigans she gets up to."

Brian laughed and returned his gaze to the computer but continued to watch Mildred over the top of the screen. There were three wire baskets stacked on the corner of her desk. She placed bills in the top basket and slipped one envelope in the second basket. Must be a check, he thought. All other mail went into the bottom basket. He'd look through everything later. A smile crossed Mildred's face and she rose from her chair.

"Look. A postcard from Chloe." She moved toward him waving the small flimsy card. "She must be enjoying her vacation."

Mildred handed it to him across his desk. The photo was of Cinderella's Castle in Disney World. "With Love from the Magic Kingdom" was printed across the bottom of the photo in white, flowing letters. He turned the card over and read the brief inscription on the back. In a few succinct words, the other *Observer* reporter described her trip and all the fun she was having with her boyfriend, Nathan. Brian smiled, not able to remember the last time he had been to Disney World. Thirteen or more years ago?

Allison couldn't have been more than ten, possibly eleven at the time. She ran up to every costumed character and gave them a big hug. And the princesses . . . Allison had been enamored by every princess they'd found. She'd stand a few feet away and act shy, like she was afraid to approach. Sarah would nudge Allison forward, and the princess—whichever one it was at the time—would bow down and greet his shy young daughter with reverence and beauty. He felt a pang in his heart and swallowed hard to keep from getting choked up by the memory. When was the last time he'd spoken to his daughter? He couldn't remember.

"That's wonderful," he said. "Glad they're having a good time."

Mildred slipped the postcard from between his fingers and stared at it again. "Hope she took plenty of photos. I haven't been down to Disney in almost forty years. I hear it's all changed."

She crossed to a bulletin board on the nearby wall and jabbed a push pin through the postcard. It stuck to the board next to the required government Equal Opportunity Employment poster. Then she made her way back to her desk. The office fell silent once again.

Brian returned his gaze to the computer and reread the email he'd received early that morning from Candice Miller. The timestamp said it had been sent at 3:15 in the morning. He wondered why she'd been up so late. The message was brief.

Brian—Do you know anything about someone named Sam Pyeong? I think he's dead, possibly murdered. Any chance you could do a little digging? I've got to be in Philly all day for a meeting. I'll explain what this is all about later.

Thanks,
Candice

It wasn't a name Brian recognized. He was the first to admit he didn't know everyone in Newark. This person could simply be one of thousands he hadn't met. Was it possible Sam Pyeong was a yet-to-be-discovered victim of the supposed "Sin Eater"?

He chuckled at the name. The whole concept of a sin eater had astounded him when Candice had first described it. The things people would do for their beliefs, he thought. Was that what this was all about? Some twisted religious fanaticism?

He rose from his desk and crossed the office to stand before the window. He slid his hands into his pockets and rocked back and forth on his heels. Newark was a quiet, unassuming city. Tiny by most accounts, particularly compared to neighboring cities like Wilmington, Dover, and even Philadelphia. Even Brian's home-town of Asheville made Newark look more like a rural community. If it wasn't for the university, Newark would just be another dot on the map. You would not expect to encounter a fanatical religious killer in a community like this.

He turned suddenly and leaned over Mildred's desk. His hands rested on either side of her computer monitor. "What do you know about Sam Pyeong?"

Mildred looked up at him, her eyes a blank stare. "Who?"

"Sam Pyeong."

Her forehead furrowed and Mildred frowned. "Pyeong? Not sure I know a Sam Pyeong."

Brian stood up straight and folded his arms. "C'mon. You know everything about everyone in town."

Mildred's eyes widened. "Are you calling me a gossip?" Her voice was filled with indignation. "Brian Wilder, I'll have you know that no one believes more in a person's right to privacy than me. I'm shocked you would even imply that I would spend my day blabbing about the affairs of others." She leaned back in her chair, folded her arms, and stared at him with ire-filled eyes.

Brian held up his hands in mock surrender. "Sorry. I didn't mean to offend. I just meant you know a lot of people in town. Maybe you knew this . . . knew of this Sam Pyeong."

Mildred shook her head. "That wasn't much better."

Brian laughed and shrugged. What else could he do?

"I don't know him," she said. "But I'll make some inquiries."

Brian started back toward his desk. "I'd appreciate that."

"What's this Pyeong character supposed to have done?" Mildred asked after him. "Is he our killer?"

As Brian sat down behind his desk, he said, "No. He might already be dead."

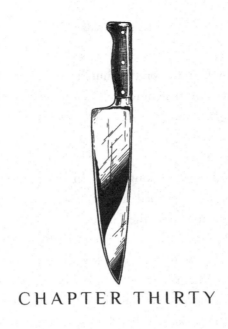

CHAPTER THIRTY

C andice closed the front door of her house, moved into the living room, and, with a low sigh of relief, dropped her purse onto the sofa. It had been a long day, and she was glad to be home. Her Friday morning had started early, with a drive through rush hour traffic up to Philadelphia for a day-long meeting between herself, her bishop, and more than two dozen other Episcopal priests from around the area. It had been a day of seminars, discussions, and closed-door meetings, which as far as she was concerned, had been mostly a waste of time. Her fellow priests, many from inner-city churches, spent most of the day complaining about the challenges of reaching the neighborhood youth, dealing with a constant stream of graffiti on the church walls, or struggling to find volunteers to serve in the church. *At least you don't have to deal with a potential religious maniac killing your flock*, she'd thought more than once.

All she wanted now was a glass of wine to go along with a hot bubble bath and an hour-long soak. In the kitchen, she opened a bottle of Pinot Noir, filled her wine glass to two-thirds, then slipped two ice cubes into the glass. It was a habit a few of her friends teased her about, but Candice loved her wine with ice.

She carried the wine glass and bottle up the stairs. She filled the tub with hot water, added some bubble bath, then went into the bedroom to undress. As she slipped out of her slacks, she felt something in her pocket. She withdrew a brass bookmark. It was shaped like a diving mermaid with a string of beads attached to the tail. One of her fellow priests—a collector of small antiques—had left the bookmark atop the open page of his Bible on a nearby table. Candice had been fixated by it all day. More than once, she'd found herself staring across the room at the emerald beads that hung over the side of the Bible.

It had been tricky to steal the bookmark without anyone seeing, but she had slipped it out of the priest's bag while everyone packed up to leave. Now, she turned it over in her fingers, let a disappointed breath slip from her lips, and said a quick prayer for forgiveness. The past forty-eight hours had left her feeling beaten, bruised, and drained. The house was still a shambles from the burglary. She'd cleaned up the food in the kitchen, but her personal possessions were still in disarray. Her late-night vigil at Andrew's house ended around three o'clock in the morning, when George convinced her to go home. He promised to remain until Andrew was awake and feeling better.

The combination of the hot bubble bath and the wine helped soothe her aching muscles and stiff joints. Although the swelling had disappeared, her head was still tender to the touch. She sipped from her wine glass and slid deeper into the water.

It still bothered Candice that the burglar hadn't taken any of her valuables. Not that she wanted her things to be stolen. But it meant her assailant was after something else. The police thought she'd simply interrupted him before he could steal anything. She took another sip of wine, then allowed the glass to dangle over the side of the tub between her fingers.

What about the murders? Two dead, both accused of a sin. If Brian Wilder was correct in what he told her over lunch, then Robbie Reynolds was "guilty as charged." But what about young Deena Cavendish? She'd have to ask Andrew about her. Even if the girl had been a liar, could it possibly have impacted someone so much that they'd kill her? She tried to wrap some level of rationality around the two crimes, but she couldn't find any connection between the victims . . . except they both suffered a sudden death by the Sin Eater. She laughed aloud. That name sounded so ridiculous, yet it was the only way she could describe the killer.

Over the next half hour, the water grew tepid and the bubbles dwindled. The wine had gone to her head. Candice climbed from the tub, grabbed a terry cloth robe from a hook behind the door, and moved back into the bedroom. Her eyes were drawn to the mermaid bookmark, which rested where she'd left it on her dresser. She picked it up and gazed at the tarnished brass object between her fingers. Would she ever rid herself of this "habit?" It was as much of an embarrassment as it was shameful.

Candice reached beneath the bed and pulled out her box of pilfered trinkets. With the plastic lid off, she stared down at the evidence of her own sin. Each object was like a little piece of her soul, torn away with every theft. The hypocrisy between her little habit and her chosen career—no, her calling—was not lost on her. She felt a grand sense of shame every time she preached on the Ten Commandments. The seventh always got stuck in her throat when she read the scripture.

She dropped the recently acquired brass bookmark into the box. Before she could put the lid back on, her eye was caught by the gold ring in the corner. She lifted it out and stared at the inscription again.

For a moment, she tried to fill in the blank letters, as if she were on *Wheel of Fortune*. *I'd like to buy an "O"*, she thought. That gave her "To" as the first word. Possibly "love" as well. Probably a wedding date at the end. April of 1998? Her mind was a bit fuzzy from the wine, so she didn't feel up to dissecting dozens of possible variations.

She dropped the ring back into the plastic box.

She reached for the lid, but then paused. Candice dug her fingers through the pile of trinkets and picked up a black digital voice recorder near the bottom. She held it between her fingers, recalling where she'd gotten it—Alex Brennen's study on the night she went to ask him about sin eaters.

Curiosity got the better of her and Candice pressed a button on the side of the device. A young female voice came from the speaker. It had a tinny echo to it, as if the person speaking wasn't talking directly into the microphone.

"—a rough week. I can't get the baby to sleep through the night and—"

Candice stopped the recording. The voice wasn't one she recognized. What was this a recording of? A conversation between friends? She pressed the fast forward button, then pressed play. This time she heard a male voice.

"—a change in her over the past few weeks. I think she's cheating on—"

Again, she stopped the recording and fast forwarded further. When she pressed play, she heard another male voice.

"Thanks for agreeing to see me on such short notice." She gasped. That voice she recognized: Robbie Reynolds.

Another voice spoke. Female. "I had back-to-back cancellations today. Otherwise, you'd have had to wait until Monday. Have a seat."

Candice expelled a quick breath. She knew that voice as well. It was Samantha. She suddenly realized what she held in her hand. The private counseling sessions of Samantha Blackwell. The recording continued to play.

"I needed to talk someone . . ." Robbie said. ". . . before tonight."

"What's happening tonight?"

Candice heard Robbie take a long deep breath. "We've been having sessions for a number of years."

"I know," Samantha said.

"And you've always kept everything we talk about confidential, right?"

"Of course," Samantha said. "Why do you ask?"

"Someone else knows about my . . . problem."

A desk chair squeaked. Candice could picture Samantha leaning forward with her hands resting on the desk.

"Who?" Samantha asked.

"I don't know. For a year and a half, I've paid thousands into an offshore bank account."

Candice moved the recorder closer to her ear to listen more intently.

"Blackmail?" Samantha said.

"I get an anonymous phone call once a month to remind me a payment is due."

There was a long moment of silence, and Candice thought the recorder might have stopped. She glanced at the screen and saw it was still playing.

"Why would you pay it? Why not call the police?" Samantha said.

"I think we both know why I can't go to the police," Robbie said.

"That's a lot of money, were you—"

"Of course, how else would I come up with that kind of cash?"

There was another moment of silence. Then, Samantha asked, "What's happening tonight?"

"Tonight, I meet my blackmailer."

Candice pressed stop on the device. She'd known Samantha for as long as she'd been in Newark. Even referred some of her parishioners to Samantha . . . including Robbie Reynolds. As far as she knew, Samantha never recorded sessions with her clients. So, why was this session on the voice recorder? And how had it ended up on Alex Brennen's desk?

She fast forwarded again, then pressed play. What she heard this time froze her blood.

"You don't look like you've slept much," she heard Samantha say.

"That's the understatement of the decade." It was her own voice. A recording from Candice's evening visit to Samantha's office on Monday.

"Have you pilfered anything lately?"

Candice's chest tightened as she listened to herself stammer a response. "No . . . well . . . I . . . it was . . . maybe . . ."

She stopped the playback and let the voice recorder slip from her fingers. It fell back into the box among the other trinkets. She rose from the floor, pulled her robe tight to her body and wandered over to the window. The sun had set, and the street beyond her yard was cast in shadows. She felt as if a cold finger had just run down her spine. Her stuttering words were practically a confession of guilt. A revelation of her sin. And Alex Brennen had had ample time to listen to a recording of her own words admitting that she was a thief.

WEEK
2

CHAPTER THIRTY-ONE

Saturday

B rian had just finished cleaning up from breakfast when the doorbell rang. He glanced at the clock on the microwave and wondered who would be coming to visit at 7:15 on a Saturday morning. He glanced out the window and was surprised to see a black Dodge Charger parked in front of the building on Main Street. It was Chief Jenkins' unmarked police car. He moved across the apartment and down the stairs to open the door.

"Bit early for a social visit," Brian said as he stepped aside and gestured for Lyle to enter.

The police chief remained on the sidewalk. "I'm not staying. Stephanie O'Connell has gone missing. Her and her baby Kristen."

His face looked grim. "Her husband called us last night in a panic. We found her car an hour ago at White Clay Creek State Park. Mick's up there now, prepping for a search of the park. We could use every able body we can find. I was passing by and thought I'd stop to see if you could help."

"Absolutely. I'll grab my hiking boots." Brian said.

Brian watched Lyle turn and walk toward his car. Brian began to push the door closed when he saw Lyle pause and turn back. Lyle took three steps and was back at the door; arms folded across his chest.

"I know you've been talking to Mick about the two murders," Lyle said. "I'm assuming he's shared more with you than we've made public to the rest of the press."

Brian remained silent, his expression neutral, not nodding or acknowledging the statement. It was public knowledge that he and Mick were good friends. It wouldn't be a far stretch to assume Brian received insider information about ongoing investigations.

"I know I don't need to tell you this," Lyle said. "But after that debacle with the *Post-Gazette*, I'd appreciate it if you could be judicious with those details that are not yet public knowledge."

Brian smiled. "Are you referring to the *Post-Gazette* connecting the murders? Does that mean the two murders are indeed connected?"

Lyle's arms dropped to his sides, and he glared at Brian. "I didn't say that."

Brian stared at Lyle for a moment with all the seriousness he could muster, then laughed. "Don't worry. I've got you covered." He gestured for Lyle to leave. "Get going. I'll meet you out at the search site."

Brian climbed from the Mustang and glanced around the parking area for the state park. Parking was at a premium in the lot, with cars already filling most of the spots. There was one car that caught Brian's eye as he moved toward the gathering crowd at a nearby picnic pavilion. It was a forest green Nissan Sentra. The police had cordoned it off by running yellow caution tape around the nearby trees and lampposts.

White Clay Creek State Park was north of Newark and strad-dled the state line of Pennsylvania. There were several entry points to the park: this one being known as the Judge Morris Estate. Most of the park fell outside the jurisdiction of the city police and was patrolled by New Castle County authorities. Judging by the mix of city and county police cars in the parking lot, it looked like this would be a joint operation.

Brian wondered who'd take the lead on the investigation. The missing persons report had started in the city, and Stepha-nie O'Connell was a city resident. He doubted Lyle Jenkins would ever let the county police take over an investigation that his team started.

Mick Flanagan stood on the picnic table and gave directions to the officers and volunteers around him. Lyle Jenkins was studying a map, which had been spread across the table near Mick's feet.

". . . and her baby is nine months old. Stephanie was last seen yesterday morning at the Starbucks on Main Street. She had Kris-ten with her at the time." Mick swept his gaze over the crowd. "I'm sure I don't have to tell you how critical it is that we find her. If she's been out here all night with her baby . . ." He brushed his hair back with his hand. "Let's just hope we find her."

As Mick stepped down from the table, Lyle Jenkins waved for people to step forward. "Pair up and see me for grid assignments."

Brian, standing near the back of the crowd, began to make his way around toward Mick. As he moved, he scanned the crowd and picked out a few faces he recognized.

Most of the Newark police force was there, as were a couple members of the city council. He noted that Mayor Jacob Stuart was conspicuously absent. Brian wasn't surprised; after all, it wasn't an election year.

Huddled just beyond the far side of the table was Jack O'Connell, the missing woman's husband. His tousled ginger hair was evidence of a long night without sleep, and his frantic stare spoke of his anxiety.

Jack was the owner and chef of Tipsy McStaggers, the pub on the corner of Main and Center Streets. Standing beside Jack was Father Andrew Blake. The O'Connell's were regulars at St. Matthew's.

The priest looked just as tired as Jack. Probably had been up all night as well. He figured Andrew must have been called sometime after Stephanie was reported missing. There to provide comfort, as well as keep the frenzied husband out of the police's hair while they searched for his wife. Andrew looked as if he could kill for a cup of coffee.

Brian continued to push his way through the crowd toward Mick, but found his path blocked again and again with volunteers forming search groups and getting instructions. He stepped back to reroute himself past a trio of police officers and felt an elbow drive into his back.

He turned and found himself facing Alex Brennen, who was stumbling back from the impact.

"Sorry." Brian reached out his hand to steady Alex.

"My fault for not watching where I was going."

"You here to join the search party?" Brian gave Alex a quick appraisal. Tan khakis, a pale blue Oxford shirt, and brown suede shoes. Not exactly dressed for a search through the forest.

"Yes. Got to do my part for my fellow man," replied Alex, a smile across his lips. "You want to pair up?"

Brian hesitated. He knew they had a lot of ground to cover, and Alex seemed like he'd be a handicap. Despite his reservations, Brian eventually nodded. "Sure. Let's get our grid."

CHAPTER THIRTY-TWO

C andice stood before the door of apartment 27B and hesitated
before knocking. The apartment complex on East Delaware
Avenue was the address the church had on file for Agatha Bowman. The older four-story building retained some of the charms
of a by-gone era, like marble floors in the foyer and brass-plated
buttons in the elevator. The architecture of the lobby looked dated,
but it had an appeal that enticed the beholder to drink it all in upon
entering. On her walk over, Candice wondered if showing up unannounced at Agatha's front door was the best approach. But she
was convinced Agatha would never have agreed to see her if Candice called to arrange a meeting. The elderly woman had departed

from their last encounter in a distraught rush and had implied that any talk about her involvement in murder was nothing more than a touch of dementia. But Candice couldn't let it go at that.

A long minute later Candice finally heard the lock click in answer to her knock. Agatha peered through a two-inch crack between the door and the door jam.

"Yes?" Agatha said. Her visible eye brightened with recognition. "Oh, Pastor Miller."

"Agatha. I hope I'm not intruding. I was in the neighborhood." Candice paused when she realized how ridiculous and untrue her words were. "I wanted to stop by and see how you were doing. The other day you left the church in a hurry. I was . . . concerned."

Without a word, Agatha closed the door. Candice heard the clank of the security chain as it was unhooked. The door opened wide this time. Agatha, dressed in a floral housecoat, gestured for Candice to enter.

She was led into a small living room, furnished with a single sofa and a dark-stained rocker. A narrow bookshelf along the wall displayed a sizable collection of Precious Moments figurines, and a small stack of Harlequin romance paperbacks. A small flat-screen television was across from the sofa on a cheap faux wood TV stand.

"Please, sit," Agatha said, pointing to the sofa. She clutched her hands together. "Can I get you something? Tea, perhaps?"

Candice was about to decline the offer when Agatha turned toward the kitchen.

"I'll just put the kettle on," she said as she shuffled from the room.

Candice leaned back in the sofa. The seat cushion offered little support, obviously having seen better days. The paisley floral pattern looked like it was something from the '70s. She rose from the sofa and crossed to the far wall, where a collage of framed five-by-eight photographs hung. Candice recognized Agatha's daughter in several, as well as her two grandchildren. Near the bottom was a black and white wedding photo. A young Agatha beamed in a white wedding dress while standing next to—Candice assumed—the young Mr. Bowman. She had never met Agatha's husband. He'd passed away years before Candice arrived in Newark. Odd, even in the old wedding photo there was a haunted look behind Agatha's young eyes.

The sound of running water drifted in from the kitchen, followed by the sound of a tea kettle as it was set on the stove. Candice made her way down the hall and into the kitchen. Agatha had her back to the door. She reached up into the cabinet for a mug but was struggling to reach the high shelf.

"Let me get that," Candice said as she stepped past the round dinette table.

Agatha jumped at Candice's words. "Oh, I didn't realize you were there." She moved aside so Candice could pull down two mugs from the shelf.

"How about we drink them in here?" Candice set the mugs on the table.

Agatha hesitated, seeming lost for a moment. Then, nodded and turned back to the stove. She fiddled with the tea bag box and the sugar bowl.

Candice pulled a chair out and sat at the table. A battered shoebox rested on the tabletop, and dozens of old photographs were scattered around it. Some were black and white. Many were in color but had faded with the passing of time. Candice fingered through a pile, found one of Agatha as a teenager and smiled. The young Agatha must have been fourteen or fifteen at the time. There were two other girls in the photo as well. The three were making silly faces for the camera. Candice flipped the photograph over and found the fading words: *Martha Wilson, Janice Sullivan, and Me – June 1948.*

"Bet you turned all the boys' heads," Candice said, holding the picture up.

Agatha turned and glanced at the photo. Her face flushed. The grin that formed was filled with nostalgia. "Oh, we were a trio of troublemakers. That's what we were." She set the box of tea bags on the table. Agatha took the photograph from Candice and stared at it. "Best friends we were. We went everywhere together. Did everything together." Her grin faded to a frown. "I'm the only one left."

Candice sifted through the scattered pile and pulled out another photograph. In the black and white image, Agatha appeared to be a few years older. She was wearing a dark, mid-calf skirt, a white varsity sweater—a big *N* emblazoned on the chest—and a neck scarf tied to one side.

In the picture, Agatha was standing beside a tall, muscular man in dark slacks and a shirt and tie. His arm was around Agatha's waist, and they looked like the perfect couple. He didn't look like the elderly woman's husband from the photos in the living room. Perhaps a whirlwind teenage romance. From a time before Agatha met and married her now deceased spouse. Candice turned the photograph over and read the words on the back. *Me and Stuart Hardwick—April 1952.*

"Who is Stuart?" She had to ask. Stuart was a name Agatha had mentioned the other day at the church office in relation to the death of Sam Pyeong. "Your high school sweetheart?"

The elderly woman's eyes flashed a moment of panic, then became wistful. She reached for the photograph with a trembling hand and took it from Candice. Agatha gazed at it for a minute; moisture forming in the corner of her eye.

"Stuart? Now there was a charmer if there ever was one," she said, her voice soft and distant. "Had a silver tongue on him. A real way with words." She stared at the image, looking lost somewhere in the past.

"Were you and he an item?" Candice asked.

Agatha didn't seem to hear the question at first. Then a distant smile emerged on her face. "An item? Yes . . . for a time. He was a couple years older than me. Met him when I was seventeen, still just an innocent girl. He was a man. He drank, smoked. He was experienced in . . ." Agatha blushed as her words faded away. "Well, you know."

Candice suppressed a giggle. A woman of eighty-plus years being embarrassed to talk about sex with her pastor. It amused her. "I get it. He taught you a few things."

Agatha set the photograph down on the table and looked toward Candice. She chuckled. "Yes, I guess he did. It gave my Fred—God rest his soul—quite a treat on our honeymoon when he saw some of the tricks I knew."

For the first time since Candice had arrived, Agatha seemed to relax a bit. Her shoulders didn't look quite as tense, and her eyes were not quite as sad.

"How long did you and Stuart date?"

Agatha hesitated, as if she were drawing on a long-forgotten memory. "Two years?" Her words came out more as a question than a statement. "Maybe a bit more than that."

Candice pointed at the image, which still lay before them on the table. "How old were you in '52?"

"Eighteen."

"You looked happy."

Agatha picked up the photograph again. "I was. We used to go to the sock hops together at the high school. I'd have to sneak him in. He was too old, you know. After high school, we'd go dancing up in Wilmington. There were a couple clubs . . ." Her words fell away again as she drifted into an old memory. "'Dance with me, Agatha,' he used to say. Begged me to dance with him all the time. He loved to dance."

Candice wondered how far she could push the conversation, if she could make Agatha talk about Sam Pyeong again. "Whatever happened to Stuart?"

Again, Agatha didn't seem to have heard the question. She stared at the photo, as if she was lost in the past. Her gaze was far away, seeming like she was reliving a memory. Then her lips began to tremble, and the photograph fell from her fingers. Agatha abruptly rose from the table and turned to the stove. "Look at me. Chatting away and here I never turned on the stove to warm the water for tea."

Candice asked once again. "Agatha. What happened to Stuart?"

The elderly woman's shoulders sagged, and she gripped the edge of the kitchen counter as if to steady herself. She didn't turn to look back at Candice. "He . . . he left. That's all. He just left . . . me."

CHAPTER THIRTY-THREE

Brian pushed aside a branch, then let it snap back behind him. He wasn't concerned about it whipping back into Alex's face. His partner was stumbling on the trail somewhere behind him, cursing as another stick slipped from under foot. They'd been walking along the trail for three quarters of an hour, but Brian felt as if they'd barely made any progress at all. Alex had asked to stop and rest half a dozen times already. The way he was gasping, Brian figured they would stop again any minute.

The intertwined tree branches above them blocked the sun and cast the forest floor in shadows. The temperature in the shade had lowered by at least ten degrees. Despite the chill, there were sweat stains on Alex's shirt. Brian halted, leaned against a tree, and took a swig from his water bottle. He glanced down the trail to watch Alex's slow and laborious approach.

"Ah . . . good . . ." Alex spoke between gasps. "I was . . . hoping we could take . . . a break."

Brian nodded, then peeked at his watch. 11:24. He'd hoped to be further than this. Alex leaned forward and placed his hands on his knees for support. His labored breathing cut through nature's tranquility like a freight train through a funeral parlor. Brian considered moving on without the university professor but recalled Mick Flanagan's direction to avoid separating from your search partner.

Alex stood back up, reached into his back pocket, and pulled out a black leather cigar case. He slipped a cigar from the pouch and fished a lighter out of his front pocket.

"Hope you don't mind." He bit the end and spit out the tip. "This'll do wonders for me."

Brian nodded, then wandered a few feet up the path to put a little distance between himself and the cigar smoke. Alex rambled on about how this was his first search party, and how he hoped they'd find the missing woman. Brian tuned him out and scanned the surrounding forest. There were over 3,000 acres of state park to search.

What were the chances they'd find Stephanie and her baby . . . if they were even here? He thought for a moment about Jack O'Connell. He seemed to recall Mildred commenting a few weeks ago about Jack and Stephanie getting into a very public shouting match at the restaurant. It was no secret that Jack worked long hours. He was a bit of a control freak and couldn't bear to have anyone else run things. According to Mildred, Stephanie felt as if her husband was neglecting her and their new baby. Brian tried to push the suspicious thoughts out of his head, but the recent deaths in town made murder top of mind.

Brian glanced back at Alex, who was talking as if oblivious to the fact that no one was listening. He was about to urge Alex to finish his cigar so they could continue with the search when a faint sound caught his ear.

"Alex," he said. The man didn't seem to hear, so Brian spoke again, this time with more urgency. "Shut up."

A momentary flash of anger crossed Alex's face. "Excuse me?"

Brian waved for him to be silent, then strained to hear the sound again. When he did, it seemed louder. It was a faint cry. The sound of an infant crying. "Do you hear that?"

Alex hesitated with his response. "I think . . . yeah, I do."

Brian charged forward into the underbrush in the direction of the cry, paying little heed to the brambles that thrashed at his legs. "Come on."

Alex struggled along behind him, cursing a long stream of expletives while trying to keep up. Branches snapped and dried leaves crunched beneath their feet. Brian trudged up the slope, pausing often to listen for the infant's cry. He made an occasional adjustment to his direction and then moved on. Behind him, he heard nothing but gasping, grumbling, and the sound of nature being trampled underfoot.

Pausing near a thick-trunked oak, Brian heard the cry again, loud, and close by. Then, a crash and a yell came from behind him. He spun around and looked down the hill at Alex, who had stumbled and fallen into the underbrush. "You okay?"

Alex rolled among the leaves and clutched his ankle. "No. I think . . . I think it's sprained."

Brian sighed and started to move back down the hill toward his injured partner.

Alex waved him off. "Go. I'll be fine."

Brian nodded, then turned back toward the infant's cry. He scrambled further up the hill. The baby had to be close. Ahead, a fallen tree lay across the ground, forming a low wall in his path. As he approached, he heard the baby's cry coming from the other side. Brian rushed forward and stepped cautiously over the fallen pine.

Nudged against the trunk of the fallen tree lay a baby, tightly swaddled in a blanket. The beige cloth was wrapped around the child like a papoose. Only the face was exposed. The infant's cheeks looked flushed from exposure. *How long have you been out here? All night?* Despite the chilly air, the bundled baby looked to be otherwise warm and protected. A baby stroller lay on its side a few feet away.

What was more shocking was what lay beside the baby in the underbrush. The woman was partially covered by leaves and dirt. Dressed in a light windbreaker, jeans, and hiking boots, she looked as if she'd come prepared for a peaceful walk in the woods. But apparently, it wasn't meant to be. Her arms were outstretched, and her legs twisted. She was facedown, her long blonde hair matted with dried blood and a crater where the back of her skull should have been. A dark pool of coagulated fluid stained the leaves around her head.

A column of ants marched in a military-like formation across her back, scavenging crumbs from the broken loaf of brown bread that rested between her shoulders. Each tiny soldier foraged for a morsel and retraced its steps along the pale-yellow windbreaker and off into the underbrush. They seemed unconcerned by the horror which resulted in their meal.

Brian scanned the scene with a careful eye and took in as many details as possible. He pulled out his mobile phone and snapped a quick picture to give Mick a record of where the baby was in relation to the body. Then he scooped the bundled child into his arms and swayed side to side, hoping to soothe its cries. He turned to step back over the fallen tree trunk, wanting to get out of the immediate crime scene. As he lifted his foot, he glanced downward. He froze and stared at the back of Stephanie's jacket. Crimson markings were scrawled across the fabric. His eyes traced each rough letter.

CHILD KILLER.

CHAPTER THIRTY-FOUR

It was twenty minutes past noon when Candice drew her Subaru onto the shoulder and climbed from the car to see why the parking lot for the White Clay Creek State Park was blocked by a county police car. Dozens of people were milling about near the entrance to the park. Was there a community event she didn't know about?

She'd awoken that morning with every intention of meeting with Andrew for their weekly chess game. But the more she thought about him, the more she felt ill-prepared to see him. She wasn't sure what to say about the other night. How should she address his drinking? Should she address his drinking? After meeting with Agatha earlier in the morning, Candice chose to skip the chess game. She was in no shape for any more drama. A forest run was what she needed to clear her head.

She locked her car and walked over a grassy knoll to get an unobstructed view of the parking lot beyond. Of all the times she'd visited the usually serene park, Candice could not recall ever observing this much activity. People were huddled in small clusters around the asphalt lot, some with heads bowed. The black coroner's van was parked nearby. What was going on?

As she surveyed the commotion below, Candice toyed with the digital voice recorder in her jacket pocket. Its cold plastic casing was smooth to the touch and slipped from finger to finger with ease. She feared another break-in attempt at her house might result in the recorder's discovery. She'd pocketed it for safekeeping on her way out the door. What she planned to do with it was still an outstanding question. If word got out about her "habit", it could mean the end of her career. Just like Andrew's binge drinking could ruin his. Spiritual leaders were supposed to have self-control and be able to overcome sin in their lives. She was far from overcoming her little "habit" and, if Candice was honest, far from even trying. She'd never admit it to anyone—barely even to herself—but she'd become addicted to the thrill of her kleptomania.

A white canopy tent had been erected near one of the trailheads leading into the forest. Mick Flanagan was speaking with two other officers, his hands gestured toward the tree line. New Castle County EMS parked an ambulance at the far end of the lot. A stretcher was being rolled across the parking lot by two EMTs. Alex Brennen was strapped in and covered to his waist with a white sheet.

Candice moved cautiously along the perimeter of the asphalt lot and worked her way toward the ambulance. She eyed Alex from a distance. It was like she was seeing him for the first time from a new perspective. Not as an amiable college professor, but as man who might have dark ulterior motives for every action. Candice recalled Robbie's words on the recording she'd heard. "Tonight, I meet my blackmailer." She wondered again how Alex obtained the recording of Samantha's sessions. What did he do with them? Did Samantha know about the recordings? She shook her head as if to push aside the thought. Candice refused to believe that Samantha would knowingly allow anyone to record her therapy sessions. Far too much sensitive information. Is that why Alex recorded the sessions? Did he use this information to his advantage? Candice gasped. Was Alex blackmailing Robbie Reynolds?

Alex turned his head and caught her eye. He waved and smiled. It was a friendly, welcoming smile, but Candice wondered what corrupt undertone might linger beneath it. She moved toward the stretcher, doing her best to disguise her suspicion.

"What happened?" she asked. The EMTs continued to push the stretcher but slowed their pace.

Alex waved his hand in dismissal. "Just a sprain. Guess I wasn't cut out for traipsing through the woods."

"What? Oh, yes. Sorry to hear that, but I was wondering what . . . happened *here*." She pointed to activity all around them.

He didn't respond but leaned down to massage his ankle. His shirt sleeves were rolled up, revealing a blood-stained bandage wrapped around his right forearm. Candice's heart skipped a beat as she recalled the bloodied steak knife the police had taken as evidence from her home after the burglary.

Alex noticed her stare, and quickly rolled his sleeves down. "That's nothing," he said, as if she'd been worried about him. "Did that the other day. My fall caused it to bleed again."

"What happened here? Why all the police?"

"A search party for a missing woman and her child," Alex absently said, as if it was of little concern to him.

Candice rested her hand on the stretcher's cold stainless steel arm rail. "Did they find her? Is she dead?" Her words came out in rapid-fire fashion. "What'd they find?"

"It's not pleasant."

Her heart raced as she wondered what the police discovered. Candice had a quick flashback to the Cavendish kitchen. The bread. The accusation written in lipstick. Had the police found the same thing here? What sin was the victim accused of? If the poor woman had been killed sometime in the night, she would have lain in the forest for hours. She shuddered at the thought of dying alone among the bracken and the trees. No goodbyes to loved ones. No prayers being said. Just the hard cold ground. The insects crawling over dead flesh. Nocturnal animals sniffing a rigid corpse to satisfy some primal curiosity.

What a terrible way to die.

She glanced back at Alex to find him glaring over her shoulder. His lips formed an angry scowl. Candice turned, looking toward the nearby ambulance. Toni Brennen stood near the emergency vehicle's open rear doors. She looked sheepish and a bit unkempt. Her hair had been hastily pulled up into a bun, and her clothes were wrinkled and frumpy. A black purse dangled in front of her, the straps gripped tight in her white-knuckled hands.

When the EMTs stopped by the ambulance doors, Toni stepped forward to grasp her husband's hand.

"Are you okay, Alex?" Toni said.

He pulled his hand away from his wife's. "What're you doing here?"

Toni allowed gravity to slowly draw her hand back down by her side. "I came to see if you were okay."

"Are your chores done?"

Her eyes averted downward as she shook her head. Alex turned to the nearest EMT. "Could you give us a moment in private?"

The EMT tried to dissuade him, but Alex remained firm, emphasizing that "a sprained ankle never killed anyone." The EMTs moved around to the side of the ambulance while Candice stepped away to give the couple some privacy, but she kept watching from the corner of her eye.

Toni's gaze was turned toward the ground while her husband gestured and spoke vehemently at her. His eyes looked on fire, and his face was red with rage. Toni's bottom lip quivered under Alex's words. Candice couldn't hear what he was saying, but she was certain it wasn't edifying. She studied Toni, noticing the sallowness of her face and the way she bit her bottom lip.

An awkward sense of pity rose within her as she watched the couple. Candice barely knew Alex and Toni, so she had very little context from which to judge any perceived abuse. She'd intervened once before at her previous church with what she suspected was an abusive relationship. Assumptions had been made and signs misread. Candice had been young, fresh out of seminary, and ready to make an impact on people's lives. But her youthful eagerness had been her downfall. Her accusation not only lacked evidence but had been completely unfounded. She'd only been trying to do what she thought was right. After an awkward year following the incident, the congregation requested she be replaced.

The EMTs pushed the stretcher into the ambulance. Alex went on glaring at his wife, who stood a few feet away. Toni's gaze was still tilted downward, her fists clenched, knuckles white.

"Funny running into you here."

The voice startled her. Brian, arms folded, met her gaze with a smile when she turned.

"It's true what they say about you," she said.

"And what's that?"

"If anything happens in Newark, expect Brian Wilder to be there. You're that perpetual face in the crowd."

Brian frowned and turned his eyes downward. "This is one time I wish I hadn't been here."

Candice lifted one eyebrow and tilted her head, hoping he'd take the hint and tell her more. His face was pained, lips drawn in tight and eyebrows low and close together.

"I found the body," he said. Brian went on to detail the events leading up to his gruesome discovery. For her part, Candice absorbed every detail and tried to fit them into the larger puzzle that had formed in her head. When he told her about the words scrawled in blood on the woman's jacket, she couldn't control the shudder that ran through her shoulders.

"What was her name?"

"Stephanie O'Connell," Brian said.

"I hear she had her baby with her. Is the baby . . . ?" she asked.

"They took her to the hospital, but . . . the medics think she'll be okay."

"Thank God," she muttered. She caught sight of the ambulance as it pulled out of the parking lot and onto the road. The red flashing lights disappeared behind the nearby grassy knoll. Candice surveyed the parking lot, looking for Toni, but Alex's wife was nowhere to be found. She knew Toni hadn't gotten into the back of the ambulance with her husband. Did she have a car parked nearby? She had certainly disappeared fast enough.

"What brings you here?" Brian asked.

Candice returned her gaze to him. "I came to take a run through the park." She glanced down and suddenly felt self-conscious about her attire. The pale gray polyester of her joggers suddenly felt more form fitting than she realized. She tugged at the bottom of her windbreaker, wishing it would cover more of her hips. A warm flush rushed up her face. "Didn't the O'Connell's go to St. Matthew's? Is Andrew here?"

"He went to the hospital with the baby and Jack O'Connell."

Candice felt a sudden sense of relief. She had to admit that she just couldn't face Andrew right now. She didn't know if he was aware that she'd been the one to find him passed out from his night of binge drinking. And although she'd toyed with the idea of telling Andrew about the voice recorder she'd taken from Alex's house, the possible consequences had overruled that train of thought.

Her hand slipped into her jacket pocket, where the cool plastic of the voice recorder met her fingertips.

Her expression must have exposed her anxiety because Brian asked, "Is everything okay?"

"Yeah . . . well . . . actually, no. It's not okay." All morning, the voice recorder in her pocket had seemed to get heavier with every passing minute. Now the burden felt overwhelming. The recorder placed her in an uncomfortably compromising position. How could she turn it over to the police without revealing how she got it? News of her "habit" would ruin her. She'd be forced out of Newark, maybe forced out of ministry altogether. Would that be such a bad thing? After all, her doubts about what she believed had grown over the past few years. Maybe she wasn't meant to be in ministry any longer. But to be forced out because of a scandal . . .

Candice glanced at Brian whose blue eyes were filled with the intense curiosity of a journalist. He'd want to know how she got the recorder just as much as Andrew would. Brian's questions, however, might not come with that look of pity she knew Andrew would give her. Candice would never be able to look Andrew in the eye again without seeing the disappointment hidden just beneath the surface.

"I may have some information that could help the police in their investigation," she said.

Brian's eyes focused on hers. "Really?"

"But . . . it's a delicate situation. I could use some advice."

Brian folded his arms and smiled. "If I can help, I will."

After taking a deep breath, Candice withdrew the voice recorder from her pocket and proceeded to detail what she'd heard.

CHAPTER THIRTY-FIVE

Brian was first to arrive at the office complex on Academy Street. He folded his arms and leaned back against the car while he waited for Candice and Samantha to arrive. He'd called the therapist before leaving the park and explained that it was urgent they meet immediately.

"Can't you just tell me over the phone?" Samantha asked.

He'd said no, and she reluctantly agreed to meet them at her office. Candice had left the state park moments after Brian, and he figured she'd arrive shortly.

While he waited, Brian flipped through the pictures from the forest crime scene on his phone. He hadn't mentioned to Mick that he had the photos. The police might have confiscated his phone, and he wanted more time to study the images before potentially losing them completely. He stared at the first grim picture. Despite the blood and gore that oozed from Stephanie's head, the scene around the body seemed almost tranquil. Nature appeared unfazed by the tragic death that lay within it. He swiped to another photo, this one of the infant bundled in her blanket. The child had no idea of the horror that lay next to her. A silent witness that had no way of conveying what she saw.

He hadn't known Stephanie O'Connell all that well and was far more familiar with her husband. Brian had been to Tipsy Mc-Gregor's many times and had enjoyed more than a few evenings sitting at the bar in conversation with Jack. He was good-humored and easygoing if you didn't ask about the business. Brian got the impression the O'Connells had taken on a lot of debt to open the restaurant. Although it was a popular hangout for the university students, it hadn't quite paid off the way they hoped. It wouldn't be too much of a stretch to cast Jack as the prime suspect. The very public arguments at the restaurant. Mounting debt. And if there was insurance money . . . *I hope he's got a good lawyer.*

Jack's only saving grace might just be the two murders from earlier that week.

When the pale blue Subaru Outback pulled into the parking lot, Brian slipped his phone back into his pocket. He waved to Candice after she had parked and climbed from her car. As she approached, he noted the haggard look in her face, the dark shadows beneath her eyes. Her steps seemed weighted, as if she carried an unseen burden.

"No Samantha yet?" she asked.

He shook his head. "Not yet. She probably won't be long."

Candice kicked at a pebble by her right foot. "What are you going to tell her . . . about how you . . . I found the recorder."

Brian pondered her remark for a moment. Maybe this was his chance to get the truth. "Since you brought it up, how did you get your hands on it?"

Her face flushed, and she turned her gaze away from him. "I'd rather not discuss it."

"If you want my help, you need to confide in me."

Candice hesitated, then gave a nervous glance around the parking lot. "It's not relevant."

"Everything is relevant with murder," Brian said. "When Mick learns about this, he'll be asking some hard questions. I might be able to take some of the heat off you . . . if you're honest with me."

"I don't know."

"Okay. Let's start with something easier," Brian said. "What did you pick up outside the Cavendish house?"

Her jaw dropped, and her face turned ashen. She glared at him with just as much embarrassment as surprise. "How did you know?"

"My photographer took a number of pictures of the house from the street. A couple caught you picking something up."

"Damn," she muttered.

Brian waited for her to speak. No, wondered if she would speak. Would she tell him the truth? Or would she lie? He'd magnified the photo as much as he could, but never was able to get a clear enough image to see what Candice had picked up. If she told him a lie, he'd have no way to know.

She averted her gaze to stare at the ground. "A ring."

"What kind of ring?"

Candice rocked on her heels, like she was restless and uncomfortable. "A wedding ring. Gold, tarnished, and well-worn," she said.

Brian folded his arms and watched her closely. "How did you know it was in the grass?"

"It dropped out of the body bag after Andrew prayed for the girl. They jostled the bag a bit while zipping it back up."

Brian rubbed his chin, then frowned. "Why would a sixteen-year-old girl have a wedding ring?"

Candice looked up at him, her face became alive with curiosity. "That's what I wondered. There was an inscription. It was hard to read. Some of the letters had worn away."

Brian pushed off his car and straightened up as a red Mazda Miata pulled into the parking lot. The top on the convertible was down, and Samantha was behind the steering wheel. The thumping rhythm of Journey's *Separate Ways* filled the air in the car's wake. The music cut off as the car came to a halt in the neighboring parking spot.

"Let me tell her," Brian said.

Samantha climbed from the car. Her hair was pulled back into a short ponytail. She wore violet yoga pants and a T-shirt with an abstract swooping design of rainbow colors printed across the front. She approached them with a bounce in her step. Samantha looked from Candice to Brian. "What's this all about?" she asked.

"Thanks for meeting us on such short notice," Brian said. "Can we go up to your office?"

Brian leaned against the door frame of Samantha's office with his arms crossed while Candice was seated on the sofa. Samantha tossed her bag onto her desk chair, then perched herself cross-legged on top of the desk.

"What was so important that you had to interrupt my Pilates class?" she said.

Brian nodded to Candice, who pulled out the voice recorder and handed it to him. Brian pressed the play button and held it up so that everyone could hear the sounds coming from the small speaker. The recording started in the middle of a sentence. A young female voice complaining about the "oppression" she had suffered at the hands of her parents. Samantha's mouth fell open as she heard her own voice reply on the recording. The shock and horror in her eyes were evident and she gasped.

Her reply was one word. "How?"

Brian stopped the playback. "We don't know. We thought maybe you could tell us."

Samantha slid off the desk and began to pace the small room. "No idea. I don't record my sessions." She brushed back a few hairs that had fallen in front of her face. "How much is on that thing?"

"Probably a few days," Candice said. "Don't worry. We didn't listen to it. At least, not all of it."

"It is voice-activated," Brian explained. "If it isn't yours, then someone's been bugging your office."

Samantha reached for the recorder in his hand. "That needs to be erased."

He closed his hand around the device. "That might not be possible."

With her hands on her hips, Samantha glared at him. "Why not?"

"It might be evidence in Robbie Reynolds's murder," Brian said.

"Evidence? How can that be evidence?" She reached again for the recorder, this time more aggressively. "Give me that."

Brian snatched his hand away. "I'm sorry. I can't."

Samantha spun away in a huff.

He felt sorry for her, sorry for having to place her in this situation. He knew once the trust between a therapist and a client was broken, the relationship would have to end. In Samantha's case, the loss of confidence in her ability to guarantee her clients' privacy would ruin her business. And the potential lawsuits that might arise could bankrupt her. "When did you have your last session with Robbie?"

"I'd argue that you shouldn't even know that Robbie comes here, but . . . Friday. I saw him the Friday afternoon before he died."

"You might've been the last person to talk to him," Brian said.

Samantha fell onto the sofa next to Candice. "That's it. It's all over." Samantha threw her hands up in frustration. "Once this gets out, I'm finished. Years of hard work gone. I'll lose my clients, my business. I could lose everything." She placed her head in her hands and let out a loud sob.

Brian hiked his hip onto the edge of the desk. "Who has access to your office?"

Samantha pondered this for a minute. "There's Maggie. She does the billing for me. She's here three days a week. But I can't imagine her . . ."

"Who else?" Brian prodded.

"My cleaner comes in twice a week. Tracey—don't know her last name—from Nooks & Crannies Cleaning. That's it."

"Anyone *else*?" he asked.

Samantha opened her mouth, but then closed it again. Her eyes narrowed, then widened. Brian caught the momentary look of realization on her face. Then, after another moment, Samantha simply shook her head.

Candice suddenly spoke up. "Are you sure?" She turned to glare at Samantha. "What about Alex Brennen?"

The question seemed to take the therapist by surprise. Her face turned red, a combination of anger and embarrassment. She bit her bottom lip; her eyes darted from Candice to Brian and back. "I don't know what you mean."

"Oh, come on, Samantha, you're having an affair with Alex, aren't you?" Candice said.

Samantha angled away from Brian and Candice; her chin fell to her chest. "I am."

"How many couples have you helped through their infidelity issues?" Candice said, as she rose from the sofa, as if trying to put some distance between her and Samantha. "You've seen the problems it causes. You've seen the damage it inflicts on a marriage. Yet here you sit . . ." Candice closed her eyes and pinched the bridge of her nose, feeling a momentary sense of hypocrisy over her own sin. "Why?"

"I don't know anymore. When I met him a couple years ago, my love life had stalled," Samantha said. "He was breath of fresh air compared to the assholes I'd been dating. I knew he was married the first time I slept with him. It didn't matter. He thrilled me in ways that no man had ever done before. He was honest about his marriage. Didn't try to hide it, not like other guys I knew."

Candice glanced at the ceiling and let out a long breath. She touched the corner of her eye and wiped her cheek with a finger. Brian thought she might be fighting a well of emotion.

"Honest?" Candice grabbed the voice recorder from Brian's hand. "This came from Alex's house. How's that for honesty?"

Samantha's shoulders stiffened and her eyes bulged. "You stole that from Alex?"

"Yes," Candice said.

Brian glanced at Candice, but she avoided his gaze. Her reluctance to discuss where she got the recorder suddenly made sense. To reveal that she had stolen the device could open her up to legal trouble. Possibly petty larceny charges. A misdemeanor, but not something a minister would want on their record. The importance of the voice recorder's provenance wasn't lost on him. Mick had mentioned that Robbie Reynolds was paying out large sums of money. Robbie had admitted on the recording that he was being blackmailed.

Would it be too much of a stretch to assume that Alex might be the one blackmailing him?

"We should search the office," Brian said. He took the recorder back from Candice. "There might be more of these."

It only took him five minutes to find the small Velcro strip beneath the desk. It matched the piece that was attached to the back of the voice recorder. Other than that, they found nothing out of ordinary in the office.

When the search was complete, Samantha sat in her office chair while Brian and Candice each took a seat on the sofa. Samantha rubbed her eyes with balled-up fists.

Her wrinkled brow and pained gaze were a testament to the emotional toll this was taking on her.

"I wish there was another way," Samantha said. "If they're made public, those recordings could damage a lot of lives."

"Conversely, this could stop a killer who's already struck three times."

Samantha turned her head. "Three?"

"Sorry, we thought you knew," Candice said.

"Stephanie O'Connell was found dead today," Brian said.

Leaning back in her chair, Samantha's face was devoid of emotion; her gaze distant. She pursed her lips and mumbled, "It can't be."

"What?" Candice said.

Samantha spun her chair around and rested her arms on the desk. "The three murder victims? Robbie Reynolds, Deena Cavendish, and Stephanie O'Connell are . . . *were* . . . my clients."

CHAPTER THIRTY-SIX

B rian and Candice left the office and rode the elevator down to the first floor in silence. Samantha had asked to be left alone, and although Brian had further questions, he acquiesced to her request. Many of his questions were about Samantha's relationship with the three murder victims, but he doubted she'd answer any of those anyway, citing client confidentiality.

Despite the horrors of the day, Brian felt a charge of exhilaration, one he hadn't felt in years. He'd almost forgotten how electrifying investigative journalism could be. His work at the *Observer* had been satisfying, but it was humdrum reporting of day-to-day news. This was different. The thrill of running down a story, of putting seemingly unconnected pieces together to form a coherent narrative. He'd missed this.

Outside the office building, they stood by his car. The sun had set, leaving the parking lot in partial darkness; the only light came from the nearby streetlamps. They had no reason to stay, but neither seemed in a hurry to leave.

Candice kicked at a crack in the asphalt. "Can I ask you something? Something personal?"

Brian nodded absently.

"Why did you come here?"

He knew what she was asking, and, for a moment, he found himself angry that she would pry into his life. His fingers knotted into fists, but he kept his arms folded to hide his anger. Maybe if he ignored the question . . .

"Tell her," Sarah said, startling him. Her voice came from the front of his car. She was sitting—cross-legged—on the hood of his Mustang.

He spoke under his breath. His reply was short and quiet, the words for Sarah's ears only. "No."

"Tell her," Sarah said again.

Brian closed his eyes. He swallowed hard to push back the lump that formed in his throat. He let his arms drop to his sides. He looked toward Candice and was surprised to see Sarah now standing beside her.

"I'm here for the same reason you are. To find out how those recordings were made."

Sarah said, "That's not what she meant."

"That's not what I meant," Candice said. "Why are you here in Newark? You were a globally recognized journalist at the height of your career."

He didn't want to talk about this. He barely knew the Episcopal priest. His past was his own cross to bear, and bear it he had for the past ten years. Who did this woman think she was, asking him a question like that?

"Tell her," Sarah said, her voice soft and persuasive.

He pleaded with his eyes, hoping that Sarah would see the folly of her words. But she only returned his stare with her sea-blue eyes. The corners of her mouth curled up in a Mona Lisa smile. His shoulders sank, and he leaned back against the car. He didn't turn to look at Candice, just stared out to the street, his eyes lost in the light of the streetlamps.

"Ten years ago, I was in Afghanistan, embedded with a group of Marines who were serving as advisors to the Afghan army. I was doing a story for *U.S. News and World Report* on the progress we'd made against the Taliban." He glanced at Sarah who nodded, as if directing him to continue. "My wife—Sarah—was coming home from the movies with Allison, my daughter."

Brian glanced up into the sky. There wasn't a cloud above, and the stars were visible and bright. He fought against the tears he felt forming in his eyes. "A tractor-trailer ran a red light." He breathed deep to control his emotion. "Sarah was alive, but in critical condition. She died two days later." He looked to where Sarah had been standing. She was gone. "I didn't make it home in time to say goodbye."

Candice's hand shot to her mouth to stifle a sympathetic gasp. "My God. I'm so sorry," she said, her voice was soothing and quiet. She reached forward and touched his upper arm.

He fell silent, recalling how he'd dropped off the radar after the funeral. How he'd stopped returning calls from newspaper and magazine editors. How he went to pieces, barely able to sit through the early days of the trial against the truck driver. And, how his daughter—permanently paralyzed—moved out and stopped speaking to him when she turned 18.

Grief counseling helped . . . a bit. But Brian lost interest in being a globe-trotting journalist. He realized that a change was what he needed. The settlement from the trucking company was more than enough for his move to Newark, as well as starting the *Observer*. But his daughter . . .

Brian's mobile phone shattered the silence. He'd never been more grateful to hear its ring. He slipped it out of his pocket and answered. Mildred's voice greeted him.

"I can't talk long, but I've got a nugget for you," she said.

Brian strained to hear her over the background din coming through the phone. Loud music, raucous voices. "Great, what've you got?"

"Sam Pyeong. He's dead. Hold on . . ." Her voice became muffled, but Brian could just make out her words. "Tell him to keep his pants on. I'll be there in a minute."

He strained to hear her over the thumping rhythm in the background. Her voice became clear again. "Brian, you still there? Sorry. Where was I? Oh, Sam Pyeong. He died back in the '50s. Someone found his body in the alley behind the old diner in Newark." Mildred's voice suddenly boomed. "Goddammit. I'm coming."

"Mildred?" Brian said.

"Sorry. That's all I know. You might want to talk to his granddaughter. She runs an office cleaning business in Newark. I think it's called Books & Fannies . . . no, that's not right. Nooks & Crannies," Mildred said. "Gotta go. I have a wad of dollar bills burning a hole in my pocket and these beefcakes don't tip themselves. See you on Monday."

When the line went dead, Brian stared at the blank screen of his phone, trying to stifle a laugh. Mildred never ceased to surprise him.

Candice looked at him. "What was that all about?"

"It was about Sam Pyeong," he said. "Apparently his grand-daughter runs a cleaning business here in Newark."

CHAPTER THIRTY-SEVEN

It was well past ten when Candice opened the door to her cottage. She stepped into the foyer and switched on the lights, then gestured for Brian to follow. As he crossed the threshold, Candice caught his eyes darting around the room as if making a mental study of every detail. She felt as if he'd made a most meticulous inspection of her life, and within those few seconds knew all there was to know about her.

"Excuse the mess." She gestured toward the living room. "I still haven't finished cleaning up after the break-in."

Brian paused to kneel over the dried blood stains that were still in the carpet by the door. "You must not have wounded your burglar too badly." He touched the dried spots of blood with his fingers. "Blood stains aren't easy to get out. Might need to have that professionally cleaned."

Candice set her keys on the small table by the door and moved down the hall toward the kitchen. "Do you want something to drink?"

His footsteps were close behind her. "No thanks."

They entered the kitchen and she gestured for Brian to take a seat at the round dinette. The glass-topped table with its brass legs suddenly looked very dated. Candice felt the warmth of embarrassment creep up her face. The table had served her well since she graduated from seminary. She'd purchased it at a thrift store after arriving at her first church. It had never been an eyesore before, but now . . . why did that table suddenly agitate her?

"Mind if I have something?" Candice headed to the wine rack and pulled out a bottle. She poured herself a glass and turned to face Brian. "I don't normally drink on Saturday nights, but . . ."

Brian rested his hands on the table. "It's been one of those days. No one would blame you."

She sipped from the wine glass. A familiar warmth rose within her and took the edge off her frayed nerves. Candice set the glass down on the table. "Let me go get that ring."

In the bedroom, Candice reached beneath her bed and dragged the trinket box out from underneath. With the lid off, she stared in at the stash of shiny objects. Her cache of shame. A lifetime of petty theft. She shifted through the items, searching for the ring.

Ring in hand, she returned to the kitchen. The voice recorder was in the center of the table. Brian toyed with it, spinning it around and around. He looked up when Candice walked in. Arm outstretched, she opened her hand to reveal the ring.

He took it from her. Holding it between his thumb and fore-finger, he brought it close to his face. "There's a *T*. It looks like an *A*. I can't quite read the next few letters." He twisted the ring around and lifted it closer to the light that hung above the table. "Then *wit*, possibly *l*. Maybe *ve*, but I'm not sure. Another *T*, and some numbers. *4* and *1998*."

"What do you think?"

Brian set the ring onto the table and stared across at her. His gaze seemed to probe her darkest secrets. Was this how world lead-ers felt when he interviewed them? Did they suddenly feel naked and exposed?

"Do you make a habit of stealing things from people's houses?"

Candice watched the surface of the blood red wine ripple as she fidgeted with the stem of her wine glass. She felt a warm rush across her face. Her stomach twisted with anxiety. Her mouth went dry, and she took a gulp from her wine glass. The wine suddenly tasted sour to her, as if it had been miraculously turned to vinegar. She shrugged it off as a manifestation of her guilt. She gazed across the table into Brian's blue eyes. They were focused on her, piercing and deliberate. His stoic expression made her feel as if he already knew her secret, like he had discerned it long ago and was waiting for her to confirm it.

She opened her mouth to speak, but her words failed her. Syl-lables failed to flow in a coherent sentence in her mind, so Candice held back from speaking. Where should she start? Should she tell him about her first theft? It had been in high school. Her best friend—Emily Parsons—had flaunted her new sterling silver ear-rings and bragged about how expensive they were. Candice hadn't been all that enamored by them, but felt it was her duty to teach Emily a lesson about materialism. What she hadn't anticipated was how electrifying the experience had been. Those sterling silver earrings were still in the box hidden beneath her bed.

"I've got this habit. Maybe addiction is a better word. I call it Shiny Object Syndrome, but it's really just kleptomania." Her throat felt thick, like it was closing in on itself. She coughed to try to clear it, then continued. "I've never stolen anything of real value. Just knick-knacks and small trinkets."

"Even trinkets can have intrinsic value to the owner."

Candice felt a flash of irritation wash over her. Here she was, baring her soul, and he threw a remark like that at her. But a moment later, she realized he was right. What if the angel statuette she'd stolen from Marissa Reynolds's bedroom had been a gift from her dead father? Her actions may have deprived a young girl of a treasured curio linked to the memory of her deceased parent. What of all the other objects she'd stolen over the years? What value did her victims place on each? "I've been struggling with this since high school. I built up quite a collection of baubles through seminary. When something catches my eye . . . I just can't seem to overcome the urge to take it."

"You never got caught?"

Candice shook her head. "Never. Samantha's the only other person who knows. She's offered to help me, but I still foolishly think I can beat this on my own."

"I think you're wrong. You were caught. Hear me out. You steal a voice recorder from Alex Brennen. Maybe he's frantic to get it back. He searches his house and can't find it. What does he do? He remembers your visit and puts two and two together. He wants that voice recorder back. The next night, someone ransacks your house, but doesn't take anything."

It all made sense.

She thought back to her one brief glimpse of her assailant. He had the same build as Alex. Then there was the bloody bandage on Alex's arm. She'd had her suspicions, but hearing Brian lay it all out drove home the facts. The skin on Candice's neck tingled. "That bastard." Candice covered her mouth in embarrassment. "Sorry, I don't usually use that kind of language."

He waved off the apology. "Don't worry about it. You got a pencil and notepad?"

"Yeah." Candice crossed the kitchen and opened her junk drawer, rummaged around for a moment, then returned to the table with a white-lined notepad and a stubby pencil with a missing eraser.

Brian scribbled on the topmost piece of paper. When he was done, he spun the notepad around so that Candice could read what he had written. Scrawled across the top in neat block letters was the message engraved on the ring.

T A   wit 1 ve, T   – 4/ /1998

"Let's assume for a moment that Alex was blackmailing Robbie Reynolds. If Robbie threatened to go to the police, that would give Alex a motive for murder." Brian frowned, and then continued. "What about Deena Cavendish? I doubt he was blackmailing a teenage girl."

"What if she knew something about him?" Candice added. "Something bad? Could she have been blackmailing him?"

"I'm not sure if I buy that, but let's go with it for now." He spun the notepad back around and added a couple letters. "That gives us this."

To Alex wit 1 ve, T   – 4/ /1998

Candice read the letters again, then tapped on the table. She grabbed the pencil from Brian and filled in more of the blanks. "His wife's name is Toni. And since this is a wedding ring . . . we get this."

To Alex with love, Toni – 4/ /1998

Brian considered the words for a long moment. "This would place Alex at Deena's murder scene." He leaned back in his chair to ponder their conclusions. "There's one problem."

"What?"

Brian started to speak. "There was . . ." His face flushed red, and he stumbled on his words. "Uh . . . well, there were indications that Robbie engaged in . . . uh, sexual activity just before he died."

Candice was silent. She fought the urge to giggle at his embarrassment. "Kind of hard to picture Alex and Robbie . . ."

Brian frowned. "Yeah." He checked his watch. "We should tell Mick what we know, including the ring and the voice recorder."

Candice felt an unease in the pit of her stomach. "Won't he want to know how we got them?"

"Leave that to me." Brian pulled his mobile phone from his pocket.

"Isn't it a bit late to be calling?"

Brian shook his head as he dialed. "No. He's not sleeping these days. His wife is pregnant."

CHAPTER THIRTY-EIGHT

Sunday

When the alarm clock shattered the silence in his bedroom, Brian rolled over and buried his head beneath the pillow. He'd called Mick shortly after midnight to talk through the evidence of the ring and voice recorder, but Mick had asked if it could wait until morning. They'd arranged to meet at the Roasted Bean at 6:30. However, it had been well past 3:00 in the morning before Brian finally slipped between the sheets, and now he regretted the early Sunday morning rendezvous.

The Sunday morning sun peeked around the curtain's edge as if trying to nudge him awake. He cursed into his pillow before climbing from the bed. His bare feet thudded on the hardwood floor as he walked to the bathroom. The dark shadows beneath his eyes glared back at him in the mirror, a testament to his long night. He cupped his hands beneath the faucet and splashed cold water on his face.

It didn't help.

The crisp morning air caught Brian by surprise as he stepped out of his apartment. He debated whether he should run back in and grab a light jacket, but decided against it. Main Street was empty apart from a few early risers who were—like Brian—out to get an early morning coffee from the Roasted Bean.

As Brian strolled along the sidewalk, he considered the events of the previous day. The discovery of Stephanie O'Connell's corpse would be front-page news on this morning's edition of the *Delaware Post-Gazette*.

These were the moments that irked him. The earliest that he could get this story on the front page of the *Newark Observer* would be Thursday's edition. To get Monday's edition of the newspaper delivered on time, the printer usually had the presses running first thing Sunday morning. He'd had no time to get the front page changed.

When he pushed through the door of the Roasted Bean, Brian was greeted by the savory blend of a dozen coffee varieties merging into a single enticing aroma. A middle-aged woman in nursing scrubs was giving her order to the barista behind the counter. She glanced toward Brian when he entered and gave a quick wave.

He hesitated as he picked through his memories to put a name to her face. It came to him only a moment later. Ashley Fisher worked as a nurse in the ICU at the area hospital. She was a regular attendee at midnight mass at St. Matthew's Catholic Church. Andrew had introduced them once afterward. As he made his way to the counter, he smiled and returned her wave. "Nice to see you, Ashley."

When it was his turn to order, Brian asked for two large coffees and took them to a table in the corner. He only had to wait a few minutes before Mick came through the coffee shop's door. The detective's hair was disheveled, and his black T-shirt wrinkled, like it had just been pulled from the clothes hamper. Brian pushed a cup of coffee across the table as Mick sat down.

"I figured you'd need that," he said.

Mick gripped the coffee with both hands. "Thanks. Now what's this about missing evidence?"

"I've got two items that you might be interested in. I'm not prepared—at the moment—to reveal my source . . ." He placed a clear plastic bag onto the table. The ring and the digital recorder were inside. ". . . but these two items might be important to your investigation."

Mick lifted the bag from the table and studied the contents. "Care to tell me what I'm looking at."

Brian explained how the ring had been found in the grass in front of the Cavendish home, making sure to brush over the identity of who found it and when it had been found. Mick's frown grew more intense, and his eyes narrowed as he listened.

"The inscription is partially worn off, but it doesn't take much deduction to fill in the missing letters," Brian said. "As for the voice recorder—"

"Who found the ring?" Mick interrupted.

"That needs to remain confidential unless absolutely necessary. My source is willing to sign an affidavit, if need be, but would prefer to remain anonymous."

Mick yawned, then rubbed his eyes with balled-up fists.

"When was the last time you slept?" Brian asked.

"Cheryl can't sleep," Mick said. He lowered his voice to almost a whisper. "Which apparently means I'm not allowed to sleep, either."

"It gets easier. Trust me."

"When?"

Brian chuckled. "After the baby turns eighteen and moves out."

"Not encouraging," Mick grumbled. He gestured toward the plastic bag. "You realize the Chief's going to bust a nut when he hears about this."

Brian nodded. "The voice recorder contains what might be the last words spoken by Robbie Reynolds before he met his killer." Brian proceeded to detail the conversation preserved within the recorder's flash memory. He paused—for dramatic effect—before revealing that Robbie was preparing to meet his blackmailer on the night he was murdered. "Samantha Blackwell knew nothing about her sessions being recorded. She'd appreciate it if this could be kept out of the press."

Mick shrugged, then gestured toward Brian. "Why're you telling me that? You *are* the press."

Brian smiled, as he prepared to deliver his big reveal. "The recorder was found in the house of—"

Mick interrupted. "Alex Brennen."

Brian raised an eyebrow in surprise. "How did you know?"

"I haven't been sitting around waiting for you to solve my case for me. I've run a few clues to ground. At least for the Robbie Reynolds death. The other two, not so much."

Brian grinned. "Perhaps I can help you there. I discovered a connection between the three victims. They were all clients of Samantha Blackwell."

Mick's phone suddenly shrilled loudly, breaking the early morning tranquility of the near empty coffee shop. Brian noted the grim frown that quickly appeared on Mick's face after answering the phone. When he disconnected the call, Mick grabbed his coffee cup and gulped down a mouthful.

"What was that about?" Brian asked.

Mick stared across the table; the exhaustion in his face seemed to have intensified in mere seconds. "That was dispatch. Samantha Blackwell was found in her office, bludgeoned close to death." He rose from the table and looked back at Brian. "You coming?"

Ten minutes later, Brian and Mick arrived in the parking lot of the Academy Street office complex where Samantha's office was located. An ambulance was already out front along with two Newark Police cars. Mick walked off to confer with the two uniformed officers who were waiting near the door of the building. They spoke for a moment, then Mick disappeared into the office building.

Brian leaned back against a nearby police car as a uniformed officer cordoned off the entrance with yellow crime scene tape. A few minutes later, two EMTs rushed a stretcher out of the building; a motionless Samantha Blackwell was covered to her neck with a sheet. A clear oxygen mask covered her bloodied and battered face. A paramedic followed close behind, peeling bloodied surgical gloves from his hands as he walked.

Brian felt the cold hand of grief clutch at his heart. Against his better judgment, he and Candice had left the therapist alone in her office last evening.

If only they'd stayed . . .

As the ambulance pulled out of the parking lot, Mick emerged from the building and approached Brian with heavy footsteps. His shoulders drooped with the burden of yet another act of violence.

"You're not going to believe this," Mick said. "Come with me."

Brian followed Mick up to the second floor and into Samantha's office. A faint odor greeted him as he entered. It reminded him of a scrapyard in Mexico filled with rusted iron and copper—a drop point for a drug cartel he'd investigated fifteen years before. But there was no iron or copper present in the office before him. Just blood splattered up the wall across from the door, like a macabre star field of red. He stood in the doorway and studied the ghastly sight. The office was in disarray. The desk drawers were dumped across the floor and the chair lay on its side.

Two long smears of blood streaked down the wall by the door. A crimson handprint marred the nearby sofa. "What happened?" Brian asked.

"Best I can figure, she was attacked and beaten with some kind of blunt object, as well as stabbed several times," Mick explained. "Her body was lying there." He pointed at the large dark stain on the carpet beside the desk. "Barely alive. The paramedics aren't sure if she'll even make it to the hospital."

"Who found her?"

Mick stroked his chin with his thumb and forefinger. "The office manager for the ENT doc next door dropped by this morning to get something from her desk. She found this office's outer door open. Apparently she was friendly with Ms. Blackwell and stepped in to say hello."

"Hell of a thing to see this early in the morning." Brian continued to scrutinize the room. The dark red blood was a contrast in gore to the beige walls and carpet, like an abstract study in carnage.

His eyes fell on the five letters scrawled on the wall in blood. WHORE.

"Another Sin Eater killing?" Brian said.

Mick furrowed his brow and sighed. "Sin Eater? Did you have to name this sicko?" He turned away from the door and stepped back into the hall. "It's not a murder . . . yet."

Brian took one more glance at the horrific scene in the office before following Mick into the hallway. "Same MO as the others?" he asked.

Mick leaned against the wall and folded his arms. "Funny you should ask. There was no loaf of bread."

CHAPTER THIRTY-NINE

Candice noticed Brian Wilder standing in the back of the church as she closed out her sermon. She hesitated for only a moment before continuing with her final remarks to the congregation. This was—what she called—a "busy sermon." A generic message with little doctrinal substance that she kept in reserve for those weeks that she was too busy to write a real sermon. This had been one of those weeks.

When the service was over, Candice stood impatiently at the back of the church. As her parishioners passed, she greeted them with a smile and a few warm words that were meant to be innocuous enough to not spark any lengthy discussion. She gave the occasional glance toward the corner where Brian still stood, his gaze distant and unreadable. His grim expression worried her, and the longer she had to wait to talk to him, the more anxious she grew. Candice could tell that something had happened. Something grave. Perhaps another murder.

When the last stragglers had exited the sanctuary, Candice pulled the doors closed and turned to face Brian. He was now seated in the back row, motionless and staring toward the front of the church. She sat down next to him.

"This is a surprise," she said.

He didn't turn his head to look at her. Didn't move at all. Just spoke in a low, soft voice. "Samantha Blackwell was attacked last night."

His words drove through her heart like a sharp dagger. She fell into the bench and drew in a quick breath. "What happened?"

As Brian detailed the events of earlier that morning, Candice felt tears well up in her eyes. She fought against the sob that was stuck in her throat. This was all too much. Too much violence. Too many deaths. It was getting too close to home. This was not something Candice had signed up for when she entered seminary. Her aspirations had been to be a spiritual leader to the lost, not a witness to the carnage of a serial killer. Was Samantha the next victim? If they hadn't left her alone in the office the night before . . .

"Will she be okay?"

His vacant stare and slack jaw told her all she needed to know. "It's bad," he said.

She couldn't hold back any longer. The tears raced down her cheeks, and Candice broke into an uncontrolled sob. Brian placed his arm around her shoulders to draw her close. She cried into the cloth of his shirt. The soft cotton soaked up her tears; quickly becoming damp against her face. Samantha was her friend. A close friend. The news of her attack hit Candice harder than any of the past week's deaths.

"Sorry. It's getting a bit too real."

"I understand," he said.

She looked up and wiped the tears from her eyes. "Do you believe in the divine power of God?"

Brian hesitated. "It's hard for me to define what I believe. God is a concept that is difficult to frame within two-to-three thousand words."

"When I entered seminary, I dreamt of leading a small church just like this one." She gestured around the sanctuary. "Now . . . I'm not even sure I should be a pastor." She averted her gaze away from his and pulled her arms in around her body. Her throat felt as if it were closing. Her next shameful words barely escaped. "I don't know if I even believe there's a god."

With her blasphemy uttered aloud, Candice exhaled and let her shoulders sag. She was glad there was no one from her parish there to hear her words. Sylvia Bavistock would probably have dragged Candice into the street and stoned her on the spot. The thought brought a brief smile to her lips. "I'm not cut out for this kind of work. I was lost long before these murders started. How do you lead a flock when you don't know yourself where to go?" Again, she gestured around the church. "These people expect me to have all the answers. To have a wealth of religious wisdom at my fingertips. They expect me to know God's personal phone number."

She turned to Brian and found him quietly watching her, as if analyzing each word.

"Do they have that expectation? Or do you set that expectation on yourself?" he asked.

She folded her arms and huffed with frustration. "If I wanted to be psychoanalyzed, I'd go to Sam . . ." Her words trailed off as she remembered why he'd come to her church in the first place. Her own problems suddenly seemed petty and insignificant. She felt a rush of heat in her cheeks.

"Was it the Sin Eater?" she asked.

"Not sure yet. There was no bread left with her." Brian shrugged. "The police are processing the scene. They'll be there most of the day."

She rose from the bench and lifted the stole from around her neck. She fingered the purple satin for a moment before folding and placing it on the bench. "These robes can get uncomfortable quickly," she said, as she unzipped her cassock. "Tell me about Samantha's office."

Brian gave her a questioning glance. "Are you sure? It was pretty gruesome."

"Yes. It was just the shock." Candice slipped the robe from her shoulders. Once it was folded and on the bench, she returned to her seat next to him.

"There was far more blood than the other murders. It was almost like a frenzied attack."

A wave of nausea rushed through her. Candice bit her lip and fought back another swell of tears. Somehow, she needed to separate herself from the horror that befell her friend. Look at things with detached eyes. *Easier said than done.* She wiped away some moisture that had formed at the corner of her eye. Maybe she wasn't as ready to hear this after all. "What sin was she accused of?"

"The attacker wrote *whore* on the wall in Samantha's own blood." Brian studied her response before he continued with his description.

Candice leaned forward and allowed her hands to dangle between her knees. She aimlessly studied the pattern in the tile floor beneath her feet. The brutality of the attack weighed heavily on her mind. It sounded far worse than the other killings. Those had been senseless acts of violence, but swift. This seemed . . . she struggled to even find a word to describe it. Why had this attack been so much fiercer than the others?

A distant car horn breached the church walls from somewhere outside. It was a faint sound that would have never been heard if the sanctuary hadn't been cloaked in silence. The noise nudged a memory from the back of Candice's mind.

"This might not be the first time someone tried to kill Samantha," she said. She turned and locked eyes with Brian. "On Thursday, someone tried to run her down with a car."

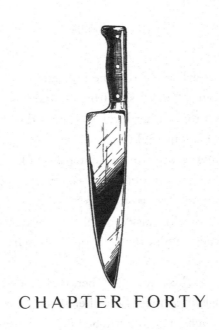

CHAPTER FORTY

Brian remained in the church sanctuary while Candice carried her folded vestments to a back room behind the altar. The silence seemed to echo off the high ceiling. The church was a stark contrast from St. Matthew's, plain and unadorned compared to the elaborate carved statues and woodwork in Andrew's church. Yet Brian found the simple architectural details to be quaint and endearing.

His gaze wandered around the church. The four windows on each side of the sanctuary were frosted glass and allowed through only a filtered version of the March sun. His eyes closed and his head nodded forward. He caught himself. His lack of sleep and early start that morning were catching up to him.

He was more exhausted than he realized.

"You need a nap," Sarah said from behind him.

Brian turned to find her leaning against the back wall of the church. "It's been a long night."

"I know." She walked to the center aisle of the church, then turned in a circle, to take in the entire sanctuary in one long glance. "Comfy little church. Not as stuffy as St. Mark's back home." She strolled forward down the aisle, stopping halfway. "She seems nice. What do they call them in the Episcopal Church? A priest? Or is it pastor?"

"Pastor, I think." Brian studied her, took in every detail. From the color of her hair to the style of her shoes. Sarah wore her favorite blouse—lavender with a stitched floral pattern that came off the left shoulder. It hung untucked over faded blue jeans, and the sleeves were rolled up to her elbows. His first instinct was to go to her, to hold her, to never let her go. It was always his first instinct. But he knew that it could never be. He could no more hold her than he could hold even the smallest fragment of the sun. Yet, he rose from the bench and approached her anyway. "You look lovely."

Sarah turned toward him and smiled. "You say that all the time." She brushed past him and moved toward the back of the church. When she reached the back wall, she turned again to look at him. Her eyes were crisp and penetrating. "You know who did it yet?"

Brian followed Sarah and halted inches from her. His eyes were dry despite his desire to cry. He needed her. Needed to feel her near him again. An impossibility, he knew, but he leaned in anyway.

She skirted past him and moved along the wall. "That only makes things worse. You know that."

Brian shrugged and bent his head forward. "I just . . . I miss you."

Sarah averted her eyes and frowned. Then, abruptly changed the subject. "You didn't answer my question. Do you know who did it yet?"

Brian folded his arms across his chest. He remembered her evasiveness all too well. "No. I've got suspicions but no concrete evidence. At least nothing that would stand up in court."

Sarah walked slowly down the outside aisle of the sanctuary. Brian matched her step for step down the center aisle, keeping his eyes focused on her.

She said, "What do you know so far?"

"Three murders and one attempted murder."

Sarah looked across at him. "Attempted? Are you sure murder was the intent?"

Brian slipped his hands into his pockets and continued to walk down the aisle. "No. But, for now, let's say it was." He saw her start to move again in step with him. He continued, "The killer has a specific signature. A handwritten accusation of the victim's supposed sin, and a loaf of bread."

She gestured toward him. "Not true. No bread at Samantha's office."

Brian reached the front of the sanctuary and spun on his heel to face back whence he came. "Either the killer slipped up, or . . ."

"Samantha's attempted murder is unrelated to the Sin Eater," Sarah added.

He stopped and pointed across at her. "Exactly. But that would be an incredible coincidence."

Sarah, who had also begun to walk back along the aisle, cocked her head. "They do happen, you know."

Brian shook his head. "Sarah, I don't buy that."

"Then why no bread?"

Brian, who was halfway up the aisle, halted. He thought for a second, then snapped his fingers. "Perhaps a copycat. Enough details have been in the news, but Mick withheld details like the bread from the public." Then he shook his head. "But no, I don't buy that either."

He started to move again. His slow steps became a subconscious effort to stall. He turned the details of each murder over in his head. Samantha Blackwell was the only connection he could find between the victims. How did Samantha fit into this picture?

Sarah reached the back of the church before him. She stood in the corner, watching him as he continued his slow trek up the aisle. "What about Sam Pyeong? Where does he fit into all of this?"

Brian shrugged as he reached the last row of benches. "I don't know if he does. If Mildred's information is correct, he died decades ago."

"Then why would an elderly woman confess to his murder?" Sarah pushed off from the wall and drifted toward him. "Why now, after all these years?"

He stood at the back of the church, watching her approach. She still walked with such grace and poise. Her ash brown hair cascaded down the side of her face like a waterfall and splashed onto her shoulder. She had been everything to him. Lover. Confidante. Wife. Friend. And mother of his child. The vacuum left in his life by her absence was oppressive. His heart ached for her even more. "That's a good question. I don't know enough—or anything—about Sam Pyeong's death to find a connection." Brian rubbed the back of his neck. "She'll hate me for it, but maybe I can send Jessica up to Wilmington to do a little research for me."

"Who are you talking to?" Candice said from behind him.

Brian spun around and felt the heat rush up his cheeks. Candice stood a few feet behind him, looking puzzled. She'd changed into blue jeans, but still wore the lavender clerical blouse and white collar.

Brian stammered. "I was . . . just thinking aloud." He knew that explanation sounded lame.

"Sounded like full-fledged conversation to me," Candice said. "I thought you were on your mobile phone for a minute. But I can see you're not."

He didn't respond, hoping the awkward moment would pass. It didn't. She continued to stare at him with expectant eyes.

"Sarah. That was your wife's name, right?" Candice asked.

Brian nodded, then moved to the nearest row and sat down. How could he account for Sarah's continued presence in his life? Was there any explanation that wouldn't make him sound like a raving lunatic? He didn't want to have this conversation, never wanted to, not even with Allison. "I took Sarah's death really hard. Hard enough that I couldn't see a life for myself without her." His gut wrenched as he recalled his anguish from those first few months after Sarah died. The nights with no sleep. The days that passed without notice. "At first, I'd talk to Sarah at her grave. Nothing crazy. Just telling her how much I miss her. But then I started talking to her at home. Just innocuous one-sided conversations."

Candice sat down next to Brian. Where he expected to find pity, he instead found compassion in her eyes.

"My daughter was in therapy—both physical and mental—to overcome the impact the accident had on her. She was paralyzed from the waist down and was fighting hard to recover and move on. I, on the other hand, wallowed in my own self-pity. My conversations with Sarah manifested into a delusion where I could see her, and our conversations were no longer one-sided. Like she was really there and had never left." He reached up and wiped away a tear that threatened to drop from his eye.

Candice reached over and took hold of his hand and gently rubbed his back as if to comfort him. It was an odd feeling for Brian to have someone hold his hand after all these years. The intimate contact was awkward yet reassuring at the same time.

"When my daughter first caught me talking to Sarah, she went ballistic. I don't blame her. Allison was moving on with her life, not letting the accident define who she was. I was still stuck in the past, not willing to let it go. I didn't want to move on. We had a few rough years. Our final big blow up happened the night before she left for college. Allison moved out and I moved to Newark."

"Have you spoken to her since?"

Brian nodded. "Yeah. On occasion. Most times, the conversations end in frustration for both of us. She's made her disappointment clear on many occasions."

Candice gave his hand a gentle squeeze. "I can't begin to understand the grief you went through. I've not found my soulmate yet, but I hope they love me as much as you loved Sarah."

Brian checked his watch and rose from his seat. "I should go. Thanks for not telling me I'm crazy."

Candice held up her hands and smiled. "Hey, I steal things in my spare time. We've all got our cross to bear."

CHAPTER FORTY-ONE

When Toni ushered Brian into Alex's study, he was fascinated by the volume of books on the shelves around the room. The floor-to-ceiling rows of leatherbound spines was an impressive collection, but he wondered how much of this was just for show. His desire to spend hours perusing the shelves was only curbed by the knowledge that he might be stepping into the realm of a blackmailer, maybe even a killer.

His gaze moved to the center of the room, where Alex sat behind an antique oak desk.

"I wanted to see how your ankle was doing," Brian said as he approached the desk and shook hands with the older man.

Alex rose to his feet, using an aluminum crutch to stabilize himself. "Much better than it was yesterday." He gestured to the crutch. "I only need this to get to my feet. Can I get you something to drink?"

It wasn't much past one in the afternoon. But after what Brian had seen earlier that morning in Samantha's office, he thought an early drink might be just the thing to calm his nerves. "Let me get it," he said, gesturing for Alex to sit down.

Brian looked around the room for a bar cart but found nothing. Not even a cabinet that remotely resembled something that would hold alcohol and glasses. Alex laughed behind him. It was a deep laugh that held none of the jocularity that Brian would have expected for such an occasion. A cold chill raced down the back of his neck.

"It's over there," Alex said, pointing to one of the bookshelves. "Behind those books. Press the left most book and the panel will swing open."

When he moved to the shelf indicated, Brian realized that the books were fake. He ran his fingers along the spines of the faux books, amazed at how realistic they looked. "Brilliant," he said. "I'd never have noticed."

"I'll take a JD, straight."

Brian prepared two drinks and carried them back to the desk. Alex downed his in one gulp, slamming the glass down on the desk with a satisfied sigh. Not being much of a whiskey drinker, Brian nursed his drink with slow sips. In his years as a journalist, Brian had interviewed two prolific murderers. Both were infamous for their crimes, almost household names. As he studied Alex over the rim of his glass, Brian felt certain that, if Alex were a killer, he would never reach that pinnacle.

His name would fade quickly with the passing of time.

He looked around at the bookshelves, craning his neck up to survey the top row of books. Then he turned back to Alex. "This is quite a library."

"That's years and years of patient collecting." Alex began to rise from his chair, but he grimaced and sat back down. "Some of those volumes are hundreds of years old."

Brian wondered if the pain was being emphasized for his benefit. "Must have cost a small fortune. I didn't realize university professors were paid so well."

Alex hesitated before answering. A hard smile crossed his lips and his eyes turned dark. "My wife's father was very wealthy. He left us a small legacy when he passed."

"She was okay with you spending her inheritance on this?" Brian said. "That's very generous."

A sudden knock at the door kept Alex from responding. He glared across the room for a moment, before loudly saying, "What?"

The door hinges protested with a faint squeal as it swung open. Toni entered the room, her hands clasped in front of her, and her head bowed. "The police are here to see you."

Moments later, Toni ushered Mick Flanagan into the room. She lingered in the doorway for a moment until Alex glared at her. She backed out of the room and pulled the door closed. When the detective saw Brian in the room, he cocked his head to the side and frowned.

"What are you doing here?" Mick asked.

"Just a friendly visit," Brian said.

"Detective, please come in," Alex said. "Would you care for a drink?"

Mick shook his head. "No." He gestured to a nearby chair. "May I?"

"Of course," Alex said.

Mick turned the chair to face the desk and took a seat. "I was hoping you'd be willing to answer a few questions about yesterday."

Alex shifted in his chair. His eyes darted around the room. Brian thought he saw a flash of fear on Alex's face, but it was gone a moment later. "I'd be happy to assist in whatever way I can."

Brian spoke up. "Perhaps I should go."

Alex dismissed the idea with the wave of his hand. "No. Stay if you'd like. We're all friends here."

Mick glanced at Brian as if waiting to see what he would do. Brian gave a faint shrug and carried his half-full glass over to the window to stare out at the midday sun.

"I wanted to get your statement about yesterday afternoon," Mick said. "You were present when Stephanie O'Connell's body was discovered. Could you tell me what you saw?"

Alex leaned back in his chair. "There isn't much to tell. I'd sprained my ankle shortly before the . . . gruesome discovery. I'm afraid I didn't see much of anything."

"Can you tell me what you did see?"

Alex proceeded to detail the minutes leading up to the discovery of the body in the forest. He talked briefly about hearing the distant cry of an infant, and how Brian charged ahead through the underbrush to search. Brian listened carefully to the narrative, searching for any discrepancy that might indicate that Alex knew more than he was telling. But the description was consistent with Brian's own memories. Alex finished his brief account with, "I never saw the actual crime scene. Just heard the cries." He gestured toward Brian. "He could tell you far more than I."

Mick nodded and rose from his chair. "I figured as much, but I can't leave any stone unturned."

"I understand," Alex said. "Is there anything else I can do for you?"

Brian watched the detective drift around the room before answering. Mick glanced up and down the bookshelves as if noting the many titles. He paused before one in particular and ran his finger down the dark blue spine. "Alcott's Fireside Lectures. Sounds riveting."

Alex gritted his teeth, as if trying to suppress a sudden moment of anger. "That is a rare 1851 edition. If you simply came to mock my collection—"

Mick spun around; his eyes focused on Alex. "Far from it, Mr. Brennen. Please step outside. I have a warrant to search your home."

CHAPTER FORTY-TWO

C andice climbed the steps to the small porch in front of the rectory of St. Matthew's Catholic Church. The Sunday afternoon sky was the perfect analogy for how she felt. Gray and dreary. An hour earlier she'd been at the hospital, hoping to see Samantha, but Dr. Rucier had been explicit in his instructions about visitors. Only immediate family, and even that was discouraged. The nurse, however, had been kind enough to let Candice peer through the glass door of Samantha's room in the ICU. A myriad of tubes and wires wove their way in and out of the bed sheets while monitors hung from the wall, counting off each heartbeat and respiration with a beep. Samantha's face was swollen and black and blue and bloodied. Candice could only stand to look at her friend for a few minutes before she could stand it no more and left.

When she left the hospital, Candice had driven around Newark like an aimless arrow searching for a target. The sudden urge to talk to Andrew struck her forty-five minutes into her drive. Candice knocked on the door and waited for a response. None came. She knocked again, this time a little harder. Still no response. A moment of concern reared its head. Just days ago, she'd found him in a drunken stupor.

Please, not again.

She tried the doorknob. It was locked. Candice glanced back at the driveway at Andrew's Honda. Maybe he was still in the church. She knocked once more, just to be sure.

When there was no answer, she moved down the steps and walked along the path that led to the church past the old cemetery. Her feet crunched on the gravel as she counted the iron posts of the ancient fence surrounding the old graveyard. The lettering on some of the headstones had faded with the passage of time, leaving nothing but illegible shapes that once were names and dates. *Ashes to ashes, dust to dust.* The cliché that even she had recited at a few funerals danced through her mind.

She reached the rear entrance of the church. It was unlocked. Along the darkened hallway, she passed Sunday school classrooms on either side. Paper cutouts of Noah, some animals, and an ark were thumbtacked to a cork board that hung on the wall.

Candice moved along the hall and halted before a door. The plaque on it read:

Fr. Andrew Blake.

No light shone from beneath the door, but she knocked anyway. There was no answer. She knocked again and leaned her face closer to listen for any sound coming from the other side. "Andrew?" she said.

She checked the doorknob. It was unlocked. She pushed the door open and glanced into the office beyond. The disarray didn't come as a surprise. Books were overflowing from the single bookshelf in the corner. Correspondence and other church papers were stacked in uneven piles on the desk, on the floor, and even on two chairs. Desk drawers were half open; one probably couldn't be closed because of the miscellaneous bric-a-brac that spilled over the brim. To the unfamiliar eye, one might think the room had been ransacked. But Candice had seen Andrew's office several times before. She knew this was just Andrew in all his disorganized glory. She pulled the door closed. Only one other place: the church sanctuary.

Candice made her way along the hall and into the sacristy—a small room where Andrew usually prepared for mass. The lights were on, and the closet that held Andrew's vestments was open. The elegant robes and stoles were hung haphazardly on hangers. Green, purple, red, and white. The rainbow of colors was accented with glimpses of gold braids. Her own vestments looked uninspired beside Andrew's.

Across the room, the door that led into the sanctuary was open. She smiled and took a step forward but stopped when the sound of sobbing reached her ears. Someone was in the sanctuary. Perhaps Andrew was comforting a distressed member of his congregation. In that case, her interruption would likely be unwelcome. And it was none of her business who was seeking solace with Andrew. They deserved privacy and confidentiality.

But . . . if she was quiet and cautious, no one would know, not even Andrew. She stepped gingerly toward the door to the sanctuary and peered into the vast space beyond. The sobbing was louder, but all the pews were empty. Only after she stepped into the sanctuary did Candice find the source of the sobbing. Someone was huddled on the floor in the aisle that ran the length of the chamber. Cries of despair echoed off the vast ceiling and walls. Candice moved a few steps closer, until she realized who the figure was.

"Andrew?" Candice said as she closed the distance between them.

She was only a few feet away from him when she saw the blood.

CHAPTER FORTY-THREE

The observation room in which Brian stood was little more than a closet. Two black metal storage cabinets were against the far wall. A bucket and mop were propped up in the corner. The air was stale, as if the room had been closed for months. An old cassette deck and other antiquated audio equipment sat on a table in front of a window that looked into the interrogation room. These days, all interrogations were digitally recorded by four cameras. But not only had the police never removed the older audio equipment from the observation room, they'd turned the room into a storage closet. The room was dark except for the light coming through the one-way glass before him.

On the other side of the glass, the interrogation room was an uninspired gray. The floor was a block pattern of gray linoleum tiles. The walls were painted gray. The metal table and two chairs in the room were silvery gray.

Everything was gray.

Seated at the metal table, Mick Flanagan waited patiently as Alex Brennen paced fitfully back and forth. His limp was less pronounced than it had been earlier that day. Brian wondered how much of Alex's helplessness had been nothing but an act. A uniformed officer stood quietly in the corner of the room, his eyes moving from side to side in sync with Alex's movements.

After several minutes, Alex halted by the table with a scowl that screamed of indignation and fury. His shoulders seemed to tense, ready to explode at any minute with a raging anger. He slammed his hands onto the table. "Where's my lawyer?"

Brian saw the officer in the corner flinch at the violent gesture, but Mick Flanagan remained perfectly still.

"Why don't you sit down?" Mick said.

Alex folded his arms and turned his back on the two officers. "I demand to speak to my lawyer."

Mick leaned forward and rested his elbows on the table. "If Mr. Sherwood arrives, I'll be glad to usher him in immediately." He drew in a deep breath. "I'd like to make it clear that you are not currently under arrest. This is just an attempt to clarify some facts."

"Facts? Facts?" Alex blurted. "How is this for a fact? I didn't kill Robbie Reynolds."

Mick cocked his head to one side. "No one said you did . . ."

Alex huffed for a moment. He looked perplexed, as if he were an actor and had forgotten his next line.

". . . yet," Mick said.

Brian smiled in appreciation of Mick's pause, which had been just long enough to disassociate his final word from the rest of the sentence. He wondered if Alex had picked up on it too.

Alex stared at the detective through narrowed eyes. He rocked back on his heels while he studied Mick's expressionless face. "What's that supposed to mean?"

Mick leaned back in his chair. "No one has accused you of murder yet." He paused, then added, "But there are a few points that need clearing up before we can say for sure that no one will make such an accusation."

Brian almost felt sorry for Alex. There was a faint sheen of sweat forming on his high forehead. Alex looked as if the seriousness of the situation had finally dawned on him. Perhaps he realized that he wasn't as untouchable as he thought.

Alex rolled his neck. "This is ridiculous. I'm a tenured professor at the university. You can't think that I would have murdered anyone . . . especially someone that I barely knew."

Mick picked up on the point immediately. "So, you did know him?"

"What?"

Mick opened his notebook and flipped through several pages. "Just an hour ago, you told me you didn't know Robbie Reynolds."

Alex stepped forward and placed his hands on the chair on his side of the table. He gripped the metal until his knuckles turned white. "I want to talk to my lawyer."

"Happy to accommodate . . ." Mick shrugged his shoulders. ". . . if and when he arrives."

Alex's seething rage was barely contained. His face was a deep red; the anger had reached a fevered pitch. He lifted the chair a few inches up and slammed it back onto the floor. The clang echoed through the room. "Enough with the questions. I've told you every-thing I know." Alex turned his back once again on the two police officers.

Brian watched with interest, wondering what Mick's next move would be. He didn't have to wait long to find out.

"Are you finished?" Mick asked. "I do have a few more ques-tions."

Alex didn't turn around. He stared at the gray wall before him.

Mick slid the lid off an evidence box that sat on the corner of the table. Alex didn't move, or even acknowledge the action. Mick lifted a plastic evidence bag from the box. Brian recognized the brass letter opener he'd seen in the crime scene photos. The short narrow blade looked tarnished. The longer Brian's gaze lingered on it, the more he realized that the rust-colored stains were dried blood.

"Perhaps you could explain why we found this at Robbie Reyn-olds's home the day after he was murdered," Mick said. "It is yours, isn't it? There are some engraved initials on the blade. They match yours. Can you explain why your letter opener was found at a mur-der scene with the victim's blood on it?"

Before Brian could hear Alex's reply, the door to the observa-tion room opened and Chief Lyle Jenkins stepped in. Brian swal-lowed hard and the back of his neck prickled. He felt like a little kid caught with his hand in the cookie jar. Brian waited for the barrage of questions, curses, and threats that he assumed were about the befall him. Without saying a word, the chief made a small gesture with his finger, indicating that Brian should follow him.

Out in the hall, Lyle Jenkins growled only two words. "Wait here." The police chief opened the door to the interrogation room and leaned his head in. "Flanagan, can you step out here for a mo-ment?"

When Mick came into the hall, his eyes went wide at the sight of Brian leaning against the opposite wall. Brian gave a quick shrug as a sort of apology. Mick regained his composure and turned to the chief. "What's going on?"

Lyle pointed at Brian and spoke through gritted teeth. "What was he doing in the observation room?"

Looking from Brian to Lyle, Mick seemed at a loss for words, like he was searching for a believable answer that the chief might accept. "Well, I—"

Brian interrupted. "Mick didn't know I was in there. I came by to see if he'd made any progress with the case. Someone told me he was in the middle of an interrogation. I stepped in there to see who he was talking to."

Lyle's glare darted between Brian and Mick. His round pudgy face was red. "I don't know which I'd get more joy out of right now." Lyle pointed at Mick. "Firing you, or . . ." His finger shifted to point at Brian. ". . . arresting you." He returned his angry stare to Mick, then growled, "Get him out of here."

Brian and Mick remained silent as Lyle stormed off down the hall. But, as soon as the chief was out of sight, Brian could no longer contain himself and began to laugh. Mick joined him moments later.

Mick placed his hand on Brian's shoulder. "Thanks for covering for me. That would've been it for me if he knew I let you in."

"Trust me. He knows."

Mick stopped laughing and glanced down the hall with a puzzled look. "Do you think?"

Brian nodded. "Absolutely. Lyle is no fool. C'mon, you better escort me out of here before he comes back."

CHAPTER FORTY-FOUR

Candice rushed to Andrew's side and knelt beside him. He was on his knees, face forward, arms outstretched, and palms turned down. The smear of blood on the marble floor in front of him looked moist and fresh. He didn't seem to notice her presence until she touched his shoulder. He turned his face up toward her. His complexion was pale, and tears streamed down his cheeks.

"Forgive me," he muttered.

She glanced down at the smeared blood. A penknife lay on the marble beside his knee. The blade was stained crimson. Her chest was suddenly tight; each breath seeming to get stuck in her throat. Her pulse throbbed in her temples. *Please God, don't let this be what*

I think it is. Candice gazed back into his eyes. They darted aimlessly from side to side. "For what?" she asked.

Andrew looked down at his hands and turned his palms over. His palms and fingertips glistened under the sanctuary lights. The cuffs of his black clerical shirt were damp from the blood that oozed from a single slash on each of his wrists.

Her stomach churned. Candice forced herself to swallow, resisting the urge to be sick. She couldn't breathe.

She fumbled in her pocket for her mobile phone. "I'll call for an ambulance," she said. "Hang on, Andrew."

"No! No ambulance," he said. His voice was weak, weaker than she'd ever heard before. His eyes pleaded with her. "Please . . ."

"Andrew, you're bleeding. I've got to do something—"

He grabbed her arm and grimaced in pain. "George . . . call George."

Candice flinched at his touch. She yanked her arm away from his grasp. Smeared bloody fingerprints remained on her coat sleeve. "But you need stitches—"

"George. Just call George." His eyes pleaded with her. "Please . . ."

The coffee was too hot to drink, so Candice set the mug down on the table and watched the steam rise. She sat, exhausted and numb. It had been nearly forty-five minutes since she and George had moved Andrew to the church rectory, and twenty minutes since she'd excused herself to the kitchen, leaving George alone to tend to Andrew's wounds.

To her surprise, George took the scene in the church calmly and without comment. He acted as if this were normal for any late

Sunday afternoon. With his composed demeanor, he took charge of the situation and barked soft commands at her, which she felt compelled to follow. Candice remembered the day she'd found Andrew passed out after a day of binge drinking. George hadn't seemed surprised by that either.

She picked up the mug to take a sip but was suddenly repulsed by the smell. She just didn't have the stomach to drink it, or anything for that matter. Candice set the mug back onto the table and pushed it away. What could be so bad that Andrew would try to take his own life? He hadn't been himself for the past week. A sudden lack of focus. His mood swings. The binge drinking. Now, attempted suicide.

George stepped into the kitchen and moved to the sink. His shoulders were curled forward, and his head drooped. She noted the blood that stained his hands. He scrubbed vigorously beneath the running faucet for several minutes. Despite having questions, Candice remained silent. When he finished washing, George turned to the coffee machine.

"You can have this one." Candice gestured to the mug on the table. "It's hot, and I haven't drunk any of it."

He looked from her to the mug and back, then took a seat at the table. "Thanks." He pulled the mug close to him and cupped it with both hands. He didn't drink it.

"Will Andrew be okay?" she asked.

"I've managed to stop the bleeding. His wounds weren't too deep. He's resting on the sofa."

She leaned forward, placing her arms on the table. "Did he say why?"

George was silent. He turned his gaze away from hers. Candice had never gotten close to George, not like she had with Andrew.

The few times that George had interacted with her, she'd felt as if he were only tolerating her presence because of Andrew.

Like she was only there as part of an uneasy truce between enemy factions.

"Please tell me," she said.

"George, give us a few minutes."

Candice turned to find Andrew standing in the doorway of the kitchen. His face was pale, and he seemed unsteady on his feet. Gauze bandages were wrapped around each wrist. Andrew moved to the table and sat in the chair next to Candice. George didn't move at first.

Andrew looked across the table. "Please."

George huffed as he rose from his seat and exited the kitchen.

Once they were alone, Candice shifted to face Andrew. There were a dozen questions swirling in her mind, but she realized it would be best to remain silent. Time to let Andrew speak on his own terms. That was what Andrew would've done if their roles were reversed.

Andrew refused to meet her gaze.

His chin dipped to his chest, and he slumped in his chair. "I owe you an apology."

Candice shook her head. "No, not at all."

He rested his bandaged hands on the table and flexed his fingers, then grimaced with pain. "How much have I told you about my life before Newark?"

"You said you served in Pittsburgh for several years, but you've never said much more than that."

Andrew's sunken eyes held a deep sadness, and she saw the conflict on his face. He had something he needed to tell her but didn't seem at all easy about it.

"What happened in Pittsburgh has been a heavily guarded secret," he said. "There are only two people in Newark who know about it."

She rested a hand on his forearm, just above the bandage. "Let me be the third."

Andrew patted her hand with his. "I served at a church in Pittsburgh's inner city. Eight years ago, I was cleaning up the sanctuary after a Wednesday night mass. I'd stepped into the sacristy for only a few minutes to put away leftover communion wafers and wine. When I returned to the sanctuary, I found a fifteen-year-old boy—Matthew was his name—standing in the center aisle. He had a gun."

Andrew paused to collect his thoughts. Candice bit her lip, waiting for him to continue. She studied the lines in his face. He suddenly looked so old. Older than she'd ever seen before. She feared the toll that reliving his past might take on him.

"I knew Matthew. His parents were regulars on Sundays. He was babbling about this horrible thing he'd done and whether God would forgive him," he said.

The words struck a chord with Candice. She'd heard something similar the previous week from Agatha Bowman. "What had Matthew done?"

"He'd just shot his parents and younger sister."

Candice ran her hand through her hair and gaped at him. "What?"

"Matthew was waving the gun and threatening to kill himself. I tried to talk to him. Tried to convince him to give me the gun. He kept walking in circles and talking nonsense. I didn't think I was making any headway with him. But while I kept Matthew talking, I inched closer to him. Thought if I got close enough, I could take the gun from him."

Andrew stopped talking and gazed into nothingness. His eyes didn't move, and he didn't blink. It was almost as if his consciousness had left his body, leaving behind a lifeless husk.

Candice said, "What happened?"

Her words roused him. "We must've struggled for a good minute. Pulling and tugging and pushing. I don't know how it happened or who pulled the trigger. My God, it was so loud." His voice cracked with emotion. He cleared his throat as if it would clear the emotion that was choking him. "It was a good thirty seconds before I realized what had happened. Matthew was lying on the floor. He'd been shot in the chest."

Candice fought the urge to cry. She leaned back in her chair and drew in a deep breath.

"The wound was gushing with blood. I used my bare hands to put pressure on the wound, hoping to stop the bleeding. I knew I needed to get help, but I'd left my mobile phone in the sacristy. If I took his hand off the wound, Matthew would've bled to death within minutes. But if I didn't get help . . ."

A pang of grief gripped Candice's heart as she listened.

"One of the other priests found me the next morning. Still on my knees, still holding Matthew in my arms. He had died sometime in the night, but I was in shock and didn't even notice."

Candice mumbled, "Dear God."

"After that, I took to drinking heavily. One Saturday night, I went on an all-night bender and arrived the next morning for Mass drunk. I made it about a third of the way through the service before passing out on the pulpit."

Candice slouched in her chair to absorb his words. She now understood why Andrew had always been tight-lipped about his past. A congregation never liked to see weakness in their spiritual leaders. An unwritten rule taught by one of her professors in seminary. "Once a congregation loses confidence in you, you might as well pack your bags and move on," he'd said in his deep baritone. And indeed, Candice's own experience at her previous church could attest to the statement's validity.

"How did you end up here?" she asked.

"The bishop sent me for treatment and rehab," Andrew said. "I was there for a year. When I was released, the bishop felt it would be better for all involved if I was transferred to another, smaller church. That's how I ended up in Newark. George was already serving as deacon when I arrived. The bishop asked him to keep an eye on me. I've strayed once or twice, but nothing like this past week."

Andrew suddenly fell forward, cradled his face in his hands and sobbed. Candice rested her hand on his shoulder, he flinched at her touch. Between sobs, he muttered, "Newark was supposed to be quiet, a safe haven. Everything was going to be fine. But these recent murders . . . too much death. Too much blood. Why? Why do they all have to die?"

The sobs grew in volume until Andrew wailed loud enough to bring George rushing back into room. Candice wrapped her arm over Andrew's convulsing shoulders, desperate to calm and comfort him.

George approached the table and brushed her arm away.

"Let me take care of this." His voice was soft, but authoritative. He gripped Andrew's shoulders and guided the sobbing priest to his feet. "I know what needs to be done. Please, just go."

Candice scowled at George, angry that the deacon was pushing her out. "I'm not leaving him." She reached out to help with Andrew.

George brushed her hand away and half-led and half-carried Andrew toward the door. "It's best for both of you if you let me handle this."

Candice opened her mouth to protest. "Don't shut me out!"

"Don't you understand?" George said. "This scandal could end Andrew's career in the priesthood. I might be able to mitigate it, but I need you out of the picture to do so. The bishop won't be happy if he knows that you're involved."

CHAPTER FORTY-FIVE

Monday

The Monday breakfast crowd at the Main Street Diner had cleared out by the time Brian and Jessica took a booth in the back corner of the restaurant. Brian had just returned from Newark City Hall. His early morning meeting with Mick Flanagan had been shorter than Brian had expected. Mick only had one real update for him on the investigation.

"They kept Alex Brennen in jail overnight," Brian said across the table to Jessica.

She fiddled with her napkin, folding and unfolding it again and again. "Took them a week and a half to arrest someone? That might be a local record."

"Don't get too excited just yet. Alex might have an alibi for the first two murders. Mick is checking it out this morning."

Jessica slouched in her seat and rolled her eyes. "So much for that record. Why'd they go after him anyway?"

"A couple things. When they searched Alex's house, they found evidence that he was blackmailing several people, including Robbie," Brian said. "And phone records showed a call from Alex's office phone to Robbie's mobile phone on the night he died. But, if his alibi holds up, there's no way Alex could've made that call."

"That doesn't sound suspicious at all." The sarcasm oozed like molasses from her lips. "Where's the FBI in all this? Don't they deal with serial killers?"

Brian leaned back and shrugged. "You know how Lyle Jenkins is. Half the town would need to be dead before he called for help."

Jessica averted her gaze and stared across the empty diner. "Fat bastard," she mumbled under her breath.

"Jess . . ."

"I know. I've got to respect the police. Blah blah." She shook her head and let out a sigh. "Any juicy details from the blackmail angle?"

"They're still sorting through that evidence. That's going to take more time." Brian sat back as Norah, one of the morning waitresses, arrived at the table with their orders. Once she was gone, he asked, "How was your morning excursion up to Wilmington? Did you find anything?"

Jessica jabbed a piece of bacon with her fork and pushed it through the syrup overflowing onto her plate from atop a stack of pancakes. "About that. Have I told you how much I hate research?"

He nodded with a smile, then cut through his omelet with a knife. He had called her the previous night to ask her to run up to the *Delaware Post-Gazette*. As the regional daily newspaper, it might contain references in the archives to Sam Pyeong, or the new name Candice had given him the other night, Stuart Hardwick. Jessica had been less than enthused by the assignment, but Brian knew he could count on her to get the job done.

"Do you know how early I woke up get to the *Post-Gazette?*" Syrup dripped from her bacon onto the table as she gestured with her fork. "Six o'clock. I didn't even know six o'clock came twice a day."

"Did you have any luck?"

"Some." She shoved the bacon into her mouth and started to chew. "It must have been a slow news week, because Sam Pyeong's murder dominated the headlines for three days. April 1952. He was found dead in the alley behind the old Newark Diner. Police found evidence that two people were involved in the killing, but there were no arrests that I could find." She sliced through the stack of pancakes with her fork. "A Korean immigrant. Mid-twenties. Worked as a dishwasher at the diner. Took some trash out to the dumpster one night and never returned. Someone found him later that evening. Beaten to death; his head smashed in. Left behind a wife and a young daughter."

Brian watched her shovel a forkful of pancakes into her mouth. It was a little like watching a five-year-old eat. He considered her brief narrative. *The murder happened behind the diner. This diner in fact. But not this diner.* If he remembered his local history, the diner on Main Street had opened and closed a half dozen times over the years and changed its name as owners came and went. He didn't know how much the building had changed since the murder. But he did know there was no longer an alley behind it. A three-story office building now backed up against the diner where the alley had been.

"What about Stuart Hardwick? Did you find anything on him?" he asked.

Jessica set her fork down on the edge of the plate and took a drink from her glass of orange juice before responding. "Not a lot. Just one brief news story and an obit from 1953. The news story came first. He was found dead in his father's garage. Police reported it as suicide. He was hanging from the ceiling joists. This Hardwick guy had been in and out of the jail. Petty theft. Assault and battery. He had a violent streak in him."

He pondered this new information. Maybe Sam Pyeong's death was a robbery gone wrong. Perhaps a chance encounter in the alley that turned deadly? 1952 would've put Sam Pyeong's death at the height of the Korean War. He wondered if there might've been any connection.

"Don't look now, but Inspector Clouseau just walked in," Jessica said as she slouched down in her seat.

Brian turned toward the entrance of the diner. Mick was standing by the front counter. The detective scanned the diner, spotted Brian and Jessica, and moved toward them. Brian couldn't help but notice that Mick was wearing the same clothes from Sunday morning. The stubble on his face had grown thicker, and Mick's hair was wild and unruly. His eyes were narrow slits, and his forehead was creased with tension.

Brian turned back to Jessica. "You should probably go."

"Why?" She gave him a hard look. "What the hell did I do?"

"Mick doesn't need your antagonism right now."

Jessica huffed as she slid out of the booth. "I wouldn't have to be antagonistic if the cops would do their job once in a while." She brushed past Mick as he approached. Brian watched her leave, making a mental note to talk to her later. Mick slid into the seat that Jessica had abandoned just moments ago.

"Have you slept at all in the past forty-eight hours?" Brian asked.

"Morpheus has to catch me first," Mick said. "I thought I'd find you here."

Brian noted the shadows beneath Mick's eyes. "You look utterly wiped."

"It's been one helluva long day."

"It's only . . ." Brian checked his watch. ". . . ten in the morning."

"Then it's been a helluva long night," Mick clarified. "Between the Blackwell crime scene and interrogating Alex Brennen . . . Coffee, please. Black," he said when Norah approached the table. He leaned back in his seat and dropped his hands onto the table as if he were surrendering to his frustration. "Had to let Brennen go. He's got two alibis; one for Robbie and one for the Cavendish girl."

"Who gave him the alibis? His wife?" Brian asked.

"No. Several colleagues from the university."

Brian rubbed his chin with his thumb and forefinger. "What about the letter opener?"

Mick snorted. "With a strong alibi, any remotely good lawyer could tear that evidence to pieces in court. Probably say it was stolen. Or my favorite . . ." Mick made air quotes with his fingers. "Planted by the police."

"Couldn't you hold him on blackmail charges?"

The detective shook his head. "Forensics has only started digging through the material we took from his house. It'll be days before I have enough to touch Brennen again. Damn it."

"Any word on Samantha?"

Mick frowned, his face grim. "Talked to the hospital this morning. She's still unconscious. They're not sure when she'll wake up . . . if she wakes up."

CHAPTER FORTY-SIX

B rian's hands hovered over the computer keyboard but didn't touch the keys. He stared at the empty white space on the screen. In little over a week, three people had died, one lingered on the edge of death, and an unsolved murder from decades ago had reemerged from the past. The usually quiet city of Newark was overshadowed by a cloud of gloom.

He felt it everywhere he went. It was in the whispers and hushed conversations on the street, in the coffee shops, and restaurants. Some mourned the dead. A few gossiped over the possible reasons for each death, and whether the victims deserved what they got.

Brian stretched his arms above his head and clasped his hands together behind his neck. He then arched his back, heard his joints crack, and sighed at the relief from the stiffness that came from his lack of sleep. His eyes glanced at the computer screen again. *This story isn't going to write itself*, he thought. But thoughts of the past forty-eight hours consumed him. The image of Stephanie O'Connell's corpse was all too fresh in his mind. Her bloody, battered skull. The army of insects crawling over her body. The helpless infant lying among leaves.

He opened his notebook and flipped through the pages, making a review of all the sorted pieces in the puzzle. There were notes on Robbie Reynolds, Alex Brennen, Sam Pyeong, and even Candice Miller. He paused at a note scribbled in the margin.

Nooks & Crannies Cleaning Co.

It was the local cleaning company that came into Samantha's office twice a week. He did an Internet search and found their website. Brian read briefly about the services the company offered, a few referrals from happy customers, and then checked the office address. They were a few blocks down on Main Street.

With a sudden swift movement, he pushed back from the desk and rose from his chair. Mildred glanced up when Brian scooped up his mobile phone from the desk and moved toward the door. Her knitting needles continued to click together, the only sound to break the silence in the office.

"I need some air," he said. "Hold down the fort while I'm gone."

"You okay?"

Brian pulled open the door and paused as a cool breeze drifted in along with the sounds of the midday bustle of Newark's Main Street. "Yeah. Want to clear my head." With that, he stepped through the door and let it swing closed behind him.

As Brian strode along Main Street, he shuffled the names of the dead in his mind. Robbie Reynolds. Deena Cavendish. Stephanie O'Connell. And what about Sam Pyeong? He seemed like the "odd man out" in this collection of victims. How much did Candice know about the Pyeong murder? She'd been tightlipped on anything other than the barest of details.

At the corner of Main and Academy Streets, Brian passed the university bookstore and then halted before an older brick office building. The front facade consisted of two bay windows flanked by three doors. The right and left doors opened into their respective offices, a law firm, and a bagel shop. The center door led to a second-floor office. He glanced at the plaque mounted by the third door.

Nooks & Crannies Cleaning Co.
Tracey Pyeong-Smith, Owner

———————

Tracey Pyeong-Smith directed Brian to a black leather sofa by the window of the second-floor office. The leather was worn and had lost its sheen long ago. She crossed to a kitchen area and picked up a coffee mug.

"Can I offer you anything?" she asked, holding the mug up as an invitation.

Brian shook his head and studied her as she poured coffee into the mug. Average height, thin, maybe in her early forties. Her shoulder-length jet black hair was straight and framed her face. She wore form-fitting jeans and a paisley silk blouse. Tracey moved to an oversized papasan chair and gingerly sank into the gray cushion.

"Pardon the state of the office," she said, gesturing to a dozen mops, buckets, vacuum cleaners, and other assorted cleaning supplies that lined the wall and nearby shelves. "We don't usually have people visit."

Brian waved her remark away. "No worries. I'm not actually here on business."

Tracey raised an eyebrow. "Are you in the habit of making social calls on complete strangers?"

He leaned forward, rested his elbows on his thighs and clasped his hands together. "I'm here to talk about your grandfather, Sam Pyeong?"

Tracey sipped from her coffee; her eyes seeming to study him over the rim of the mug. "Okay," she said with caution in her voice. "What's this about?"

"I have some questions about your grandfather. His name has come up in connection with . . . a story."

Tracey's brow furrowed. "Grandpa's been dead since 1952. I don't see how he can be connected to anything."

Brian frowned. He hadn't expected Tracey's defensiveness. But it was understandable. If a journalist he'd never met walked into his office and started asking questions about his dead wife, he'd probably get defensive as well. "I'm certainly not here to cause you any discomfort or distress. If you'd rather I leave—"

Tracey shook her head. "No. I'm fine. Just cautiously curious."

"I understand your grandfather worked at the old Newark Diner," Brian said.

"Yes, and that's where he died. He was attacked in the alley behind it."

Brian nodded, then leaned back in the sofa. "Can you tell me a bit about him?"

Tracey shrugged. "Only very little. My grandma refused to talk to me about him. But my mother told me a bit. She was just three when he died, but . . ." Tracey dipped her head and laid one hand on top of the other in her lap. When she looked up again, her voice was firm. "What do you want to know?"

"Did your grandparents live in Newark?"

"Yeah. They rented a small apartment on Chapel Street. Mun-Hee and Sam Pyeong." Tracey wiped the corner of her eye with a finger. "They came from Korea about three years before the war. They saw America as the promised land. The land of milk and honey. Of endless opportunities." She let out a sharp snort that oozed with sarcasm. "The best they could get was a two-room second floor apartment and a job washing dishes in a diner."

"Not exactly the American dream," Brian said.

"Asians were about as welcome around town as African Americans were back then."

"Were your grandparents harassed much?"

Tracey stroked her cheek. "Not much. At least not until the war broke out."

He slid forward and sat on the edge of the seat. "What happened?"

"I really don't know much. Mostly just vague details." Tracey sank deeper into the papasan chair cushion. "But my mother said there was one guy who hounded my grandparents for months. I heard of an incident where he followed my grandma home from the market one afternoon, shouting vile racists remarks the entire time. My mother was just an infant back then."

Brian felt a pang as he pictured a scared young Korean mother pushing a stroller along the sidewalks of Newark while an odious man trailed behind, reciting a litany of hideous language. "Why didn't they get the police involved?"

"They didn't want to make waves. According to my mother, this guy—what was his name? Stuart, I think—was nothing but a sleazeball troublemaker around town."

Brian's pulse quickened at the mention of the name. "Did you say Stuart?"

Tracey nodded. "Yeah. Stuart—not sure what his last name was—Hartley? Hensen?"

"Hardwick?" Brian asked.

Tracey snapped her fingers and point across at him. "That might've been it. Stuart Hardwick."

CHAPTER FORTY-SEVEN

Candice lifted her head off the pillow when the doorbell rang. Wondering who would be at her door at such an early hour, she glanced at the alarm clock on the bedside table. 1:35? In the afternoon? She stifled a moan. She'd left Andrew's church late and arrived at home around midnight and crashed hard when her head hit the pillow. She'd not slept well, still upset over how George had dismissed her the night before. All she wanted to do was help, but George had been quick to push her away.

The doorbell rang again. Candice didn't move. *Maybe if I don't answer, they'll go away.* She closed her eyes and tried to push away the ache that throbbed behind her forehead. A third ring from the doorbell caused a low moan from Candice. *I'll give them this: they're persistent.* She rose from the bed and crossed the room to the dresser. The image that met her in the dresser mirror made Candice cringe.

She'd fallen asleep in her clothes. Wrinkles crisscrossed her blouse like roads on a map. She ran her hand through her hair before heading down the stairs.

When she pulled open the front door, the afternoon sunlight besieged her eyes. She squinted at the figure waiting on her front step. "Brian? What are you doing here?"

He pushed his way past her and into her house. "It's about Sam Pyeong. It's time you introduce me to his alleged killer."

———————

Agatha poured hot water into three tea mugs and pushed one across the table to Candice and another toward Brian. Then the elderly woman sat at the opposite side of the round kitchen table. Her hands trembled when she lifted the sugar bowl and offered it to Brian. Candice cupped her own mug and felt the warmth seep into the palms of her hands.

"Had I known you were both coming, I'd have had some scones to go with the tea," Agatha said.

Brian stirred his tea. The spoon clinked against the side of the mug with a hollow ring. "I'd like to talk to you about Stuart Hardwick."

Agatha averted her eyes down to her own mug. Her head seemed to teeter from side to side. "I . . . I'm not . . . I don't think I know a Stuart Hardwick."

"Are you sure?" Brian asked.

Agatha appeared to struggle with the answer, her eyes cloudy with turmoil. "I don't think so."

"What about Sam Pyeong? Did you know him?"

"Sam Pyeong? No, I don't think . . ." Agatha stammered. Each word came out in raspy gasps. "I think you both should go." She began to rise from her seat.

Candice leaned forward and grasped the elderly woman's hand. "Agatha, please. Talk to us." The action and words came so suddenly and without thought, Candice barely believed they had come from her. "I saw the picture of you and Stuart, remember?"

Agatha returned to her seat and refused to look in their direction. She kept her gaze down, focused on the teacup before her. "Yes. I knew Stuart."

Candice stroked the back of Agatha's hand with her thumb. "You loved him, didn't you?"

The elderly woman's reply came as a simple nod of the head.

"Did you know that Stuart had been in prison?" Brian asked.

"Prison?" Candice jerked her head to look at him. On the drive over, Brian had alluded to having "new information pertaining to Sam Pyeong's death," but had not been forthcoming.

Agatha nodded again. "Yes. He was sweet, really. But . . . he had a terrible temper when the mood struck him. Stuart came from a troubled home, never got any good breaks in life. His father was killed at the Battle of Midway during the war. His mother . . . well, she turned to the bottle for consolation." Agatha sipped from her teacup.

"And Stuart turned to petty theft and violence?" Brian asked.

The elderly woman set her teacup back down on the table. "Oh, he was never violent around me. He was so sweet and gentle. A real gentleman." Agatha gave them both a wistful smile. "Had a silvery tongue, that one did. He could talk the panties off a nun." Her face flushed for a moment. "Sorry, I . . ."

Brian gave a wave of understanding. "No need to apologize. It sounds like he meant a lot to you."

"He was my first." Agatha smirked and looked away. "I never told my husband about Stuart. Didn't want him to think he was getting soiled goods, if you know what I mean."

Candice watched all of this in fascination. Brian's ability to get Agatha to open up about her past amazed her. She couldn't pinpoint how he did it. Was it the tone of his voice? The words that he said? The way he alluded to already knowing everything? If nothing else, she finally understood how Brian had become such a world renown journalist. He had interviewed government officials—both from the United States and abroad—as well as criminals, dictators, and even royalty. Brian Wilder had written vast investigative pieces that tore open some of the darkest secrets. And now she was watching him persuade a little old lady to reveal her own dark secret.

Brian rested his elbows on the table and leaned forward. "Tell me about that night behind the Newark Diner."

It seemed like Agatha had fallen into a trance. Her unfocused eyes gazed past Candice and Brian as if they weren't even there. A minute or more passed, before Agatha moved. She rose from the table and left the kitchen only to return moments later with a photograph. After returning to her seat, Agatha placed the black and white image on the table. Candice recognized it from her earlier visit.

"That's Stuart." Agatha pointed to the man standing beside her younger self in the picture.

Brian picked up the photograph and studied it. "Very handsome, I can understand why you fell for him."

"He blamed the Japanese for his father's death at Midway and despised anyone who looked Asian. Didn't matter where they were from—Japan, China, Korea—he hated them all. There weren't many Asians in Newark back then. Just a handful."

The elderly woman closed her eyes as if trying to remember every detail. "One night, Stuart took me for a drive around town. I thought we were going to find some place to be alone. But he pulled into the alley behind the diner. I asked him what was going on, and he just said, 'We're going to have ourselves a little fun.'"

Candice felt a chill across her neck, as if a breeze had blown through the room. She glanced around. The room suddenly seemed smaller. A clock ticked off the seconds like a drummer's cadence—rhythmic and loud.

"So, we waited," Agatha continued. "Ten minutes later, the diner's back door opened and out came this young Asian man—Sam Pyeong. He had his hands full of garbage bags. After he placed the bags in the dumpster, he turned to head back into the diner. That's when Stuart pulled the car's tire iron out from under his seat and handed it to me. 'Watch this,' he said. Next thing I knew, Stuart's out of the car and talking to this young Asian man, to Sam. I couldn't hear what they were saying, but suddenly Stuart hit Sam. Punched him, threw him to the ground, kicked him. I just sat there. I didn't know what was happening." Agatha fell silent, picked up the photograph, and stared at the picture. Tears welled up in her eyes.

"And then?" Brian asked.

His voice seemed to break Agatha out of her trance. She let the photograph slip from her fingers and fall onto the table. "All I remember was standing in the alley, tire iron in my hand. Stuart got Sam to his feet and had his arms locked behind his back. Sam struggled, but Stuart was too strong for him. 'Come on, Agatha. You know what to do,' Stuart said. He kept pointing out how our soldiers were being slaughtered in Korea. Kept saying 'The gooks are trying to take over the country,' and that 'they need to be taught a lesson.' Nobody talks that way anymore, and that's a good thing, but back then . . ." She took a long breath. "I can still hear his voice. 'Do it, Agatha. You know what to do. Punish the son of a bitch.'" Agatha let out a soft sob.

Candice found it difficult to catch her breath. A sudden feeling of cold arose from deep within her. She feared where the elderly woman's story was going but had to know. "What then?" she asked.

Agatha looked her straight in the eyes and said: "I struck Sam Pyeong with the tire iron. Again, and again until he was dead."

CHAPTER FORTY-EIGHT

B rian kept his eyes fixed on Agatha as the tears rippled down her cheeks. Each drop surged and declined over the creases and crevices of the decades-old flesh. Her words still reverberated in his mind. They had not been what he'd expected.

He lifted the mug to his lips and took a sip. The tea was tepid and disagreeable. Brian glanced at Candice. Her jaw was tight. She was biting her lip so hard that he worried she might draw blood.

There was not much that surprised him anymore. He'd reported on some of humanity's most horrifying atrocities. Yet Agatha's account of Sam Pyeong's death had caught him unprepared. He'd assumed that Stuart Hardwick had wielded the weapon that battered poor Sam into an early grave. He figured that Agatha knew the truth and might even have been a witness. He'd never imagined that this eighty-plus-year-old woman was the one responsible for casting the fatal blow.

"Agatha," he said. "Do you realize what you're saying?"

She nodded. "I'm a murderer."

There was a sudden movement to his left. Candice pushed away from the table and rose to her feet. She walked across the kitchen to stare out the small window above the sink, arms folded. She exhaled loudly, as if she'd been holding her breath for the past several minutes.

"Stuart was so proud of what we'd done," Agatha said, her voice soft and trembling. "Said it was our patriotic duty. We'd cleansed the city of one more . . ." Her voice trailed off as if she were ashamed to say anymore. "It was on the front page the next morning. That's when I found out he had a wife and child."

Brian stroked his chin. The stubble reminded him that he hadn't shaved in days. "You didn't come forward? Tell the police what you did?"

Agatha wrung her hands together. "I was young, scared. Stuart kept telling me that it would all blow over. That no one would ever know what we . . . what I had done. I trusted him. But then—"

"He killed himself," Brian said.

She nodded. "He left me. Left me all alone to deal with this. He took the easy way out, while I . . ." A tear streamed down her cheek. "I've tried to make up for it, spent my life trying to make up for it. Volunteering for every charity imaginable. Hoping a lifetime of good deeds could make up for the one horrible thing I did."

"Why?"

Brian looked over at Candice.

Her back was still turned away from them. Her head was hung low.

She asked again. "Why did you do it?"

"I don't know." The elderly lady's voice quivered.

Candice slammed her fist on the kitchen counter. The loud bang made Agatha shudder.

"Don't give me that," Candice said, her voice sharp with anger. "Why did you kill him?"

Agatha cowered in her chair. She squeezed her eyes closed as if trying to block out the acrimony that hung in the air.

"I wanted him to love me." Her words came out almost as a whisper. The shame, the guilt, and the horror of her past enveloped every word she spoke. "I thought if I proved myself worthy of his love that he would never leave."

Candice spun around. "Don't you dare talk about love. You killed someone for a roll in the hay." Her nostrils flared as she took a breath. "And now here you sit, feeling sorry for yourself. 'Woe is me, I murdered someone and had to live with my guilt.' Where's your compassion for the Pyeong family? You deprived them of a lifetime with Sam so you could get laid. Your selfish, petty act—"

Brian stood up and cut her off. "Candice!"

She glared at him; her hands clenching and unclenching. He saw the tremble in her shoulder, the red rage in her face.

"Leave the room, please," he said.

Candice scowled at him, then turned her gaze to Agatha. Candice opened her mouth to speak, then closed it again and stormed from the kitchen.

Brian remained on his feet for a moment. In the sudden silence of the kitchen, the tick of the clock on the wall roared like thunder in his ears.

"You've kept this to yourself all these years." Brian returned to his seat at the table. "Why come forward now?"

Agatha folded her hands and rested them—still quaking—before her. "The recent killings. I was sure I'd be next. Sure that if I didn't confess, I would end up dead." She glanced at the door. "Even my confession is a selfish act. Pastor Miller has every right to be angry. To judge me."

Unsure what else to do, Brian reached for her hands. Her wrinkled skin was so soft and warm, it seemed impossible to imagine that they had killed so callously.

Agatha looked up at him. "What's going to happen to me?"

Startled by the question, Brian let go of her. "I wish I knew."

———————

Brian found Candice leaning against his Mustang in the parking lot of the apartment building. She was staring down at the asphalt with her arms folded. When he approached, she glanced up at him, then turned away to look out at the street. Her earlier look of rage had ebbed to that of indignation. Her outburst had caught him by surprise. He hadn't known her for much more than a week, but Brian had assessed her as being more levelheaded and aloof.

"What was that all about?" he asked, as he stepped up to the car.

Her gaze seemed fixated on the traffic passing on the street. "Nothing."

"I wish I could believe that." He slipped his hands into his pockets and rocked back on his heels. "Agatha is upset. She could use some words of comfort from her pastor."

Candice snorted but didn't reply. She straightened her shoulders and turned her gaze toward him. Her eyes were moist, the lids red and swollen. A deep sense of pain lingered behind her clenched jaw. How many times had he seen a similar look before? That look of betrayal.

"Tell me what's on your mind," he said.

She was slow to answer, but after a few moments, she spoke, her voice soft and broken. "They never taught me how to handle this in seminary. Agatha is supposed to be that little old church lady. You know, the kind who comes every Sunday and knows all the old hymns by heart. She brings cookies. Not death." She pushed off from the car and turned her back to Brian. "What's happening here? People are dying at the hands of some . . ." She seemed to struggle for the right word. ". . . religious nut job. Samantha's in the hospital, fighting for her life." She gestured toward the apartment building. "And the sweetest old lady I know killed someone so she could get it on. I don't know what to do anymore. Ministry was not supposed to be like this."

Brian kicked at a stone by his foot. It hobbled across the parking lot, its odd shape keeping the stone from ever picking up any momentum. He could sense her frustration. The anger in her voice was evident, but there was also an undertone of fear, as if she were afraid of losing her perfect dream.

He recalled his first exposure to violence and death. The doubt and despair he'd felt over the reality of the human condition—it's depravity, hedonism, and corruption—still haunted him on occasion. Even his own demons rose on extremely dark nights to torment him. He had little to offer her in response but banal words of insignificance. "We humans are a self-possessed and often dangerous kind."

"That's not very reassuring."

"It wasn't meant to be," he said.

Candice began to walk toward the parking lot entrance, and the sidewalk beyond. Her steps were slow, and her head was down.

"Where are you going?" Brian asked.

"Home," came her reply.

"I'll drive you."

Candice halted for a moment. "No. I need some fresh air. Some time to think. Alone."

CHAPTER FORTY-NINE

C andice reached the front steps of her church an hour after
she'd left Brian standing in the parking lot. Her walk home
had become a meandering tour of most of the side roads off Newark's Main Street. Her mind had been so preoccupied that she
barely remembered seeing anything along the walk. She wasn't
even sure how, or why, she ended up at the church as opposed to
her house. She climbed the seven steps out front, and, when she
reached the top, turned and sat down on the uppermost step. The
concrete felt cold to the touch.

A crumpled newspaper drifted along the street in the light
afternoon breeze. She watched it cartwheel along the asphalt.

Aimless. It reminded Candice of her faith of late. She wasn't sure if she even believed in anything anymore. Not God. Not humanity. Not even herself.

Agatha's confession weighed heavily on her heart. She couldn't reconcile the gracious elderly woman she knew with the young murderess she had confessed to be. Had there been some mistake? Perhaps Agatha was confused or delusional. Maybe dementia was taking hold. How could a person who had spent a lifetime caring for others reveal herself to be a cold-blooded killer?

A few strands of hair fell in front of her eye, which she brushed back with her fingers. And what of the killer she'd come to know as the Sin Eater? Was he driven by the same frustration over sins that remained unpunished? Was the murderer not a sin eater but an avenger? And why was she sitting here, thinking of punishment and revenge? Where was her own capacity for forgiveness?

Her thoughts were interrupted by the ring of her mobile phone. Caller ID identified Brian Wilder. Probably calling to check up on her. She let the call go to her voicemail. She wasn't yet ready to talk to him, or anyone for that matter.

Candice stared at her phone screen. The background image was of Jesus handing out loaves of bread, cropped from the famous Jacopo Tintoretto's painting *The Miracle of the Loaves and Fishes*. The bread was the centerpiece to these murders. Whoever was responsible understood the meaning of the bread within the context of the sin eater mythology. They knew how to get their hands on unusual loaves of bread without arousing suspicion. And they knew that Robbie, Stephanie, and Deena were all clients of Samantha Blackwell. The only person who met those requirements was Alex. But Brian had mentioned that Alex had alibis for the first two killings. That seemed to put him in the clear, at least for the murders.

Someone else must know about sin eaters. She needed to speak to Alex again.

The early evening sun was beginning to set, creating a fiery red arch above the treetops. Candice pulled down the visor of her car to block the blinding light. She turned onto W. Main Street and drove the few blocks to the Victorian-style house she'd visited for the first time less than a week ago. She drew her Subaru up to the curb and shut off the engine. She glanced at her mobile phone on the passenger seat. No call back from Brian. On the drive over, she had tried to reach him but he hadn't answered his phone.

The curtains for the first-floor windows obscured the view from outside. It was difficult to know if anyone was home. Perhaps she should call first, instead of showing up unannounced. What would she say? She just happened to be passing. She wanted to make sure Alex was okay after his night in jail, as if a pastor should make it a habit to check up on someone accused of blackmail. No good pretense came to mind, so Candice gave up her attempt to rationalize her sudden visit, opened the door, and climbed from the car.

The Range Rover that sat in the driveway was covered in a mild haze of tree pollen. The fine particulates had shaded the car into a delicate bisque. She fought the urge to write "wash me" on the back window with her finger.

There was no other car in the driveway. She remembered that Toni had a small sedan but couldn't recall the make or model. Perhaps Toni was out for the evening.

Candice walked past the Range Rover and toward the front porch of the house.

When Toni Brennen opened the front door, Candice thought she'd detected a flicker of shock in the woman's face. Toni's eyes blinked rapidly, and she glanced over her shoulder back into the house before returning her gaze to Candice. The woman didn't say anything, just stood holding the door half open.

"I'd like to talk to Alex, if he is home," Candice said.

Toni remained momentarily frozen; her mouth opened and closed without speaking. Then she said, "He's indisposed. Perhaps you can come back later?" Dark shadows lingered below her blood-shot eyes. Her hair was pulled back, frazzled, and lifeless.

"I'd prefer to speak to him now." Candice inched forward; a subtle push to get past the gate keeper. She didn't want to walk away without talking to Alex and getting some answers. Samantha deserved as much. "It's important."

The woman's shoulders tightened, and the corner of her mouth twitched. After a brief hesitation, Toni opened the door and gestured for Candice to enter.

The door closed behind them with a low thud, which Candice found irrationally loud when compared to the hush that hung over the house.

Toni led her into the living room, which was shrouded in shadows because of the drawn curtains. A fire crackled in the fireplace and the room was hot and stifling. The moment she entered the room, Candice felt drops of perspiration form on the back of her neck. She slipped her windbreaker off and laid it over the top of the sofa.

"Can I get you something to drink?" Toni asked as she crossed the room to the sidebar, which held an assortment of bottles and tumblers. An ice cube clinked against glass as Toni dropped one in a tumbler.

Candice didn't respond right away. Something was different about Toni. Her clothes were rumpled and dirty. Slight streaks of grime covered the front of her gray slacks. In past encounters, Toni had been quiet, shy, subservient, but always proper. Now she seemed disheveled, and yet, there was a confidence just below the surface that Candice hadn't seen before.

Toni reiterated her question. "What would you like?"

"Nothing for me."

"Suit yourself." Toni turned, raised her glass ever so slightly in a faux toast, and then swallowed the bourbon in one gulp. A grimace quickly followed, as if the flavor was distasteful to her. "What do you want with Alex?" The tone was stark, almost condescending.

Candice eyed Toni with suspicion. Did she know about the blackmail? Was Toni in on the scheme? "I have a few questions for him. His insight into religious practices might help the police solve the murders."

Toni swirled the ice cube around in the glass. It clicked over and over like a loud clock, counting off the seconds with rhythmic repetition. Toni's glare didn't waver. Her dark eyes seemed to consider Candice like a malignant carcinoma on her skin.

"The police sent you here?"

"Oh no, I—"

"He's indisposed," Toni interrupted.

"You mentioned that. Perhaps you could tell him I'm here." Candice folded her arms and returned the stare, trying to be as intimidating as possible. But she couldn't match the intensity of Toni's gaze. A faint memory from her last visit to the house inched to the surface. The smell of fresh baking had been in the air. A chill raised the hair on her neck. She wondered if her next words would be her last. "Look, why don't you tell him I'd like to ask him about his involvement with Samantha Blackwell?"

If she had expected some kind of reaction, Candice was sorely disappointed. Toni remained still; her eyes never wavered from Candice. If anything, it seemed as if those eyes grew darker, as if fueled by some underlying malevolence. The force of their individual wills collided in the space between them. Although she knew it was probably imagined, Candice felt her chest tighten as if invisible hands were squeezing her lungs.

They continued to stare at each other; eyes locked, mouths firm and resolute.

Then, to Candice's surprise, her opponent flinched.

Toni turned back to the bottles and refilled her glass with more bourbon. "Fine. You want to see Alex. You can see Alex." Toni threw her head back as she downed the freshly poured liquor, again in one gulp. Then, with sudden ferocity, Toni spun back around, the half-emptied bourbon bottle in her hand. She heaved the bottle across the room. Candice threw up her left arm up to protect her face but misjudged the trajectory of the bottle. The glass caught her in the right collar bone; the impact came with a crack and a knifelike pain. Bourbon soaked her blouse and the bottle shattered when it hit the floor. She stumbled backward, collided with the end table, and toppled a lamp.

Toni lunged toward her. A wine bottle was in her hand. Candice tried to backtrack, but her foot tangled in the cord of the lamp. She fell toward the floor, screaming as the corner of the end table dragged across her back. There was a swish of air as the bottle came within an inch of her head. Candice clamored to her feet, stumbled forward, and, by sheer instinct, threw out her right hand to brace herself. She remembered her injured collarbone the moment her hand touched the floor. Pain raked over her shoulder, and she screamed again.

The floor rushed at her. She rolled onto her back. Tears stung her eyes and streaked down her cheeks. A blur raced toward her. She kicked out in blind fear. Her foot hit something soft. A yelp of pain followed immediately after. Keeping her right arm close to her chest, Candice scrambled to her feet again. Her eyes were still blurry with tears and pain. The front door. She had to get to the front door. Once outside she could run unimpeded. Just had to reach the front door.

Candice rushed blindly toward the foyer. Her left shoulder clipped the corner of the archway and sent her stumbling into the hardwood of the front door. Her hand groped along the door to find the doorknob. Her head was suddenly jerked back as Toni grabbed a handful of hair. Candice yelped in pain. With a fierce push, Toni shoved Candice's face forward into the door.

The impact left Candice momentarily dazed. She flailed her arms and managed to reach behind and grasp Toni's wrist. Candice dug her fingernails into the flesh. Toni screamed and released her hold. Candice again cast about for the doorknob. Then a sudden pain shattered her conscious mind, and all went dark.

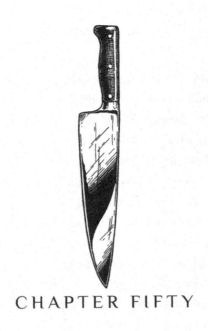

CHAPTER FIFTY

B rian stood in the hallway studying the door to Samantha Blackwell's suite of offices. Yellow crime scene tape was still stretched across the door, like a feeble barrier designed to stop nothing. He pondered the wisdom of the action he was about to undertake. Mick would be furious if he found out, but he'd forgive Brian . . . eventually. Chief Jenkins, on the other hand, would probably have Brian arrested.

It wouldn't be the first time he'd been cuffed and hauled off to jail. Once, years ago, Brian had been in the middle of an interview with a South American dictator when a rebellion broke out. He'd been rounded up by the rebels along with the dictator and many of his staff and thrown in prison. The living conditions had not been ideal, and the food atrocious. But the rebels treated him far better than they had the dictator. Three days later, the military put down the coup, and Brian was released. He figured a few days in jail in Newark would be delightful compared to that.

He glanced up and down the hall, then slipped a set of lock picks from his pocket. It was early evening, but he wasn't sure how many offices in the building would still be occupied. He'd have to work quickly if he hoped not to be discovered. Brian slid the picks into the lock and manipulated the locking mechanism, then tried the door handle. Nothing. *Damn.* As he fiddled with the lock again, Brian wondered when he'd last had to pick a lock. Three, maybe four years ago? He tried the handle again. Still nothing. He gave a quick look up the hall toward the elevator, then returned his gaze to the task before him. If this kept up much longer, someone was bound to catch him. He bit his bottom lip and leaned closer to the door.

There was a faint click from the lock as Brian pushed, pulled, and tilted the lock picks. The sounds were barely audible, yet Brian thought they were as loud as the crack of a pistol shot. *Someone must hear that.* The third time he tried the door handle, it turned, and the door swung open. With one final glimpse over his shoulder, Brian slipped beneath the crime scene tape and into the office beyond. With the door closed behind him, Brian waited for his eyes to adjust to the dimly lit waiting room. There were no windows in this part of the office suite to provide natural light. He moved quietly through the room and down the interior hall to Samantha Blackwell's office.

The door stood open, and the office looked much like it had the day before. The blood still stained the walls and carpet. A faint silvery powder covered the doorknob, the edges on the desk, the base of the desk lamp, and just about any surface where a fingerprint might be found. The laptop computer that had been on the desk was gone, probably being scoured at this very minute by county forensics.

The only other thing missing was Samantha Blackwell's beaten and battered body.

Brian moved across the hall to a small alcove where he knew Samantha's part-time admin worked. Three black metal file cabinets stood next to an L-shaped desk. The cheap wood veneer reminded him of something he could find at Walmart. The drawers of the file cabinets were unlocked, probably left that way by the police. He pulled the top drawer open and began to finger through the files.

The drawers of the first cabinet were mostly accounts payable and accounts receivable paperwork, all filed according to month and year. The second and third drawers contained client files, exactly what Brian had come to find. He paused to again consider what he was about to do. His next action would potentially violate the privacy of Samantha's clients. What would be the difference between himself and Alex Brennen? Brian frowned at the thought. He'd come here in hopes of answering the question of the sins found at the crime scenes. Alex was a blackmailer, pure and simple, out for nothing more than personal gain. Was motive enough to make the distinction between himself and Alex?

He stepped away from the file cabinet and turned to walk back into Samantha's office. He was startled to find Sarah standing behind him.

With his hand on his breastbone, he caught his breath. "Don't sneak up on me like that."

She snickered and held out her hands in a questioning manner. "Do you realize how absurd that sounds?"

He rubbed the back of his neck. "Yeah."

Sarah pointed to the file cabinets. "Aren't you going to look?"

"I can't," he said. "It's a privacy thing."

Sarah rolled her eyes. "No, it's not." She took a step closer to him. "You're not like him. You never were, and you never will be."

He reached back and placed a hand on the middle cabinet. "These people have nothing to do with this. Why should I dig into their dark secrets?"

"They are dead, like me. They won't care if you look."

***

There hadn't been much to see in Deena Cavendish's file. A few cursory notes about her first visit, but everything else had been related to personal contact details, billing, and insurance. He did discover that Deena had been coming to Samantha for therapy for over a year. A guidance counselor at Newark High School had first recommended that the girl see a therapist. The notes in the file mentioned numerous incidents—mostly related to the girl's compulsive lying—that led to the recommendation. This confirmed what he already knew about Deena. She was a liar, just as she'd been labeled by the Sin Eater. Absent from the file were any notes related to treatments or progress. Samantha must have kept her ongoing notes elsewhere. Maybe on the laptop.

He slipped the file folder back into the drawer and then pushed it closed. Moving to the drawer labeled M-R, Brian fingered the files near the back until he found Robbie Reynolds's folder. This folder was thicker than Deena's. According to the notes, Robbie had been coming to Samantha for two years. He initially came to her about an addiction issue, or a pair of addictions if Brian was interpreting the notes correctly. Gambling and sex. Like the young girl's folder, there were few notes about progress. Robbie had a reputation of being a womanizer and a frequent visitor to the casinos in Philadelphia and Atlantic City. There were no surprises in the folder. Brian slipped the file back into the drawer, realizing that, as with Deena, the Sin Eater had chosen an appropriate sin.

He was about to search for the final file he'd come to look at when his mobile phone rang. He cursed under his breath as he yanked it from his pocket to silence it. *Of all the stupid things to forget.* He placed the silenced phone back in his pocket and remained still, listening to see if any of the building's occupants had come to investigate the sudden noise. Nothing.

Brian resumed his scan of the files in the same drawer until he found a folder labeled: O'Connell, Stephanie. She'd been the victim that most puzzled him. He didn't know Stephanie all that well, which made her sin—child killer—a mystery. He opened the file and scanned through the paperwork. Stephanie had started coming for therapy nine months ago, citing depression and difficulty sleeping. He finished reading through the remainder of the initial visit notes. When he closed the folder, he understood the sin left near Stephanie's body.

Brian tried to push the drawer closed, but it jammed and wouldn't latch properly. The mechanism to secure the drawer was designed to only engage when all drawers were properly fastened. He noticed that the bottom drawer was open slightly, just enough to stop the other from closing. Brian gripped the handle and pulled. Unlike the other drawers where folders were hung from siderails, this drawer contained several files stacked on top of each other in the bottom of the drawer. The siderails on the drawer were intact. So why leave the files in a disorganized bundle? Had the police left it like this during their search? He pulled each folder out and set it aside on the floor. Once empty, it was immediately clear that this drawer wasn't as deep as the others. He ran his hand over the painted sheet metal that served as the bottom of the drawer. It flexed when he put pressure on it, far more than he would've expected. He felt along the seam where the sheet metal met the sides of the drawer.

Near the back, he found a paperclip that had been bent out of shape. One end of the thin paperclip disappeared into a tiny hole in the bottom of the drawer. A makeshift handle. Brian extracted the sheet metal drawer bottom to reveal a hidden compartment, approximately three inches deep. It contained three bundles of paper, each held together with a large black binder clip.

Brian removed the first bundle and gave it a close examination. It contained envelopes and notes that appeared to be personal in nature as opposed to business correspondence. They were all addressed to Samantha. He grabbed one at random and slipped the folded note from the already opened envelope. As he glanced over the words, his face grew warm with embarrassment. It was a handwritten love letter, and quite graphic in nature. His eyes reached the bottom of the short note and read the signature. Alex.

He pulled another from the pile and found it to be like the first. The letters weren't dated, but the envelopes all contained a postmark. He skimmed through the pile, checking the dates in the upper right corner of the envelopes. The first pile spanned about a year. He reached into the drawer to replace the letters when he noticed the pile near the back of the drawer. The address on the upper most envelope was typed, not handwritten like the others.

He slipped the folded note from the envelope. The postmark was dated three months ago. The notepaper was beige, and the crease looked precise, as if someone had gone to a great deal of trouble to make the fold as perfect as possible. The words on the note were brief and to the point.

Stay away from my husband, you goddamn whore.

CHAPTER FIFTY-ONE

Candice felt something nudge her back. Behind her eyelids, white flashes of pain emanated from deep within her skull. The nudging came again. Something round and hard pressed into the center of her spine, almost as if probing her. She struggled to open her eyes, but even that action sent pain raking through her head. The nudge in her back came again.

Through parched lips, she grunted, "Stop."

Her mind was a jumble of confused memories and random sensations that she couldn't quite piece together. Her face rested on something cold and hard. An earthen smell invaded her nostrils. She licked her lips and caught the taste of grit and dirt. Her head throbbed with pain so strong that it turned her stomach. Candice was afraid she'd throw up but fought to keep down the bile that rose in her throat. She tried to move her hands, but they were bound behind her back. Whatever was used to bind her wrists was tight and cut into her flesh.

"Are you awake?" said a voice behind her.

Candice thought she recognized the voice, but her mind was still hazy and muddled. "No," she said.

She opened her eyes to a find herself lying on a concrete floor; dust and dirt coated the chilled surface. The air in the room—if it was a room—was crisp, and she shivered. Somewhere in the distance, Candice heard a faint whoosh, like she'd hear when the gas heater in her house turned on. There was not much light to see by, and with her vision still blurred, Candice could only make out shadows and silhouettes. She rolled over onto her back and yelped at the pain in her head and right shoulder. Both were sharp, stabbing pains, and she fought against a blackout. When the agony subsided a bit, she stared at the dark sky above her. Was it sky? It was dark like night, but she could see no stars.

Candice closed her eyes tight and reopened them. Her blurred vision cleared some, and she could now see parallel lines across the darkness above her. Joists?

Was she in an attic, or maybe a basement? *Probably basement. Attics don't usually have concrete floors.*

A face interjected itself in her vision, disturbing any further study of what hung above her. As her eyes adjusted their focus, and the face became clear, she recognized the gaunt features of Toni Brennen.

Toni's eyes were wide and bloodshot; her left eyelid twitched. But she smiled, comforting and somewhat ghastly at the same time.

Her pallid complexion was speckled with tiny red dots. Strands of her hair hung from her head, like brittle pieces of straw.

"How's the head? I didn't mean to hit you so hard." Toni's left eye twitched. Her voice was soft, almost apologetic. "I got worried when I couldn't wake you earlier. You were out for a lot longer than I intended."

Candice squeezed her eyes closed as pain throbbed from the back of her head. "What happened? What did you do?"

"You've been a naughty girl." Toni swung her hand into view. Her fingers clinched tight around the handle of an aluminum baseball bat. The barrel of the bat glistened a dark red. Toni tapped Candice's chest lightly with the bat's bloody end cap. "You couldn't just leave it alone." Toni spoke like a kindergarten teacher lecturing a five-year-old. "We were doing just fine until you showed up. Then you had to bust in talking about that—" Toni seemed to search for the right word. "—that whore."

Candice turned her head from side to side, trying to survey the room. The movement caused more pain in her head and right shoulder. There was not much to see. A gray block wall was on her left. To her right, she found an eclectic collection of junk piled along the far wall. An old box spring with the cloth covering removed, a disassembled bicycle, a folding beach chair with a torn seat, and an old metal gas can, among other things. A staircase led up to a closed door. The wood of the ramshackle stairs looked gray with age.

"Where's Alex?" Candice asked.

"He's here. Do you want to see him?"

Before Candice could reply, Toni leaned forward, gripped her left forearm, and dragged her up and around until her back was against the nearby wall. Candice screamed in agony. The pain of the sudden movement tore through her head like a red-hot poker and ripped the breath from her lungs. Her vision went blurry again, and Candice could only make out a silhouette in her periphery. The wall was cold, and the pocked rough stone surface jabbed into her back.

Toni gestured to the right with the baseball bat. "There he is."

Candice heard a deep groan. She squinted to push away the cobwebs that still clouded her eyesight. As her haze cleared and the silhouette came into focus, Candice was horrified by what she saw. She now knew where the red spots on Toni's face came from.

Alex was slumped on the floor a few feet from Candice; his hands bound behind his back like her own. His trousers were torn and filthy. His shirt was in no better shape. Streaks of maroon violated the white fabric with stains that bleach would never be able to erase.

It was his face that was the most shocking, though. Alex's bottom lip was swollen and split; blood dribbled from his open mouth. There was a gap between his bottom front teeth, his left cheek looked distended, and his chin was skewed. The skin around his left eye was blackened and bulging; the swelling encasing the eyeball in a grotesque pouch of battered human skin. A contusion had ballooned on his high forehead; the blackish-purple hue stood out in contrast to the rest of his pale skin.

Candice gasped as his head turned toward her. Alex tried to speak but struggled to form words with his broken jaw. All that came out was a raspy wheeze and blood-colored spittle. Red gore ebbed from his crushed nose and covered his upper lip. She averted her gaze and tried to erase the vision from her mind, but she had no doubt that this moment would haunt her for years to come. Her head spun. *Gotta stay focused. Mustn't pass out.* There was almost a rhythm to the pounding in her skull. The pain radiated from the base of her neck through her head and behind her eyes.

"Where am I?"

Toni straightened her back and thrust out her chest, as if taking great pride in what she was about to say. "Our basement." She stretched out her arms. "You are in my domain now."

CHAPTER FIFTY-TWO

Toni's laughter drowned out all sound, including the gurgling from Alex's breathing. Candice screwed her eyes shut in hopes of fending off the pain that Toni's delirious mirth inflicted on her head. It felt as if someone had driven an ice pick into each ear. Candice swallowed back against rising vomit; the acidic regurgitation burned her throat.

The laughter stopped abruptly, and before Candice could open her eyes, she felt cold metal press against the bottom of her chin. She snapped her eyes open as the end cap of the baseball bat nudged her head upward. Toni stared down at her, eyelid twitching, jaw clenched. Candice gulped down a breath. *Is this my moment to die?* She waited for her life to flash before her eyes like in so many stories, but nothing came. Perhaps that was all just a fictional plot device that didn't happen in real life, or . . . maybe her life just wasn't interesting enough to warrant a deathbed review. Had her life been as empty as it felt right now? An unfulfilled existence plagued her, the "going through the motions" of a calling she now wasn't sure she'd ever had.

She pressed herself back against the wall to place some distance between her and the baseball bat. The half-inch difference didn't provide any additional comfort. Toni lowered the bat; the end cap rang as it hit the floor. Candice flinched at the movement, anticipating the worst. Her only hope was that it would be quick. She didn't want to linger like Alex.

"Don't worry," Toni said. "I'm not going to kill you." She tapped the bat on the concrete floor a few times. "I should kill you, especially after you mentioned that whore's name in this house." Toni stepped back a few feet and brought the bat up to rest on her shoulder. "But I need you. Someone must live to tell the tale. You get to tell the world how the brilliant Alex Brennen was beaten by a stupid woman."

The words should have brought comfort, but Candice felt nothing but terror. Was she destined to be the only survivor of some twisted murder-suicide of a deranged wife and her adulterous husband?

"Can't we talk about this?" she said. "There's got to be another way."

Toni snorted. "Another way? Like what? Remaining married to this bastard?" Toni brought the bat down onto Alex's left shin with a crack. He screamed, which was the most reaction Candice had seen out of him since she had awoken.

"Do you know . . ." Toni started to speak, her voice low and conspiratorial. ". . . he used to lock me down here in the basement as punishment when I did something wrong. He'd leave me down here for hours. No food. No water. No bathroom. No light." She gestured around the room. "Not that I'm complaining. It's the lap of luxury, as you can see."

Although she'd already studied the basement earlier, Candice couldn't help but glance around again. The second inspection was just a as gloomy as the first. There was nothing in the basement that could even remotely be considered comfort, not even a chair to sit on. She couldn't begin to imagine what it must have been like to be locked in this dismal place. The loneliness. The isolation. The humiliation. How many hours of Toni's life had been spent here in this bleak chamber?

Did each hour chip away at her already-fragile spirit until she reached a breaking point?

Candice had no idea what the woman may have been like in her early years. Perhaps Toni and Alex had been happy once. Maybe even in love. She felt a sudden moment of pity. A life with Alex had driven Toni to become a killer, her final act one of revenge against her abuser. Candice looked at Toni's victimizer, now turned victim. Alex whimpered in agony. His left foot twitched and a fresh stain of blood was forming on the left pant leg. The hit from the bat had been hard and the crack loud. *His leg must be broken, bad.*

Using the bat as a cane of sorts, Toni paced the floor. Tap, tap, tap. The hollow ring of metal on concrete proceeded each step. Tap, tap, tap. She stopped and spun around. "You can blame the police for this." Toni pointed the bat at Candice. "I gave them all the evidence they needed to convict him of the murders. The letter opener. The ring. My God, his initials were on almost every clue."

"What went wrong?" Candice asked, desperate to buy time. *For what?*

Toni waved her hand in dismissal. "He never told me his schedule. I didn't know he'd have an alibi for the first two murders." She gently tapped Alex's left foot with the bat. His whimpers turned to grunts of pain.

He tried to speak again through his battered mouth, but the words were slurred and unintelligible.

"I had to resort to this," Toni said, pointing to her husband. "You have no idea what I had to do—how I had to debase myself— just to get the police to arrest him." Toni turned her back on Candice and hung her shoulders low as if she were suddenly ashamed. "Did you know that Robbie Reynolds was a sex addict? That was the only way I could get close enough to him. He wouldn't even let me in the house until I offered to give him a blow job. He was more than willing to drop his pants for that, even if I wasn't as pretty as the hookers he picked up at the casinos. Then, when he was too preoccupied, I drove the letter opener up into his heart." Toni glanced over her shoulder at Candice. "Sorry. I don't mean to offend your religious sensibilities with my filthy sex talk."

Candice felt a twinge of anger. "Robbie was my friend."

"You should choose your friends more wisely."

"And the girl? Why did she have to die?" Candice asked. "She had her whole life ahead of her."

Toni turned back to face her. "Deena? She was such a little liar. She tried to get me kicked out of the church a few years back by telling everyone I had a lesbian lover. Imagine that. Me, a lesbian? Alex would've locked me down here indefinitely. Imagine the blow to his ego if it got out that his wife had turned to a woman for satisfaction because he wasn't man enough. It was lucky that Father

Blake saw through Deena's lies. She made a public apology, but I could never forgive her."

"You took that young girl's life just to get back at her for what she did?"

"No, silly. This was always about Alex. My revenge for the years of infidelity. The years of being locked in this basement. The years of him calling me stupid. Killing Deena was just a bonus. Killing two birds with one stone, so to speak."

The ache in Candice's head worsened. Her vision blurred, and Toni split into two. The diplopia brought on a fresh wave of nausea. Despite her best efforts, she could no longer hold back the bile that rose in her throat. She slumped to the left as best she could and retched on the concrete floor. Her heaving sent a new rash of stabbing pains through her head. Candice struggled to control the convulsions, to stop the violent motion from inflicting further torment.

Once the nausea subsided, she gulped down a lungful of air. The sour odor of her own vomit made her cringe, but the coolness of the fetid oxygen soothed her throat. Her chin was moist, and she wished her hands were free to wipe away whatever remnant remained. Candice felt drained, her strength gone and her head spinning. She tried to straighten herself up but could only achieve a half-slouched position against the wall.

"O'Connell. What about her?" It hurt to speak. Her throat was raw and still burned from the acidic stomach bile that had assailed it moments before.

Before Toni could answer, a doorbell rang somewhere in the distance. Toni glared up at the stairs, pursing her lips in irritation. "Who could that be?"

For the first time since awakening, Candice felt a glimmer of hope. Could she shout loud enough to be heard by someone at the front door? What would Toni do if she tried to raise the alarm? She had no doubt that Toni would kill again. She'd already killed three, and possibly a fourth if Samantha didn't survive. What would one more body mean to Toni? Nothing. Candice feared she had little chance to get out of this alive if she didn't try.

The doorbell rang again. Toni walked toward the stairs, then stopped. She seemed to ponder something. Her head cocked to one side, and then twisted back toward Candice. She leaned the baseball bat against the stair rail and moved across the room to an old workbench. Toni rifled through the jumble of small metallic objects and tools until she found what she was looking for. Then, in a few quick steps, she was kneeling before Candice.

Toni held up a swath of cloth, which once may have been white, but was now gray with grime. "Can't have you calling for help." She shoved the rag into Candice's mouth and tied the gag around the back of her head. "Be right back."

CHAPTER FIFTY-THREE

It took several minutes, as well as several rings on the doorbell, for Brian to get someone to answer at Alex Brennen's house. Candice's voicemail had raised alarm bells. After all, the letters he'd found in Samantha's office suggested she was walking straight into danger by coming here.

When the door did open, it was Toni Brennen who greeted him. He kept his expression neutral as to not convey his surprise at her appearance. Her clothes were wrinkled and grimy as if she'd been kneeling in dirt. Although her hair was pulled back, some strands had come free from their bounds and looked frazzled. The once-timid eyes were now wild and held his in an intense gaze.

"Sorry to disturb you," Brian said. "I was hoping to speak to Alex. Is he home?"

Toni didn't respond at first. Her jaw clenched and unclenched while she seemed to contemplate an answer to his question. When the answer did come, it was short and to the point. "No."

He studied her face, connecting the tiny specks of red on her skin with his eyes. Then his gaze moved past her and into the house. Something on the sofa caught his eye. "Bummer," he said. "My friend Candice said she was coming here to speak with him. I'd hoped to catch them both at the same time."

Toni's eyes narrowed a fraction, but otherwise her face betrayed nothing. Brian brought his gaze back to her face and the flecks of red on her cheek and forehead. The spots were small enough, that in the right light, they might not even be noticed. But the overhead light in the foyer blazed a bright white that brought everything into sharp focus.

"They're not here," Toni said. "Maybe she was meeting him at his office. Perhaps you should try there."

With that, she closed the door.

He stepped from the porch and walked up the street to give the impression that he was leaving. But once in the shadow of an old oak, he paused to make a phone call. It was time to bring in the calvary. He called Mick Flanagan.

Even as he communicated his suspicions to Mick, Brian knew his evidence was flimsy. It would be hard to justify a police raid on a home with what little he had. It "could've been blood" on Toni's face. It "might have been" Candice's coat he saw in the living room. Mick was hesitant to ask for a warrant without something more concrete, but the detective agreed to meet up with Brian and confer about the situation on the scene. "I'll be there as soon as I can. Don't do anything until I arrive," Mick said just before ending the call.

Brian stood on the sidewalk about half a block from Alex Brennen's home. He watched the Victorian-style house from a distance, wondering if he had the luxury of waiting. He couldn't hope for Mick to arrive for—at the least—twenty minutes. If that had been blood on Toni's face, twenty minutes could be too late. There was no doubt in his mind that he had seen Candice's coat sprawled across the back of the living room sofa. There could only be one reason why Toni would lie about Candice.

He hurried back to the house and took the porch steps two at a time. But when he reached the door, he froze for a moment. What was he going to do? Ring the doorbell again? Force his way past Toni when she answered? *Strategy. Think strategy.*

He peered into house through the sidelight beside the door. A pale blue curtain covered most of the narrow window, blocking much of his view. But Brian found a slim gap between the fabric and the window frame. Most of the foyer was visible, as well as the hall leading to the back of the house, but not much else. There was no one in view. He tried the door handle, but it was locked. Trying to pick the lock was out of the question. He'd never had much luck with Yale locks.

He stepped off the porch and glanced to the right and left. A row of tall hedges lined the right side of the yard, a natural fence to separate the property from the neighbor's. It might provide him some cover from preying eyes. Brian darted around the side of the house. The first window he came to was too high. He had to stand on his toes just to reach the sill. Near the back corner of the house, however, he found two large windows side by side. He peered through the glass. The room within was Alex's library. But it had changed in the last twenty-four hours. Books had been pulled from the shelves and were sprawled across the floor. The furniture had been tossed, some of the fabric torn. The mess within the ransacked room seemed to form a ring around the desk, which was still where it had been the day before. Centered on the desk was a round loaf of dark bread with a knife driven through the top.

The casement windows looked old, perhaps the originals from when the house was built. He ran his hand along the tarnished metal of the window sash. Maybe if he could get some leverage . . .

Brian studied the latch on each window through the glass. Both were secure. He could try to pop one of the latches, but that would take time. *Leave this as a last resort*, he decided, and rounded the corner to the rear of the house.

He came to a screened-in porch with a sloping roof. A half-wall rose to waist height on all three sides and was topped with a flimsy screen up to the roof line. The door into the house from the porch was an old French door. The wood sash was painted white, and the beveled glass panels were frosted. But what caught Brian's eye was the tarnished brass knob and lock. Like the door, it looked as old as the house.

Brian rushed to the outside door that led onto the porch, but found it locked. He gave it a hard tug. The white metal door held firm. He glanced into the porch again. To his surprise, Sarah was seated on a teak bench on the other side of the screen.

"You're about to cross that line again," she said.

He paced in front of the screen window. "I know."

"Is it worth it?"

He halted by the window and stared at her. When she was alive, Sarah had always been his North Star. A rational voice in an otherwise chaotic world. Her quiet composure had been one of the reasons he loved her so much. Her words of wisdom had always seemed well beyond her years. She was his compass, his truth, and his light in the darkness.

He gazed into her eyes. "Yes."

"Then do it."

With that, Brian thrust his fist through the screen.

CHAPTER FIFTY-FOUR

Moments later, Brian stood in the doorway of a small laundry room just off the porch. The door into the house had given way easily to his shoulder, and now he paused to allow his eyes to adjust to the dim light. A washer and dryer came into focus to his right, along with a utility sink. A basket full of clothes sat on the slate gray floor in front of the washer. Across the room, a three-panel door—dingy, white, and scuffed—stood open. Beyond that, a long hallway extended into the house, ending at the front door. The light in the foyer blazed bright and cast the section of hallway closest to Brian in shadows. He stepped forward cautiously, careful to ensure that his footfalls made only the slightest sound upon the hardwood floor. He glanced into an opening on his right. The lights were on in the kitchen, but there was no one around. The kitchen counters were spotless; nothing looked out of place. He scanned around the room and noticed that the butcher block was missing one knife.

Brian crept forward until he reached an open door midway up the hall on his left. The voices were louder and seemed to be coming from beyond the open door. He peered around the doorframe to find a set of wooden stairs leading down. The basement. The light from the hall only cast enough illumination for him to make out the first few steps. But he could hear the voices clearly.

". . . as stupid as you thought," said a woman's voice. There was a twinge of sadistic rage in the words.

There was a loud thud followed by a deep grunt of pain. A man's voice grumbled something unintelligible.

"See? Even now, he refuses to admit that I outsmarted him," the woman said again.

Brian recognized Toni Brennen's voice. But it was different. Angry, full of venom.

"Do you know how long I've waited for this moment?" she said. Another thud, another groan.

"Stop it! Hasn't he suffered enough?"

Brian's eyes went wide. That voice, he knew. Candice Miller. She was down there, but in what shape? Her voice sounded weak, and her words slurred a bit. He'd planned to listen from his concealed position until he had a better handle on the situation, but now he needed to act. Brian moved through the door onto the first step.

There was another thud, but this time the grunt that followed was louder and followed by a desperate moan. Brian took the next step with caution and now had a full view of the basement.

Alex—battered and bleeding—was resting against the far wall. Toni loomed over him with a baseball bat, her feet straddling his legs and a murderous gaze locked on his face. One other detail was caught up in Brian's quick assessment: Candice Miller was also propped up against the wall, hands behind her back.

Toni drew the bat back and thrust it forward into Alex's chest, like she was using it as a battering ram to break through his rib-cage. Alex's head bobbed with the impact and yet another agonized groan filled the basement. A spray of red mist expelled from his mouth.

"Stop! Please have mercy," Candice pleaded. "All these deaths. All these innocent people. You killed them just to get revenge on him? You're no better than he is."

Without moving, Toni turned a fiery gaze at Candice. "Innocent? They were all sinners. Isn't that what a sin eater does? Rid the world of sin? Alex obsessed over the concept for decades. I had to listen to his twaddle constantly but was never allowed to speak about what I loved." She paused; her voice became soft for just a moment. "Like mathematics. I was never allowed to talk about my passion, about what I left behind. About what he made me leave behind." The rage returned to her voice. "So, I used his obsession against him."

"But Stephanie O'Connell?" Candice asked. "Why did you choose her? You've left her child motherless. What sin could she have committed to make that acceptable?"

Brian took two more steps downward; this time ensuring that his footsteps were heard. "She had an abortion when she was a teenager. She'd struggled with the guilt ever since. She never told her husband. The guilt got too overwhelming after their first child was born." He turned his gaze toward Toni. "That's why you labeled her a child killer. Was it jealousy that made you choose her? Because you didn't have kids? Couldn't have kids?"

Toni didn't seem surprised to see him. Her venomous eyes only glanced at him for a second before returning to Alex. "We tried, but I couldn't . . . It made me angry that she threw away her child's life when I couldn't even have one."

"How long have you known that Alex was blackmailing people?" Brian asked.

"About a year. I found his recordings one afternoon when I was cleaning his study. He'd left his desk drawer unlocked, which was something he'd never done before."

Brian took another step down. The basement floor was only five steps away now. "And Alex's affair with Samantha Blackwell?"

"About the same time. I heard one of their . . . heard them on one of the recordings." Toni's voice cracked with emotion. "Alex must have forgotten to turn off the recorder."

"You started listening to them?"

Toni gave a slight nod. "I figured out how to open his desk drawer without a key. You've no idea how fucked up people are in this godforsaken city. The things I could tell you . . ."

His next step down was slow and cautious. Brian didn't want to give Toni a reason to be on her guard. "I get it. You were mistreated, abused. I can't imagine what it's been like. But this isn't the way."

Toni bit her lower lip as she seemed to consider his words. Her right arm—the one that held the baseball bat—went limp and the bat's end cap touched the floor. "You're right," she said. "You have no idea what it was like. How humiliating it was to sit down here for hours simply because I burned his toast." She slouched forward and stared down at Alex. "Or because I didn't use enough starch when I ironed his shirts. Do you know what it's like to be told that you're stupid and useless?" A tear streaked down her cheek. "I loved him once. But he was only after my father's money. When he couldn't get that, I became nothing to him. All the years I've wasted. All because of him. I thought I could start over. Get him sent to prison. Leave town and go somewhere to start anew. But . . ." She straightened her back and stood tall. The forlorn look vanished from her face. A maniacal smile formed on her lips.

"You know, I used to play softball in college," Toni said. "Even held the season record for homers one year." Her fingers tighten their grip on the bat. "I wonder if I've still got it."

Toni drew the bat back over her shoulder and shifted her feet into a batting stance. Brian leapt down the remaining three steps and lunged toward her. He stretched his arms forward to tackle her. Toni caught sight of his approach and tried to adjust to counter the attack. As she twisted around, the metal club spun in a wild arc. Brian's shoulder crashed into her chest just as she brought it down to block him. The baseball bat clipped him in the thigh as they tumbled across the concrete floor. He skidded through the dust and grime, slamming into the wall. Brian yelped in pain and lost his grip on Toni. She tumbled away from him in the impact. As he rolled over and tried to stand, he heard the clang of metal against concrete.

When he looked up, Toni hovered over him, a carving knife gripped in her fingers. He guessed it'd be a perfect fit for the empty slot on the knife block he'd seen earlier in the kitchen. He swung a quick glance around, hoping to find a weapon. The baseball bat was on the floor, out of his reach.

"What's one more?" she said.

"Drop the knife!"

The order came from the stairs. Brian turned to find Mick crouched on the steps. The detective's gun was drawn and aimed at Toni. She remained motionless for several seconds. Brian's gaze locked with hers. Toni's eyes were vacant, as if the effort to kill her husband had broken the last vestige of humanity remaining within her. There was nothing left. Just dark emptiness in her stare.

Her arm began to move. Slow and steady like an automaton. Her hand raised into the air; the knife held high in a white knuckled grip.

Mick barked his command again. "Drop the knife!"

Brian stared up at the point of the stainless-steel blade. Even in the dim light, it flared with brilliance. The edge caught what little illumination was available and amplified it with a glint that seemed impossible. Her face gave nothing away. No intention, no emotion. What was she going to do? Kill him in cold blood?

Her arm reached full extension, then twitched before beginning a downward sweep. The gunshot reverberated off the walls.

CHAPTER FIFTY-FIVE

"She's still alive," Mick said, his fingers on Toni's neck to check for a pulse. "Are you okay?"

Brian struggled to rise to his feet. Pain radiated across his thigh and down his leg, but he didn't think anything was broken. "Yeah, you cut that a bit close."

Two uniformed police officers appeared at the top of the basement stairs, guns drawn.

"Get an ambulance over here. Pierson, you stay upstairs and secure the house. Thompson, grab the first aid kit out of your car," Mick said.

Pierson nodded, and both officers rushed back up the steps and disappeared.

"How did you know I was in the house?" Brian asked.

"When I couldn't find you on the street, I figured you decided not to wait for me."

Mick rolled Toni onto her back. She groaned. Brian noticed the growing blood stain on her shoulder. He turned his attention to the other two occupants in the room. First, Brian scrambled over to check on Alex. His battered face was a horror to look at. Any skin that wasn't bruised and bloodied was ashen gray. Brian feared what he would find when he checked for a pulse.

His fear came true: There was none. He lowered his head and said a brief prayer to a god he didn't know and didn't understand. "He's dead," Brian said.

He then moved over to Candice. Her head was turned, her eyes pinched closed. Tears streamed down her cheeks. She flinched when Brian touched her shoulder. When she opened her eyes and met his gaze, the sense of relief he expected to see wasn't there, just terror.

He saw it immediately. The pupils that didn't match. One was larger than the other. Other than basic first aid, he'd never taken medical training, but knew that unmatched pupils were a sign of something bad, very bad. "You'll be okay," he reassured her. "Let's get you out of here."

"My head's killing me," she said.

Brian helped Candice to her feet. Her legs faltered at first, but he held onto her until she was able to rise. She was unsteady, so he leaned her against the wall while he untied the rope that bound her hands. "You think you can walk?"

Candice rubbed her raw wrists. "To get out of here? I'd crawl."

Thompson raced back down the stairs, first aid kit in hand. Brian turned to Mick, "I'm taking her upstairs. Get her some fresh air."

Mick tore open the first aid kit and yanked out a large pressure bandage. "Fine, but don't go anywhere. I've got a lot of questions that need answering."

Brian wrapped his arm around Candice's waist so she could lean on him. She seemed weak; her footing unsure. They made slow progress across the basement toward the stairs.

"What were you thinking? Coming here by yourself," Brian said.

"I thought I had it all figured out. It couldn't have been anyone else but Alex," Candice said, her words slurred. "I didn't realize it was her until it was too late. She bakes. The first time I was here, the house smelled like fresh baked bread. She told me she'd just finished baking." Candice started to cry. "I didn't pick up on it. Not until I was here. How could I have been so dumb?"

They reached the stairs, and Brian guided her up the first few. "Don't think about it. Let's just get you to the hospital. In a couple weeks, you'll be back on your podium, giving the best sermon of your life."

"No," she said. "No more preaching for me. I've decided to leave the church. To leave ministry."

Brian paused halfway up the steps. It felt as if she was leaning most of her weight on him, like he was the only thing keeping her from falling. He looked at her. "Why?"

Her reply came slow, the words a little slurred, a little emotional. "I don't believe. After all that's happened, I have no faith left. Not in God. Not in humanity."

Brian understood better than she might have realized. His faith—tenuous as it was—had almost been decimated by Sarah's death. He'd gone through the same questioning, the same doubt that Candice was going through now. But unlike her, his career was not based on—or even required—faith in an unseen deity. He appreciated the dilemma she faced.

How could a minister lead a congregation on a journey of faith without having any? The hypocrisy would be too much for any self-respecting minister to bear.

They reached the top of the stairs and Brian helped her out into the bright lights of the hallway. Candice screwed her eyes closed against the glare. After a moment, she opened them again, tried to take a step forward, and stumbled. Brian was at her side and caught ahold of her. She clung to his shoulder until she regained her balance.

"Come on, let's get you outside," Brian said as he began to lead her toward the front door.

Candice leaned more of her weight on him. Her feet shuffled along the hardwood floor. "You are a nice guy." She poked his chest with her finger to emphasize each word. "You need to find someone. Someone who will take care of you."

He rolled his eyes. Apart from the slurred words, it sounded like the same speech that Sarah often made during his lonelier periods. "Just a little further. We'll get you to the hospital and get you fixed right up."

"Seriously, you need someone. You deserve someone."

Brian grit his teeth. Was delirium setting in? Was she succumbing to her injuries?

Ahead of them, the front door was open, and a cool evening breeze blew into the foyer. The darkness outside was lit by flashing red and blue lights from the police cars and a newly arrived ambulance. "We're almost there," he said.

"You came for me. Like my knight in shining armor," Candice mumbled.

Brian drew in a deep breath. Yep, she was definitely becoming delirious. "I got your voicemail and thought you might be in danger."

"Knight in shiny armor. I'm so glad I met—" Her words abruptly stopped, and Candice's body went limp. He clung to her and guided her gently to the floor.

"Help! I need help in here!" he shouted.

WEEK
3

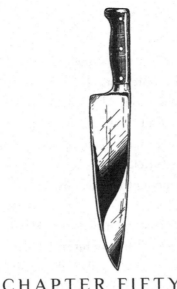

CHAPTER FIFTY-SIX

Monday

B rian pushed open the church door and stepped out into the
Monday morning sun. He stood at the top of the stairs and
surveyed the traffic moving along Main Street. He was surprised
by how empty the church had been for Alex's funeral. A few people from the university were present, but it seemed that most had
decided to stay away. News of what happened had spread fast, and
Brian wondered if many were trying to distance themselves from
the carnage.

Despite the emptiness of the church, he'd felt claustrophobic
and needed some fresh air. He hated funerals. They reminded him
of how frail human life could be. It wasn't just about the fact that

everyone dies; it was the fact that some can die before their time. That fact bothered him more than any other. His wife was one whose time had come too soon. All the plans they'd made, all the things they still had to do, and all the love they had yet to share had been wiped away in one instant. *Gone before her time.* Sarah's had been the last funeral he'd attended.

He'd considered skipping this one, but . . . he felt he was obligated to be there.

It had been a week since the incident in Alex Brennen's basement. Brian's leg—still sore from the hit he'd taken from the baseball bat—was improving, but he still walked with a slight limp. There'd been no broken bones, just a soft-tissue injury that the doctor said would heal. The bruise just above Brian's knee looked a lot worse than it actually was. At least that's what he told anyone who asked.

He preferred not to mention how much ibuprofen he required to fall asleep, or the difficulty he still had navigating the stairs of his apartment. He heard the door open behind him but didn't turn to see who had come out of the church. Moments later, Mick was standing next to him.

"You okay?" Mick asked.

Brian nodded. "Yeah. Just needed some fresh air."

"Not sure I've ever seen a crowd that small for a funeral." Mick rubbed his chin with his forefinger and thumb. "I read your story in Thursday's *Observer*. Nice recap of the case. I couldn't help but notice you didn't mention the recordings of Samantha Blackwell's therapy sessions."

"Didn't see the need. She'll have her hands full enough—once she's back on her feet—getting her practice going again. I didn't want to make matters worse for her."

"Toni's signed confession to the murders is all I needed," Mick said. "I turned the case over to the county prosecutor yesterday. I've been told to drop the blackmail investigation as well. Something about wiretapping laws and nonconsensual recordings." Mick leaned toward Brian. He lowered his voice to almost a whisper. "My guess is there were a few influential people caught up in Alex's scheme, and the city doesn't want to embarrass them with an investigation."

Brian snickered. "You're probably right." He fell silent for a moment as he contemplated the reason this had all happened in the first place. "I can't help but think this could have all been avoided if someone had spoken up about the abuse. I barely knew Alex and Toni, but I saw the signs when I first met them a few weeks ago."

"Robbie was already dead. It was too late." Mick placed his hand on Brian's shoulder. "Don't worry yourself about it. You didn't know." Mick thumbed at the church doors. "You coming back in?"

"Yeah. In a minute."

Mick turned away to re-enter the church. Then turned back. "By the way, Chief Jenkins said he won't charge you with breaking and entering . . . this time." Mick smiled. There was a heavy thud as the door closed behind him.

Candice was asleep when Brian entered her hospital room. Most of the color had returned to her face since the last time he'd seen her. It was a huge improvement from when he'd sat at her bedside through that first night. The head injury she'd received had been serious. An epidural hematoma, that's what the doctor had called it.

"Another hour and she'd have been dead," Dr. Rucier had said after emergency surgery relieved the pressure on Candice's brain. "She's still got a long recovery, but at least she's alive."

Brian walked to the bed and took hold of her hand. An IV tube snaked around her arm and disappeared under the sheets, only to reappear at the head of the bed where it attached to the bottom of an IV bag hanging on a bedside pole. Wires of varying colors wound out from under the sheets as well, hooked to the heart monitor hanging from the wall. A white bandage was wrapped around her skull, covering the entire top of her head. She still looked frail and fragile. She opened her eyes at his touch and gave him a weak smile.

"You didn't happen to bring a pizza with you," she said, her voice hoarse.

"Sorry. I'm not sure I could sneak that in here without someone catching me."

"Bummer. I've been craving pizza all day. Have you talked to Andrew? He hasn't come to visit. I was wondering if he was okay."

Brian had anticipated the question but was still unsure how to answer. Although George Hardy was light on the details, he'd explained that Andrew had been admitted into a mental health facility for treatment. He wouldn't say where. Knowing that the Catholic Church frowned heavily on suicide, Andrew's professional future was very uncertain. Candice had her own recovery to worry about, and Brian didn't want to add to her stress.

"He's taken a sabbatical," he said. "How are you doing?"

"I'm in the hospital with a new hole in my head. How do you think I'm doing?"

Brian snorted at her joke. "At least you still have your sense of humor."

Her smile faded, and she closed her eyes. "That's about all I have."

He gave her hand a gentle squeeze. "I wouldn't say that."

"Oh yeah? They shaved my head." She gently touched the bandage covering her scalp. "Do you have any idea how long it will take my hair to grow back?"

Brian laughed, struggling to imagine what Candice would look like bald. "Wear it like a badge of honor." He fell silent as another question surfaced in his mind. The real reason he'd come to visit. "Do you remember what you said to me as I helped you out of the basement?"

She squinted and bit her lip as if trying to recall the memory. "It's a bit fuzzy."

"Are you still planning to leave the church?"

Her eyes became distant as she pondered her answer. "I'm not sure I have much choice. I can't exactly be a minister of the faith without faith."

He released her hand and folded his arms. "That's where I think you're wrong. You've had a small setback, that's all. You came up against something that made you doubt yourself. But don't let it push you away." He looked across the room and saw Sarah standing by the window. He felt a warmth rise from his heart when she smiled at him. He fought back a tear. "I've found that the greatest part of life's journey is rediscovering the things that you've lost. This week, I discovered how much I miss investigative journalism. As tragic as this has all been, I . . ." He was suddenly at a loss for words. How could Brian explain the euphoria he felt as the pieces of the puzzle fell together? Or the thrill he had with every new revelation? He found no way to convey the excitement that came with his pursuit of the truth behind each death, each a mystery begging to be solved. "Give it another chance. You might surprise yourself."

CHAPTER FIFTY-SEVEN

Wednesday

B rian shifted on the black leather sofa, trying to ease his discomfort. The office in which he sat was dark and felt un-
inviting. The woodwork of built-in bookshelves to his right was
a stained ebony. The large desk across from him was stained to
match. The shades for the windows behind the desk were drawn,
blocking the Wednesday late afternoon sunlight. The wall across
from the bookshelves was bare except for several framed certificates
and diplomas. The lack of color and personal items made the office
feel very clinical.

Seated beside him, Sarah crossed her legs and rested her clasped
hands in her lap. She looked calm and contented even though

Brian was beginning a journey that might end in their parting. That thought made him queasy. Was this such a good idea? He failed to see how his life could move on without her. Sarah was so ingrained in his mind that she was a part of him, a part of who he was. The mere idea of letting her go felt to him like having a lobotomy.

Sarah reached over and touched his hand. "It'll be okay."

Brian couldn't look at her. "I'm afraid to lose you."

"I'll always be a part of you." Her voice was a sweet sound to his ears.

"This won't be easy," he said.

"You can do this. It's time to begin the process of moving on."

"I know." He turned to look at her. "I love you."

The door to the office opened, and a tall, thin man in black slacks, a white shirt, and a bright colored tie hurriedly strode in. He was clean-shaven, and his dark hair was slicked back. He paused by the sofa and held out his hand. "Sorry to keep you waiting. I'm Garrett Verney."

"Brian Wilder."

Garrett rounded the desk and took a seat in the black leather office chair. "I'm familiar with your work. But I'm puzzled about why you came to West Chester for a consultation. I could recommend several good therapists in the Newark area. It would save you the hour-long drive."

"It's mainly a desire for privacy. Newark is a small city. Word gets around easily."

"I understand," Garrett said.

"You were recommended by a friend, Rebecca Stanchion."

Garrett's face lit up at the mention of the name. "Oh, yes. Rebecca lives two blocks over. She's consulted me numerous times for her books. She's very thorough on her research. Always wants every detail to be correct. But I'm sure you didn't come here to talk about her. What can I do for you?"

Brian looked to his right and found Sarah still sitting there. She nodded as if to say, "Go ahead." He leaned forward, clasped his hands, and let them hang between his knees. He looked up at the therapist and said, "This is about my wife. My dead wife."

That night, Brian stood before the windows of his second-floor apartment and gazed down on Newark's darkened Main Street. Most of the storefronts and restaurants had closed hours ago. An occasional group of college students wandered along the sidewalk, heading toward the university campus. He hadn't been able to sleep. His afternoon meeting with Garrett Verney had gone well. That first hour had merely been an introduction. But Brian had agreed to meet with Garrett on weekly basis. His first step toward letting Sarah go.

He thought about everything that had occurred over the past two weeks, how the archaic practice of sin eating had been per-verted into a maniacal symbol of vengeance. He felt pity for Toni because she saw her only escape to be the murder of innocent lives, and her husband as well. Despite everything that Alex had done, Brian didn't believe that he deserved to die. But there was one last loose thread that still nagged at the back of his mind.

Agatha Bowman.

"What are you going to do about her?" said a voice to his left. "You're thinking of letting her go, aren't you?"

He turned to find Sarah standing beside him. She was once again wearing the red silk dragon kimono he'd bought her in Japan.

"There's no point in turning her over to the police now," he said. "The only evidence would be a confession that could easily be chalked up to senility. She's lived with the guilt for decades. Why make her suffer further during the last days of her life?"

Sarah turned to glare at him. "When did you become a judge and jury? You don't have the right to decide who deserves punishment and who doesn't."

"But—"

Sarah snapped at him. "No! The Pyeong family deserves closure. Agatha is a sweet lady who's dedicated her life to serving others. But that doesn't excuse a brutal murder. It's a hate crime, pure and simple. There is nothing you can say to justify not telling the police what you know."

He spun toward her to make his rebuttal, but she was gone. Her last words still echoed through the darkened apartment, gnawing at the back of his mind.

Brian sighed and reached for the phone. His call was answered on the fourth ring.

"Do you have any idea what time it is?" Mick said.

"Were you still up?"

"My wife is pregnant. Of course I was still up. What do you want?"

Brian drew in a deep breath. "I've got some information that might help you crack a cold case. A decades-old murder."

ACKNOWLEDGMENTS

You might think that writing a novel is a lonely, solitary experience. But in reality, it takes a village to write and publish a book. I'd like to take a moment to acknowledge and thank my "village."

First and foremost, I want to thank my wife, Diane, for her love and support throughout this process. Her patience and understanding of my need for "space" while in the throes of writing a novel is truly appreciated. I couldn't ask for a better partner on life's journey.

I'm also grateful to the writers in my critique group: Christine Schulden, Sarah Fisher, Ellie Searl, Marietta Fisher, and Paul

"Elizabeth Warren" Popiel. Their criticism, both encouraging and critical, was invaluable, and helped form a cohesive narrative out of a jumble of disjointed words.

I'd especially like to express my gratitude to my editor, Helga Schier. Her developmental edits and plot suggestions were instrumental in taking this novel to the next level. She can work magic with her red editing pen. As always, it was a true pleasure to work with her.

And finally, thanks to the whole team at CamCat Books for once again taking a chance with me. It is always a delight to work with such a dedicated team of knowledgeable and committed professionals. You all are awesome.

FOR FURTHER DISCUSSION

1. This novel take place in a small town in Delaware. In what ways does the location play an integral role in the story?

2. Who did you first suspect of being the murderer? Why?

3. Of all the characters who were killed in the book, whose death impacted you the most? Why?

4. When you discovered that Sarah was dead, what did you think she was? A ghost? Brian's guilty conscience? Or something else?

5. Discuss the way religious institutions are portrayed in the novel.

6. How do you think Candice's struggles with her faith tainted her objectivity when investigating the murders?

7. At the end of the book, Brian decides to reveal to the police what he knows about Sam Pyeong's murder. Do you think Agatha Bowman should go to jail over what she did sixty years ago? Why or why not?

8. Why do you think Brian has clung so tightly to the memory of his dead wife, Sarah?

ABOUT THE AUTHOR

M ichael Bradley is an award-winning author who was born and raised in southern New Jersey. He started life as a radio disc jockey, working at stations in New Jersey and West Virginia. After spending eight years "on-the-air," he realized that he needed to get a real job. He spent the next twenty or so years working in Information Technology.

Never one to waste an experience, he uses his familiarity with life on the radio for many of his suspense novels. His third novel, *Dead Air* (2020), won the Foreword INDIES Award and the IBPA Benjamin Franklin Award. The novel has been called "absorbing and filled with shocking twists."

When he isn't camping, working, or writing, Michael hits the waterways in his kayak, paddling creeks, streams, and rivers throughout Delaware, Pennsylvania, Maryland, and New Jersey. He lives in Delaware with his wife and their two furry four-legged "kids," Preaya and Willie.

AUTHOR Q&A

What inspired this book?
Although the concept of sin eating sounds made up, it truly was practiced in the eighteenth and nineteenth centuries in parts of England, Scotland, and Wales. Several years ago, I stumbled upon a brief article entitled *The Worst Freelance Gig in History Was Being the Village Sin Eater* on a website called Atlas Obscura. I was intrigued by the concept. The premise was simple. As described in the book, the sin eater was considered the lowest of the low in the community, and lived in such poverty that he, or she, was willing to risk their immortal soul for some bread, some ale, and a small amount of money. At the time, I had no idea that this information

would ever make it into one of my books. I filed the article away as a resource for possible use in the future. Fast forward to the end of 2019.

Most mystery or suspense books start with a "What if . . ." question. As I began to formulate the plot for this book, my "What if . . ." ran something like this, "What if a killer used the symbolism of the sin eater as a calling card?" And from there, the story grew into what you have just read. Fun fact, the last known sin eater passed away in the United Kingdom in 1906.

Are there real-life models to your characters?
Brian Wilder is a character that has been with me for almost twenty years. I've written a couple short stories that featured him as the main character, but this is the first time I've given him the spotlight in a novel. Even in his earliest versions, he's had a tragic backstory. Perhaps more tragic than this current incarnation.

I was aiming for a savvy, well-travelled journalist. When I first created Brian, I think I may have modeled him a bit on David Muir from ABC News. But that was years ago, and Brian has changed quite a bit since then.

The model for Candice Miller is tougher to find. I think she resembles me in her struggles questioning her faith. Unlike Brian, Candice was new to me for this book. I got to know her as I wrote. With every word, I gained new insight into who Candice was. Her backstory developed as I went along, which meant I had to go back and re-write quite a bit to make it all fit.

I'll let you in on a little secret. There is an early draft of this book where Candice dies in the end. Luckily, some good friends and my excellent editor convinced me to let her live.

I'm glad I did.

What was the most fun about writing this book?

The biggest thrill I had while writing this book was meeting all the characters. I don't mean Brian and Candice. I mean the side characters that pop up for a scene or two and then are gone. Many of these characters will probably never show up in another book, but it was such great fun to get to know them as I wrote their scenes. Although each of those characters gets just a moment or two in the spotlight, they have a deeper history that never gets told in the book. Some of them may return in a future book, but most will disappear once the final page is turned.

What was the greatest challenge when writing this book?

I started writing this book about a month before the COVID-19 pandemic lockdowns began. One of my writing habits was spending two nights a week at a nearby café with a small handful of other writers. Although noisy and often crowded, the café was a place where I was extremely productive. I'd often get more work done in the few hours a week there than any other time during the week. When the pandemic hit, going to the café was no longer an option. I had to readjust to doing all my writing at home. With the café, it was easy to tune out the surrounding noises and distractions to focus on what I was writing. It was not as easy to do that at home with my wife and dogs around. The first few months were rough, but I eventually was able to adjust to a new norm and press on with writing the book.

Also by Michael Bradley

Dead Air

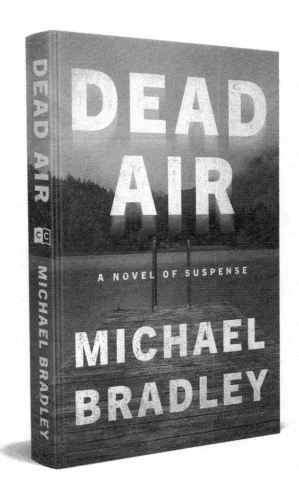

If you've enjoyed

Michael Bradley's *None Without Sin*,

you'll enjoy

S. K. Waters's *The Dead Won't Tell*.

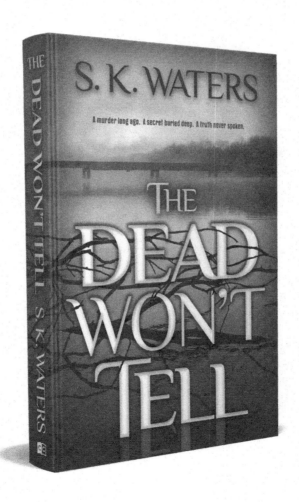

PROLOGUE

July 25, 1969, 12:41 A.M., Hunts Landing

Acrid sulfur from the fireworks faded with the nighttime breeze. Dr. Theodore Wexler held up his glass—red flashes from the police cars on the Quad pulsed chestnut in the bourbon. *Pulse. Pulse.* The cadence matched his heartbeat, steadier now, settled after this disrupted day of jubilee.

"Damn."

Twenty hours ago, Armstrong, Aldrin, and Collins had splashed down into the tranquil waters of the Pacific, and the town erupted in celebration. Engineers from Hunts Landing College—a small school on the Tennessee River—were instrumental in getting those men home safe. Their success ensured prestige and rewards. Theodore, the college president, had spent his day dreaming of accolades and endowments.

Now, however, his thoughts simmered.

Pulse. Pulse.

Wexler House sat elevated above the Quad. From the French doors of his study, he could inspect every corner of the common. He sipped twenty-six-year-old Pappy Van Winkle. The bourbon had been a reward, purchased three years ago when the college won the NASA contract. Saved for today and stored in a particular nook in the cellar, Wexler had intended it for tonight's party.

Instead, only after the guests left, and he could brood in peace, did he send Cyrus to fetch the Pappy. Now the bottle sat half empty.

Earlier, there'd been some fracas on the Quad. He'd observed the squad cars arrive with disinterest. If the incident involved any students, campus police would handle the situation. He would deal with the aftermath in the morning.

No, his thoughts returned to the thick manila envelope on his desk, its contents strewn on his blotter.

Oblivious to the fiery liquid trickling down his throat, he sipped and contemplated. The implications of those papers tumbled through his thoughts as if he stood in the shadows of a snow-covered mountain, unable to escape the avalanche hurtling towards him. Yes, avalanche. The appropriate metaphor. The contents of the envelope could bury the college.

"Damn and damn again."

Like a chess player, he considered his first move, his second move, then a third, before discarding them all as futile and unlikely to save the school from exposure. Glass empty, he refilled it, three fingers' worth. His sister Nevelyn, who'd taken over management of the household (and Theodore as well, if he would be truthful) after Theodore had been widowed, would disapprove. At the moment, though, he didn't care a bit about what Nevelyn thought. He turned back to the open doors. There were more red lights now, from more squad cars than the campus police had in its fleet. Someone must have called in the town cops. With a scowl, he downed his drink. Allowing himself one final "Damn!", he swept the cursed papers into his desk drawer, and went out through the French doors.

CHAPTER ONE

Wednesday, March 11, 2015, 9:01 A.M., Hunts Landing

Abbie Adams's loose fist hovered two inches away from the engraved nickel nameplate reading *Sylvia Van Cleave*, and she wondered again if last night's nightmare, where Sylvia fired her, was coming true.

A summons from the editor of *The Hunts Landing Times* was rare. The last time, a reader had disputed a Sunday feature on worker conditions at the town's old cotton mills, calling the article an utter disparagement of her dear granddaddy Puckett, one of the town's more infamous mill owners. Abbie had done the research on the piece for Will Irestone, the paper's primary reporter, and even though she had double-checked every fact, the Pucketts had persuaded the paper to amend the article with more favorable language.

In Hunts Landing the memory of old money ran long, and its advertising dollars stretched far.

She gripped the strap of her shoulder bag, inhaled, and knocked.

At the terse "Come in!", she pushed open the door. Stacks of storage boxes littered the floor, Post-it notes covered the windows, and whiteboards crammed with scribbles dominated the walls. The cluttered office satisfied Abbie's sense of Woodward and Bernstein.

Sylvia Van Cleave's fingers flew over her keyboard. Her linen suit and silk blouse were crisp and professional, and the reading glasses perched on the tip of her nose only added to her flair. She extended a hand to the only empty chair but didn't stop typing with the other. One finger poised over the return key for a moment before she pressed it. "Abbie!" the editor smiled. "Thanks for coming in. We're in crisis mode today."

Part of the knot in Abbie's stomach loosened. At least Sylvia hadn't led with "You're fired."

Sylvia fished out a brown file folder from the messy pile on her desk. "Will crashed his Jeep into a cement truck last night."

Abbie gasped. "Is he all right?"

"On the one hand, yes," Sylvia said. "A mild concussion and a broken nose from the airbag. The bad part is that the truck crushed his leg. He needs a complete hardware reconstruction. Dammit," Sylvia shook her head. "There's no story in Hunts Landing worth speeding in the rain, but that's exactly what he did last night. No more marathons for Will, and that's going to really piss him off. Anyway, he goes into surgery in a few hours, after he's stabilized."

Abbie realized she didn't know much about his private life, only that he was a bachelor. "Is anyone with him?"

"His sister is on her way." Sylvia handed her the folder. "I've farmed out his other assignments, but this one requires your touch. We're starting a new series for the Sunday edition. The history of Hunts Landing. Events that may have gone unreported or were reported only scantily. Will's begun the first piece, but it's not finished, and we've already sold the advertising. Waiting for his return isn't an option. Good news for you, you get the by-line."

A by-line! Writing credentials were currency in this business. Terrible that the opportunity came only because of Will's injuries, but gee, *a by-line. By Abbie Adams.*

Sylvia motioned toward the folder. "This first story is an unsolved murder from 1969. Campus police found the body of a young Black woman, Rosalie DuFrayne, near the river, cause of death, blunt force trauma. The police investigation was . . . half-hearted. Even this newspaper didn't seem to care much about the story. You'll find the reporter's notes and an unpublished article draft."

"Why unpublished?"

"No idea. Caleb Jackson covered the murder, but he died in 1989. His editor, Ozzie Etherington, passed four years ago. We can't ask them." She leaned forward. "There are two interesting angles to this story. The first one is the date. July 24, 1969. Do you remember the significance?"

"Of course," Abbie said. Anyone who'd grown up in Hunts Landing knew all about the day the astronauts came back from the moon. Hunts Landing scientists built the rocket systems that carried the Apollo crew into space, and the town still beamed with pride. July 24th was a day of celebration, starting with a parade and ending with parties that lasted all night long.

"That night," Sylvia continued, "there was a party on the college Quad, next to the river. Two hundred yards away, someone brutally killed Rosalie DuFrayne."

Abbie opened the file and found a photograph on top, a yearbook photo perhaps. Rosalie DuFrayne had been a looker, her light brown skin giving her a Creole look. "The police didn't do much of an investigation?"

"Next to none. That should be high on your list. Racism might have been one of the reasons why the authorities didn't sufficiently investigate the murder and why the paper's coverage was, well, let's say 'anemic.' I believe that's the aspect that Will was exploring."

Only because he didn't grow up here, Abbie thought. As a historian with an addiction for the truth, she wanted to dive right into any and every angle of the story, but as a resident of Hunts Landing, warning bells pealed in her head. Perhaps forty-five years put enough time and distance between the present and the racial turbulence of the past. Or did it? Given the viral nature of stories with a racial angle, she wondered why the paper even wanted to touch the topic now. Especially after the Puckett fiasco. "Don't you think this is a little risky for the paper?"

"It's part of the history of Hunts Landing," Sylvia said. "The murder of a Black girl that the police barely investigated and this very paper ignored? That's a story."

Abbie leafed through the folder. "You mentioned two interesting angles?"

"A more human aspect of the case. The victim's mother, Miss Etta DuFrayne, was the Wexler family cook. Rosalie worked with her mother at the Wexler's party the night she died."

Abbie felt the blood drain from her face. "She worked for the Wexlers."

"Yes."

"And this is the first story in the series?"

"Yes."

"Why?"

"Funny thing about family-owned papers," Sylvia said. "They get to stick their hands in the editorial side of the house. The owners asked for *this* story."

"Did you know it was Dr. Wexler who shot down my thesis?" Abbie swallowed the sudden trickle of bile she tasted at the back of her throat.

The editor hesitated. "Yes, I knew. But your Dr. Wexler was only nineteen at the time of the murder. Miss Etta worked for his father, Dr. *Theodore* Wexler. The question is, can *you* be objective about that family?"

"I don't know!" Abbie blurted before she could stop herself. She wanted this assignment, wanted the by-line.

Sylvia took a seat on the armrest of the only other chair. "The board wants this series to tell the untold history of Hunts Landing, and the Wexlers are news in this town. I can't farm this out to someone who doesn't know the place. I need *you*. And you can be objective. Stick to the facts. What happened the night of July 24, 1969? Why didn't the police investigate thoroughly? Why did the paper ignore the story? How were the Wexlers involved? I smell something funny here, and the Wexlers are in the middle of it." Sylvia glanced at her watch. "I've got another meeting. Your deadline is next Wednesday."

All Abbie had to do to get the by-line was go buy a jumbo bottle of Pepto Bismol to quench the nausea in her gut. After all these years, the Wexler name could still turn her stomach upside down. She tucked the file folder into her satchel. "Any tips on where to start?"

"Go talk to Will at the hospital. Room 2427."

"He's about to go into surgery. They won't let me in."

Sylvia stood in dismissal. "Tell them you're Will's baby sister."

Wednesday, March 11th, 7:37 AM, Santa Monica, CA

Joss Freeman didn't know which crisis he should tackle first; his missing cat, his girlfriend's empty closet, or the phone call he'd just finished.

Lincoln's missing pet carrier combined with the tangled mess of empty wire hangers only partially explained the cat's disappearance. Harriet loathed the long-haired Persian. Joss had never persuaded her to even pet the animal, let alone attempt to coax Lincoln into a pet carrier he had no intention of getting into. So why would she take him? And why did she leave, with no phone call, no note?

It wasn't the first time he'd missed a flight home.

Joss left two voicemails. Harriet would return the calls when she was good and ready.

He opened the sliding glass door to the balcony. A few blocks away, the Pacific sparkled, a view that usually soothed him. Not today. Not when his career hung by a thread. The third crisis.

Shows got cancelled all the time, but none whose hosts had as many social media followers as Joss did. At this moment, the news was going viral on Twitter and Instagram. *America's Stories cancelled. What will @JossFreemanHistorian do next? #IsHistoryDead?* And some idiot would certainly post some Photoshopped meme of him in a gruesome state of demise.

The channel had called while his plane was in midair, and he hadn't returned the call until he'd landed and was far enough away from LAX that he could drive on autopilot. Stuck in gridlock, he'd been prisoner to the words coming through his car's speakers. *Shift in programming. America's Stories doesn't fit into the new concept.*

The ocean was just far enough that he could smell the salt in the air but couldn't quite make out the whitecaps on the water. *What to do next.*

He'd never been one to kowtow to the network establishment, which was why he was so unsuccessful yesterday. The six-hour flight to New York. The four-hour wait in the lobby of National Media Corporation's headquarters. Finally, the scant five minutes during which he attempted to enthrall programming executives with the reasons they should renew *America's Stories*.

Facts had always been his friend. The data was irrefutable. He'd never lost an advertiser. He had more social media followers and friends than all the other series on NMC combined. He couldn't define his ideal viewer because he didn't have one. Retired grandmothers commented on his posts as often as the high school girls suddenly acing history. Joss loved being able to transform the dull, dusty names and dates from history books into vibrant stories that educated and entertained.

His viewership reflected that.

His numbers were better than any other NMC series. Yet, those programming executives delivered the rebuke in seemingly innocent words: *America's Stories doesn't fit into the new concept.*

Joss didn't even know what that meant.

He didn't have many appealing options. He could pitch to one of the big networks, or he could go the indie route. Either option would compel him to spend more time on the business end of things and less time creating, and, well, creating was the fun part. None of his choices tickled his fancy.

His doorbell chimed, and he buzzed in whoever it was without checking. Harriet, maybe? His heart leaped at the possibility.

Instead, his long-time producer, Ursula Quinville, swept in, a short dynamo with a backpack slung over her shoulder, sunglasses on her head and readers tucked into her cleavage. "What the hell did you say in New York?" She breathed.

Ursula never wasted time on silly things like 'how was your flight?'. At the moment, Joss didn't know if he appreciated that characteristic. "All I did was pitch them the profile for a new series. *America's Stories II: 500 Years of Amazing Tales.*"

"And all they did was cancel your old one! Zeesh, Joss, how many times to I have to tell you to leave this stuff to me?" She flung her backpack down onto his sofa. A shoulder strap snagged her readers, which tumbled under the coffee table. "I mean, what were you thinking? To appeal to that fraction of the audience that still thinks all true American history begins with Columbus?"

Joss thought it best not to mention the spectacles. "It's the same problem we always have with pre-Columbian events. No written record."

"Oh, shut up. You hypothesize on camera all the time. You're the king of 'what if.'" Ursula plopped herself onto the sofa next to her knapsack and dug for her phone. "We've got one chance to fix this," she said, and felt beneath her throat for her readers. "Aw, dammit."

Joss knelt and reached for the missing glasses. "How do we fix it?"

"How do we .. ?" Her head trembled with the effort at self-control, and Joss could have sworn her jaw was about to become detached from the rest of her face. She pointed a single finger at him, once, hard. "*We* do nothing. *You* will do whatever the new director of programming wants you to do. Which is . . ." she used the same finger to swipe on her phone—"a treatment on missing treasures from the Civil War."

Joss stifled his groan. "C'mon, anything but the Civil War."

"Civil War, Joss. Missing treasures. The new guy's named Kenetsky and according to his Twitter account he's a buff. You pitch him a week from Friday."

The countdown timer ticked in the back of his head. *Nine days times twenty-four hours a day* . . . "What am I supposed to come up with in a week?"

"You've gotta dazzle him. Any ideas?"

Too many, not necessarily good ideas, ricocheted through his skull like pinballs run amok. "I need more than twelve seconds."

"Don't take too many. You've only got nine days." She picked up her backpack and slung it over her shoulder. "Call me later." With a kiss on his cheek, she left.

Joss locked the door behind her. *Something new? In nine days?* Did Kenetsky have any idea what he was asking? It took *weeks* of planning, research, prep, and shooting to develop a documentary. The pinballs were heading towards tilt.

He knew next to nothing about the Civil War, other than that it was an overplayed subject in the documentary universe. He didn't have time to do a 101 course on the topic.

What about Abbie Adams?

When they were undergraduates, Joss had shared a house with Abbie and four other students who were at school on athletic scholarships. He and Abbie were the sole academics in the house, spending endless late nights with boxed wine and arguing the finer points of history. During those early years after graduation, they'd remained fairly close. Close enough to manage cross-country visits, although once she'd had her kids, those trips were harder on her. He'd even stood in for her husband, Zach, deployed in Iraq, at her daughter's christening.

The Abbie he'd known in college, assiduously passionate about everything historical, who fleshed out multiple research topics before selecting one, just for fun, might be the just person Joss needed. He wasn't ashamed to admit that, more than once, he'd taken one of Abbie's rejects to use for his own assignment. Joss was good at telling the story, in fact, he wasn't just good, he was great at it, but finding the story to tell, that's where Abbie shined.

Of course.

Abbie was what he needed now. She'd help him come up with something sexy enough for Kenetsky. He activated his headset. "Siri, call Abbie Adams."

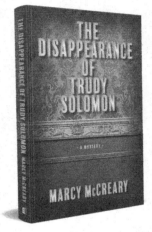
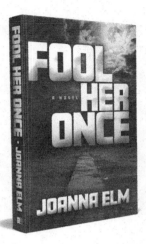